BETWEEN THESE BROKEN HEARTS

ALSO BY LEXI RYAN

These Hollow Vows
These Twisted Bonds
Beneath These Cursed Stars

BETWEEN THESE BROKEN HEARTS

LEXI RYAN

STORYTIDE
An Imprint of HarperCollins*Publishers*

HarperCollins Children's Books, a division of HarperCollins Publishers,
195 Broadway, New York, NY 10007

HarperCollins Publishers, Macken House,
39/40 Mayor Street Upper, Dublin 1, D01 C9W8, Ireland

Storytide is an imprint of HarperCollins Publishers.

Between These Broken Hearts
Copyright © 2025 by Lexi Ryan
Map copyright © 2021 by Lexi Ryan
Map art by Aaron Stratten
All rights reserved. Manufactured in Harrisonburg, VA, United States of America. No part of this book may be used or reproduced in any manner whatsoever without written permission except in the case of brief quotations embodied in critical articles and reviews. Without limiting the exclusive rights of any author, contributor, or the publisher of this publication, any unauthorized use of this publication to train generative artificial intelligence (AI) technologies is expressly prohibited. HarperCollins also exercises their rights under Article 4(3) of the Digital Single Market Directive 2019/790 and expressly reserves this publication from the text and data mining exception.
harpercollins.com

Library of Congress Control Number: 2024042857
ISBN 978-0-06-331195-4

Typography by Chris Kwon
25 26 27 28 29 LBC 5 4 3 2 1

First Edition

———◆———

For the ones who feel trapped in their darkest night. I see you.
Take my hand. We'll wait for the sun together.

———◆———

ABRIELLA

Another day of searching for my sister. Another day of chasing ghosts.

Rage is my constant companion. I've stopped trying to contain the rumbling shadows that swirl around my feet and fingertips. I no longer care whether Abriella, queen of the shadow fae, appears gentle or brutal, kind or intimidating. My sister is gone. My court is falling apart. And if the winds don't change soon, all will be lost.

"We are running out of time," I say, spinning away from the setting sun to scowl at my visitors.

"You think I don't know that?" When Hale Kendrick's ice-blue eyes meet mine, they contain the fury of a tempestuous sea. "You think it doesn't haunt me every day I fail to find her? Every day I fail them *both*?"

The ache in my chest intensifies at the reminder of my selfishness. I'm not the only one whose sister is missing. Kendrick lost the woman he loves and his sister, Felicity, in the same day. He hasn't rested since, and the dark circles beneath his eyes hint at the exhaustion his posture never reveals.

Months. We've been at this for *months* and have nothing to show for it.

I thought this time would be different, but now I realize desperation was making me see what wasn't there. The rumors of Jasalyn sightings hurt the stability of my court as much as they hurt my heart. Some say she ran back to the human realm. Some say she is hiding out in the Seelie Court. Too few believe she is with me, staying in the safety of the Midnight Palace until her eighteenth birthday.

Every rumor, every speculation makes me rage. And I can't even defend my sister by sharing the truth because seers across the land have whispered prophecy about the shadow princess, and one hint of the truth of the ring and her blood magic connection to Mordeus would be the end for me. The end of everything good I've tried to bring back to these people.

Claim the princess and control the court.

"You said you had a lead. That someone had seen her. Was it lies?" I demand. That's why they're here, after all—to update me on their latest efforts to find Jasalyn.

Kendrick's friend Natan nudges his spectacles up the bridge of his nose and steps forward. "It was more of the same," he explains. "Someone knows someone who saw her—but tracking the rumors didn't yield anything."

Of course it didn't. We can never find anyone who saw her with their own eyes. And I am unable to search for her myself because I have to remain at the palace and pretend she isn't missing at all. We've had a trusted shifter take her form to make the occasional appearance on various palace balconies, but without Felicity's special gifts, we can't risk allowing anyone close enough that they might suss out our deceit.

I shake my head, the same questions that have haunted me for months spinning through my head. "If we can't find her because of the ring's magic, why are there any memories of her appearing at all?"

Natan shakes his head. "This ring—it's a conduit to some of the most powerful and complex magic I've ever seen. Perhaps the magic is changing. Or perhaps the rumors are just rumors and that's why we can never find a true source."

My gut folds in on itself at the hopelessness of it all, but I keep my chin up, my face impassive. We haven't lost this yet. Haven't lost *her* yet.

"With all due respect," Kendrick says, folding his arms, "finding her might prove futile without this mythical stone your seer claims can nullify the ring's magic."

My temper flares, my shadows surging alongside my rage. Because he's right. The idea that we could have found her and simply don't remember is as devasting as anything. And even if that hasn't happened already, if I don't track down the Stone of Disenchantment, that is exactly the challenge we have before us.

Finn, my king, my love, my bonded partner, places a hand on the small of my back, and I draw in my first full breath since Elora's chosen king returned with more bad news.

"Misha is investigating a lead on Felicity," Finn tells Kendrick, smoothly shifting the subject away from my futile search for the stone. I'm glad he's clearheaded enough to share this latest bit of news. If someone could give me a small shred of hope regarding *my* sister, I'd want to hear it.

Finn looks to me and I give a subtle shake of my head. We

won't give this male more hope than that. Not until Misha brings Kendrick's sister back safely.

"Misha's team still believes she lives," I tell Kendrick. Like me, he'll have to sustain himself on scraps of hope, and when those scraps aren't enough to put a dent in the fear and grief these months have planted in our hearts, we plow forward nonetheless.

Kendrick squeezes his eyes shut for a beat. "I choose to believe the same. About them both."

"We're running out of time," I say. "On Jasalyn's eighteenth birthday, she'll be lost to us forever, and the future of the shadow court right alongside her."

CHAPTER ONE

JASALYN

They don't fear me in this body. Obedience comes with hesitation. With doubt. So I teach them the cost of their uncertainty, burning their fields and their homes with the flames that should be mine to command, burning it all to ash and painting the horizon in the reds and oranges of my rage.

She locks her power away from me, even now. Even weak as she is. But I will command it when the time is right. The seers have foretold this. They think they can steal my destiny. They think they can keep me away from my rightful life, my rightful court, my rightful throne.

I will take it all back or I will burn it to the ground.

"Princess. Pretty, pretty princess. Wake up now, you foolish girl."

The words are too far away. A shout from a distant realm. A call from the shore to my submerged body.

Sleep has me in its grasp. Weakness weaves around my bones, worming its way into my muscles, forbidding me to do so much as open my eyes.

The ring. I know it's the magical ring that is stuck on my hand making me so useless. Pushing me closer and closer to death. I'm teetering on the edge, peering into the abyss, craving the relief from this whole-body ache.

"Come now. Enough of this."

A cup is pressed to my lips—cool ceramic prying them apart before something hits my tongue. Thick, warm, and sweet.

My eyes flutter open to see the faerie leaning over me, a steaming mug in her hand. "I need to go to Feegus Keep," I tell her. Tell *myself*. I shouldn't need to be reminded. Mordeus is using me—to kill hundreds, to bring himself back to life—and I won't be the reason he returns for good. Kendrick thought Feegus Keep might hold the Sword of Fire, a sword that he says will open a portal to anywhere you want to go, a sword that can kill *anyone*. I need to find it and end Mordeus. I can't undo my mistakes, but I can do this.

I look around the room. It's not too dark to make out the silhouette of the short, stout female at my bedside, but it's dark enough that I never would've chosen this place to rest if it weren't for the ring's magic weakening me.

I pick through the cobwebs of my thoughts, trying to remember how I got here. I was staying with Kendrick and his friends at Ironmoore, an Eloran settlement, when the town was attacked by a wyvern. That night I dreamed the most awful thing—about Kendrick being someone else, about him working with Mordeus.

Then I found out that every session of torture Mordeus made me endure in his dungeons was blood magic, and that now, because of that and this ring, Mordeus has some level of control over my consciousness. He used me to do horrible things. This ring makes me a murderer with death's kiss, and some of those deaths I chose. The people who worked for Mordeus and tortured me in those dungeons? I wanted to watch them die.

I never would have guessed that I was personally resurrecting Mordeus with each life I took.

The female snaps her fingers in my face. "No more sleeping. You've done enough of that."

"Who are you?" I ask, my voice raspy from lack of use. "Where am I?"

She flicks her fingers and the lantern at my bedside flames to life. "Climb out of this bed now," the faerie commands, yanking the piles of blankets off me. Her thinning gray hair is pulled into a knot at the crown of her head and her pale skin has a yellow undertone. She flicks my arm with her thumb and forefinger.

"Ouch." I rub away the sting, but I do feel a little more awake. Is this her house?

When it became clear that my horrible dreams were actually Mordeus's memories, I left Kendrick. I climbed into a farmer's wagon and was far from Ironmoore when I remembered my goblin bracelet and asked Gommid to take me somewhere I could sleep. Somewhere I'd be safe. Where did he bring me?

"Now."

My mind is too fuzzy to piece it out and I'm too tired to argue, so I sit up and swing my legs over the side of the bed.

I vaguely remember Gommid grumbling about my foolishness, about how he warned me about the ring. The last thing I remember is ignoring his rant and crawling into a soft bed. *This* soft bed? Maybe, but I was too feeble and sick to pay much attention to my surroundings.

How long did I sleep? I feel better than when I called for my goblin, but weakness still nips at my heels. Maybe I just need some food. It's been too long since I've eaten anything.

You need the Sword of Fire. You need to find Mordeus and fix what you've done.

Coffee. Food. I just need something in my stomach, and I'll be okay. *Then* I can find my way to Feegus Keep and hunt down the sword that legend says can kill anyone.

Food. Sword. Mordeus.

I still have the ring. I can do this. I meet the elderly faerie's eyes and let the Enchanting Lady's thrall fill my voice as I say, "Could I trouble you for some dinner?"

She shoves the steaming mug into my cold hands, ignoring my request. "Hurry now. Drink more of this."

I bring it to my lips, greedy for more of the sweetness she used to wake me. "Thank you." I sip, and this time I'm awake enough to identify the flavors dancing on my tongue. Warmed chocolate spiced with cinnamon and clove.

The concoction soothes my riotous stomach as it goes down.

She studies me. "I trust you slept well."

"I—" I shake my head. Who is this female? She called me *princess*. How does she know who I am? "Yes, thank you. Could you please make me some food?"

She rocks back on her heels and frowns as she looks me over. "Stick with the drink for now. It's too soon for food."

I frown at my ring. This ring makes everyone do my bidding. The only ones who have been immune are Abriella and Kendrick.

And now this faerie. "You don't want to make me food? Even if that's what I want?"

She props her hands on her hips. "You should consider yourself lucky I didn't kick you out of my house. Ungrateful child."

Her house. Does Gommid know her? Did he know he was bringing me to her house? "I'm sorry. I thought..."

"You think I should be bowing at your feet because of that ridiculous ring. I know."

I instinctively check my mind for the shields Misha taught me to hold in place before realizing it shouldn't matter. I shouldn't need my shields when I'm wearing my ring.

"If you hadn't noticed, goblins are immune to that particular enchantment." She sticks out her hand. "Fherna, pleasure to meet you."

I blink at her as I take her hand. *A goblin.* Of course. I should've realized sooner. "I've never met a female goblin before."

"You probably have. You just weren't paying attention. Just because our male folk spend their time escorting ungrateful creatures around doesn't mean there are no females. Didn't your mother teach you about the birds and the bees, my girl? About how babies are made?"

I bite my bottom lip to hold back a laugh before I realize—I feel like laughing. The cloying sickness from wearing the ring during the day has dissipated.

"It's the drink," Fherna says. "It mutes the pull of the magic."

My heart sinks and I put down the mug. "I need my magic. I need—"

"Don't be foolish," she says, nudging the mug back toward me.

"Your enchantment is intact. The drink mutes the magic's ability to draw from your life force."

I glance down to my mug and then back up at her. I don't know anything about this creature, so I'm not sure I should trust her so readily, but I've already come this far—sleeping in her bed and drinking her offering. I might as well listen to what she has to say. "Explain?"

"Magic is life, my dear. Life is magic. A ring that powerful was brought into being only because you sacrificed so much of your life to have it, but magic takes on the qualities of its creator. A magic like this is *hungry*. It takes and takes. It will draw from you until there's nothing left."

I shake my head. "I have until my eighteenth birthday. I have—"

"Don't misunderstand," she says, "that ring won't kill you. He's worked too hard to let that happen. But he wants it to keep you hovering around death until your bargain is complete."

I set the mug down on the bedside table and gather my thoughts. It's getting easier. Whatever she put in that drink is allowing me to think clearly for the first time since leaving Kendrick and the others. "Why are you helping me?"

Her face goes solemn. "Because if I don't, everything changes." She nods to my cup. "If you plan to find a way to defeat Mordeus, you best finish that."

My breath catches. "How do you know all this?" This is why Kendrick never wanted to use the goblins. *They know too much*, he said. It seems they do.

She narrows her eyes. "I understand your exposure to goblins was limited when you were a child, but nearly four years you've lived in this realm. How do you understand so little about the creatures around you?"

I know that goblins are always collecting information. I know that they are the keepers of the history of the realm. "Then tell me, will I find what I'm looking for—will I find a way to defeat him—at Feegus Keep?"

She barks out a laugh. "We know facts. We know history. We aren't seers."

"You just told me everything changes if you don't help me."

"That's not seeing. That's logic."

Nonsense. Why do goblins always speak in nonsense? I take another sip of the warm chocolate and reframe my question. "Is the Sword of Fire at the keep?"

"It was once, if the rumors are true. Mordeus was said to have used great magic to shield the sword from anyone but himself."

"And I can use it to destroy him?"

"The girl asks so many questions but has given me nothing in return."

I turn up my palms. "What do you want? My hair? Nail clippings?"

She wrinkles her pointed nose. "I cannot be bought with such tawdry scraps."

"Then what?"

"I want you to wake up," she snaps. "To *fight*."

"I'm *trying*. I've only just found out about Mordeus using me to come back. I came here only to rest before I leave to retrieve the sword." I fold my arms across my chest. "If you want me to fight, tell me how. Tell me my plan will work."

She purses her lips. "The Eloran Sword of Fire can be used to destroy anything or anyone if she who wields it is deemed worthy."

"Deemed worthy by whom?"

"By the sword, of course."

"If I'm deemed worthy, it could kill Mordeus? And it could take me to him?"

"If you're deemed worthy, it could kill *anyone* and take you *anywhere*." She shakes her head. "But you're asking the wrong questions."

I don't have time to argue with her. She doesn't understand. I force myself to set down my mug—no matter how delicious it is, I have more important things to do than linger over a treat. I push out of bed. "I need to go."

She harrumphs. "You're welcome, by the way."

I wipe a hand over my face and shake my head. "I'm sorry. Thank you for letting me sleep here."

"And for the drink?"

I nod and force a smile. I slept in this female's house without permission. The least I can do is show a little gratitude. "Yes, thank you for the melted chocolate. It was truly delicious."

She rolls her eyes. "Delicious? You didn't notice anything else?" When I don't immediately understand, she gives a heavy sigh. "Did you notice that you now have the strength to stand when before you couldn't even open your eyes?"

I frown at the mug and then toward the dark window. "The drink did that? I thought nightfall was bringing my strength back."

She cocks her head to the side. "You have no idea just how insidious that ring is, do you? You've slept day and night, too weak to know time is passing you by."

I tug at the ring, not that it matters. It won't budge. I'd hoped that the weakness would abate in the nighttime hours, but if what she's telling me is true— "Do you have more of this? If I don't get what I need tonight?"

"I don't exactly keep it on hand, no."

"Do you have the recipe? Where can I find the ingredients?"

"The recipe doesn't have to be so precise. I just added the chocolate and spices to make it more enjoyable for you." She shrugs. "The forest is the easiest place to find what you need. If you're not too squeamish."

"Too squeamish for what?"

Her eyes light up, and when she smiles, the chocolatey drink is smeared across her teeth. "To drain the beating heart of an innocent magical creature."

Nausea surges into my throat and this time it has nothing to do with the ring. My mug holds the dregs of the concoction. "Blood? You had me drink blood without telling me?" Moments ago I was ready to lick the cup clean. Now I want to retch the contents up and onto the floor.

"You feel better, don't you?"

"I . . ." I close my eyes and focus on my breath until the nausea settles. "I didn't know I was drinking blood."

"You eat meat. I don't see the difference."

"The difference is that this is disgusting."

"You didn't seem to think so before." She huffs. "It doesn't matter. You'll do what needs done when the time comes."

"I thought you weren't a seer."

"I'm not. I'm an optimist."

I hang my head and draw in a long breath. Yes, if the alternative is letting Mordeus use me to destroy my sister's court, I would do worse than drink blood. "What kind of magical creature?"

Her grin is nearly feral. "Have you ever heard of the wolpertinger?" She waves a hand and an image appears in the air between us. The creature looks a bit like a large bunny, complete with soft fur and floppy ears, but tiny little antlers sit on the crown of its head and thin, gossamer wings sprout from behind its front legs.

I shake my head. "It's practically defenseless." A shiver of revulsion shudders through me as I try to imagine drinking blood from the tiny creature's heart. "I don't think I can."

"You killed dozens of Mordeus's faithful for vengeance alone."

My back stiffens. "They weren't innocent."

"You found a way to justify their deaths and you'll find a way to justify this. If you want to survive, that is. Remember, you need not just the blood, but its *life*—you must take so much blood that you stop the creature's beating heart. For the longest-lasting effects, make sure you drink the blood while it's fresh. The magic fades the longer it's separated from its life source."

I stare at the ring and think of Skylar's suggestion from the night before I left Ironmoore—that if all else failed, we rid me of the ring by cutting off my finger. I would be free of it and wouldn't have to worry about sleeping for days on end.

What would be the harm in a missing digit when I'm already so scarred and the days ahead of me are so few?

But I need the ring. I need it to get into Feegus Keep, and I need it to find the sword. Surely Mordeus wouldn't let an item so powerful go unprotected. I can't conceivably *fight* my way inside. I need to be the Enchanting Lady and I can't be her without this cursed ring.

The irony doesn't escape me. I traded everything for this ring—not only my sister's most sacred magical book but every day of my life once I turn eighteen. Now the ring is exactly the tool I need to find the sword that can get me to Mordeus and kill him once and for all, while simultaneously being the very thing that has kept me too ill to do more than sleep.

I will get what I need tonight. If all goes well, I'll find the Sword of Fire and be able to confront Mordeus before the sun rises. Once he's taken care of, I can figure out what's next.

I can't let myself think about that now. I traded everything for vengeance, and I can't allow my mind to drift to what happens when there's no more left to take.

"Feegus Keep," I say, "it's near here?"

"You're still asking the wrong questions."

"Please."

She lifts her chin. "Chase the moon through the woods and beyond the lake. You won't miss it."

"Thank you," I whisper. She nods and turns to leave the room.

I glance down at myself and realize the pants and boots that I was wearing when I fled Kendrick and his friends are already scuffed with soot, like I've crawled through a fire-ravaged forest. "How long was I sleeping?" I ask her back.

She peers at me over her shoulder and arches a wispy gray brow. "Over eight months."

Everything inside me recoils in denial. "That would mean my birthday's in—"

"Eleven days."

CHAPTER TWO

FELICITY

"Shouldn't you be in bed?"

The words take me by surprise, pulling me into my body as if my thoughts had taken me elsewhere. I turn my attention to the voice behind me to find my brother, standing in the palace's moonlit garden and smirking at me. Konner's pale blue eyes and white-blond hair are a match to mine, but he spends most of his time wearing the fierce expression of a fighter. Not tonight, though, and the sight of his smile fills my chest with warmth.

"You're back!" I hop off the stone ledge and run to him.

Konner pulls me against his chest and squeezes me hard. "It's only been two weeks. I promised I wouldn't be gone forever."

I frown as I pull away. He's right, of course. It hasn't been that long, but part of me feels like I've spent my whole life with this gaping hole in my chest where my twin brother should be. I shake away the thought and squeeze his hands. "And I'm glad for it. I've been a little lost without you."

He chucks me on the chin and smirks. "Really? Because I believe the last thing you said to me was to pull my head out of my ass before I lost my chance to marry the sweetest girl in all of Elora."

"I mean, that advice clearly came from a place of love and adoration."

"Sure it did." He tips his head toward the palace, and it's natural to head down the path by his side.

The stars are so bright tonight, as if the clouds from earlier in the day scattered at the approach of the moon.

"Do you want to tell me what has you wandering the gardens when the moon is so high in the sky?"

"Nightmares," I admit. "I came out to clear my head before going back to sleep."

His eyes are solemn when he glances toward me. "Want to talk about it?"

I bite my bottom lip. I hate to take myself back there, back to the loneliness and heartache that haunts my dreams, but this is Konner. I can tell him anything, and usually feel better once I do. "I have these recurring dreams that I'm . . ."

He waits a beat, then arches a brow. "Go on."

I cringe. Is there any way to say it that doesn't make me sound and feel pathetic? "That I'm all alone in the world."

"Felicity," he murmurs. "You know you're not."

I shake my head. "Maybe it's because you've been gone and Aster hasn't visited from Elora in an age. I don't know. But the dreams are so real. I'm living in Faerie. On the run and hiding. I don't have any family or friends, and I can't even take my true form because it's too dangerous." I sneak a look at him, just to see if he thinks I'm crazy, but he's looking up at the same stars that have been giving me comfort tonight and nodding.

"It makes sense."

My chest squeezes tight. I didn't realize I needed him to take my silly dreams seriously. "It does?"

"Well, yes. The only thing that matters to you more than Elora, more than *home*, is family. Your love is your motivation for all you do—whether it's preparing to join the Seven or giving guidance to your friends. Your truest nightmare would be to have all that taken away from you." His eyes, so much like mine, are tender when they scan my face. "What would the point of any of this be if you didn't have your family?"

That fist around my heart loosens. "They make me feel raw. The dreams. Raw and terrified that I could've been there instead of here." I swallow. "They just feel so real. What do you suppose it means?"

"Perhaps that you feel powerless against these unknown enemies that have been trying to find a way into our palace." His lips curve into a facsimile of a smile, but I see the pity in his eyes. "Or perhaps it just means you have the best twin brother in all the realms."

I cough out a laugh and swat his arm with the back of my hand. "Oh. I'm sure that's it."

He cocks his head to the side. "I am sorry, for what it's worth, that you're having nightmares. If it were up to me, there would be no bad guys and we would never have to leave the palace."

"I don't understand how they can hate us so much." I wave a hand toward the palace. "This is all for the good of the realm. To protect those weaker than us. Why would anyone be against that?"

His gaze shifts back to the stars and he sighs. "Sometimes I think we've done you a disservice by keeping you here. We've done such a good job protecting you from the evils of the world that you can't even comprehend their existence."

"I'm not that naïve."

He shakes his head. "No. You're full of hope and belief. And that is just what Elora needs." He flicks my nose, then slides his arm through mine. "Don't change yourself, sister. Change the realm."

He leads me through the heavy servants' door and into the late-night quiet of the palace corridors. The halls are lined with paintings from the finest artists in Elora and lit by the glow of flickering sconces that line the halls.

He stops at my chamber door. "What if I told you someone gave me something for you before I left Faerie?"

My stomach pitches. "Did he?"

He pulls a pale green velvet pouch from his pocket and hands it to me.

I loosen the strings, dump the contents in my hand, and my breath catches as I find myself staring down at the most beautiful pair of earrings I've ever seen. They're bloodred rubies wrapped in fine gold vines with tiny emeralds as leaves. "Why in the world did he think to send me such a lovely gift?"

"I believe they're a sign of his affection. Not that anyone needs reminding."

I study the earrings again. "Did he send a message with them?"

"A message?" He shakes his head and my stomach sinks.

I shouldn't expect so much. He's very busy, with more demands on his time than I can wrap my head around. I should accept the gift and be grateful.

Konner's lips twitch and he nods to the doorway behind me. "I'm pretty sure anything he has to tell you he'd like to tell you himself." Before his words sink in, he takes me by the shoulders, turns me around, and nudges me into my chambers. The door closes behind me with a soft click.

Just inside the door, the breathtakingly handsome king of the Wild Fae waits with a finger to his lips, and it almost doesn't stop me from squealing.

His grin slowly grows as he looks me over. "Felicity." My name is an exhale. A discovery. A relief. The dark waves of his hair are mussed, as if he couldn't keep his hands out of it while he waited, and his skin is deeper golden than the last time I saw him, a testament to hours spent in the sun during our time apart, but those russet eyes I love so much are the same.

"I missed you," I whisper, and the ache in my chest slowly drains away.

His gaze flicks to the door and then I'm in his arms, spun until my back is to the wall and my face is cupped in his big hand. "Not as much as I missed you."

I tug my bottom lip between my teeth.

"You didn't have to do this. I don't need any gifts."

His callus-roughened fingers tickle my palm as he lifts one earring, then brings it to my ear. "That's too bad because I want to give you them all." He slides it into place before taking the other. His fingertips scrape across my earlobe, and I shiver.

"Have you thought any more about what we discussed?"

My stomach flutters at the memory of our last conversation. "I thought maybe that was the faerie wine talking. If my brother has been pressuring you to think this way, and you don't want—"

He presses a finger to my lips. "I am in love with you, Felicity. I have been since the first time I laid eyes on you."

My cheeks flame hot and I drop my gaze. "I don't know why."

"Because you're beautiful. And kind. And loyal. You're more than I ever dreamed I would find in a partner, and I am prepared to do whatever your mother asks to have you as my wife. But only if that's what *you* want."

He dips his head and sweeps his lips across mine. They're so soft and the kiss is so gentle, and I arch my back, pressing onto my toes as I part my lips beneath his. I want more. Our time together has been full of stolen moments and fleeting kisses, and never enough time alone.

Felicity, you have to wake up.

The words have me pulling away and looking around. "Did you say something?"

He arches a brow, amused. "While I was kissing you?"

"I mean, in my mind?"

I think I hear my name again, but this time it's little more than a distant echo. More like a memory than a sound.

Misha cocks his head. "Are you okay?"

I focus and hear nothing. *Feel* nothing but the presence of the male before me. I shake my head. "I'm fine. Just a little tired, I think."

"You aren't sleeping," he says. "More nightmares."

I shrug, as if it's nothing. "Can you stay? The maids always keep the guest room ready." Not that I wouldn't prefer he stay in my room, but Mother would never hear of it.

His throat bobs and regret shines in his eyes. "There have been developments in Faerie and threats against my court. I've spent too much time away, and it's weakening the magic of the throne."

Something twists in my chest, hard and tight. "Of course you need to be home. I can come to *you* sometimes."

He slowly shakes his head. "Not until it's safe. I won't put you in danger."

"I'll be fine."

He steps back. "Felicity..."

I see the resolve in his eyes, and it guts me. "I am not some delicate thing you need to protect. I *love* you. I don't want to lose you."

"Then wait for me." His expression is so patient, even though I'm asking something I have no right to ask. I knew who Misha was when we first began our relationship, even before the rumors of a court takeover came to light. I knew what his responsibilities were and what his priorities had to be.

"The people who want to steal your court while it's weak—they will do anything to spread their lies across your kingdom and remove you from that throne. Good is at a disadvantage against evil because we have morals. We have lines that we will not cross. They do not."

"They don't have this, though," he says, stroking the side of my face with his thumb. "Because they will never know a love like this, they will never have as much to fight for as I do."

Tears streak hot and wet down my cheeks as he lowers his mouth to mine. And for the first time his kiss isn't fleeting. He angles his head and parts his lips and pulls me close. The kiss is deep and full of all the love and promise I could ask for. This is a kiss of *I'm coming back for you*. A kiss of *I will win because of this love*. A kiss of devotion.

I let him wrap me into his arms and try to push it all from my mind, but when I tuck myself into bed, I still feel off. Still hear those words like someone was taking me by the shoulders and shaking me. *Felicity, you have to wake up.*

The wail of the siren pulls me from sleep, and I bolt upright in bed.

A siren.

The breath leaves my lungs.

They're here. They've breached the palace walls.

Before my feet can hit the floor, my door flies open and my handmaid rushes to my side.

"Milady, we need to go to a more secure room."

I shove my feet into my slippers and reach for my robe. "Where is Konner?"

The maid glances over her shoulder to the open door and then back to me. "We must hurry. We don't know where the intruders are or who their target is."

I toss my robe onto the bed and kick off the slippers.

"What are you doing? We must go."

"I'm getting dressed. I need to find my mother. They're here for the Seven, and none of us survives till dawn if they succeed." I try to speak with resolve and authority, but the last comes out with a hiccup. My eyes are burning. A weak little girl can't face her biggest enemies and survive. And I need to do more than survive today. I need to protect the people I love. My mother. The Seven. And the whole realm with them.

"Please," my handmaid pleads behind me. "Please come with me and we will find safety. Our best guards are protecting your mother."

I shake my head vehemently. "It has to be me. I can protect her. The oracle showed me." So many years ago. I was barely ten and had nightmares about the male who would come for my mother—the male the oracle showed me defeating.

I don't know how I know this is the day or why I'm so sure this palace raid will bring him with it, but I don't question my gut as I remove my sleeping gown and shove my arms into a fresh shirt.

When I've yanked on my fighting leathers and I'm reaching for my boots, I see my handmaid wringing her hands, her bottom lip shaking. "Please," she whispers.

"Go to the basement and to the back of the armory. It is the safest place in the palace."

She glances toward the door, and I know she wants to, but she shakes her head. "Not without you."

"I am in charge here," I say, and this time when I inject command into my words my voice stays steady. "And I am telling you to go without me."

"I can't. I would never forgive myself if something happened to you. Your mother would never forgive me."

"And I will never forgive *myself* if something happens to her." I hold her gaze for a long time, willing her to understand.

"If something happens to you—"

I can't waste any more time trying to convince her, so I wave a hand and use my magic to make her move. Her body goes limp for a beat before she walks out of the room, arms hanging at her sides. She might hate me for it, but she will forgive me later.

Only if you don't get yourself killed.

I yank on my boots and make quick work of the laces. Then I open my bedside drawer and wrap my fingers around the special blade I keep there.

With a deep breath, I run. The castle is full of shouts. Of people running and being ushered to safety. Chaos is in every direction, but I run toward the receiving hall, where I already know the Seven will be guarding the dais that allows us to communicate with the people of Elora from the safety of the palace.

I tear through the halls, weaving through the people who are running in the opposite direction—toward shelter. Only when I turn into a private back hall does the crowd clear. I pick up my pace—sprinting now.

You need to wake up.

The voice makes me skid to a halt.

I can't help you unless you wake up.

I spin around, looking for the source of those words, and find nothing. No one.

Images flash in my mind—like I'm in two places at once. Images of a blue-eyed little boy chasing me up a tree while I giggle with delight. Images of fields of grain outside the kitchen window and my mother's laughing face.

No. That's not my mother. I don't know that woman with her brown hair and green eyes. And yet the sight of her makes me ache in a way I can't explain. Makes me worry in a way that doesn't make sense.

I dig my nails into my palms, hoping the sting will ground me. *This is an illusion. Don't let their manipulative magic deter you from your mission.*

I feel my mother's presence before I see her.

"Felicity!" she calls.

But as her attention fixes on me, a stranger lunges for her. I attack, using my blade in a way that is at once familiar from my training and foreign because I've never known the feel of slicing into flesh before.

"Felicity," the male says before falling at my feet.

I meet his blue eyes and gasp. *Hale.*

How do I know his name? Why do I want to beg the gods to trade my life for his?

Your brother needs you.

I spin around, looking for that voice again.

Konner races into the room and pulls me into his arms.

And I stiffen. I stiffen because I can't seem to remember what the oracle showed me that brought me here tonight. I can't remember why I killed that male on the floor.

Wake. Up.

This isn't right. None of it. I'm not supposed to be here.

And I know as clearly as I know my own name that the male holding me against his chest might be my biological brother, but he isn't the male raised by my side, and I've spent my whole life running from him.

CHAPTER THREE

JASALYN

THERE IS NO MANTRA, NO measured breathing, no ring that could allow me to explore Feegus Keep without this horrible pit of fear in my belly. I've been here for hours and it's no better now than it was when I walked away from my goblin and turned my Enchanting Lady smile on the guards at the front gate.

The halls I've roamed show no sign of the atrocities that are committed inside these walls. Somewhere deep beneath these winding corridors, with their meeting spaces and utilitarian bunk rooms, is the dungeon where Mordeus held me, where I spent the worst weeks of my life.

Thanks to my ring, the guards only saw the Enchanting Lady. They had no idea how much I was shaking on the inside. But any boldness I might feel from these successes—entering this stronghold and exploring it freely—is dampened by the feeling that I'm being followed.

I look over my shoulder again, and again I see only those who seem to belong here. I glance toward the windows at the end of the stone hall to estimate how much time I have left before the sun rises. The moon is still high, but I could spend the entire night searching for the sword and still not see every room in this place. Its endless, curving stairwells alone are too much, and that's not even counting the levels beneath the surface I've been avoiding.

You slept for eight months. You can't afford to let fear slow you now.

Down the hall someone is coming toward me, whistling. Her robe is cinched around her waist and there's a towel thrown over her shoulder as if she's just come from the shower.

"Excuse me!" I call, jogging toward her. She stops and flashes me a bright smile. "I'm looking for the Sword of Fire."

The Sword of Fire is supposed to have a special magic that can take you anywhere you want to go and kill even the strongest immortal. Kendrick was hoping we could find the mythical sword at Feegus Keep. He wanted it so I could find and kill Erith, the wicked leader who's brought harm on so many Elorans. *I* want it to find and kill Mordeus.

"You are so kind," she says, stepping toward me like there's a magnet drawing her my way. "I want to help you. Anything you need."

I grapple for my patience. I need this ring to get these people to do my bidding, but the fawning I've encountered with each person I've spoken to has become tedious. "Tell me where I can find the Sword of Fire."

She shakes her head. "I don't know what that is, but I'll help you look."

I manage to contain my sigh of frustration. So far no one I've spoken with knows anything about the sword. It makes sense that Mordeus wouldn't have told everyone stationed here about the valuables they're guarding, but surely *someone* knows.

I try again. "Where does Mordeus keep his most valuable possessions?"

"He was wise, though perhaps not as wise as you. He keeps them throughout the court and some in the Eloran Palace."

"What about the sacred items he's stored here?"

"I don't know." She frowns and shakes her head. "I'm so sorry. Let me help you look?"

"Can you tell me where I can find the person who would know?"

"Commander Rieckus knows all the secrets of the keep."

"And where can I find this Rieckus?"

"She resides below the earth, behind the dungeons, where she can keep an eye on the prisoners. She can be cruel, though, and I don't want you to be hurt."

The dungeons. Despite the horror grasping at my throat, I treat her to a smile. "I promise I won't be. Now go to bed and get some rest."

She nods eagerly. "Of course. If that's what you'd like."

I would do anything to avoid going down to the dungeons, and it's tempting. Maybe what I'm looking for isn't even here, but I don't want to leave before asking the commander. At the very least, perhaps she can give me an idea of where to look next.

Behind me, a sword sings as it's pulled free from its hilt.

I unsheathe my dagger and spin, finding a wide-eyed male. "Milady, I only thought perhaps I could offer you *my* sword?"

My heart races. *You are the Enchanting Lady. No one will hurt you so long as you wear the ring. Breathe.*

"It is not made of fire, but it was my grandfather's and has protected me well through the years."

I shake my head and turn toward the basement stairs I've been avoiding. "Keep your sword. That's not what I'm looking for."

I could leave and come back. I could find Kendrick and the others again. Then I wouldn't have to face this place alone.

But my dream still haunts me. *Not dream*—Mordeus's memory of making a deal with Kendrick. Kendrick was to keep me from destroying myself while I was rotting in that cell, and that's exactly what he did. He pretended to be human because he knew I couldn't trust a faerie. And he kept on pretending when we were reunited. He *lied*.

I can't risk trusting Kendrick again. Not if there's any chance he's working with Mordeus. He lied to me. About wanting to help me escape the dungeons. About who he is. I can't trust him. So I will do this alone.

The guards who line the halls of the dungeons are no danger to me, I remind myself. They will see the Enchanting Lady and do her bidding.

I take a step and then another. The ring's magic is supposed to chill my heart and mute my fear. But the fear and numbness were coming back even before I left Kendrick, and *this* fear blares too loudly to be muted entirely.

This will be worth it. If I find the sword in these dark halls, the terror clutching my heart won't matter.

With each step down, I feel less and less like the Enchanting Lady with the heart of ice and more and more like the fourteen-year-old girl Mordeus broke. I look over my shoulder—once, twice—because I can't shake the feeling that someone is following several steps behind. But still I go. Because I don't have much time left. I have eleven days.

I haven't let myself think about that since I left the goblin's home. *Eleven days until I'm gone. Eleven days until I lose everything.*

I want to run far from this place and these memories of pain and terror, but I don't have enough time to waste, and I won't let him win.

If it's been eight months, how do you know Mordeus is still in the Eloran Palace? How do you know you won't lose consciousness at any moment when he uses you to grow stronger?

I shove away the thoughts and step onto the final stair, reaching a trembling hand to the door.

I know what I'll find on the other side. Pain and terror, darkness and despair.

"Jasalyn, stop!"

I spin and watch Kendrick take form on the steps behind me. "You've been *following me*?"

There's an odd hum behind the door. The din of the prisoners' cries? A vibration of some sort?

"I needed to be sure you were safe," he says, taking another step toward me. "You don't have to go down there. You're in danger here."

As if I can believe anything he tells me after the lies he's already spewed? Why is he even here if he isn't working for Mordeus?

"How long have you been here? Are you *working* with them?"

His throat bobs. "I thought you might come, so I placed a magical signal to alert me if you did. When I came, I didn't want you to run and make me forget I found you at all. But I couldn't leave you." He glances over his shoulder as if trouble might be headed down after us. "I couldn't risk you being around these people without anyone to protect you."

"*Protect me?* You want me to believe that's what you really care about? After everything?"

"Tell me what happened. Tell me what made you run."

I pin my mouth shut. I don't want to argue. I don't want to risk falling under his spell, don't want to risk my own fears and loneliness leading me back to him.

If I get on the other side of this door, the ring's magic will ensure he doesn't remember he ever saw me.

I reach for the handle and brace myself for the horrible sound and stench I remember, but when I release the latch and swing the door open, I'm greeted with more of that low humming.

Before my eyes can adjust to the darkness, red slits of light come charging at me.

Not humming. Growling.

I'm thrown into the wall of the stairwell as Kendrick shoves his body in front of mine.

A flash of light leaps from his hand and pulses around us.

The creatures freeze in their charge—dark-haired beasts like overgrown dogs with huge teeth and angry snarls.

In the next moment, they're charging again. This time, Kendrick directs his magic at me, and I don't even duck. I know before I feel it that he's protecting me.

A shield of air wraps around me, blocking the bloody maw of the beast that lunges at my face.

Kendrick draws his sword and slices across the throat of one creature before plunging into an eye of another. They keep coming at him, their teeth snapping at his face, claws reaching for his flesh.

I see the strike coming before he does. He's gutting one beast when the last remaining attacks him from behind. I surge forward, drawing my own blade, but I'm trapped, locked in place by the shield of protection wrapped around me, helpless to do anything but watch as the creature slices across Kendrick's neck with bladelike claws and sinks its teeth into his side.

Kendrick's cry of pain echoes off the walls and tears my chest in two. As I pound helplessly on the invisible shield, he plunges his dagger into the throat of the final snarling beast. It falls to the floor with an ear-piercing cry before Kendrick drops to his hands and knees.

His breath comes in ragged gasps. As he collapses fully onto the floor, the shield around me falls.

I rush to his side and drop to my knees. Blood gushes from his wounds onto the stone, mixing with the blood of the hounds. The flickering lights coming from the stairwell lanterns illuminate the increasing pallor of his skin.

He grabs for my hand but his grip is weak. "Jasalyn." His eyes flutter closed.

Everything inside me tells me to save him, but can I even trust him?

He tries to reach for me and his entire body recoils in pain at the movement. "I'm sorry. I'm sorry I couldn't protect you from Mordeus. I'm sorry I didn't—"

"No." I shake my head, as if I can keep him here by stubborn will alone. "You will *not* say your goodbyes today."

"Why did you leave me?" The question is so quiet, the words so weak that my eyes fill with tears.

"You're fae," I whisper, helplessness clawing at me. "Why aren't you healing?"

I tear the fabric from the inside of my jacket and press it to his side, putting pressure on the worst of his wounds.

"The Barghest's venom. It slows healing."

"You're going to be okay. I'm going to take you to the palace." I snap a thread on my goblin bracelet and swallow back another wave of tears. "My sister's healers can . . ."

Kendrick's eyes flutter open as he weakly rolls his head from one side to the other, and my heart sinks into the floor when I realize what he's trying to remind me of.

My goblin won't come. Kendrick is too injured. His injuries too grave. Goblins can't interfere with life-and-death moments.

His eyes close again.

"Stay with me," I beg. "Open your eyes, Kendrick. I need you to stay with me."

But his eyes remain closed, his breathing shallow. Too shallow.

"Help!" I shout up the stairs. "Someone help! Quick!"

We're surrounded by bloody carcasses of the beasts that'd been pinned in this cellar. Beasts that would've torn me apart if Kendrick hadn't appeared. What was he doing here? Was he really looking for me or was he working with these people? Was he helping Mordeus?

I fill my lungs and shout as loudly as I can this time. "Hurry and help me!"

I can feel the blood from his side seeping between my fingers and see his breaths slowing.

Just when I think I'll have to leave him to get help, I hear footsteps on the stairs.

"My lady?" The male peers down at me and his eyes go wide as he takes in the carnage. "Are you hurt? Let me help."

"My friend is hurt," I say, making sure I have his attention, making sure he is hearing the Enchanting Lady speak. "I need a healer and fast."

He gives a jerky nod, then turns to head back up the stairs before I remember—the ring. Just as it's working to make him do my bidding, it will work to make him forget me the moment he's out of my sight. Forget me and forget to fetch the healer I need.

"Wait!" My heart is racing and the whooshing in my ears makes it hard to think straight. There's so much blood. "Please don't leave me. I . . ."

"Of course not." He rushes back down the stairs and gazes longingly at me. "I'll stay as long as you want."

I could have him keep pressure on the wound while I go for help, but once I'm out of his sight, how do I know he'll continue to care for Kendrick? He'd likely completely abandon him. Or worse, identify Kendrick as an intruder and kill him.

Are you an intruder, Kendrick? Or are you working with Mordeus's people?

I shove the questions from my mind. I can't think about that right now.

"I need you to call for help," I tell the starry-eyed male. "Get someone's attention and have them get a healer." Because if *he* tells the person, they'll be able to remember their task, even if they don't remember me.

"I don't know if anyone can hear me from here. If I go to the top of the stairs—"

"No." I draw in a ragged breath. My heart feels like it's climbing into my throat. *Calm. Stay calm.* "Go up partway, but only so far that you can still see me."

"You're really afraid," he murmurs.

"I need that healer. Please. Find someone to fetch a healer, but don't leave my sight."

CHAPTER FOUR

JASALYN

He's going to live. He's going to be fine.

My hand shakes as I slowly and painstakingly stitch Kendrick's side, keeping one eye on the needle and one on the steady rise and fall of Kendrick's chest.

The Feegus Keep healer was confused when she was summoned to my side—not the dungeons, it turned out, but another godsforsaken section of the keep where they trap the death dogs they use for security—but she *did* finally arrive, and not a moment too soon.

Like the others, she was happy to do my bidding once in my presence and administered an antitoxin as well as a potion to help Kendrick heal. Once his breaths grew deeper and the color returned to his face, I plucked a thread on my goblin bracelet again. Only then did Gommid arrive, happily accepting a handful of a sentinel's hair as payment in exchange for whisking us away to the Ironmoore infirmary.

My plan had been to take him to the Midnight Palace, but I decided it was too dangerous—for him, for me, for my sister.

I thought if I brought him here, to Ironmoore, at least he'd be around his people and I could leave him in their capable hands. But the moment I looked into the glazed eyes of the village healer, I knew I couldn't walk away. I couldn't take a chance that they might forget to watch him for reactions to the antitoxin once the memory of me faded.

I commanded the healer to place a sentinel outside the infirmary doors and not allow anyone through. Then, once she'd done all she could to clean his wounds and relieve his pain, I sent her away and began the tedious process of stitching him up. I've probably spent thousands of hours with a needle in my hand stitching fabrics of all kinds, but nothing could have prepared me for stitching up such a ragged wound. What it's like to work around the blood. The feel of the needle piercing flesh again and again.

"Jas?"

I flinch and pause before making my next stitch. Kendrick's fighting sleep, his ice-blue eyes doing everything they can to focus on me. "Shh," I murmur. "You're okay. Just rest."

"You aren't real. We search and search, and it's never you." His eyes float closed, the healing tonic pulling him under again. "Do you have any idea what I'd give up to find you?"

My heart twists painfully. *You betrayed me.*

But then somehow he was there when I needed him. He risked his own life to save me. And so here I am, making sure he lives through the night even without knowing if he'll hand me over to Mordeus if given the chance.

I release the needle and thread and shake away the trembling in my hands.

"I don't know where she is," he says, the words so quiet I'm almost not sure I heard him right. He's fighting sleep but can't seem to pull from its grasp. "Help me find her. Help me save her. I have to find her before Mordeus takes over and we lose her forever."

The words are a blade twisting in my chest. I can't reconcile any of this with the male who lied to me. I can't let myself forget that he worked with Mordeus. And I can't let myself forget Mordeus's memory of Shae and the agreement he made with Mordeus.

When the time is right, we'll bring her to you.

A dozen times tonight, I've reminded myself of his friend's promise to Mordeus, of Kendrick's lies—about why he was in the cell across from me three years ago and about who and what he is.

I don't want to believe he's working for Mordeus, that he had any part in that deal his friend made, and I never would've doubted before his lies were revealed, but now I don't know.

His eyes fly open and he gasps, sitting halfway up. "Jas . . . Is that really you?"

I press a palm to his chest, urging him back down before he tears open his partially stitched wound. "You need to be still."

He settles back, lids fluttering as he trains his gaze on me. I turn to the counter and pour him another shot of the pain tonic. The healer said he needs to sleep if he's going to recover, and *I* need him to sleep so I can think straight.

"Drink this," I instruct, lifting his head and tilting the small glass to his lips.

He does as instructed, and within moments his body goes limp.

"I miss you," he murmurs. "Never knew what this was like. Never thought the gods would give me someone like you. Never thought they'd be cruel enough to take you away."

Tears burn my eyes. I miss him too, but if I can't trust him what does any of that matter? I watch his face, waiting for him to slip the rest of the way into sleep. When he does, I take a steadying breath and return to my work.

"Jasalyn?"

I jerk awake, my eyes snapping open at the sound of my name. When did I fall asleep? And for how long?

Kendrick's sitting on the side of the infirmary bed, squinting against morning light coming in the window. The last thing I remember was watching him rest. I'd finished stitching him up where I could and I was trying to convince myself I could leave. Trying to convince myself he'd make it through the night.

"What happened?" he asks, looking around.

I squeeze my eyes shut against the horrible onslaught of emotions his voice brings. How can a sound that evokes such comfort and peace also cause such pain?

He looks around the room, taking in all the healer's potions and ointments before returning his attention to me. "Did I find you at the keep? Are you hurt? Are you—"

Of course, he doesn't remember saving me thanks to the ring. "I'm fine." My jaw is tight. This is so hard—wanting to curl into his arms while also wanting to run from him, knowing his recovery means everything to me while also knowing how horribly he betrayed me. "You're the one who's hurt."

"Death dogs," he says, glancing to his side. "But you're okay?"

"What do you remember?"

His jaw works and his blue eyes scan me again and again. "I thought you'd go there months ago. We'd been looking for you to no avail, so we set a magical alarm of sorts—to notify us if you arrived there. It'd been so long that when the magic activated, I didn't remember what it was at first. I got there as fast as I could." He searches my face. "Did I find you or did you find me?"

"You found me." *You followed me to make sure I was safe. And you saved me.*

"We've been worried out of our minds. Your sister—"

The blood drains from my face so fast I go lightheaded. "Stay away from my sister."

He jerks back as if I hit him. "Jas, I don't understand what's happening here. My last notes in my journal tell me we'd spent the night together. We were still planning to find the sword. You wanted to help us." His throat bobs as he swallows. "What happened? Did someone capture you? Where have you been?"

He doesn't remember our last conversation just like he won't remember this. "I left."

The confusion on his face sends an ache through me. "Why?"

"Because I know the truth."

"What truth?" He shakes his head. "I don't know what happened. Tell me so I can make it right."

I push off the floor. "I don't want to do this again. I just stayed long enough to make sure you'd be okay, and you are, so I'm going now."

"Don't go." He looks around, as if he might find the answers he needs. "I've been losing my mind with worry. I close my eyes and think of how I failed you. I wonder endlessly where you've gone and fear what could be happening to you. Please..."

My heart tugs hard but I ignore the feeling. I can't let him manipulate me with his pretty words. "I can't trust anything you say." I stare at the floor because looking at him hurts too much. "You are the last person I ever thought could hurt me."

"I never meant to. Anything I did..."

I swallow hard. Why isn't this easier? He betrayed me but leaving feels impossible. "We're in Ironmoore. You might feel stronger by now if I'd taken you to the healers at the Midnight Palace, but I didn't think my sister would respond kindly to discovering a traitor in her midst."

"Traitor?" He coughs. "What's that supposed to mean? Will you please just *talk* to me?"

I meet his eyes, and my heart surges into my throat. It hurts to breathe. "What else do you call the person who lied to me? What else do you call the male who betrayed me for his deal with Mordeus?"

His face falls. "Jas..."

"That's right," I whisper. "I know. I know the faerie ears aren't a glamour at all. I know about the deal you made."

He leans forward, the heels of his hands on his knees. "That's why you left? Because you found out I'm fae? And found out Mordeus asked me to keep you alive?"

I curl my nails into my palms, relishing the sting. "How can you say that like it's nothing? Like I'm overreacting?"

"It's not nothing, and I know that." He holds out a hand as if

I'm an injured animal who might strike if he's not cautious. "How could I tell you the truth? How could I admit I only pretended to be human in that cell when you hate the fae *so much*? I needed you—*still* need you—and I didn't want to scare you."

Anger surges and I cling to it. "*That's* why you lied? So I wouldn't be scared? Try. Again."

"Not at first, but I wanted to tell you the truth and, honestly, after everything that happened before you left, everything you were learning about Elora and the history, I thought you were going to figure it out soon anyway. But I never guessed it would make you run from us." His voice dips, goes raspy. "I'm sorry."

"And what about your deal with Mordeus? Did you think I'd figure *that* out too?"

He squeezes his eyes shut and pinches the bridge of his nose. "I will never forgive myself for not seeing through that request." When he looks at me again, it feels as if he's looking right into my soul. As if he's begging me to look into his. "Can you blame me for taking that deal? I didn't know what Mordeus had planned or what he was doing to you. All I knew was that in return for him freeing my queen, I had to keep a girl alive. A girl who was so scared and whose kindness I could feel from my cell. A girl I came to care about a great deal. Once I met you, I would've done whatever was necessary to protect you even if it hadn't been part of our agreement."

"But you weren't *protecting* me. You were as good as those bars keeping me locked there. You gave me false hope. You might as well have been the one holding me down while he carved his knives into my skin."

Kendrick flinches. "If I could change things . . ." He shoves off the bed and stalks toward me. "No. I'd still keep you alive. Maybe I would've tried harder to kill him, but I wouldn't have let you give up."

I hang my head and hate myself for how reassured his words make me feel.

"I don't have it in me to let you give up. I didn't then, and I don't now." He comes closer, his fingers brushing my arm.

I jerk away before his touch can melt me. Even though I need it. Even though part of me would happily lie to myself forever if it meant I could forgive him, forgive it all, and go back with him. *But I can't.* "Maybe you never meant to hurt me, and maybe I could forgive that deal, but the company you keep says a lot about you."

He straightens. "I don't know what you mean. Is this about the others? Skylar? Remme? Did one of them do something?"

"I don't know about them." I shrug. I want to trust them but every time I trust again, I'm made a fool. "Your friend Shae."

His face turns stoic. "What about Shae?"

"I saw him in my dreams—in Mordeus's memories. He promised to bring me to Mordeus when the time was right. I think . . ." Why am I here? Why am I trusting him? Why do I so badly want to believe Kendrick doesn't know about Shae's exchange with Mordeus? Isn't it just as likely that Kendrick was in on it too?

But I don't believe that. I can't.

"I think he has something to do with this blood magic that's connected me to Mordeus—he's involved with bringing Mordeus back."

"Tell me what you know."

Can it hurt? Explaining all this? Either he's in on it and already knows or he's not and needs to understand his friend is a liar. "I had these dreams—dreams where I was Mordeus." I lick my dried-out lips. "I thought they were just nightmares. Just my twisted subconscious making me feel as dark and ugly inside as he is. But then Natan told us what he'd found out about the blood magic and the ring and the connection between me and Mordeus, and it started to click. They weren't dreams. They were *memories*. And the memory of your friend Shae? He told Mordeus he'd win my trust and bring me to him so that Mordeus could 'rise again.' What does that sound like if not using me to bring Mordeus back to life?"

"And you're sure the male from your dream—from the memory—was Shae?"

"When I saw him in my dream, I didn't have any idea he had any connection to you, but I would never forget that face. Those eyes. Then, that last morning in Ironmoore, I saw him sitting in the kitchen and it all came together for me." I flick my gaze to Kendrick and take in the angry lines on his face. "You don't look surprised."

"I won't pretend that what you're saying isn't hard to hear." He paces the length of the small infirmary. "Shae and I grew up together. Once, we were best friends. He's pulled away since I was tapped as the next Eloran king, but it's still hard to believe he'd betray us like that."

My stomach twists with a painful combination of hope and doubt. I want to trust Kendrick. I want to believe what he's saying, but the lure of the Enchanting Lady's magic doesn't work on him, so I have no way of ensuring his honesty.

"Shae's always had a dangerous kind of ambition. The day the oracle told me I was the Chosen, he lost it and wrecked the entire barn. He thought it should be him."

"And you trusted him after that?" He's so close I can feel his warmth, but I don't let myself move any closer.

"He apologized. He said he'd always believed that he was destined for greatness, but that after he had his meltdown he realized he could find that by my side." He scratches at his scruffy cheeks. "I think I believed him because I wanted to."

"But now you believe me?"

He stops pacing and his chest expands with a deep breath. "We haven't seen Shae since the day you left. He went to Elora to try to find another way into the palace. Or so he said. He never came back, and we thought he'd been captured, but . . . I don't know. Something's been bothering me about all of it. After he disappeared, I started realizing things with him haven't been adding up lately. Little things. Times he disappeared or wasn't where he was supposed to be. I've been worried about him, but part of me has been equally suspicious as new information has come to light."

"Like what?"

"That ring isn't randomly stuck on your finger. Mordeus needed you to be unable to remove it so he could better control you. We first thought the attack on Ironmoore came from the Seven trying to put a stop to our revolution, but Natan has gathered enough intel that now we know they weren't behind it—at least, not as a whole. We suspect the wyvern attack had a different purpose entirely. Historically, wyvern cries have been used to unlock dormant magic and we think that night was all about unlocking the magic that would keep that ring on your finger."

I nod, but I'm all jumbled up inside. Kendrick and his friends have been spending the time I've been away trying to figure out how to help me. How to free me from this ring. That doesn't fit with the story I've been telling myself. That doesn't make sense if they've been working with Mordeus. "What does this have to do with your friend Shae?"

"Someone still would've had to *send* the wyvern. Who knew you were in Ironmoore with us who would also know to use Isaak to get the wyvern into camp in the form of Crissa? Only Shae." He holds my gaze for a long time. "So, yes. Yes, I believe you. But I wish you would've told me instead of running away."

I scan his face over and over. I trust him, but it's too late. I'm running out of time. I don't have enough to waste wishing I'd handled things differently.

"Stay with me," Kendrick says, dropping into a crouch before me. He lifts his hand to my face, then drops it again. "Let me prove myself. Your sister has been losing her mind trying to find you."

Abriella. I set my jaw. "My sister is better off without me."

"Never." His face goes hard. "Don't say that."

"You wouldn't understand."

"My sister is missing too. I understand precisely how awful it is. Knowing you failed to protect your own, knowing they're out there somewhere and you're failing them again?"

"See, and I didn't even know you had a sister." *Because you don't know him at all*, I tell myself, but only because I'm struggling to remember that. It's nearly impossible when he's this close, when only hours ago I thought he was going to die in front of me.

"Felicity's my sister," he says. "The shifter who went to Castle Craige in your stead."

I flinch. "You didn't tell me that."

"And maybe I should have." He grimaces, and I can see the apology in his eyes. "She was adopted and raised at my side. But even if I'd shared that part, I was afraid that you'd question my story too much if you knew I had a fae sister."

"Did she go missing from Castle Craige?"

He nods solemnly. "Eight months ago. We've been searching for you both."

Guilt cuts through me. "Did someone take her thinking she was me? Did—"

"No. She'd been found out and thrown into a cell, made to take her true form. The others think she's been captured by Erith, but I can't let myself believe that."

"Why?"

The anguish on his face guts me. "Because Erith is her birth father and he's wanted her dead since before she was born. The oracle prophesied long ago that she would be the one to kill him."

Nausea surges in my throat. Another person whose life will be cut short because of me.

"We're going to find her," Kendrick says, his voice hard. "I refuse to give up, just like I've refused to give up searching for you."

"If Erith took her, then you'll need the sword to get her back. Or the portal that allows you into the Eloran Palace. Right?"

"None of the Seven would allow a prisoner to reside in their precious palace. They are too scared of their enemies to allow them that close. But we have a promising lead that Misha's investigating now."

My mind spins as I try to piece it all together. It's like trying to read a book without half the pages. *That's what happens when you sleep for eight months.* I wring my hands. "So your sister is missing, and my sister . . . she knows I had Felicity pretend to be me?" I can just imagine Brie's panic the moment she found out the shifter wasn't me and realized I was missing.

"She didn't believe you had anything to do with it at first, but Felicity told her enough that she had to believe it."

My stomach feels like it's filling with stones as I imagine how hurt and betrayed Brie must've felt when she found out the truth. "And how do you know all this?"

His smile is small and sad. No sign of the dimples I love so much. No trace of happiness in his eyes. "Because your sister and King Misha tracked us down and asked for our help. So we've been searching, but with that damn ring in our way, it's like chasing a ghost. There have been rumors of sightings but nothing we could confirm, and of course Abriella has had to pretend you were safely in the palace the whole time."

Because if the people of her court knew she can't even keep tabs on her own sister, it would make her look weak.

"Where *have* you been?" he asks.

"Sleeping," I whisper, but when his panicked eyes meet mine I know he's thinking the same thing I am. That maybe my *consciousness* was sleeping for the last eight months, but that doesn't mean my body was. Not when Mordeus's consciousness is linked to mine. Not when he's used me to do his dirty work before this ring was even stuck to my finger.

"This is why you can't leave." The aching rasp in his voice is worse than the words he spoke when he was bleeding out and slipping away. "We can't risk losing any more time."

It would be so easy to stay. Walking away is embracing the loneliness of my mission. But if I stay, I'll be distracted by Kendrick's mission, and I can't let myself do anything else until I take care of Mordeus. "I know you need me to kill Erith, and I'm sorry that your sister was captured because of me, but I can't worry about that right now." I step around him and toward the door.

"This isn't about *Erith*. This is about *you*. And there are things . . ." He pauses as if he can't find the words. "You need to understand what Mordeus has planned."

I hesitate before turning back to him. "What do you mean?"

He swallows. "Before Felicity was taken, she told them your secret." His eyes are so sad, and it's like seeing him bleeding all over again. I want to fix it. "She told them what you traded for that ring. That your life ends on your eighteenth birthday."

My stomach sinks, another stone added to the pile in my gut. "Oh." Why does the idea of my sister—of *Kendrick*—knowing make the sacrifice suddenly seem so real?

"How do we undo it?" he asks, voice raw. "What do we have to do?"

I shake my head. "It's done. We can't undo anything."

The pain that moves across his face makes me wish for a different life in a different world under a different set of stars. "You just want me to accept that I lose you in less than two weeks? No. I refuse. We will find a way to reverse it."

"All that matters is that I end Mordeus before that day comes, and if I'm going to do that then I need your special Eloran sword. I couldn't find it at Feegus Keep, but I haven't—" *I need to go back and find that commander to see if she knows where it is, and I need to do it before that goblin's potion wears off and I'm lost to sleep again.* I draw in a deep breath. "I've stayed too long. I'm wasting time. I shouldn't even be here. I never should've stayed."

"I'm glad you did." When his fingertips brush my shoulder, my body goes rigid, but I don't have it in me to pull away again. "Don't do this alone. It's too dangerous. And the sword—"

"The sword is all that matters. It will take me to Mordeus and it will kill him." I will destroy him for what he did to me. For what he turned me into. I curl my fists at my sides, determined not to fall apart. Exhaustion is creeping back.

"We never stopped looking for the sword. We need it more than ever now that we believe Felicity might be trapped in another realm. But while you've been gone, we've learned Mordeus hid the sword—spelled it so only he could see it. Even if it was right in front of our eyes, we wouldn't know it."

I reel back as if I've been punched in the chest. When I try to draw breath, nothing comes. How am I supposed to face Mordeus without the sword? I'm not strong enough. I was never strong enough to make a difference when it came to him.

"I'm sorry. I know that's not what you wanted to hear."

Finally, I drag air into my lungs, but the panic rumbles inside me, crushing all my plans. "I'll find another way."

"Do you understand why we need to work together? Your sister's been as obsessed over finding you as I have. She will be *so glad* to see you again."

To see me and then watch me die in days. To see me and be that much closer to danger because of Mordeus's connection to me.

I can't let that happen.

I point to the opposite side of the room, where cabinets line the walls. "I'm feeling weak," I say, and it's not a lie. "The healer left a healing tonic over there." Also not a lie, though the only tonic there is for Kendrick. "Would you get it for me?"

"Of course." He strides to the other side of the room, and I reach for the door.

"You won't remember any of this." This time when I walk away from Kendrick, it's harder than every step I took toward Mordeus's dungeons.

CHAPTER FIVE

FELICITY

I FEEL THE SPELL HOLDING me under and fight against it. Fight with my mind and my magic until I'm working my sticky eyes open and seeing flashes of the room around me. The stone walls. The figure watching me from the corner. The thin mattress under me.

My mind is a collection of puzzle pieces that don't fit together. My childhood in the palace. Running through the fields with Kendrick. My mother's adoring smile. The paralyzing fear of knowing how quickly my father will kill me if he ever finds me. Misha's breath on my neck before he kisses me good night. Misha spitting words at me as I'm dragged away.

I'll let you rot in my dungeon for a few days before I listen to more of your lies.

The last has me gasping for a breath that pulls me back into my body. Back to myself.

I jump off the bed and fall into a heap of weakness on the stone floor.

A figure in the corner moves toward me. "Easy now. The body grows weak after months of sleep."

Who is he? Where am I?

Misha will come for me, something says from the corner of my mind, and I have to shove it away. Misha hates me.

Misha wants to marry me, another part of my mind protests. That. Isn't. Real.

The figure takes another step forward but he's still too cloaked in shadow for me to identify. "Go back to sleep. It's better there. I promise."

"You got into my head," I say to the stranger, but the words slur together, slow and sticky as molasses. "You planted a whole life there." And it wants to pull me under again. To pull me back into that dream reality where I have a family and a future and a home.

I didn't realize quite how lonely I was until I was made to know a life where I wasn't.

"I was merely showing you how things could've been," the stranger says. "Perhaps how things could still be if you let them."

Kendrick bleeding out at my feet. "I'll pass," I say, voice raspy, like I haven't used it in ages. Sleep and dreams call to me, promising refuge. How long have I been a prisoner of these dreams? How long have I been a captive? Months, like the stranger said?

"You'll *pass*?" His dry laugh echoes off the stone walls of the room—no, *cell*. "Yes, because your life pretending to be anyone but yourself was so much better?"

Better? No. It wasn't better. And the idea of sinking back into that world where I had my mother's love, where Misha adored me for being myself and no one else? Yes, it's so tempting to return to that. But my survival depends on me resisting it.

A torch on the wall flames to life, illuminating the stranger as he crouches in front of me. The sight of him makes my heart twist.

Blond hair and ice-blue eyes just like mine. Just like the male in the illusion. Just like my twin brother.

"Konner." I say the name like it's precious. Like he means something to me. And I hate myself for it.

He must see the push and pull of conflicting emotions on my face because he smiles. "Hello, sister."

I squeeze my eyes shut against the wave of affection threatening to drown me. He taught me how to wield a sword and shield my mind. He held my hand while we stood at our mother's sickbed. He—

No.

Our mother was murdered by our father and all those childhood memories are nothing more than strategically placed fantasies to confuse me.

"Why?" I ask. And I hate myself for how much I like having him here. Hate myself for how much I want to talk with him. To *know* him.

My real family.

"Why what? Why show you the life you could have? Why try to make my sister—the twin I once shared a womb with—see the truth?"

"Why haven't you *killed* me?" I have to force the words out. Have to remind myself that's the real question here.

"Maybe I want you alive," he says, shoving his hands into his pockets. "You think you're the only one who had a lonely childhood? I could've used a sister. A friend."

"Or maybe you want to ascend into the Seven and you can't kill me if you want to survive the fire portal."

"You think I have an entire palace at my disposal and not a single person who would get blood on his hands for me?" He shakes his head. "Besides, I've been doing our father's slaughtering for years. He never intended to allow me to ascend." Sighing, he studies me. "I'm not so different than the brother in your dreams."

I can't just sit here and listen to him, so I scan the walls of the cell, searching for a door, a window—anything I could potentially use as a path to escape. "Except that you want me dead."

"I know that's what you think, but you're wrong."

"You and Erith want me dead. That's why he killed our mother when he found out about me. That's why he sent his soldiers looking for me."

"You are assuming so much."

"Do you deny the oracle told our father that his daughter would kill him? Do you deny he wants me dead?"

"I don't, but I am not our father."

"And yet here I am. In some dark cell with no way out." I push off the floor—I need to get away from him—but I have to cling to the side of the bed to help myself up. *I'm too weak.*

He stands and cocks his head to the side. "Have you tried asking nicely?" He waves a hand, and I feel strength pour back into me. I gasp as I'm able to straighten. "There," he says. "A gift from your loving brother."

I cough out a laugh. Legs that can hold me up are a start, but they won't get me out of a doorless, windowless cell. "You're just going to let me go if I ask? It's that simple?"

He shrugs. "Maybe not. But not for the reason you think." He studies me for a long time and I study him right back. All those illusions he planted in my mind are so strong that it's hard to see him for the enemy I know him to be. "You're stronger than I expected. I'll give you that."

I glare. Stronger? He just had to use his magic to give me the strength to stand.

"Your *mind*." He rolls his eyes. "It took more energy than I expected to keep you dreaming."

"What do you want from me?"

"I want you to rest until it's time."

"Time for what?"

"Don't worry about that."

I narrow my eyes, cocking my head to the side as I study him. "You don't know, do you? You have spent your life doing everything he asks and he can't even tell you his plans."

I see a flash in his eyes—something like frustration, anger. "I am not his puppet."

Thunder rumbles in the distance, and faster than I can follow, Konner is behind me, one arm wrapped around my waist, the other hand at my throat, a heavy wave of sleepiness thrown over me like a blanket.

In front of us, a tall, olive-skinned man, the silver lines on his forehead flashing.

"I suggest you release her before I show you what *real* magic can do."

Misha? Is that him or am I hallucinating? No. This has to be a dream. He hates me.

Konner tightens his hold and his magic surges, pulling me back into sleep. I cling to consciousness like a cat sinking its claws into its captor. The edges of my vision go dark.

Another crack echoes through the room, and then Konner drops his hand from my neck. He flies against the opposite wall, smashing against it with a thud.

My knees hit the floor, then my hands. Konner falls to the ground in a heap beside me.

"Hurry," Misha says, extending a hand.

I stare at it, skeptical. Is this another one of Konner's illusions?

"Easy." His big hand spreads across my back and I want to press into the warmth of it—into him. I want to go back in time to the moment I kissed him good night before the palace was attacked. I want to curl into his arms and never leave.

The thought is so pathetic it tears a sob from me. *He never wanted you. He wanted the woman he thought you were. The only place he wanted the real you was in your dreams.*

"Just breathe." He rubs gentle circles on my back. "You're okay. I'm here."

He slides an arm underneath mine and pulls me to my feet.

"Are you ready?"

I blink at him. "Ready?"

A hint of a smile on those beautiful lips. "To get out of here."

And that's the first moment it occurs to me that I don't know how he got to me. Or even where we are.

He makes a fist and then flicks his fingers toward the wall. A spinning disc of light appears, growing larger and larger. *A portal.*

But before we can take a single step, Konner surges to his feet, standing between us and that glowing portal—between us and freedom.

"I should've killed him," Misha mutters, but when he releases me to deal with Konner, another figure appears in the room, dark and menacing.

He grabs Misha from behind and puts a knife to his neck. "How does it feel to be king of a magical realm and find yourself powerless in this one?"

"Orlen," Konner growls. "Don't show off."

Powerless? Misha is anything but. And yet . . . I reach for my own weak, unconditioned magic and find myself grasping at air. There's no magic in this room.

When Konner grabs me again, I barely register it, too stunned to spin from his grasp.

Misha is locked in place with that blade against his neck. I see the anger in his eyes.

The man holding Misha—Konner called him Orlen—he's a *silencer*. It's a rare and highly valued kind of magic and so long as he's able to wield it, we won't be escaping through any portals.

"You think he wouldn't kill you?" Orlen asks Konner, his blade biting into Misha's skin.

"Everybody calm down," Konner says, still holding me in front of him like a shield.

"I'm only protecting you, Kon," Orlen says, and I wonder what he means by that. Who is this male to Konner? "He's going to ruin everything."

A trickle of dark red blood stains Orlen's blade, and rage boils inside me, but then I realize Misha's staring at me *hard*, trying to tell me with his eyes what he would say into my mind in any other circumstance. His gaze flicks to the sword strapped at Konner's waist before coming back to meet mine.

"Sol will kill you with her bare hands if you take him out," Konner tells Orlen. "We need—"

In a sudden burst of movement, Misha frees himself from his captor's hold, and I act without letting myself think. I shift in Konner's grasp, throwing my weight just like Misha taught me, then grab my brother's sword. When I lunge at Orlen, I have only a split second to make my choice. This stranger or Misha. Only one will make it out of here alive.

I plunge my blade between Orlen's ribs.

He stumbles back and slides down the wall. His dark eyes meet mine.

Those eyes condemn me for this choice.

With a sob, I yank the blade free before driving it home again—this time at the hollow of his neck. He gasps and gags and then falls to his knees, then onto the floor. Blood pools onto the stone around him and bubbles out of his mouth.

I'm frozen. I can't take my eyes off him.

The moment Misha's power returns, the energy in the room changes. He throws out a hand toward Konner, but before his magic can land a blow, Konner disappears.

"We have to get out of here before he comes back. Before he brings another one like *that*," he says, sneering at the dead male on the floor.

I can't move. I took a life.

"Felicity!" Misha snaps. "Are you listening to me?"

I tear my gaze off Orlen. Off the pool of blood and those lifeless eyes. "What?"

He slides an arm around me and yanks me roughly against his side. "Just hold on."

The portal appears and Misha drags me through it and into—a living room?

As quickly as the portal appeared, it closes behind us.

I look around, trying to get my bearings. *Misha just created a portal inside what was surely a well-warded cell.*

"We'll stay here for the night," he says, probably noting the confusion on my face. He collapses onto an upholstered chair and looks me over, something like worry and relief in his expression. "We both need rest."

CHAPTER SIX

JASALYN

I lean against the infirmary door and choke back a sob.

Kendrick won't remember any of that, and I should be glad. I should call my goblin and go back to the cottage where I've been sleeping and see if I can stay another day to sleep off this weakness.

And then what? How am I going to find the sword now if only Mordeus knows its location? And if I can't find him and end him, what was the point of any of this? If he lives and I die, then the only thing my sacrifice brought me was the very thing I would've laid down my life to avoid.

I wish I could talk to Abriella. She would know what to do.

The ache is so sudden and so strong, I nearly fall to the ground.

I had three years with her at the Midnight Palace where I avoided her at every turn. I did everything I could to avoid looking at her or talking with her or even being near her.

Now the risen sun means I have ten days left and I want time with my sister more than anything.

"Jasalyn?"

I jerk my head up and see Natan walking toward me, his hair tied back, his glasses glinting in the morning light. For a moment,

I forget about the ring, forget that he'll be under my spell, and a combination of panic and gratitude fills my heart. Panic because I shouldn't be here. Gratitude because I'd missed him without realizing it. Natan, Remme, even Skylar—they all became my friends during my time with Kendrick.

"You look upset," he says. "How can I help?"

I shake my head and rush down the infirmary steps before he can open the door. I don't want Kendrick to see me. "I was just leaving."

He frowns. "We've been looking for you. Are you safe? Have you seen Kendrick?"

Usually people are so enamored with the Enchanting Lady that they forget anything that's been on their mind. It doesn't mean Natan's not under my spell, but he's definitely resisting it. His conscious mind is pushing to the forefront despite the ring's lure. "I saw him," I admit.

He beams. "And you're staying?"

"No. Natan, I . . ." I scan the quiet roads around the Ironmoore square. "Are you staying here?"

He shakes his head. "No. Our team left the village not long after you disappeared."

Last time I was here, the place was half charred from the wyvern attack. Now the destroyed buildings have been torn down but few have been erected in their place. This is why Kendrick and his friends wanted my help. Their oracle showed Kendrick an image of me slaying the wicked Patriarch of the Seven that rule Elora. It gave them hope for the future of a realm that has had little for a very long time.

They will have to find another way.

"I'm only here because I sensed Kendrick was," he says. His forehead wrinkles with thought and his glance skips back to the building behind me. "You brought him to the infirmary. Is he okay?"

I swallow. "He will be."

"And you?" When he asks this, I realize he's avoiding my gaze. It doesn't eliminate the Enchanting Lady's power completely, but it lessens the effect. Knowing Natan, he's probably learned everything there is to know about enchanted rings in the last eight months and he's using that knowledge to his advantage.

"I'm fine." That might've been believable if I didn't choke on the word. With a final glance toward the infirmary, I start walking. I don't want to repeat my reunion with Kendrick if he comes out those doors again.

Natan follows—whether because he wants to talk to me more or because he's compelled by the ring, I'm not sure, but I don't question it. I might as well use his company to my advantage.

"Kendrick told me that no one but Mordeus knows where the sword is, but I need to find it or find another way to get to him."

"You're running out of time." It's not warning or censure. It's said in a tone of understanding, something close to sympathy that makes tears prick my eyes. "But even if you only have days left, I don't want you risking your life to go after Mordeus. None of us want that."

"So I'm supposed to just . . . what? *Enjoy* my last ten days of life without worrying about the consequences of what I've done? You just want me to let it all go?"

His throat bobs. "I don't want that either. Mordeus will be too powerful once he takes over your body."

The world spins a little and I have to dig my nails into my palms to steady myself. "Say that again."

"Mordeus will be too powerful once he takes over your body," he says, the need to blindly obey the Enchanting Lady making him take me literally.

"But I'm dead in ten days. What would he want with a dead body?"

"Not a dead body." He shakes his head, and I can tell he's trying to resist the need to give me what I want.

"What do you mean *takes over my body*?" I ask.

"It's your gift," he says, as if that makes any sense. "Your body will go on as long as there's a consciousness attached. And he needs your body because his cannot sustain life. He's in limbo right now—his consciousness resurrected without a body that can hold him."

"You're telling me that *Mordeus* will be in me? My body, his mind?" Everything in me rejects this notion. And yet I know what it's like to have his mind inside me. I've known for a while now. *I'm going to be sick.* "Why didn't Kendrick tell me this?"

"He didn't want you to know," he says, pointedly staring at the ground. There's more that he's not telling me. More that he doesn't want me to know.

"Natan, look at me," I say. He grimaces but obeys. "Why didn't Kendrick want me to know about Mordeus taking over my body when my time runs out?"

His eyes glaze with the power of my enchantment and I know

I'll get the truth. "He didn't want you to hurt yourself to prevent it. He still believes there's a way to reverse all of this."

"And you've been researching for him, right?"

"Of course. Looking for where they've hidden Felicity and how to help you. Every day."

"In all that research, have you found a way to cut off the connection between me and Mordeus?"

"There isn't much out there on blood magic. The Elorans banned it years ago and the Seven either destroyed or confiscated every book written about it. We know from history that blood magic is used to connect the magic or life force of two individuals, and that the scars appear when the magic is called upon."

I nod. He told me all this the day I left them, not that it makes it any easier to wrap my head around.

"And since Mordeus performed countless blood magic rituals, he connected your life forces over and over again so he could call on that connection again and again."

"Have you learned anything *new* since I saw you?"

"I've been researching instead about interconnected souls—what happens when the consciousness of two individuals are bound together as he seems to have bound yours. It is that interconnection that allows him to take over your body for periods of time and it's also what will allow him to stay there once you cease to be."

"Because of the ring. We're connected because of the ring." I look down at my finger. We all should've listened to Skylar when she suggested cutting off my finger to get it off me.

"No," he says. "The ring strengthens the bond between you,

but it's the blood magic that keeps you connected. And the two together make it a complicated knot I have yet to learn how to untangle."

I can see why Kendrick might think I'd hurt myself to avoid this. I lived through those days of wanting to disappear, wanting to cease to be. How ironic that only now that I finally want *more* do I need to release this life for the good of everyone around me.

"So it's hopeless? All I can do is wait and pray to the cursed gods that one of you will plunge an iron blade into this chest the moment he takes over?"

The devastation in his eyes isn't about the ring or the enchantment he's under while speaking to me. It's not even about the destruction Mordeus will bring on this realm when he has the power of my body. Natan cares about me. They all do. And I lost eight months that I could've been working with them to find a solution. Lost it because I couldn't trust anyone. Lost it because, despite this ring that won't come off my finger, my fear was controlling me.

"We've missed you," Natan says, as if he can read my thoughts. "And I won't stop looking for a way to reverse the connection the blood magic created or for a way to get you back the life you traded for that ring."

But it's the blood magic that connected us—the blood magic that will mean more loss than just *my* life. "Natan." My head snaps up and I stare at him. "If Mordeus can tap into me—if my consciousness is connected to his—wouldn't the opposite be true? Couldn't I tap into his consciousness and find out where the Sword of Fire is?"

"If he can access your consciousness, then yes. You should be able to access his as well."

Bile surges in my throat at the thought, but if it's the only way . . . "How?"

Natan lifts his chin, his eyes going wide. "Dreams, maybe?"

I shake my head. "I can't control those. Or I haven't been able to before, but . . ." But if I could meditate myself into a conscious dreaming state, I might be able to. My sister's desperation to save me from my own darkness meant tutor after tutor who taught me techniques to manage my anxiety and control my own mind, including a dozen different kinds of meditation I used only when forced to.

I hated it all, even when I knew I needed it. It felt like they were all trying to *fix* me, and I resented them knowing I was broken.

You're not fine, but you're not broken either. Fear isn't a measure of cowardice, and pain isn't a measure of weakness. You are brave and strong and anything but broken.

I shove the memory of Kendrick's words aside and focus on my plan.

"If I can meditate until I'm conscious dreaming," I tell Natan, thinking out loud, "I can get in his head and find out where the sword is."

"I can help you." He beams and rubs his hands together. "Remember how I took you deep into yourself to find your powers? It would be like that—me guiding you down into the proper state of consciousness. That way you'd always have one hand on your own mind."

I want to accept. Not only do I want the help, I crave the

company. I only have ten days left but when I think of facing each one alone I'm suffocated by loneliness. But it feels too risky to involve my friends in any of this. My decisions allowed Mordeus to cause so much harm already, so my priority has to be getting rid of him before he can do more to hurt my sister's court. Kendrick and his friends are so focused on getting rid of Erith and I don't know if I can do what I need to if my attention is divided. Besides, I can't risk any more people getting hurt trying to protect me.

"Thanks, Natan. Why don't you get everything ready back at the old house, and I'll meet you there?"

I can see the resistance in his eyes—part of him knows he shouldn't walk away from me, but he can't resist the Enchanting Lady, so he nods obediently and heads to the house.

CHAPTER SEVEN

FELICITY

"How . . . ?" I croak. The single word feels like swallowing crushed glass through unused vocal cords.

"I'll explain everything later," Misha says, turning his back to me and heading to a small kitchen area, where he pours water into a kettle.

I nod, but inside I'm a mess. I killed someone. And while part of me understands that I did what I had to do to protect Misha, and ultimately myself, the rest of me howls with devastation.

"You hesitated," Misha says, as if reading my thoughts. They're probably written all over my face. "You've never taken a life."

It's not a question so I don't bother answering.

"I appreciate it," he says, and I realize he's been watching me as I fumble through my chaotic thoughts. I catch sight of dark circles beneath his russet eyes before he turns to put the kettle on the fire. Has he lost sleep since I was taken from his dungeon cell? Does that have anything to do with me?

Unlikely, Felicity. You fooled him.

I'm still not convinced this isn't an illusion.

He turns his back to the kettle and catches me staring, so I glance around the cottage. It's small and tidy, and the fire crackling in the hearth fills the space with warmth and light. On the wall opposite the kitchen, there are two doors, to a bedroom and a bathing room, if I had to guess. "We won't be found here?"

"By your brother? I certainly hope not. As for the human who owns this place, she's traveling and I had a friend shield it so no one can track us here so long as we're inside."

A friend? I'm surprised Misha didn't do it himself, but I don't bother asking why. I'm too tired. Deep-in-my-bones tired. In my heart. "If you don't want him tracking us—tracking *me*—when we return to Faerie, I'll need to take another form. Assuming we aren't planning to stay within this shield forever?"

He shifts and withdraws a small pouch from his pocket. "I know. I brought hair."

I frown. If I want to take someone's form, I have to fall asleep with one of their hairs clutched to my chest. When I was locked in Misha's cell, I told him about how I shift but I didn't tell him about the hair. "How?"

"Your brother." He shakes his head. "Kendrick, not the prick from that cell. We found him and his friends after you went missing, and we've all been working together to find you and Jasalyn. Hale told me what you'd need to take the princess's form again."

"The princess is missing?"

He squeezes the back of his neck before tilting his face up to the ceiling. "The ring you told us about—it doesn't just give her the kiss of death. It makes it so people bend to her will, and when she walks away no one can remember her. And now apparently Jasalyn can't remove it. So they don't know exactly when she went missing, and they can't remember why she left or what was said or happened to make her go. Your brother was smart enough to make some notes, but he has no notes about whatever made her leave."

"That ring is controlling her. More than she knows."

"Kendrick confirmed as much." He squeezes the back of his neck. I've never seen him look so exhausted. "Meanwhile, the shadow court is on the verge of civil war. Mordeus's followers are preparing to move against the queen. If her enemies know the princess is missing, they'll use it against her to sow doubt in the crown. So long as Jasalyn wears that ring, we'll never truly be able to find her, especially with Mordeus having some level of control over her body and actions. What's worse is that she doesn't even know what will happen on her birthday."

I frown, wondering if I'm misremembering what I learned through her memories. "You mean because of trading her immortal life for the ring?"

He blows out a long breath and holds my gaze for a beat before speaking. "Because Jasalyn is a phoenix and once her life ends, Mordeus will be able to harness that power through their connection and take over her body. Mordeus's resurrection will be complete when his spirit takes her body on her eighteenth birthday."

"A phoenix? As in the bird that burns and rises from the ash?" I've heard of such a thing but never had reason to believe it was more than a myth. "And she doesn't know?"

"That's why we need you. We need to find her and tell her what Mordeus has planned—to save the princess and the Unseelie Court."

That's why he came for me—because they need me to help them find Jas. Not because he's in love with me or even because he forgives me.

"The shadow queen has found a tool that will help us rid her of the ring, and with your special gifts, you could help us retrieve it."

"What tool?"

"It's called the Stone of Disenchantment. It could nullify the ring's magic."

"So if we nullify the ring's magic then Mordeus can't take over her body?"

The look in his eyes tells me his answer before he speaks. "Unfortunately, the link between Jasalyn and Mordeus goes much deeper than a magical ring. Using the Stone of Disenchantment is only the first step, but we have to start here."

I give a shaky nod. I'll help. However I can, I'll help. But the confirmation that Misha came because he needs my help and not because he cares lands like a blow.

"We can talk about all this tomorrow. You need to rest." The kettle whistles and he turns away from me, removing it from the fire before busying himself over steaming mugs in the kitchen.

"It feels like I've done nothing but rest for months. Unless you still hate me and prefer I'm silent."

He brings a mug to me. "Drink this, Prin—" He catches himself and clears his throat. "Felicity."

I roll the warm mug between my cold hands, staring at it instead of at him. How many times did I long to hear my name from his tongue? I just hoped it would be said with the same tenderness he used when he called me Jasalyn. "Thank you."

"For the tea or for rescuing you after eight months of captivity?"

My head snaps up. *"Eight months?* You waited eight months to come for me? Was that supposed to be some kind of punishment?"

His eyes go wide for a beat. "Are you always so grateful when someone saves your life?"

"Why do I doubt you *wanted* to?"

"I don't do anything I don't *want* to do." He folds his arms. "You are lucky we found you at all. Lucky you left traces of blood behind in your cell that we could use to track you, lucky that we had a collection of very talented magic wielders at our disposal who could help, and lucky we didn't give up when we came up empty-handed in realm after realm. Then once we located you behind some artfully crafted wards, we had to begin the process of determining how to access that cell—a task that required a combination of powerful portal magic, sacred stones, and a vast knowledge of the layout of a massive prison in an unknown land." He flashes a cruel smile. "But please accept my apologies if we didn't manage all that fast enough for you."

I grimace. I need to stop giving him more reasons to loathe me. "I didn't mean . . ." I take a breath and push to standing. "I'm sorry. I really am grateful."

I open the doors opposite the kitchen and discover I was right. One is a bathing room and one is a bedroom. A tiny one. With only one bed. One very small bed.

Of course.

"I'll sleep on the sofa," I say, already turning to leave the room.

"You'll sleep in the bed," Misha says before I can get far. "You're the one who needs to dream."

"Right. Okay. I only need to sleep long enough to dream." I open the pouch and withdraw a single strand of chestnut hair. "Where did you get these? We're sure they're hers?"

"Abriella's goblin provided them, though I hate to imagine what he required for such a favor."

"There's nothing the queen wouldn't give for her sister."

Misha grimaces. "And that's why Jasalyn's disappearance is so troubling. If she falls into the wrong hands . . ."

"So long as she wears the ring, she'll be able to escape anyone who tries to catch her." I glance down at my clothes—a basic cotton tunic and pants—and try not to think of how they must've changed me while I was stuck in that illusion-fueled stasis. They'll be too big once I'm back in Jasalyn's form, but that's a problem for after our return to Faerie.

I kick off my boots and climb onto the bed. It's not particularly comfortable, but it won't matter. I can sleep anywhere.

Misha steps to the side of the bed, snaps his fingers, and a bedroll appears on the floor.

I roll to my side and frown at him. "You're sleeping in here?"

"I've been tasked with bringing you back. The best way to assure that is if I don't leave your side."

He removes the sword from his back and a bandolier of knives from his waist, eyes on me the whole time.

"I can feel you staring at me."

"Interesting."

I turn my head to glare. "So stop?"

His cocky smirk tilts up the side of his mouth. "Stop looking at you? Or stop being obvious about it?"

My stomach flip-flops. Is he looking because he *wants to* or for some other reason? "What are you doing?"

He skims his eyes down the front of me, then slowly back up. "Didn't we just cover that?"

My insides tremble with something I don't want to identify. "Why?"

He shrugs, giving me his back. He drags his shirt over his head and tosses it on a chair. I try not to watch. I can't very well complain about him staring at me and then stare at him. Even if taking my eyes off all that golden skin feels next to impossible. His skin glows where it's been kissed by the sun, and my hands itch to run across his broad shoulders.

He turns and I look away. "Like what you see?" he asks.

I roll my eyes. As if I don't care. As if the memories of his touch don't haunt me. "You're not bad. For someone so old."

He grunts. "Try not to drool on the sheets."

Seriously? "Keep dreaming."

"This is truly your natural form?" he asks.

All the warm wiggles in my stomach go cold. I lock my gaze on the ceiling. "We can't all be like the princess. No matter how much we might want to be."

"Why?" I hear the frown in his voice.

I throw my arms out. "I was born this way." Born this way and *not* willing to apologize for it. "Ask the gods if you're so determined to find an answer."

It's true that I deceived him by pretending to be Jasalyn, but I never meant for either of us to catch feelings. I certainly wouldn't ever ask to fall for someone only to have them disappointed when they discover my true appearance.

"That's not . . ." He shakes his head and lowers himself to his sleeping roll. "Get some sleep."

I shift to put out the lantern at my bedside, but it goes dark before I can reach it. "Magic is rather convenient, isn't it?" I ask, if only because lying here in the dark so close to him tangles my insides into knots of nerves and longing and grief for what I lost with him but also never had.

"Magic just is," Misha says. "Sometimes it's as much a weakness as a benefit. I would think you'd understand that. It's not like you're human, though you certainly had me convinced there for a while."

I want to ask if he understands why I did what I did now that he's met Kendrick and knows more about what's happening with the princess. I want to ask if everything he felt for me is gone. To ask if he thinks he could ever—

I smash the thought before it can go any further.

"I had to be careful about using my magic my whole life," I explain. "The Seven have their elders watch for suspicious amounts of magic use. As elves living in a fae-excluding Elora, we had to hide. It was a careful balance between using enough to learn and not so much as to pull unwanted notice toward my family." I clutch the strand of Jas's hair to my chest. I'm not sure why I'm telling him all this. It's not like he cares what my childhood was like or why I am so unpracticed at wielding my magic.

Just when I think he won't reply at all, his voice breaks through the darkness. "I can't imagine what that would be like. The few times I've had to avoid using mine, I felt like I was holding my breath. Magic is life. Suppressing it feels like death."

I close my eyes. I'm afraid to sleep. Afraid that I'll open my eyes and discover this is all just another illusion planted by Konner. Or worse, that sleep will bring visions of blood pouring from Orlen's lips when I pulled my sword from his chest.

"Why you?" I ask, if only to avoid my own thoughts. "Why not send a sentinel or one of my brother's team?"

The silence stretches. I hear him shifting on his bedroll and wonder if he's rolling toward me. Wonder how much of me his keen fae eyes can make out in the darkness. Wonder how much of him I could see if I had the courage to look.

"We needed someone powerful enough to get into the prison and break into the minds of those who guard the wards," he says. "Only once the wards were down could I portal in and out. I had the gifts we needed to do the job, and since we don't know who we can trust, it made sense for me to come."

I don't know what I wanted him to say. That he couldn't handle knowing I might be in danger and he insisted on coming for me himself? That there was nothing so important as saving the woman he loves? I am ridiculous. My relationship with Misha was as fake as the one in my dreams.

But then something he said clicks and my breath catches. I sit up in bed. "Misha."

"What?"

"You said you met Hale and his group?"

"Yes. They found us." A beat. "Why?"

"Who . . ." I press my hand to my chest to steady my racing heart. "Who was with him?"

"I don't remember all their names. A female, a couple of males."

"Just two males or three?"

"Just two," he says, and my pounding heart steadies.

"No one named Shae? Green eyes, scars on the side of his head?"

"No. Their friend Shae disappeared the day Jasalyn did. I don't know any more details."

Shae wasn't with them. I can only hope that since he disappeared, Hale found him out and knows what a traitor he is—knows he wanted me to die. "Good."

"Why?"

I focus on keeping my breathing even. "Shae tried to get me killed. I think he's working with Erith."

"We all thought Erith was behind your abduction. Your brother works for him, right?"

I hesitate, recalling my conversation with Konner. *You are assuming so much.* "I think so."

"And he didn't kill you. They had you for eight months and kept you in stasis rather than ending your life the way legend says your father always planned to. So if Shae wanted you to die when you went after my Hall of Doors, if he was trying to get you killed on behalf of Erith, but then Konner kept you alive all these months . . . what changed?"

I shake my head. "I don't know. Konner told me he doesn't want the same things as our father."

"And you trust him?"

My heart aches in my chest. Yes, I trust Konner. But I trust the Konner from the dreams he planted. Which means I can't trust the real Konner at all. "I don't know."

"We'll figure it out. What matters is that you're with us now."

I force myself to lie back down. "Good night, Misha." Emotion surges in my chest as I whisper the next words. "Thank you for coming for me despite . . . everything. I'm lucky to count you as a friend."

He grunts. "Don't get ahead of yourself, shifter."

CHAPTER EIGHT

JASALYN

The cottage is empty when Gommid brings me back. I'm already feeling weak in a way I can no longer blame on the long night, but I can't bring myself to hunt the creature Fherna showed me.

I wish she were here so I could warn her away. I don't know what will happen and I don't want to endanger her if she returns while I attempt to tap into Mordeus's consciousness. Unfortunately, waiting isn't an option when I don't know if she'll be back in minutes or days.

Unwilling to waste more time, I settle right in to my conscious dreaming efforts—lighting a candle, pulling the curtains to block out the midday sun, and making a comfortable place for myself to sit in the middle of the small cottage living room.

The truth is, I was never very good at conscious dreaming. The two times the instructor successfully pulled me down into that state of consciousness, I clawed my way back out. I didn't like what was lurking in my head. The shadows. The darkness. The pain. The rage and the fear.

Both my emotions and Mordeus's, I understand now.

But today is different. Today I'm searching for something.

Today I have a purpose and, if I'm successful, an escape from years of terror.

I cross my legs and let my eyes float closed, focusing on my breathing to remove my mind from my physical surroundings and turn it inward.

Here, you can visit memories you thought were long forgotten, the instructor told me. But I only found memories of wicked silver eyes and blood and pain.

This time, when those silver eyes appear in my mind, I focus on them, connect to them, remind myself of all the dreams I've had from those eyes and shift my consciousness into the other side of them.

The rage here whips around with such abandon, I nearly lose my grip on my own mind, but I hold tight, focusing a thread of my consciousness on myself, the smell of the candle in this room, the feel of the cushion under me, and I send the rest of myself slithering toward his darkness and rage, wrapping around it like a snake.

I see the Throne of Shadows, see my sister sitting on it, crave the feeling of taking it from her. Of ending her for stealing everything that I worked so hard for.

Seeing the world from these eyes, *feeling* Mordeus's greed for power crawling beneath my skin, it makes me want to abandon my mission. But I can't. I *need* the Sword of Fire.

The moment I lock my thoughts onto it, the images shift, and I'm standing outside a blacksmith's hut just beyond the edge of the forest. It's overgrown by bushes and trees and time, a relic of Oberon's kingdom that was never rebuilt.

I take in all the details I can. The shape of the dilapidated building, the curve in the gravel road beneath my feet, the view of the palace in the distance.

My palace.

She doesn't belong on that throne. She is a disgrace to the Unseelie Court—practically a human and residing over shadow fae.

Everyone who bows to her will lose their head when I take back what's mine.

Maybe I'll kill her slowly. I wonder if the sounds of her pleas for mercy will be as sweet as her sister's were.

I jerk awake with a start, and a blade clangs to the floor at my feet.

"Jasalyn?"

Abriella sits up in bed and blinks at me, then at the blade on the floor.

How did I get here? Why was I carrying a knife?

"Jas, where have you been?" She throws back the covers with shaking hands, her gaze dropping to the floor before shooting back to me. I backpedal, trying to get away from her. Trying to get *Mordeus* away from her.

Every muscle in my body aches, the ring reminding me I'm cheating death. This pain is the cost of the power I craved when I made that bargain with the Eloran witch.

"What are you doing with my dagger?" Brie asks. She's moving slowly, like I'm a timid, wild creature she doesn't want to scare away.

I shake my head, taking another step back. Then another.

The room is dark except for the starlight coming in from the windows overhead, but despite her caution, there's nothing but trust in her eyes as she pads toward me. Barefoot, half asleep, vulnerable. "Brie," I whisper. I'm shaking. *Trembling.* "I don't know how I got here."

She reaches for me, dropping her hand before it can touch my shoulder. "What do you mean? Are you okay? We've been looking for you. Let me call the healer to look you over."

What was I doing in my sister's chambers with an iron blade? "Where's Finn? Shouldn't he be here to protect you?" *Please tell me I didn't hurt him. Please tell me he's okay.*

"He's in the Court of the Sun. Sebastian needed help and since I didn't want to leave . . ." She looks me over. "You're sick. It's the ring, right? Kendrick says it makes you sick."

I was holding a knife over my sleeping sister. She needs to be hard with me. Not gentle.

"I'm fine." I take another step back. "Brie, you need to have wards that keep me out."

She shivers and wraps her arms around herself. "What are you talking about?"

"You're not safe around me. You need to set up wards to protect yourself against me—against anyone who might be . . . using me."

The confusion falls off her face. "You mean Mordeus." She holds my gaze and sighs softly. "I know everything—even about the connection between the faceless plague and your blackouts."

Shame washes over me—hot and heavy. The faceless plague. That's what they called all the unexplained deaths throughout the court. It had been going on for months, and we had no idea that Mordeus was the one responsible. That *I* was the one responsible.

"I'm going to make it right," I promise. "I know where to find the Sword of Fire, and I'm going to use it to get to Mordeus and kill him. For good."

"How will you do that?" Brie asks, and the pity in her eyes makes me curl my nails into my palms.

I steel myself against the surge of emotion flowing through me. "It won't bring all those people back, but I won't let him take any more lives through me. I'll do whatever it takes."

"Whatever it takes?" She ducks her head to catch my eyes. "Like trade everything for a magical ring that gives you death's kiss?" The rage in her voice sends a chill up my spine. Brie doesn't talk to me like that.

"I'm sorry. When she asked for the Grimoricon, I thought it would be worth it, but I know it wasn't mine to take. I'll get your book back too."

"You think I'm upset about the book? You *cut your life short* for that ring!"

She really does know everything. I wish she didn't. I didn't want her to be burdened with the truth.

I've made so many mistakes.

But I don't dare say it now. I don't want her sympathy. Not when it could make me crumble. "It doesn't matter. I only need to live long enough to kill him."

Abriella's nostrils flare and she shakes her head. "No. You need to live much, much longer than that."

"I traded it all away," I admit, but the truth is I'm only brave enough to say the words because she already knows. "It's too late."

"You are a child of Mab. There is no ring, no witch, no promise big enough to take away the magic that will feed your immortal years if you choose to live."

She's wrong. "It's done, Brie."

"Where have you been? We've been so worried. We've looked everywhere, but . . ." Her gaze drops to my ring.

But they wouldn't remember even if they had found me.

"Stop looking. There's nothing you can do for me. Just . . ." My chest aches. I miss her so much. I wish I could stay. "Protect yourself."

I look down at my feet. My boots are caked in mud. *I don't know how I got here. I don't know where I've been.* I need to think, but my mind is too foggy, as if I'm still half trapped in the dream where I am the wicked king, and I want nothing more than to destroy the human girl who stole my life and then my throne. "When I leave, you'll forget this," I tell my sister. "We need to find a way to make you remember. You aren't safe around me." I could write a note, but would she take it seriously? I need to leave a warning she'll remember. I can't risk her ignoring it.

"I'm strong enough to protect myself," Brie says. "And besides, your magic ring doesn't work on me like it does on the others. Kendrick and I talked about it."

I squeeze my eyes shut. The ring doesn't enchant Brie or Kendrick because of how they feel about me, but their memories are still affected. "Even if you can resist my commands, that doesn't mean you aren't vulnerable—especially when you're sleeping. And it doesn't mean you'll remember this." I bite my bottom lip. "We need to leave you a message for after I'm gone."

She shakes her head. "I don't want you to leave." But I can see that what I'm saying is finally registering, and she knows I'm right.

My mind races, trying to find the best way to get the message through to her once I'm gone. "It needs to be in blood. Your blood." Finn won't ignore a message written in Brie's blood. Her bonded partner would do anything to protect her—even from me.

"Jas . . ."

"Please? Do this for me?" I've fed her so many lies in the last few years, what's one more? "Just until I figure out a way to fix it?"

She gives a shaky nod, then pulls a small blade from beneath her sleeping gown. "I will ward my chambers against you but not the palace. We're working on something that could help you. Promise me you'll return, promise you'll check in with me."

I can't promise her that, but does it matter? If she won't remember this anyway? "So long as you ward anywhere you rest."

She slices into her palm without so much as a grimace. I use my finger as the quill and her blood as the ink, then I paint the words on her bedroom wall.

WARD AGAINST JAS. MORDEUS IS USING HER.

CHAPTER NINE

FELICITY

Misha is gone when I wake up and there's no sign he was ever there, but I can hear footsteps beyond the closed bedroom door.

I dreamed of Misha as he was in the illusion. Of the way his lips parted and his eyes went darker the first time I unbuttoned his shirt and put my hands on his strong chest. *We shouldn't . . .* he said. But in this dream, his words were cut off as blood bubbled from his mouth and down his chin and his face shifted to become that of Orlen, the male I killed.

Usually I don't remember any dreams of my own, but the illusion Konner planted in my mind is strong enough that my own dream stands as vivid in my mind this morning as the dream with Jasalyn's memory.

I climb out of bed and look down at the form I've taken. Jasalyn's body is small, and my pants are so big I have to fold and roll them at the top to keep them from falling. My top slips off one shoulder, but unless Misha brought clothes for me, they'll have to do for now.

Stepping out of the bedroom, I find Misha standing at the big window in the kitchen, the morning sun catching on his dark hair and making it shine. I slip into the bathroom before he can turn around.

I take care of my needs and clean up, avoiding the mirror and ignoring the pit in my stomach that comes with not knowing when I can be in my own skin again. It had been so long since I'd been myself, I'd stopped noticing the discomfort of being in another's skin, how every movement and step feels a little off.

When I exit the bathroom, Misha's waiting and looks me over, some emotion I can't identify playing at his lips.

Yes, he thought he was falling for Jasalyn and now he's looking at her again. But this time he knows the truth.

I swallow. "Good morning."

He arches a brow and stalks toward me. "You had nightmares."

I cringe. I was probably thrashing in my sleep. "Sorry."

"Yours or hers?"

"Mine," I whisper, and he frowns. "I know. I was hoping we'd get something useful too, but it was only a memory of a tutor teaching her to meditate."

Nodding, he skims those russet eyes over me again. "I still can't quite believe it. You're an entirely different person—from the way you look to the way you smell to the energy you bring into a room."

"Yeah. That's the gift."

"I still should've known," he says quietly.

He couldn't have, but I won't argue. "Is it weird for you?" I have no business asking, but it seems I can't help myself.

His jaw is hard as he folds his arms. "What do you mean by that?"

I swallow. Serves me right. He doesn't owe me any explanations for where his emotions are right now. "Nothing. It's . . . never mind."

"Do you mean is it strange to see you in the body of my best friend's little sister after you made me believe I'd fallen in love with her?"

My breath catches. *Love.*

It wasn't real. He thought you were Jas.

He leans against the counter and studies me with a brow cocked in question. He's going to make me own up to my real question.

"You wouldn't have fallen for me if you'd known I wasn't her."

His jaw ticks. "No. I don't tend to fall for females who lie and scheme their way into my bed."

I bow my head. I deserve that. "Right."

His exhale is audible. "But to answer your question, not really. I was never attracted to Jasalyn before you posed as her, so the way I feel when I look at you would be the same whether you're in this form or that of your great-grandfather. Not that my feelings are any of your business."

Before I can reply, a goblin appears in the room and Misha nods to him. "We're ready."

The goblin turns to me and cocks his head to the side, giving me a nod. A silent acknowledgment of who I am, and who we both lost.

Misha looks back and forth between us with a frown before realization dawns. "That was your goblin—that brought me to you in the cave, that took us back to the castle when you were hurt so badly. He's gone now?"

"Nigel was sometimes my very best friend." *And sometimes my only friend.* My eyes burn with tears I won't shed.

"Goblins make sacrifices only when they're certain," Misha's goblin says before offering me a hand.

"Let's go," Misha says, voice uncharacteristically gruff, and when he takes my other hand, I swear he gives it a subtle squeeze.

I close my eyes and hold my breath while we spin and fall and surge back to Faerie.

When we are fully corporeal again, we're in a vast room with soaring ceilings and crystal chandeliers. The black floors are polished to such a shine I can see my reflection in them, and the dais holds a massive, polished ebony throne. Before I can get my footing, I lose my balance and fall on my backside. I mentally curse my lack of grace.

Misha, of course, landed easily on his own two feet and looks down at me with something like disdain. Wondering how he ever fell for someone like me in any form, no doubt.

"Felicity!" The sound of my brother's voice pulls my attention off the Wild Fae king. Hale scoops me off the floor and pulls me against his chest so hard I might object if it weren't exactly what I needed. "I knew you were still alive. I couldn't explain it. I just knew it." When he puts me down, he draws back to study me. "How are you? Did they hurt you?"

My throat goes thick with tears. "I missed you too," I whisper.

"Don't start with that," Skylar gripes from across the room. "No teary reunions today."

"She faced her father and survived," Remme says. "That's worth celebrating."

I shake my head. "I didn't see my father."

Hale frowns, then looks to Misha for confirmation, as if *he* might know better than me.

Males.

Misha presses his lips into a thin line. "I only saw her brother. Another male appeared as we were trying to leave—a silencer that Felicity killed before he could kill me."

"Yeah?" Skylar says. She nudges Hale out of the way and pulls me into a hug. "Always knew you had it in you. Good work."

I huff out a dry laugh and squeeze her in return only to be passed to Remme, then Natan. *You aren't alone in the world. This is your family.*

When Natan releases me, he chucks me under the chin, just like he did when I was a little girl.

The shadow queen steps forward, red hair framing her face, and her king consort steps behind.

My whole body tenses. The last time she looked at me, she wanted me dead with every fiber of her being. This time, she's no less intimidating, but the energy rolling off her is more like determination than wrath.

I bow my head. "Queen Abriella."

She looks me over, conflicting emotions twisting her lips. "I won't pretend I like it when you are in my sister's form, but for now it's necessary. Misha's filled me in on what you know."

I look back and forth between them, frowning in confusion, before I realize they likely have a mental connection. He's probably been speaking into her mind from the moment we arrived.

"Allow me to apologize for not initially believing your story," the queen continues. "Thank you for agreeing to help us find her, despite how poorly I treated you. It's far past time we bring Jas home and put a stop to all that Mordeus has put into motion."

I look around the group, wondering if any of them are thinking what I am. What if something happened to Jas? What if they've been unable to find her not because the ring makes her so elusive but because she's dead?

There's a fire in the queen's eyes when she says, "She lives, and now we can get to work gathering the tools we need to locate her."

"Misha told me about the stone. Tell me how I can help."

Abriella and Finn exchange a look and when she turns back to me, she nods. "I'm throwing a ball in two nights' time. I need you to appear as my sister, as if you never left."

"A ball?" I look around. I can't be the only one who thinks the timing on this is absurd. "Right now? With everything else happening?"

"I need you to be seen," Abriella says. "There are rumors that my sister has died or that she's on her deathbed. Rumors that she's working with the rebels. Rumors that she and I are estranged. The kingdom needs to see that their princess is well. They need to know that she can step up if Mordeus or his followers find a way to strike me down."

"So soon?"

"I would do it sooner if I were confident I could get the necessary players to attend," she says.

I bite my bottom lip. "Who will I see at this ball? Who knows your sister well enough that I need to worry they might see through me?"

Beside me, Misha grunts in annoyance and looks me over. "You are physically Jasalyn in every way. Have you ever truly had to worry about that?"

"Look who's still angry about being duped," Skylar says. Hale flashes her a look, warning violence, and she rolls her eyes but shuts her mouth.

"You know you can do this, Lis," Hale says. "No one can do it *but* you."

I turn back to the queen. "If we're taking this risk, I want to make sure it's worth it."

"The ball serves two purposes. One, having the princess be seen. Two, launching our plan to find Jas. Searching for someone wearing a ring like that? It's been like searching for a ghost. I know she was here last night—she came to warn me about Mordeus—but maybe that's not the only time I've seen her. Maybe we've found her a dozen times. Maybe one of us finds her every day." She shrugs. "We would have no way of knowing because the ring's magic makes us forget. I need the Stone of Disenchantment for a spell so that when we do find her, we can nullify the magic that is keeping that ring on her finger and remove it once and for all."

Hale touches my arm to get my attention. "This ring is doing worse than making us forget if we find her. It amplifies the blood magic Mordeus used on her and acts as a conduit between Jasalyn and Mordeus. It's allowing him to control her. It's how he killed so many of his followers—fae who had pledged their lives to him—in order to fuel his resurrection."

I draw in a shaky breath, not wanting to argue with the shadow queen but needing her to understand what I do. "In the memories

I saw? The people she killed? That wasn't Mordeus. That was Jas. She wanted them dead. And she wanted to be the one who did it."

"And Mordeus did everything in his power to make sure that's exactly what she'd do," Natan says. "Every time she took the life of one of his pledges, she was unknowingly funneling the power of their life force right to him, and most importantly, it was something Jasalyn wanted badly enough that she'd be willing to trade her immortal life for it. Resurrection requires unthinkable sacrifice, and this is how he made that happen."

"How did it get stuck?" I ask. "And if Mordeus is somehow behind her getting the ring, why not make it stick from the first moment she put it on?"

"We suspect the ring became affixed after enough pledges had been assassinated to bring him back," Natan says. "The last time Jasalyn wore the ring before it got stuck, she had a blackout, during which she went to Feegus Keep and wiped out the legion there. By then, the faceless plague had been circulating the court for months and hundreds had fallen to it. So at that moment, they didn't want her to be able to remove the ring anymore."

"So he could better control her," I murmur.

"Exactly," Hale says, face grim.

"A change like that would need to be triggered somehow," Natan says. "We believe it was triggered by the cries of the wyvern during an attack on Ironmoore."

"And, worse," Hale says, "is that we believe Shae was behind it. Shae sold her out. He sold *us* out."

"He tried to get me killed." I risk a glance toward Misha. "While I was staying at Castle Craige he burned most of the hair

I had left, cornering me into moving on the portal faster than I wanted."

Skylar's nostrils flare and her anger burns in her eyes. "We will find him and deal with him. He won't get away with this."

"The more pressing matter at the moment," the queen says, bringing us back to the topic at hand, "is my sister and retrieving the Stone of Disenchantment. Rumor was that the last such stone was destroyed in the Great Fae War, but my seer told me one remains in my court. After weeks of research, we've tracked it down. It belongs to a lord just south of the capital—one who just so happens to want my sister to marry one of his sons."

My eyebrows shoot up. "And he'll give you the stone in exchange?"

She draws in a breath. "He doesn't know we want it. Given how great our need is, I prefer not to show our hand, lest he use it to manipulate the crown." She looks to Skylar, who nods and takes over.

"We tried to access the stone ourselves last new moon but were unsuccessful."

"And by access, you mean steal," I say.

Skylar shrugs. "We made it into the main house, but couldn't penetrate the safe where we suspect Lord Pandian keeps the stone."

I frown. "Skylar is the best thief I've ever met. If she can't get in, I don't know what you think I can offer."

The queen flexes her hands into fists—the only sign of her aggravation. "Lord Pandian keeps his manor secure in a way that rivals the Midnight Palace. We need to get inside that safe, and to do that, we need the one thing he wants from us: my sister."

I lift my chin. "You want me to pose as Jasalyn and pretend I'm considering the marriage offer so I can get access to their manor?"

"You made it work with the king," Skylar says, nodding to Misha, who flashes her a glare that would melt a lesser faerie.

I'm still not following. "They aren't going to open their precious safe for a potential bride."

"Probably not," Abriella says, "but we do believe it's magically keyed to Pandian and his sons, so if you could get close enough to one of his sons to get what you need to take his form..."

My brother is quiet, but his eyes are begging me to accept. "I'd do it myself if I could," he says softly.

"We're running out of time," Abriella says. "The ball will give us the opportunity to fight the rumors that Jasalyn is missing by having you there, and you'll get to meet Lord Pandian's sons. Be charming, be endearing, and above all get a hair from one of them and flirt enough that when you invite him to secretly meet with you, he won't be suspicious."

"You'll have me go there while he's gone," I say, piecing it together. After all, we can't have two of him walking around the main house.

"I'll tell you everything I remember about the manor and the main house," Skylar says.

"And who will be Jasalyn? To go to this secret rendezvous?"

"Jasalyn will be unexpectedly detained by her sister," Remme says. "And will send a trusted servant to let him know—after making him wait a bit first."

This time I meet the queen's gaze. "And you're sure you can find her once you get the stone?"

"I suspect that if we don't find her first, she'll come to us, as she did before." Again, she exchanges a look with her king. "After all, she shares a consciousness with Mordeus, who wants me dead."

The queen must sense my hesitation, even if she doesn't understand it, because she adds, "In exchange, of course, we'll give you whatever it is you need to start a new life when this is all over."

"We want access to your Hall of Doors," Remme says, sneaking a glance at me before looking back to Abriella again.

"My debt is to Felicity," she says, holding my gaze. "What is it that *you* want?"

I want to give my brother what he needs without risking his life. I want a family again. I want a life where I don't always have to be on the run.

And then a small traitorous part of my brain whispers, *I want to go back to my life at the Eloran Palace*, and I shove it away.

"You don't have to answer now," Abriella says. "Think about it and let me know."

"Tell her you want the Hall," Skylar says, nudging me. "We can't find the sword and that's the only way to get to—"

"With respect, Skylar," Hale says, cutting her off with the authority in his voice, "Mordeus has us against a ticking clock. He has to be our priority. We've waited this long to deal with Erith. He can wait a few more days."

Skylar bows her head, showing deference to Hale in a way that reveals what he is to her, and to Elora: the rightful king. The one chosen by the oracle to protect the Eloran queen. "Understood," she murmurs.

"My sister is tired," Hale says to the group now. "Let's get her some well-deserved rest so she can help us find Jas."

Later that night, long after settling into Jas's room, getting a proper bath, and changing into princess-appropriate attire, I'm roaming the halls to track down my brother when I find Misha instead.

Standing in front of the windows in a cozy sitting area, he stares out at the night sky, hands clasped behind his back.

Because I know I shouldn't do it when he's aware or when anyone else is watching, I let myself take a moment to admire the breadth of his shoulders and the way his hair falls in subtle waves that refuse to be tamed.

Really, as beautiful as he is, it's the smiles that I miss the most. The ones that were just for *me*.

Just for Jasalyn.

I clear my throat to get his attention and he turns to me, giving me a quick and appraising once-over.

"Abriella was telling the truth, you know. She will grant you a favor after you retrieve the stone."

I bow my head. "Perhaps we should wait until we know if I'll be successful before we worry about that."

"Your friends seem so sure that you should use the queen's Hall of Doors to kill Erith, but that's not what you want."

"Like Hale said, we need to worry about Jasalyn and Mordeus before we worry about Erith. Jas is running out of time."

He's quiet so long, I lift my head to see if he's walked away. He's still there. Still watching me. "That's not why, though. You risked so much to try to find my Hall for the same reason Remme suggested Brie give you access to hers. Why do you dread the idea of using her Hall?"

The blood drains from my face. "Since when do you read minds?"

"I don't need to read minds when it's right there to read on your face." He cocks his head to the side and studies me. "Why are you so afraid of gaining access to that portal, Felicity?"

"It's complicated."

"It doesn't need to be."

I've spent years keeping this secret to myself. Telling Shae was a mistake that kept me from sharing it with anyone else. After that, the only person I had to talk about it with was Nigel. "When I found out my true identity, my mother sent me to the Eloran oracle." I'll never forget my other visit there. How desperate I was for answers—hopeful that I might leave with a solution. Instead, I left terrified, with an image in my mind that I haven't been able to scrub away even all these years later. Hale on the ground, blood oozing from his chest and puddling around him.

"She showed me that I would kill Erith, but my vision didn't stop there. She showed me Hale dying. The two events were intertwined. And I knew better than I knew my own face that killing Erith, following through with that fate my brother so desperately needed me to embrace, would lead to Hale's death."

"So you ran and spent three years in hiding?"

"I wasn't hiding from my fate. I was hiding from my father."

"Why not just tell Hale the truth?"

I bite the inside of my cheek. "Because I was sure he would tell me to do it anyway."

"And did he?"

I meet Misha's gaze and hold it. "I haven't told him." I turn back to the view, studying the sparkling sky on the horizon. "I don't want him to sacrifice himself. I don't want to be the reason we lose him."

"You won't be. Even if this future she foretold comes to pass, it won't be *because* of you. You can't prevent all the horrible things in the world from happening."

"Then why did she show this to me?"

He sighs. "I don't know. I don't really understand your oracle. She shows you possible futures and you either work to ensure they come to pass—like your brother wanting to see Erith killed—or you fight to change the course of fate—like you avoiding your fate as Erith's assassin to protect Hale."

I shiver. "Do you have any idea what it's like to live in fear of your own future?"

"Unfortunately, I do." Misha's gaze slides over my face. If I didn't know better, I'd think that was sympathy in his eyes. "But if I've learned anything from having a seer in the family, it's that fate is a slimy thing. People like to think of it like a fixed point, but it's always changing." He waves a hand toward the view. "You see that temple? The star that sits at its peak, almost as if it was made to go there?"

I nod and attempt a smile. "We are in the Court of the Moon, so perhaps it was."

"Not even Mab herself can keep the stars fixed in place in the sky. Tomorrow, we could come stand here and it would seem nothing has moved. Maybe even the day after and the day after that, but we know from the scholars who chart the night skies that the star that sits atop that temple tonight won't be there in two moons' time. Fate is like that."

"I have hoped for nothing more," I whisper.

"That's why I think you should tell your brother the truth," he says, and I cut my gaze to him. "And if after you speak with him you decide you want to kill Erith the moment you're done helping them get Jas back, I will go with you."

I draw back, confused. "Surely there are many places you'd prefer to be than by my side."

"Well, yes, but time with you will make me appreciate them all the more."

I cough out a laugh. "Why are you being so nice to me?"

He turns and studies me for a long time, eyes sweeping across my face so many times I wonder if he can see the real Felicity waiting beneath. "Everyone in this world has a fate they would personally rearrange the stars to avoid." His gaze settles on my mouth for a beat before he takes a step back. "Don't think I am so different."

CHAPTER TEN

FELICITY

Hale's sitting on the patio alone, glass of amber liquid in front of him. I feel a long tug in my chest. I've missed my brother so much. For all his flaws, he made me who I am. Every bit of courage and strength I have, I have because he instilled it in me. Our mother would've coddled me until I grew soft and useless, but Hale wouldn't have that. I used to think it was because he wanted someone to go on his adventures with him, but I think he knew I would need to be tough, that someday I would need the kind of strength and resilience I would never learn tied to our mother's apron strings.

The sun has long past set, but I doubt he noticed.

The chair across from him groans against the stone as I pull it out to sit. "Figure it out yet?"

He blinks at me as if noticing for the first time that he's not alone. "Figure what out?"

I shrug. "Everything. You look deep in thought."

He scrapes a hand over his face. "There's a lot to think about." He cuts his gaze to me. "I'm sure the same is true for you."

I huff out a humorless laugh. "My thoughts are spinning

so fast I can hardly keep up with them."

"Tell me . . . about where you were—where you thought you were?"

My stomach twists. "He locked me in a dream of some sort. I was living in the Eloran Palace, training to be one of the Seven. I idolized my mother, and I . . ." *I was in love with a man who loved me for who I am rather than who I was pretending to be.* "And there was my twin too. Konner and I were close."

"So he painted a pretty picture for you so you wouldn't fight your way out."

I shake my head slowly. "But it wasn't all pretty. I was always worried that Konner was going to be hurt serving the palace. And then the palace was under siege, and I ran to protect my mother." I hold my brother's gaze and remind myself he's the only real brother I have. The only one who counts. "You were there, and you were trying to kill her. I hated you so much in that moment that I didn't hesitate." The tears I was determined to hold back spill down my cheeks.

He reaches across the table and grabs my hand. "It's okay. It wasn't real."

But it felt so real. "It wasn't until I plunged the knife into your chest that any memories of this life even flickered for me." I blow out a breath. "I don't understand why he would plant that. Why show me killing someone I love? Why risk my mind rejecting that moment?"

"And why show you a life full of worries? Why not just make it all good?"

"And that doesn't even address the biggest question of all," I say, pulling my hand out from under his and leaning back in my chair. "Why am I still alive? Erith's wanted me dead since before I was born, and they had me for months. Why did they let me live and why did they plant those fake memories in my mind?"

"The memories could be nothing more than a manipulation," Hale offers. "By the way you describe it, it felt real to you. That will inevitably affect the decisions you make. Maybe they need you alive for some reason but thought they could control you through the memories."

I nod, but I'm not convinced. Nothing makes sense to me right now.

"Lis?" When I lift my head, Hale studies me for a long time. His throat bobs before he finally speaks. "There are so many days lately where it feels like fate is against us. But seeing you here? Knowing you haven't been taken away? I'm hopeful again. For the first time in a long time."

"Do you think they'll find Jasalyn?"

"I've spent *months* scouring this court. Not that it matters." He sets his jaw and glares at nothing. "It's maddening. Anyone she's seen won't remember her."

"And you're sure she's . . ." I trail off. The question is too cruel.

"She's alive. I set wards at Feegus Keep that would alert me if she went there. They were triggered, and I went searching. All I remember is being attacked by a pack of death dogs they had locked in the basement, and then when I woke up, I was in the infirmary at Ironmoore, all stitched up. I could *smell* her. I know she'd been there." He braces his forearms on his thighs and hangs his head. "I felt it in my gut."

"You really have feelings for her, don't you?"

He shakes his head before lifting it to meet my gaze. "I have feelings for a lot of people. For Jasalyn I have . . . I'm in love with her, Lis. And I lost her." His chuckles darkly and throws back the rest of his drink. "I fucking lost her and if we don't find her and undo what Mordeus put into motion with the blood magic, with that ring . . . I'll never get her back."

I don't see how they're going to do all that beyond finding the princess, but I don't need him to explain it to me now. *One problem at a time.*

When he lifts his gaze to meet mine, he can't hide his exhaustion. "I was taking notes while she was still with us—once the ring wouldn't come off." He pulls a leather-bound book from inside his vest and drops it on the table. "One of the last notes I wrote to myself the day she disappeared was that I needed to tell her the truth about who I am. She thought I was human."

"You think she left when she found out."

"It's possible. I've been walking around thinking she hates me, but I think she's the one who got me to the infirmary and stitched me up after those death dogs tried to tear me apart. And if I'm right about that, maybe there's a chance she'll forgive me."

"We'll find her." My heart aches for my brother, but I can't help but wonder if he's abandoned his mission from home. I have to ask. "And when we do, what will you do then? You've been chosen to protect the next Eloran queen. Will you refuse that call to be with Jas?"

There's nothing but torture in his ice-blue eyes. "Crissa's still missing too." The Eloran queen, like all Chosen queens of the realm, is human, and her mortality makes her vulnerable. Maybe even more vulnerable than Jas, who Mordeus needs to keep alive for the time being. "The whole thing is a *mess*. There are so many people counting on me, and yet I can't think about anything but getting Jas back." He stares up into the night sky. "Tell me what you saw in her memories. What did he do to her in there?"

"Don't do that to yourself."

He scrapes a hand over his face. "I'll kill him. Once we have Jasalyn back, I want to find Mordeus and end him for good. It's the least I can do for her."

He's so focused on Jasalyn, this might be the perfect time to tell him why I won't kill Erith. The truth sits heavy in my chest. I could tell him. Maybe I should, but I can't bring myself to do it.

Exhausted. Confused. Emotionally wrecked.

But when I close my eyes, sleep eludes me.

I would give anything for a sleeping tonic, but I can't bring myself to leave my chambers to ask for one. I can't stomach the idea of running into Misha again.

I wander my room, brushing my fingertips across the cool marble of the fireplace mantel and opening the drawers in the desk one by one. I'm not sure if I'm hoping to find the herbs I know would help me sleep or if I'm looking for a distraction, but when I see the contents of the bottom drawer, my chest feels too tight.

My nose tingles with the threat of tears as I pull the playing cards from the drawer.

I miss Nigel so much. When I felt lonely as a child, he was

always there. Even when he wasn't, knowing he'd come at a moment's notice always gave me comfort.

I pluck a thread on my goblin bracelet just to remember what it feels like, then press the cards to my chest as if they might bring back my friend.

"I was beginning to think you'd never call," someone says behind me.

I spin around and squeak when I see a spindly-limbed goblin sitting on the foot of my bed.

He looks me over, assessing. "You are quite conscious. Finally."

"Who are you?"

"Squird Anglos the Third, at your service." He hops off the bed and bows from the waist. "But you can call me Squird. Nigel told me the rhyming bits become tiresome otherwise."

Joy rises into my chest and a bubble of laughter slips from my lips. I can imagine Nigel saying just that. "It's nice to meet you, Squird."

"Nigel asked me to look after you if anything ever happened to him. I would've introduced myself sooner, but I couldn't come until you called. What can I do for you this fine evening?" He frowns out the window. "Rather, this night when you should most definitely be sleeping."

I clutch the cards harder to my chest. Nigel assigned another goblin to look after me once he was gone. Of course he did.

"I don't know how to play," he says, nodding to the cards in my hands, "but I'll learn if you'd like."

I smile. It's hard to tell a goblin's age by their appearance—they all seem to have the same sparse, thin hair and plump belly—but

I can tell Squird is young. He hasn't become as tight-lipped as his brethren. I set the cards on the desk. "Maybe another time."

"Do you need to go anywhere?" He bounces on his toes, eagerness making his eyes shine.

I bite my bottom lip. I don't want to take advantage if he's too young to know better, but . . . "I had a question."

He waits for a beat, then looks around the room. "And you lost it? Or do you expect me to guess? Perhaps Nigel never told you that goblins don't read minds." His eyes widen. "Or maybe he did? He is one of the smartest goblins I've ever met. I bet he knew all your questions before you spoke them aloud."

I stifle a laugh, bowing my head to hide the smile I can't keep from my face. "I'm just trying to figure out the best way to ask." Goblins can be so literal, and I'm guessing Squird might be worse than most. "Why didn't Erith have me killed when I was captured?"

Squird wrinkles his nose like this is a foolish question. "Because he didn't know where you were."

"You mean to say Erith wasn't the one who captured me?"

"Erith would never get so close to one fated to end him."

"I thought Konner—or whoever took me from Misha's dungeons—did so on behalf of Erith. But perhaps they were working for someone else instead." Konner would be devoted to the Seven, having grown up in the palace. It doesn't make sense that he wouldn't have wanted Erith to have access to me, and yet I think he was trying to tell me that he wanted me alive.

"No one in that palace works for anyone but themselves," Squird says.

"What about the dreams Konner planted in my mind? If he

wasn't working with Erith—or perhaps is even working *against* Erith—why not use those dreams to make me hate my father? To make me act on my supposed fate when I woke? And if it wasn't that, then why keep me asleep at all?" I've been thinking out loud again, and I realize my mistake when I lift my head and see Squird's big, panicked eyes. "Sorry," I mumble.

He looks around, as if he realizes he's already said too much and wants to make sure no one witnessed his blunder. "I should go."

"No, don't. I—" But he's already gone.

CHAPTER ELEVEN

JASALYN

The feeble old crone who occupies the chambers in the southernmost tower of the Midnight Palace doesn't rise when I enter the room. I grit my teeth at the insolence but don't let myself lash out against her. Good seers are hard to find, and Karmyn is one of the best. In return for her skills, I allow her to march to her own beat. Even when it makes me want to break her neck and watch the life drain from her eyes.

"It's taking too long," I say, fighting to keep my voice down. "Abriella should've brought me the book by now."

"She will," Karmyn says. "You simply need to be patient and she will bring everything you ask right to your throne."

I clench my fists at my sides. The human peasant brought me the mirror already, just as Karmyn said she would. She took the bait when I bought her sister, just like Karmyn said she would. Now she will bring me the Grimoricon, and after that the crown. "Patience. Fine. If I can finally rule this court from the throne, I will find some patience."

Her blue-gray eyes go unfocused and she slowly shakes her head. "No. You don't live to rule from the throne."

"What?" I throw my power out at her and lift her from her chair. "What did you just say to me?"

Only when she claws at her throat do I loosen my magical hold, allowing her to draw in breath. "I told you before I cannot control whether you will like what I see. You made me promise to give you the truth regardless."

I did. I've executed half a dozen seers in the last year alone after discovering they were telling me what I wanted to hear instead of the truth. When I brought in Karmyn, this was the promise I asked. In return, I released her son from my dungeons and provide a meager allowance to feed her grandchildren. I release my magic completely and she sags, her body going limp with relief. "Tell me. When did you first see this?"

"Only now, Your Majesty."

"Why not before? What's changed?"

"The fate of a whole realm can change on something as small as a shift in the winds. I cannot tell why I get visions when I do."

Death. Death before I claim what is rightfully mine. Death before I come into my full power by wearing my brother's crown. "I won't have it."

I lost three more days to sleep before Fherna woke me again, or so she told me. This time, she dragged me to the dark forest while I was still groggy with sleep, the memories of my dreams making me feel like I was seeing the world through Mordeus's eyes.

"I can't keep breaking the rules for you," she mutters as she leads me deeper into the trees. "Risking everything for a fool who would give in so easily to a bargain that's still incomplete."

"What rules? Bargain with whom?"

She jerks to a stop and turns her glare on me. "Bargain with that Eloran witch. Did you forget what you traded for that cursed thing?" she asks, waving to my hand.

"I can't forget that," I answer in a whisper. I want to know more—about what she means by "incomplete" in regard to the bargain, about what she knows about the witch. If the bargain isn't complete, does that mean I can find the witch and get back what I traded?

My mind is swimming with half-formed questions, but it takes all the strength I have to follow her, and part of me already knows she's right. I need to hunt. If I'm too weak to ask questions, I'm too weak to find Mordeus.

The forest is thick and not even the night's bright moon can break through the tree cover. I pull a glowstone from my pack and let its light seep from between my fingers as I clutch it to my chest.

"I can only take you a little farther," Fherna says. "You must trek through the forest alone and find the wolpertinger. Drink the blood from its beating heart and you will have the strength to do what needs to be done."

The darkness of the forest feels like it might swallow me whole.

She holds aside a cluster of branches and turns back to me. "Just beyond these trees, you'll find a grand redwood. She soars higher than any other tree in this forest, and at her base is the entrance to the wolpertinger's burrow. The creature sleeps. When you reach it, make haste, for it will sense any hesitation. If it wakes up before you grab ahold, this hunt will turn much more difficult. Just remember: With your blood you can overcome the flame. You are built to wield the sword."

"You'll show me?" I ask, but then she's gone. The branches she moved for me remain parted, as if the forest itself is inviting me to come deeper.

"Go, Jas," I whisper. "Just go."

Each step is a battle with my body and my mind, but I put one foot in front of the other until I'm standing before a soaring redwood, the promised burrow waiting at its base.

I slide my iron dagger from my side and fall to my knees.

Dropping my glowstone in the leaves, I take a breath, brace myself, then plunge my hand inside the burrow until it collides with a mass of soft fur.

Move quickly. Do not hesitate.

I grip my dagger in my hand, preparing to strike, and grab the creature. I wrench it from its den, but as I hold it in front of my face and prepare to plunge the blade into its chest, I freeze.

The wolpertinger is nothing more than a ball of fluff with a flat face, floppy ears, and a long tail that coils around my wrist. Its tiny tongue darts out and licks my palm, and round, innocent brown eyes blink up at me.

A sob surges up my throat and I make myself shove it back down.

Life gives life. Do this for your sister. Do this for all the souls who would be tortured under Mordeus's rule.

I ready my blade and the ball of fluff begins to vibrate in my hand, like a purring cat.

"I'm sorry," I whisper.

It opens its little mouth, as if to beg for its life, and the purring vibration intensifies until I can barely hold on. In the next moment, it shifts, and all the fluffy hair turns to spikes digging into my flesh, its soft brown eyes glow green and angry, and long fangs shoot out from its gaping maw.

It surges for my neck.

The spikes pierce my skin and my grip goes slippery with my own blood, but I hold tighter, bring my dagger to its throat, and slice, hard and fast.

The creature goes limp in my hand, soft and furry again. Was it ever anything else?

I can't let myself wonder. I need to finish what I've started.

I drag the blade down and rip the creature's tiny heart from its chest, thrusting it to my lips before I can think better of it. The first taste of its blood—coppery and salty, with an underlying sweetness too much like decaying fruit—is almost enough to make me abandon this mission, but I force myself to bite into the tough muscle. Blood squirts hot and viscous onto my tongue, and I gag.

Drink. You have to drink.

The words sound like they're coming from Fherna. I don't know if it's my imagination or my memory or if this horrible act has made me lose my grip on reality, but I obey. Every swallow is easier as the weakness and misery of the ring's curse ebbs. I need this strength. I need to find Mordeus.

Only when I've sucked the gristly muscle dry do I let myself stop. I drop it to the ground and then lie down beside the soft carcass of the wolpertinger, and I cry, big, jagged sobs that are gobbled up by the trees around me.

I'm stronger, and I'm not afraid of anything in this forest as much as I am of myself, as I am of what I've become.

I want to see Kendrick.

It's risky and pointless, but I don't care.

I don't know if Death's coming tonight—when I intend to get that sword and use it to kill Mordeus—or in a week, when my bargain for the ring will bring me to the end of my life. But I feel her hovering, her fingers a handsbreadth away, ready to steal the very breath from my lungs.

I ask Gommid to take me to Kendrick. I just want to see him one more time. I just want to say goodbye.

"He's here?" I ask when the world materializes around us again. We're in the gardens behind the Midnight Palace.

"Kendrick the Chosen is inside. He's taken the chambers next to yours, but you'll have to take yourself there. As threats have escalated, your sister has warded the whole palace against goblin travel."

I knew Kendrick had spoken with my sister, but I didn't expect he'd be *staying* here. "Thank you, Go—"

But he's already gone.

The palace is buzzing tonight, the doors to the ballroom stand open and torches glow on every terrace, revealing the partygoers who mingle and sip on faerie wine. Something tugs hard in my chest at the normalcy of it all. This is what my sister's life should look like—palace balls and hundreds of guests who adore her.

Every pair of eyes locks on me as I head inside. Gommid said she warded the palace against goblin travel. He didn't say anything about her warding against me. She said she wouldn't, and yet as I head into the palace I find myself hoping that she did more to protect herself than she promised when I woke up in her chambers.

I don't reply to any of the fawning compliments or meet any of the longing stares of my sister's guests. I head straight for the stairs, stopping only briefly at the landing that overlooks the ballroom.

My heart aches as I stare at the gathering below.

I spent three years dreading or outright avoiding my sister's balls, and now I would give anything to stand by her side through just one. When the female at her side turns, my breath catches. A shifter pretending to be me? Would they dare around so many people? Or did they find Felicity?

Felicity makes a better princess than I ever did. I take a step back from the rail, not wanting to risk any of the partygoers seeing two princesses in one night. Not that it would matter for long, since they would forget as soon as I left their sight.

The halls seem bigger than before as I navigate my way through them toward the chamber next to mine. When I get there, I enter without knocking.

Kendrick's sitting shirtless in bed, leaning against the headboard with a book in his lap. He jerks his head up, his eyes widening, his lips parting. He scans me as if he's looking for injury, skimming over my riding leathers and taking in the sword at my back and the daggers on my hips.

The sight of him and the feel of his eyes on me make me warm deep in my stomach but cold in every part of me that remembers I can't climb in beside him. *Shouldn't.*

I do it anyway, removing my sword from my back and sitting right beside him, so close my arm's pressed against his. My heart aches too much to deny myself.

He stares at me like he can't quite believe I'm real. Maybe because I'm not. I'm not who I used to be, and I won't live long enough to become anyone new. I'm not anyone anymore.

"Jasalyn." My name, said with relief, with gratitude, with worry.

I curl into his side and rest my head on his shoulder. "It was just a bad day," I whisper.

"Where have you—"

I shake my head. "Don't. I don't want to do this again. I'm fine. I'm working to fix what I broke. I just . . ." I wrap my fingers around his arm, reveling in the size and strength there. I'm safe. Right here. Right now. I'm safe. "I wanted to see you."

"Like you did before."

I lift my head. "You remember?"

Kendrick pulls me onto his lap, moving me like I'm no more than a child, but I don't care. I let him wrap his arms around me and rest my head against his chest. Hands stroking my back, he buries his nose in my hair and breathes in deep. "I might not remember it, but I knew why I'd gone to the keep and when I found myself in the Ironmoore infirmary, the scent of you was still there. It's clung to me since. And now . . ."

His chest shudders with his next inhale. "Tell me you aren't going to leave this time."

I can't lie to him, but I won't waste this night rehashing the same conversation we had in the infirmary. "I'm here now," I say, hoping that will be enough.

"We have a plan for the ring." He touches a finger to my lips and I shiver. "Once we have the Stone of Disenchantment, I'll be able to kiss you again."

I close my eyes. I'd like that. Just once before this is all taken away from me, I'd like to know Kendrick's kiss again.

I lightly brush the pads of my thumbs on the bruises beneath his eyes. "You aren't sleeping."

He cocks his head to the side. "How could I possibly sleep when everything that matters is so unsure?"

"Crissa," I say. They still don't know what happened to their queen.

He huffs out a breath that was probably supposed to be a laugh, but there's no amusement in the sound. "Yes. I should be losing sleep over my queen. I should be losing sleep over the fact that we haven't had one hint of where she might be and over the future of the realm I've been tasked with saving." His jaw works for a moment before his arms tighten around me, but instead of feeling like a prison, they're like a blanket, offering warmth and comfort without trapping me. "But I'm losing sleep over you, Jas. I've been out of my mind trying to find you."

His eyes are so blue. So pure. They are the eyes that saved me, his is the voice that saved me, even when his hands couldn't.

"You didn't have to pretend to be human."

He stiffens because, of course, he still doesn't remember that I know. "What do you mean?"

"You didn't have to be a human for me to trust you." I skim my fingertip across the delicately pointed shell of his ear and he shivers. "I would've needed your friendship in those dungeons whether you'd been fae or human or goblin. I'm not angry that you're fae. I'm angry that you lied."

"That's why you left? Because you found out who I am?"

It hurts—being erased like this, knowing that in so many ways this ring took my life before the date I agreed to. "I don't want to have this conversation again. I just want . . ." I close my eyes and breathe in the scent of him. Leather. Soap. Fresh air.

"Tell me." His fingers are so gentle as he tilts my face to look at his. "Tell me what you want and I will bend the world to give it to you."

I want to kiss you. I want to stay here in your arms and forget everything that's broken—everything I've broken. I want to lose myself in this moment. In you. To feel like I did during our night together—to give you the same feelings you gave me. "I want to touch you."

His nostrils flare and his lips part. "Jas . . ."

I slide my hand down his bare chest, relishing the heat of his skin, the tickle of his chest hair beneath my fingertips. "You don't remember, but we spent the night together before I left." I find the waistband of his soft sleep pants and skim a knuckle across that spot where skin meets cotton.

His eyes float closed and he shivers subtly beneath my touch. "I don't remember"—his voice is the rasp of desire brushing against need—"but I have my journal. I know . . ." He swallows. "I would trade a hundred useless memories for the one from that night."

"You don't need to trade anything." I slip my hand beneath his waistband and watch his eyes darken as I find him. I don't know what I'm doing, not exactly, but my cousins whispered about this enough to give me an idea. And it's easier than I would've guessed to know what he likes—what makes his lips part and his breath hitch, what makes his hips lift just slightly from the bed. "This?"

He releases an unintelligible sound that makes want and heat curl together low in my belly. "Gods." He holds my gaze and traces my lips with the pad of his thumb. "I must be dreaming."

I explore the warm skin tentatively at first, but then with more confidence. He fights to keep his eyes locked on mine, but when he loses himself to pleasure, head pressed into his pillow, neck arching, something like pride flows through me. I feel like I'm glowing.

He pulls my hand away and before I can wonder why, he's wrapping an arm around my waist and rolling us so I'm on my back and he's above me. He scrapes his teeth down the column of my neck, then kisses his way across my collarbone and down to my chest, pressing his open mouth to my breast and licking me through my shirt.

He draws back, throat bobbing. "You're bleeding." He searches with eyes and hands across my belly, over my chest, and down my arms before reaching my wrist and finding the bleeding punctures from the wolpertinger's spikes.

I didn't even notice I got blood on his pants. "It doesn't hurt anymore," I promise.

He brings my wrist to his lips and kisses the tender spot. "Let me get a bandage for this."

If he leaves, he'll forget this. I'm not ready for that yet. "I'm fine. I just want you to stay with me. To hold me."

He scans my face like he's looking for answers, like he might remember this if he just tries hard enough. "I'll hold you as long as you'll let me."

I skim my fingers across the stubble of his short beard, making my own efforts to remember this moment, though there's no chance I'll forget.

He lies on his side and pulls me against him, my back to his front. I let myself stay in the warmth of his embrace until the candle beside the bed flickers in the last of its wax, until his breath falls into the shallow rhythm of sleep.

"You won't remember this," I whisper, and the truth of it is like the worst of the darkness on the loneliest night. I thought I knew loneliness in the depths of my despair, during those years before I got the ring, but that can't compare to the loneliness of knowing nothing I say or do now will be remembered. I will walk away and be erased. "I love you," I say softly. I slide off his bed, not letting myself hesitate, even when he reaches for me in his sleep.

CHAPTER TWELVE

FELICITY

"You see the male to my right who keeps creeping closer?" the shadow queen asks me. The ball is tonight. After having just two days to prepare, I am here as the princess—here to prove all is well at the Midnight Palace, here to prove that no one but the queen and the princess herself control Jasalyn. "Gray hair and yellow tunic?"

Beyond the dais, where we stand, the ballroom floor is crowded with noble guests not just from the shadow court but also visitors from the Court of the Sun and the Wild Fae Lands, but I easily spot the male in question. He has long gray hair, gray eyes, and pale skin with such a milky pallor I wonder when he last saw the sun. I give the queen a subtle nod.

"*That* is Lord Pandian. He's the one with the Stone of Disenchantment, and the males on either side of him are his sons." The sons in question have golden hair but are otherwise as pale and nondescript as their father.

"And you're sure they won't suspect anything if Jasalyn is suddenly interacting with them after years of avoiding everyone?" She already told me that the dais is protected by a sound shield, but speaking so freely about this here still makes me nervous, so I keep my voice low.

"That entire family is too swollen with arrogance to suspect anything but my sister's adoration."

"They're all staring at me," I say. She knows I don't just mean the lord and his sons. Everyone in this ballroom is appraising me on some level—from curious gazes to outright gawking.

The queen's lips twitch. "Of course they're staring. They want to tell everyone they know that they saw the princess for themselves. They will find every reason that you are or aren't her."

"Do they suspect? Why? How? I haven't even talked to anyone yet."

"The true princess could be by my side and these fools who want to believe she's missing would still see her as a fraud. We're not here to convince those who have already decided one way or the other. We need to convince those who don't want to believe the rumors."

I swallow hard. It was one thing to pretend to be the princess at Castle Craige when there was no reason for anyone to suspect anything was amiss, but now the stakes are higher.

"Misha will be here soon," Abriella says, and my heart kicks into a faster beat. I haven't seen him since the day we arrived at the palace. "He's promised me he'll stay by your side all night."

"And how much did he curse you when you gave him *that* order? He hates me."

Her smile turns to a grin and her eyes dance in amusement. "With an intensity I've never before seen him display."

"That's not comforting."

She scoffs but doesn't look at me. She's still scanning the crowd. I know without asking that she's looking for signs of trouble, as are the dozens of sentries both in and out of uniform throughout the ballroom. "Misha is a king. I wouldn't dare give him orders. It would be inappropriate."

I drop my gaze to my hands. "Do you think he will pursue a relationship with your sister—once she's home?"

"You think he might want to pursue Jasalyn because of what happened between the two of you?" She tuts. "That wasn't about Jas. Misha had never shown any interest in my sister before you took on her form."

"But when we spoke at Misha's ball, you said—"

"I said I'd *hoped*, but that was me daydreaming. It wasn't based in anything. I mostly just liked the idea of her . . ." Her eyes go glossy with tears and she swallows. "I liked the idea of her being well enough to fall in love. My sister and my best friend—can you blame me?"

"I suppose not."

"Besides, now that I've met Kendrick . . ." Sadness flashes across her features so quickly that I almost question if it was there at all. "What I would give to know if my sister gets the same look in her eyes when she talks about him as he does for her."

"We'll find her." Even as I say it, I feel the ticking clock of her bargain closing in on us.

Abriella rolls her shoulders back, then her gaze shifts to the steps behind me. "Misha, we were just talking about you."

"Are you giving away all my secrets?" he asks.

The hair on the back of my neck stands on end. I can feel him looking at me, so I slowly turn. He's absolutely regal in his dark tunic—a blue as deep as night with shimmering maroon and cyan stitching. This is *King* Misha. His royal facade. The male who rescued me from my twin was *warrior* Misha. Two sides of the same coin, each equally skilled. Each equally magnetic.

"Good evening." He might hate me, but there's no question that I still feel *everything* for him. I wish Abriella hadn't spoken about it with me. I don't need anyone lending my foolish heart an excuse to cling to unrequited feelings.

"Ready to parade across the ballroom, *Princess*?" He uses the title like a barb, like he's reminding me of everything I'm not.

"Are you ready to pretend you like me?"

His gaze is so potent as it scrapes over me, I feel it like a touch. Like calloused fingertips across my skin. "You're not the only one who can play a part when necessary." He turns on his heel and leaves the balcony with the confidence of a male who has every reason to believe he'll be followed.

"Have fun," Abriella says with a wink.

I hurry my steps to catch up with Misha before he can exit the queen's sound shield. "You know, a polite escort would walk at a pace I could keep up with," I say to his back.

He slows and offers his arm.

I hold his gaze for a beat before I take it, ignoring the way my whole body lights up when I'm in contact with him. *He hates you*.

"I'm sorry you have to escort me," I say as he slowly leads me down from the dais and to the ballroom floor. The apology is kinder than railing against him for emotions he's more than entitled to. It's fairer than all the heartbroken, unfair accusations I want to hurl at him. It's less pathetic than everything I want to ask him for.

I lock those thoughts away before they can do something humiliating like flash across my face.

He cuts his gaze to mine. *We need someone near you all night who knows the players in the court.*

My eyes widen as I register that he's not *speaking* the words but— *You're in my mind.*

He arches a brow. *Did you forget? Or do you only remember my more remarkable talents?*

My cheeks heat. If I didn't know better, I'd think he was flirting. Seeing me in Jasalyn's form must be messing with his head. *You didn't speak to me this way when I stayed at Castle Craige.*

Only the once. His throat bobs and he tears his gaze from mine. *It seems the connection that materialized between our minds that night was never severed.*

I feel it now—the path between us, the connection not so much like the thread I'd imagine. More like a rescue rope, thick and durable.

I'm not sure how I feel about that, I admit, and even though I can feel the connection and know I control my end of it, I still find myself asking, *Can you hear my thoughts?*

His russet eyes are so magnetic I couldn't pull my gaze away if I wanted to. *Only the ones you feed me.*

The tension between us buzzes with everything unspoken.

Perhaps I'm not as good at shielding as I once thought.

He smirks. *Or perhaps you don't want to keep me out as much as you once did.*

What's that supposed to mean? Is he referring to my feelings for him? Really? Rude. *You're sure no one else is available to escort me tonight?* The group Abriella pointed out is only steps away. *What if they think we're together and I don't get close enough to either son to get what I need?*

His gaze flicks to mine. *If you're so worried, you should probably stop looking at me like that.*

Like what?

Like you know how my mouth feels on your skin and you're wondering when you can feel it again.

I gape at him and he lifts a shoulder as if to say he can't help how I'm feeling.

Stay close, he says as Lord Pandian notices our approach and turns to greet us.

"King Misha," the lord says, acknowledging him with a curt nod before turning his full attention to me. "Princess, how lovely to see you in attendance tonight. You look stunning, as usual." He takes my hand, lifting it to his lips and leaving a slimy trail behind.

Do not *wipe your hand on your skirts,* Misha mentally warns me. *No matter how much you might want to.*

I'm not socially inept. You'll remember I fooled you *without an issue.*

Trust me. I remember.

Lord Pandian tugs lightly on my hand, bringing me forward. "Princess, it is my pleasure to introduce you to my sons—Leon and Ezra."

"Good evening," I say, bowing my head politely toward each of them. "Thank you for joining us."

Ezra steps forward and takes my hand, bringing it to his lips as his father did. "The pleasure is ours, Princess."

"It's a relief to see you well," Leon says, taking his turn adding his own slippery kiss to the back of my hand. "We'd heard you'd befallen a terrible fate."

"Which rumor was that?" Misha asks. His eyes dance and his lips quirk as if he's trying to hold back an amused smile. "Did you hear the one where she was kidnapped by the sea dragon or the one where she ran away with her goblin lover?"

As far as I know, neither of these is a rumor that's been circulating, but that's precisely why Misha's using these examples—to make the rumors that hit a little too close to home seem equally ridiculous.

Ezra clears his throat and blushes. "Neither. We, uh . . ." He glances at his father, then to me, then to his brother. "We'd heard that—"

"What matters is that you're here and you're well," Lord Pandian says. "I hope you'll take some time from your evening to get to know my sons. Perhaps you can start with a dance." He gestures to the dance floor.

I brighten my expression, as if this is just what I want to hear. "I—"

"The princess isn't dancing tonight," Misha says. "Too many people to greet, you understand." He's already pulling me away.

What are you doing? I ask Misha as I shoot a disappointed glance in Ezra's direction. *They are ready to hand over just what we need.*

We don't want to be too eager, he says into my mind even as he greets another guest. *We'll get what we need in good time. Ezra wants to convince you to dance with him before his brother has the chance.*

And this is a bad *thing?*

His father wants Leon with the princess. His jaw ticks. *But Ezra thinks he can get you alone. Thinks he can seduce the princess, and he has some . . . well, he thinks rather highly of himself.*

You're in his mind?

His shields are little more than tissue paper—but I'm not sure if that's because he's too foolish to bother with them or because he's magically weak.

Wouldn't it be faster to let him follow through with his plans?

Misha's brows shoot up. *You want to be seduced by Ezra tonight? He thinks if the princess winds up pregnant she'll have no choice but to marry him.*

When I visibly shudder, Misha's amusement shimmers through our connection. *Charming. Am I not supposed to win them over, though? Let them believe I'm entirely charmed by them?*

Ezra wants what he can't have, so we need to work with that.

Misha leads me to an older couple with bright eyes, long braids, and ebony skin. "Lord and Lady Felhaus, please allow me to introduce you to Princess Jasalyn." He steps back so I can take the lady's offered hand. "The Felhaus family was living in the Unseelie settlement in my territory during Mordeus's rule."

My face falls. They were refugees. "I'm so sorry to hear you had to leave your home," I say, squeezing the female's hand.

"King Misha took good care of us," she says, "but we are so happy to be back in the shadow court now. We just hope your sister knows she can count on our village to stand behind her should . . ." She looks to her husband, who gives a curt nod, but she lowers her voice before continuing. "Should the rumors of Mordeus's return and his growing legions be true."

Should I act like I know of these rumors? I ask Misha.

It would be impossible to miss them at this point. Acknowledge the offer but keep it optimistic.

I press a hand to my chest and give her a sad smile. "Let's hope that's not necessary."

Soon, Misha's ushered me away to a female who helped run the school at the settlement and her partner, who blushes fiercely when Misha reminds her how much he loves her paintings.

When he smiles down at me, the moment is so superficially similar to so many moments in the illusion that my heart stutters.

Suddenly I'm back in the Eloran Palace, back in Misha's arms as he leads me in a dance I've been practicing since childhood.

The room spins as my mind is drawn taut between my reality and my memories—*no.* Not memories. The illusion Konner planted in my mind.

Someone calls Misha's name, and he smiles and lifts a hand in greeting. *You should go for a while. Jasalyn has never stayed through an entire ball. She avoided these things, so you should slip away just as she would.*

He's right, and if I were thinking straight, I would've thought of it first.

You'll tell Abriella?

I already have. I'll come find you later to sow the seeds we've planted.

I nod and retreat toward the servants' entrance Abriella showed me before the ball—the easiest place to escape if the crowd becomes too much, she said.

If only she'd shown me how to escape my own thoughts.

I'm sitting on what feels like it must be the only quiet terrace in the whole palace when Remme finds me.

"Hey, you," he says, taking the seat opposite mine. "How are you holding up?"

The sincerity in his voice tells me it's not just a throwaway question, and suddenly I'm blinking back tears. Hale's friends always tolerated me, but I never fully felt like they were mine as well. I've spent my entire life just outside every circle I longed to be a part of. *Until that illusion. Until that alternate reality I lived and breathed for months.*

"Not so great then, huh?" He pats my hand on the tabletop, then squeezes it.

I worry my bottom lip between my teeth. "I'm walking around with those memories from the illusion—fake as they might be—and feeling this overwhelming sense of homesickness." I turn toward the stars in the distance to hide my face. "How pathetic is that?"

"It's not pathetic at all," Remme says. "No one can blame you for having complicated emotions about all of this. What counts is your actions. You're here. You're fighting for what's right, even though he made that feel so wrong."

"He said it wasn't fake. That it was what *could've been*, and I know he's messing with my head but I . . ." I swallow the lump of emotion surging up my throat. "I wonder if that's true. If I'd been raised in the Eloran Palace, would I be so sure of their righteousness? Would I think that Hale's mission was misguided?" I close my eyes and draw in a long, slow breath. My thoughts feel too heavy. "Am I so mentally weak that I believe whatever the people around me feed me? And if that's true, how can I trust that any choice I make is my own?"

"Felicity," Remme says. I keep my head bowed, too aware of his full attention on me. "Felicity, look at me."

I meet his unwavering gaze.

"He wanted to get in your head. You are confident and steadfast, and he wanted to mess with that. But you don't need to worry about this." His smile is a little amused and a little lopsided as he shakes his head. "Did you forget why you were living on your own for three years? Did you forget where the tension between you and Hale came from? You made your own choices. We told you to kill Erith, and you wouldn't. You aren't some silly child who mindlessly bends to the will of those around her. You have grown into a mighty female who wasn't afraid to reject the destiny those she loved most were begging her to embrace."

This time, when I draw a breath, I finally feel like I can fill my lungs. "Thank you."

"I'm only reminding you of the truth. You know I don't do that motivational speech crap." His chair screeches against the stone and he rises from the table. "I thought for sure you were lost to us, but your brother refused to believe it. He believed in you. He still does. That guy you shared a womb with? He doesn't know you at all. He used his magic and his own agenda to make you think he does and to make you question yourself."

"I just don't know where I belong."

He flicks my nose and I swat his hand away. "You're going to figure it out. And we'll be here to help."

As he straightens, Hale stumbles onto the terrace, looking dazed.

"Hale?" Remme says, stepping toward him. An owl shrieks in the distance. "What's going on?"

Hale drags a hand over his face. "Jasalyn was here."

"Where?" he asks. "How do you know?"

"She. Was. Here." He drags both hands through his hair and turns in a slow circle, as if she might reappear.

Remme and I exchange a look. "You remember?" Remme asks. "What happened? What did she say?"

Hale drops his hands to his sides and curls them into fists. "I *don't* remember. I just . . . damn it, I *know*. She was here. I can smell her. I can . . ."

When he stops turning, I gasp. "Hale. You're hurt." His pants are smeared with blood. I jump up from my seat and rush toward him. "What happened?"

He looks down at himself, as if in a trance. "It's not mine." He wipes at the blood on his trousers and lifts it to his nose. He flinches. "This is Jasalyn's blood."

"You're sure?"

He nods. "She's hurt. We have to find her."

Remme blows out a breath. "And now we finally can."

Hale squeezes his eyes shut. "Finally."

"How?" I ask, looking back and forth between them.

"We can use her blood to track her," Remme says.

"But the moment she gets away from us, we won't remember that we found her."

"I will," Hale says, and he's so sure it makes my heart ache for him. His eyes are desperate when they reach mine. "You have to believe me. This was her blood."

Remme's sigh is resigned as he turns to me. "Looks like we're going to have to accelerate the plan, Lis. If we're going to use that blood to track her while it's still fresh, we need that stone tonight."

CHAPTER THIRTEEN

JASALYN

When I saw the boarded-up blacksmith's hut in Mordeus's mind, I knew exactly where I needed to look for the sword. It's close to the Midnight Palace and not far from the tavern where I tracked down one of Mordeus's guards and made one of my first kills as the Enchanting Lady.

As I leave the palace, the fog is so thick I can barely see my own hand in front of my face, but I trek forward nevertheless, determined to make the most of the energy my forest sacrifice provided me. "Your death won't be in vain, little guy," I murmur, and then instantly shove away those thoughts when my stomach heaves. Better not to think about it.

Twigs snap under my boots and an owl calls in the distance, but the area is otherwise eerily silent. This kind of silence in this part of the capital at night isn't natural, and I have to wonder if protective wards have been erected around the sword to scare even the insects away.

After I've been hiking long enough that I'm questioning my memory, I finally spot the roofline of the shack. As I creep closer, I hear it—the low wheeze and whoosh of an animal's breathing.

So the wards haven't scared away all *the creatures.*

I still can't see more than a few inches in front of my face, so I can only use my ears to navigate around the creature. I'm close. I can't explain it, but I can feel the sword calling to me, can feel the lure of the snapping flames and the waves of heat. I don't want to detour too far. Then again, I don't want to bother a sleeping animal I can't see either. I turn to my left, but my foot snags on a branch and before I can get my balance I'm stumbling to my hands and knees on the forest floor.

A heavy *harrumph* comes from my right, and then a cry so loud the forest seems to split in two around me. The creature's close enough now that I can hear it breathing—a snorting inhale and wet exhale that reminds me of a sleeping dog. But I already know this is no dog. It's big enough to be—

A line of fire barrels toward me, and I roll onto my side to dodge it, then lie on the ground staring at the scorched earth beside me. I can't stop shaking. Why did I think this would be so simple? Wasn't the disaster at Feegus Keep enough to remind me that my ring can't do anything to help me against monsters? I'm foolish enough to deserve the painful end I'm sure is coming for me.

Stand up, Jasalyn. Take a breath and stand up.

I grab the fallen limb behind me and hoist myself over to the opposite side, ducking behind it as I draw my sword from my back.

A sword against a fire-breathing monster. I'm as good as dead.

I remove my dagger from my thigh and spin it in the air above my head before blindly hurling it toward the dark form hulking toward me. The sharp cry that pierces the air tells me

I've hit my target. I just don't know how well.

It roars again, and this time when fire bursts from its lungs, it's directed at the sky. That's when I see it. Them? So much like the death dogs in the basement of Feegus Keep—except this one has three heads. Right, and *breathes fire*.

I drop behind the limb again, but I'm too late. The head on the right spotted me.

The creature lunges, swiping at me with claws the size of my head. I retreat but not fast enough, and one of those claws finds purchase in my thigh, digging in and tearing into leather and flesh as it cuts through me. Pain radiates from my thigh and out to every inch of my being. With a scream, I scramble away before it can land another blow.

I wish I were like my sister. I wish I weren't so utterly human and had even a little magic at my disposal. But all I have on my side is my size, my ability to move through a forest with such dense trees and undergrowth.

When the monster opens its mouth again, I know this time he will strike home with its flames. I don't let myself think or hesitate.

I run.

I pump my legs as hard as I can, ignoring the searing pain in my wounded thigh as I weave through the narrowest openings in the trees to force the three-headed beast to find another path to get to me. Its angry roars follow me and then slip farther away.

When I sense I've put enough distance between us, I strip off my vest and press it against my bloody thigh before hanging it on a branch above me. I cut away the bloodiest part of my pants, then do the same with that fabric, leaving it on a tree just a little deeper in the woods. I can't block my scent, but I can scatter it—confuse the monster before I take a different path.

Only when I see it turning toward my lures do I circle back, following that inexplicable pull toward the closed-up hut—toward the sword—through the dense underbrush.

By the time I reach the dilapidated building, the pain in my leg is so intense I can't make out the sound of the three-headed creature in the woods anymore. All I can hear is my weakening heartbeat and the labored whoosh of my breathing.

I want to collapse. Oblivion offers me her hand and it's so tempting. I could curl up on the ground right here. I could stop fighting and give in to my exhaustion.

But I'm too close to give up now. I tear off the rotten boards and throw them behind me, then shove at the stone door with all my might until it slides clear, revealing the prize inside.

Orange and red flames lick the cavern ceiling and heat the air. At first, I think that's all it is. Nothing but a fire waiting on a ledge in this crumbling hut. But then I look closer.

The sword is right there in the hottest, bluest part of the fire. In the flame. Made of flame. The Sword of Fire *is* fire.

I'm too close to give up now. I put one foot in front of the other as I approach the sword, but it's like willing myself into an oven. The closer I get, the more desperate I am to retreat.

I'm shaking. Whatever rush of energy I had while fleeing the monster has all but left me and my leg throbs with every step, but still I need to try. Reaching the sword is the only thing that matters now.

I've never felt fire so hot, and as I surge forward, the heat burns, threatening to sear my lungs and blister my skin.

If I give up now, he wins. If I give up now, he could get to my sister. If I give up now, all the horrors he'll bring upon this realm will be my fault.

With eyes that fight to close against the scalding heat, I search for the hilt—or some other part of the sword meant for holding—and see nothing but white-hot flame. Flame that repels me even as it calls to me.

Mordeus. Grab the sword and have it take you to Mordeus.

Maybe it's an illusion. Maybe this is all a trick of magic to protect the sword from theft.

In the forest behind me, I hear the cacophony of breaking limbs and underbrush. *It's coming back.*

With a final searing breath, I reach for the hilt, yanking my hand away when the flame threatens to engulf my hand.

The three-headed beast roars just outside the hut, and when I turn, it's in the doorway, blocking my exit, exposed teeth and angry red eyes promising death.

Trapped between the beast and the lethal fire at my back, I see death in both directions. Death by three hungry, snapping jaws, or death by the sword's endless flame.

CHAPTER FOURTEEN

FELICITY

I feel Misha's presence before I see him come onto the terrace. Maybe it's that connection in our minds growing stronger the more we're around each other. Or maybe I'm just that aware of him.

"Let's go," Misha says. "Ezra's growing impatient."

I push back from the table, glad to be done waiting. If they find Jasalyn tonight, they need that stone. "Well, hello, Misha. My evening's been fine, thank you for asking."

He arches a brow. "I imagine it's been better than mine. Trust me, I would've much rather been watching the stars out here than mingling in there." He scans me as I stand. "Are you ready?"

"As I'll ever be." I blow out a breath. "Let's go get what we need."

"You need more than a strand of hair. You need enough of his attention that he'll accept your invitation."

"Right," I mutter, smoothing out the wrinkles in my gown. "Simple."

"He's been standing in the same place all night, constantly scanning the room for you. Go to the window near where he's speaking with his father. Make it look like you're using the view as an excuse to get close to him. Sneak looks but—"

I roll my eyes. "I can manage to act coy for a few minutes, but I appreciate the instruction."

He grunts. "How quickly I forget."

I squeeze my eyes shut for a beat, then sigh and look at him again. "I am sorry, Misha. I didn't like lying to you."

He shoves his hands into his pockets and surveys the distant, moonlit horizon. "Spare me the apologies. I know why you were doing it, and as insulting as it is that you thought you could seduce the location of my Hall of Doors out of me, I understand why you tried."

I stare at his profile for a long time. The full lips and thick brows, the faint glow of the silver webbing on his forehead, the sadness in his eyes. He's so close I can smell him. The pine and rosewood. The clean male scent that intoxicates me. "I needed the information," I say, "but I didn't intend to seduce you for it. Seduction was my brother's ridiculous plan. I hoped to figure it out on my own."

He cuts his eyes to me, like he can't help it. "Then why? Why . . . everything else?"

I open my mouth and then close it again. Why indeed. *Because you're irresistible? Because the way you looked at me made me feel wanted for the first time in my life? Because I was weak?* I swallow the lump in my throat. "I didn't expect it to happen. Males don't fall for me. But I wasn't taking into account that I'd be Jasalyn to you. I mean, obviously I knew you'd think I was her, as that was the only reason I was there at all, but I forget that males have such a weakness for females who look like"—I breathe through the embarrassment heating my cheeks. I wave a hand to indicate Jasalyn's form—"like this."

He scoffs, then strides away. "I've never had a weakness for Jasalyn," he calls without turning back. I don't know what that is supposed to mean, so I make myself bite my bottom lip before I can embarrass myself by asking.

Even though I gave Misha a hard time about instructing me on how to get the attention of the lord's son, I follow his instructions to a T: going to the window as if drawn by the view and then sneaking a glance toward Ezra.

His eyes are already on me, and I duck my head bashfully.

He's nodding at something his father is saying, but I can feel his attention like a heavy coat in the summer.

The second time I glance his way, Ezra excuses himself from his father and comes to stand by my side at the window.

"Hello," I say. If only I could will myself to blush.

"How has your evening been, Your Highness?" His eyes look me up and down over and over again. Greedy. Like he wants to gobble up the princess and doesn't know where to start. Being an Echo gives me the empathic gift of detecting the relationship between people and how they feel about each other. Even if Brie hadn't told me, I'd know now that though Ezra and Jas have no history, Ezra is desperate for her—but not in any romantic or affectionate way. He wants control of her.

"Long," I say, trying to emulate a personality that's the necessary mix of Princess Jasalyn and the flirtatious girl she's never been. "I don't much care for crowds. It's hard to have a good conversation with so many people around."

"I couldn't agree more." He stops a waiter and takes two glasses of wine from his tray before handing one to me. "The wine helps," he says with a wink.

His eyes never leave mine as he drains half the glass in two swallows. When he nods to my glass, I take the world's smallest sip. I need to stay alert. "Thank you."

His face falls. "You don't like it. Can I get you something else? Anything?" He's nervous. I see it in the way he keeps wiping his palms on his trousers, in the way he pulls his bottom lip between his teeth. "Perhaps some tea or refreshments? I can call for your servants."

I clasp my hands at my waist, trying to look as nervous as he seems. Not that it's difficult. I don't like being here. Don't like the slimy feel of Lord Pandian's eyes on me every time he looks this way. "I'm fine. I don't need a thing."

"I hope you'll forgive me for saying so, but you look tired. Though no less beautiful than when you're rested."

I bow my head enough to look up at him through my lashes. "You don't have to say that. I know I'm rather . . . plain." *Jasalyn, please forgive me for putting such a gross self-loathing sentiment in your mouth.*

His eyes go wide, and I know it was worth it. "Not at all, Princess. To say you are plain is like saying that the sun is irrelevant or the raging sea is idle."

"I am humbled by your praise," I murmur.

"I've never been particularly interested in the lessons our tutors gave in literature, but your beauty could inspire me to write poetry." His doughy white cheeks flame red, and now he's the one ducking his head and looking embarrassed. "But I needn't go on. I'm sure many males have told you as much."

You only need a hair and a rendezvous, not a marriage proposal, Misha says into my mind. He seems . . . irritated?

I'm not sure when he returned to the ballroom or where exactly he's standing, but I don't let myself look for him.

"May I tell you something in confidence?" I ask Ezra.

He snaps his gaze back up to meet mine. "Anything. I am, you should know, a male you can trust—with your secrets and with your life."

He lays it on a bit thick, doesn't he? Misha grumbles in my mind.

I ignore him and give all my attention to Ezra. "My sister is a bit protective. So while you say you believe others have given me compliments like yours, it's not true. Abriella fears males will take advantage of me if they get too close, but in truth . . ." I dart my eyes to either side of him, as if to make sure we won't be overheard.

"In truth?" he asks, encouraging me to go on.

"In truth, I get lonely. I could use a friend. Someone who can speak to me openly and who makes me feel safe." I duck my head again. "Someone like you."

Makes you feel safe? Misha scoffs in my mind. *You just met tonight. How—*

"Not someone *like* me." Ezra touches two fingers beneath my chin and tilts my face up to his. "Let that friend *be* me."

I school my expression, biting back my smirk. *I know what I'm doing.* "I like that idea," I say softly. "You have . . ." I reach up to brush an imaginary piece of lint from his shoulder and tuck a stray hair into my palm. I smile up at him. "There."

His eyes warm. "May I call on you?" he asks. "Soon?"

"I don't know if my sister would allow it." I glance at the queen over my shoulder. "Sometimes it's better to ask forgiveness with her—rather than permission."

He frowns. "Should I arrive unannounced? Or perhaps you'd like to visit my father's manor?"

"I would rather . . ." I shake my head and give a half-hearted laugh. "Foolish to wish for things I cannot have."

He cocks his head to the side. "Tell me what you wish for and allow me to make it so."

I take a breath, as if gathering my courage. "I wish we could be alone tonight."

I feel Misha's tension through our connection. *You're pushing it.*

Ezra's eyes widen. "Tonight?"

I wave a hand. "I know. Impossible."

He swallows. "Nothing's impossible. But my father—" He glances over his shoulder at the male in question. "There's a certain way he believes things should be done, so I need to time this right." He frowns. "That is, if you think you could get away after the ball?"

I take a few rapid breaths. "I can. I know how to sneak out."

"We'll have our alone time then." His gaze drops to my mouth, his eyes dancing with happiness. "I know just the place."

"What. Was. That?" Misha looks downright angry when he finds me in Jasalyn's chambers.

"Change of plan," I say, pulling up my pants again. I slipped away shortly after Ezra and I made arrangements for our rendezvous, and Hale and Natan helped me track down clothes to wear in Ezra's form. They keep slipping off Jasalyn's small frame. "I'm going after the stone tonight."

Misha fists his hands at his sides. "That wasn't what we agreed on."

Part of me knew he wouldn't like this, and that's exactly why I didn't tell him before making plans with Ezra. "Why do you care, Misha? Tonight, tomorrow? Either way, I take Ezra's form and retrieve the stone."

"I can have more *eyes* at the manor tomorrow. Eyes that can make sure nothing goes wrong. People who can step in and protect you if needed."

"Yes, but Jas visited Hale tonight. She must've been bleeding because her blood was on him, and they want to use the blood to track her while it's still fresh."

The anger falls off his face. "He's sure it's hers?"

"He won't consider anything else."

"That doesn't mean this is safe."

"I'll be fine," I say, trying to ignore the knot in my stomach. I want to do this. For Jasalyn. For my brother. I *need* to do this to convince myself I'm still committed to this cause, to convince myself that Konner's manipulations haven't swayed my loyalty. "I don't have much time to dream between now and the high moon hour he'll be away, so if you would let me sleep, I'd appreciate it."

"I'm going with you."

I cough out a laugh. "Are you kidding me? How will you do that? Are you secretly some sort of shifter?"

"If you go in there and they catch you trying to retrieve the stone, they'll lock it down so tight we'll never have a chance of retrieving it. Without the stone, Jasalyn is as good as dead, and if she dies, Mordeus will take her body and destroy everything that's worth saving in this court and then in this realm."

I fold my arms. "You think I don't know all that?"

"I don't need to go in with you. I just need to be close. I need to be in your head and know that everything isn't going to shit."

"Can't you do that from here?"

His jaw ticks. "As of late, not consistently, no."

"Fine. You can come and wait outside if that's what it takes to convince you I'm not going to screw this up."

"Good."

I settle onto the bed, and he doesn't move. I wave to the door. "You can go?"

He glances at the clock and frowns. "I could help you fall asleep easily, if you'd like. It's a gift of mine."

My brows shoot up. "Wow. That's a line I never expected from you, *Your Majesty*."

He tries to scowl but his lips twitch. "Does your mind only visit the gutter in my presence, or does it have a full-time residence there?"

"You bring it out in me," I say, then regret how flirtatious the words sound.

Misha closes his eyes for a beat, and in the next the wind in the trees outside grows both louder and more comforting, the leaves rustling in a way that's almost their own song.

The tension in my muscles releases and my eyes float closed.

I part my lips to tell Misha how nice this is, how relaxed I feel, but I hate to interrupt the lovely melody that's washing all my cares away. I'll tell him in a moment. Just one more moment.

CHAPTER FIFTEEN

JASALYN

The three-headed beast snarls, long streams of saliva dripping from its lips.

Die before you can fix what you broke or die taking Mordeus with you.

I don't let myself think. I plunge my hand into the flame and grab the Sword of Fire.

Flames snap at my flesh, devouring it and incinerating skin, but I force myself to hang on.

"Take me to Mordeus," I demand of the sword with the last of my will.

A swirling black vortex opens as the beast lunges toward me. I hurl myself into the darkness and the old blacksmith's hut disappears.

I drop the sword to the stone floor and clutch my ravaged hand to my chest. It's bright red and raw and already covered in blisters and pustules. Seeing it makes the pain scream louder in my head. I tear away part of my shirt and wrap it up.

Blood oozes from my thigh onto the stone floor and my hand pulses with pain. The agony and the despair work together, trying to pull me under, but I fight it. When I draw in a breath, putrid rot hits my nose, and I jerk into awareness, blinking as I look around.

The smell is sickening, a scent so thick it shoves itself into my nostrils and clings to the back of my throat, threatening to make me lose the contents of my stomach.

I'm in a dark room open to a long corridor, and moonlight pours in through a high window, illuminating a corpse on a stone bed. *Mordeus.*

I push off the ground, stumbling when I try to put too much weight on my injured leg. Weakness from blood loss threatens to pull me back to the floor, but I limp deeper into the room, following the scent every instinct tells me to turn away from.

The sight of him is worse than the smell. His flesh hangs from his skeleton as if it's no longer properly attached. The bone of his left arm protrudes from where the flesh has been cut away—or maybe even eaten.

His cheeks are gaunt and when I get close enough to look, there's nothing but squirming maggots where those horrible silver eyes used to be.

He's not resurrected. This body is the picture of death. How could any magic, great or small, bring him back in this vessel?

The moment I'm convinced that's impossible, I realize his chest is moving. Barely. But slowly—lifting and falling with the telltale movement of shallow breath.

He lives.

A shudder racks my shoulders. *He lives.* How can such a horrific, pathetic creature make me want to run? Want to curl into myself and hide?

I don't let myself back away or even take my eyes off him. Because his hands are folded across his stomach, and on one finger is a ring that's a match to mine.

He orchestrated all of this. He's been using me and manipulating me every step of the way.

I reach for my blade with a shaking hand. Maybe I should go back for the Sword of Fire, but I don't think I'm strong enough to pick it up, and I can't risk sacrificing my remaining good hand. There's no way a body this ravaged, this *weak*, could survive my iron-and-adamant blade.

I might not understand how this corpse can ever become the fearsome faerie who will steal the throne from my sister and rule the shadow court, but I don't need to understand. I will end him before he has the chance.

Every muscle in my body trembles as I lift the blade over my head, prepared to strike, to cut out his wicked heart and toss it into the sword's flame so it can never be used again.

I swing the blade down, and it sinks too easily through rotted flesh and decaying bone.

Laughter sounds behind me, low and devious.

I yank my dagger from Mordeus's chest and spin around, blinking as the shadows part to reveal a laughing fae male. His face is so familiar, but I can't place him. He strides toward me, gobbling up the ground with his long legs until he stands before me.

"You can't kill something that's already dead," the faerie says, nodding to the corpse behind me. His white hair is tied back, and he smiles as he watches me clutch my blade, adjusting my grip on the cool metal hilt, preparing to strike.

An eerie wind swirls around me, wrapping around me and

lifting me from the floor before returning me to my feet.

"Look how pretty you are. A face that will win over the masses." His smile is so patient, almost grandfatherly. I struggle but can't escape the hold of the wind.

I'm wearing my ring. How could I forget my greatest strength?

"Back down," I command, infusing my voice with every bit of the Enchanting Lady I can muster. "Let me go."

"Not yet. We should talk first."

Why isn't it working? Is it because I'm so injured? Why would the magic work any differently now? I hold his gaze and try again. "Drop your shield for me. I need you to listen to what I have to say."

His lips quirk and he chuckles. "Do you think I would create a magical ring and allow it to enchant me as it does others?"

Create. This male created my ring. He's responsible for this curse. "Who are you?"

"He promised you would bring me that," he says, nodding to the Sword of Fire blazing in the corner. "I've been waiting."

I don't know who he is, but I recognize his voice from my memories. No. *Mordeus's memories.*

"Erith," I whisper. I don't know how I'm so sure or what memory this knowledge comes from, but I know the male smiling at me is the Patriarch of the Seven. The male Kendrick needs me to kill.

He cocks his head to the side. "I'm dying to know, though, how you overcame the effects of the ring—how you have the strength to be standing before me now."

I only fortify my mental shields and glare in response. I'm not about to tell him about the wolpertinger or Fherna.

"Fate is a slippery beast, and sometimes you need to go to

extreme measures to make it work in your favor." He glances toward the sword and smiles again. "It's been a long journey, but it's all proving worthwhile."

"You helped him return and now you're protecting him." I look to Mordeus and then back to Erith. I knew Erith was evil, but what does he stand to gain from making my ring? "All for the Sword of Fire?"

"Don't worry yourself, little princess. You don't need to know the details." He lowers me back to the floor and flicks his wrist. A doorway appears. On the other side of it is my childhood bedroom, the place my mother tucked us in each night before the house was burned to the ground in a fire. "Don't fight it. You deserve to rest."

Everything will be better if you come home, it seems to say. *Step this way and the pain will fade. The fear will melt away. You'll be safe here.*

"No," I breathe. I came here for a reason, and I'm not leaving. I'm not giving up. I won't let the people I love pay the price for my mistakes.

I tighten my grip on the iron-and-adamant blade in my hand, and I charge at Erith.

It's only as the blade plunges into his chest that I realize he didn't even dodge the blow.

"Do you really think I would've let you keep that blade if it was a danger to me?" he asks as we stand there, eyes locked, connected through this blade I refuse to release.

"How?" I say the word on an exhale, my body growing weaker by the moment.

"Isn't it fun when prophecies come to pass?" he asks, eyes dancing with nonsensical delight. "Make sure you tell your friend who fancies himself the king of Elora. He's been waiting for the moment you'd put this blade in my chest." Then, as calmly as if he were brushing crumbs from his shirt, he wraps both hands around mine and removes the blade from his chest.

I let my hand drop to my side and stare. There's no blood. No *wound*.

Is this a trick? Perhaps Erith isn't here. Perhaps this is some enchantment Mordeus set into motion to protect his corpse from harm? Am I dreaming? Maybe I'm curled up in the blacksmith's cottage, delirious from the pain, and all this is a hallucination.

I'm too weak to think straight and drop onto the floor, clutching the dagger as if it can protect me. This isn't real. I need sleep. Sleep and then I'll be able to understand what's happening. Sleep and then I'll wake up and make sense of everything.

"That's right," he murmurs, his voice the soothing melody of an old lullaby. "Rest now. Go to bed like a good girl, and I will make the pain go away."

And with that, a blast of his magic shoves me toward the door. I stumble but fight my way back to my feet. I feel the bedroom's tug pulling me away, but I know that if I surrender to it, I'll never come back. If I let myself sleep, this will be the end.

I lunge for the Sword of Fire, prepared to wrestle it from his grasp if he reaches it before me, but Erith flinches away from its unyielding flame. I exploit his hesitation. Wrapping my raw and blistered fingers around the flaming hilt, I make myself think of the bedroom at Fherna's house. My hand is nothing but red-hot, searing pain, and when Erith's magic sweeps in to retrieve the fiery sword, I can't hold on. I roll through the portal even as consciousness fades.

CHAPTER SIXTEEN

FELICITY

I almost feel sorry for Ezra. He's spent his whole life trying to get out from his brother's shadow and prove himself to his father. One memory of a family hunting trip was enough to understand what makes him tick better than weeks of observation ever could.

"What if he changes his mind and doesn't go to meet her?" I ask Misha as I adjust my tunic for the third time in as many minutes. I underestimated the size of Ezra's shoulders when I picked out the clothes I'd wear, and the too-narrow fit across my shoulders is making me feel pinned in.

"Skylar is prepared to meet him, and she'll let me know when he arrives."

"I still can't believe you talked her into dressing as Jasalyn's handmaid."

Misha smirks. "Does she always have such a temper?"

"Oh, always. That's just Skylar being Skylar."

"There it is," Misha says, nodding to the gates ahead.

"It's bigger than I expected."

"Abriella says they guard their wealth more fiercely than Mordeus guarded the throne."

I roll my eyes. "Of course they do."

He gets a strange look on his face for a beat, then smiles. "Skylar says he's there. She'll let him wait a few minutes before going in to tell him the princess is running behind. Ready?"

I nod, but I'm not. Even with all the coaching I'm still not convinced I can walk into this manor in the middle of the night and walk out with an invaluable magical stone.

"I'll be close—just keep yourself open to me. Share what you're seeing and I'll guide you."

"Okay."

Misha gives me one last look before riding away. He'll loop around to the back side of the manor and stay there in case anything goes wrong.

With a breath, I spur my horse ahead. When I reach the gates, I wave to the guards without slowing down.

"Back so soon?" the younger-looking of the two bald males asks.

"I forgot something," I say, hoping Ezra isn't the kind of person to never speak to the help.

"Flowers," the other calls to my back. "If you want to win her heart, take her flowers."

"Or jewelry," the first says. "Females enjoy jewelry."

This time I don't respond but head through the gates and to the front stairs. I hop off my horse and toss the reins to the sentinel standing there.

"Shall I take this to the stable for you, young lord?" he asks.

"I'll be right back out," I promise, striding up the steps, my heart pounding as hard as if I'd run here.

You're doing fine. Misha's voice in my mind steadies me. *When you get through these doors, you'll see a hall to the right. Go down to the end and take a left.*

The doors open for me, revealing Ezra's brother, Leon, waiting on the other side. "Why are you back already? She didn't show, did she?"

I did not count on him sharing the meeting with his brother, Misha says in my mind.

Me either, but I can't change that now. "I forgot something," I say. Then, remembering how the brothers treated each other in the memory, I brush right past him and stroll down the hall.

Where am I going, Misha? I can't exactly get the stone while he's following me.

Next right is a sitting room with a small bar. Go in there, pour yourself a drink, and sit down. See if you can shake him.

When I turn into the room in question, Leon follows me, chuckling when I pour myself a glass of amber liquid from the decanter at the bar. "You are such a coward. You can't face her without drinking your face numb."

He is really the worst, I tell Misha. *No wonder Ezra's so desperate for a way out.*

I throw myself into the chair and glare at Leon over my glass. "Don't you have somewhere better to be?"

"Look at you *sitting there* when the princess is waiting for you. What's wrong, brother? Worried you won't be able to perform?"

"You don't know what you're talking about," I mutter. The empty phrase was one of Ezra's favorite defenses against his family in my dream memory.

The amusement falls from Leon's face. "You were lying the whole time, weren't you? You never had a meeting with the princess. You just wanted me to think you'd bed her, so I'd stay back."

This is going to be a mess when Ezra returns and has no memory of this conversation, Misha mutters in my mind.

Now, I can actually do something about that.

I bring my drink to my lips but make my hand so unsteady that I slop it onto my pants on the way up.

"Or maybe you've already had her. Just that quick. Maybe it was so bad she sent you away." Leon folds over in laughter, delighted by this possibility.

"Maybe she said she wants to get married first," I say, slurring the words. "Maybe it's just a matter of time, so you should be more respectful to me."

"Because you'll be the next king of the shadow court. Right. Keep telling yourself that. She might be dumb enough to bed you, but she's not dumb enough to marry you."

King? What is he talking about? Jasalyn's husband would never be king.

I feel Misha's anger through our connection. *Unless something happened to her sister, forcing Jas to become the queen.*

Claim the princess and control the court—do you think that's what this is about?

"I don't have time for your delusions." Leon strides by me, swatting my glass on his way out and spilling most of the contents onto my pants.

"Jackass," I mutter.

Leon only laughs.

Placing the glass on the side table, I force myself to settle into the chair and not turn around to watch him go. I count to twenty, then do it again.

Any idea where he went? I ask Misha, who's gone alarmingly quiet in my mind.

No. I can't get into his head from out here.

Could you if you were in here?

I could if his shields are as weak as his brother's.

Good point.

I push out of the chair and take my glass back to the bar, listening for the sound of anyone approaching, but all I hear is the creaking of an old house and the groan of the wind in the trees out back.

I'm headed to the stone.

I don't like this.

You've mentioned that a few times now.

Pardon me: I didn't like it before. Now that we know they're after more than just the princess's hand, I hate it.

We still need that stone. The others are working on the tracking spell this very moment.

I keep my steps as soft as I can while still keeping my movements casual.

There, on your right, Misha says.

I risk a look over my shoulder before turning the knob, stepping inside, and closing the door behind me.

The room is bigger than I expected, with a table and four chairs in the center. Not just a room to store valuables but a place to bring guests and show off your priceless possessions.

My gaze lands on the safe in the corner, a freestanding copper unit that reaches Ezra's chest. My heart stumbles from its steady jog into a sprint.

Use your hand to open the safe, pocket the stone, and then get out of there.

I stop in front of it, something knotting in my gut and telling me to turn back. Intuition or cowardice?

Come on, Felicity. The sooner you get it, the sooner you can leave.

I position my hand—Ezra's hand—against the outside of the safe, pressing my fingertips into the cool metal as the mechanical bolt whirs, then retracts.

I pull my hand away and the door swings open, revealing gems and jewels of all kinds.

Did you know you block when you get stressed? Misha asks. *Let me see.*

I focus on relaxing enough to open the connection between us and look at the contents of the safe.

Misha curses. *That's a bigger stockpile of fire gems than I've seen in ages.*

But where's the stone?

I try to focus on the safe's contents but can't shake the sense of revulsion that comes over me every time I redirect my focus.

Something feels wrong about this. Could it be spelled to repel me?

It's possible. Are you okay? Do you need to leave?

Not when I'm this close.

See the white box tucked behind the gems?

I feel dizzy, but sure enough in the back corner there's a white box with a pearlescent sheen. My stomach surges into my throat as I reach for it, but I work past the discomfort and close my hand around it. Maybe this horrible feeling will fade once I get it away from this safe.

I drop it onto the table in the middle of the room, and Misha's immediately in my mind. *What are you doing? You need to get out of there.*

I need to make sure it's the stone.

I release the clasp on the side of the box and flip open the lid.

"What do you think you're doing?"

My head snaps up as Leon strolls into the room. *Misha. Trouble.*

Leon narrows his eyes and sniffs. "I knew Ezra was acting strangely. Not like himself at all." He cocks his head to the side. "You don't smell like a shifter. So this must really be my brother's flesh."

"I don't know what you're talking about." I blink and his blade is at my throat. "Leon, what are you doing?"

"I heard about the creatures who take over their host's bodies. Old magic, but if the stories are right, you'll run from this host if I cause you enough pain."

I jerk away, ready to run for my life, but I can't. He has me locked in place with his magic, and he grins the moment he sees it register in my eyes. When his blade plunges into my shoulder, I scream.

He pulls the blade free before dragging it down my arm. He plunges it through my hand. "This is going to be so satisfying."

If my body were in my own control, I would crumple. I'm not strong like my brother. I'm not fearless in the face of pain, and this—this pain laced with anticipation of more to come—is brutal.

But then Leon's blade clatters to the floor and he gulps like he can't get air.

Misha's eyes blaze as he yanks Leon off me, holding him with one hand on either side of his head. "You drank too much tonight," he says, staring into the male's watery eyes. "You don't remember anything after leaving the ball, only that you were so jealous of the attention your brother was getting from the princess that you drank yourself mindless."

"Heard something strange," someone says down the hall, steps coming closer.

Misha releases Leon, letting him crumple to the ground. His eyes dart to the door for a beat before a blast of magic shimmers through the room and a portal appears. I try to move toward it, but whatever magic Leon used to paralyze me still lingers and my movements are strained and jerky.

The doorknob turns and Misha wraps me in his arms. In the next moment we're tumbling into a grassy field. Misha lands on top of me, and before I can appreciate the sensation, he rolls to sitting, resting his arms on his knees, breathing hard.

"We'll wait here until Pretha can come open a portal for us," he says.

I clutch my wounded arm to my side and look around. "Where are we?"

"In the pastures behind the Pandians' barn."

I want to ask why *he* can't open a portal to get us back to the

Midnight Palace, but something tells me he wouldn't appreciate the question.

"You asked why I insisted on coming," he says. "That was why. Lark told me to be cautious tonight."

And since Lark has visions of the future, he would have very good reason to take her warning seriously. I cough out a laugh. I feel practically manic. My blood is buzzing with the thrill of having survived while still pumping like I need to flee. "Maybe just warn a girl next time?"

"What would you have done differently if I'd said, 'By the way, my niece said the bad man thinks he can torture you out of your body and to please not let him accidentally kill you'?" Exhaustion lines his face, and while I know he just expended an exceptional amount of magical energy, I'm shocked to see him so spent.

"*You* knew what that meant?"

His full lips quirk in amusement. "I had no idea what any of it meant, but that's not unusual for Lark's visions. I just knew you were in danger. I figured it would be better if you weren't alone."

I shift, slowly testing my muscles before moving to sit up. "Thanks."

"Look who can move again."

I flinch. "The stone. I left it on the table."

Misha pats his side. "I grabbed it before we left."

"Leon's more powerful than I thought if he could hold me still like that."

Misha shakes his head. "No, I was starting to feel it even in the short time I was in there. You must've set off some trap when you entered the room. I'm guessing some substance the brothers are immune to."

"Crabknot seed," I mutter. "It paralyzes anyone who breathes in enough of it. If the family uses it for security, they probably eat the roots regularly so they aren't affected by the seeds." I knew something was off, but I was so focused on my mission I didn't stop to think about what I was smelling.

Tonight could've ended very differently if Misha hadn't been so close.

"I'm glad you came," I say.

"Good to know my company is preferable to death. Even if only slightly."

I want to laugh but the pain in my arm and shoulder are too intense.

He studies me, brow furrowed. "They have a healer waiting for you at the palace."

"Leon won't remember?" I ask.

Misha winces. "Not my best work, but it will do."

"And what about Ezra? Will he be suspicious that Jasalyn never showed?"

"Skylar doesn't think so," he says. "She told him the princess changed her mind because she didn't want her sister angry with her. We'll probably need you to take Jasalyn's form again tomorrow to lock the story in."

A portal appears in front of us, and Misha helps me stand, an arm wrapped around my waist as we step through it and into a bedroom with the familiar black stone floor of the Midnight Palace.

Pretha's waiting for us on the other side. "Are you okay?" she asks, looking her brother over. "Did you use too much magic?"

He cuts his gaze to me for a beat before looking back to his sister. "I'm fine. Is the healer on her way?"

Pretha takes in my arm and cringes. "I'll hurry her along." She slips out of the room, leaving me and Misha alone.

He rolls his shoulders as if his whole body is feeling the effects of draining so much magical energy. And his sister was worried about him using too much?

This is the same male who moved us from the caves deep beneath Castle Craige and to my room in a blink. The same male who conjured a whole thunderstorm just to show off for me and give me an excuse for my wet undergarments. Something's going on that he's not telling me.

"Can't you usually open portals at will?" I ask, if only to distract myself from the pain.

He scrapes a hand over his face and lets out a long breath. "Usually."

The door creaks open and the healer bustles in, coming to my side, and I realize that even if there is something happening with him and his magic, that's as much as he's going to reveal.

CHAPTER SEVENTEEN

JASALYN

Go to bed like a good girl, and I will make the pain go away.

Erith's words echo in my head as I force my eyes open to take in my surroundings. I smell rot and animal feces. It's damp, cold, and so dark, the charred ceiling half caved in, one wall entirely burned away, exposing the entire place to the darkness of the night.

A squeaking sound comes from the pile of debris at my fingertips, and I scramble back as a rat scurries away from me.

I drag myself toward the missing wall, leaving a trail of blood behind me. I'm losing too much, and if I don't find a way out of here I will die. I have no idea where I am. I wanted to go to Fherna's cottage, so why did the sword send me here?

My head is too heavy, and the night is too dark. I can't die here. I haven't fixed what I broke. Mordeus is breathing, and I may not understand how resurrection works in a rotting corpse, but I won't fail again. I can't. Abriella deserves better.

Leg throbbing, head spinning, I prop myself up on a fallen beam and rip away the bottom of my shirt to wrap around my wound. My eyes fall closed, and time folds in on itself. I'm in my sister's arms while our house burns around us.

Hold on. I've got you.

I fight for consciousness and Kendrick is scooping me into his arms, and I know I'm still dreaming because mighty wings tear from his back and we're flying through the night. I know I'm dreaming because I've never been so happy to see the stars.

Someone's touching me. A palm on my forehead. Cool fingers on my cheek.

"She's burning up." I burrow into a warm and solid chest. *Kendrick.* Yes. I want to sleep more and dream of Kendrick.

"Is it the ring?" another voice asks. Abriella? What is she doing here?

"Maybe? Probably? Do you think Felicity got the stone?"

"I won't consider an alternative, but even if she could bring it to us, I won't risk casting the spell outside of the palace walls. There are too many unknowns here."

"No goblin is going to transport her in this condition," Kendrick says. "So unless you're aware of a portal nearby . . ."

"We don't have the time."

I'm lowered down and the warmth of those arms is taken away. I cry out and reach for them without opening my eyes. I'm too cold.

"I'm sorry, Slayer. We need to get your fever down."

Slayer. The nickname tugs on threads in my mind, trying to pull memories to the surface. Mordeus's dungeons. My constant fear. Kendrick's reassurance. The way the pet name changed years later, the way I'd begun to feel powerful when anyone called me that.

"I'll run a cool bath."

My throat is raw. As if I've been screaming for hours. I'm covered in sweat and my bones feel like they're coated in ice. I pry open my gummy eyes and see Kendrick kneeling beside me.

"There you are." He smooths back my hair. "The ring is making you sick, but you're safe now. We're going to get rid of it and you're going to be okay."

"The sword . . ." Why am I so tired? I did what the goblin said. I killed the wolpertinger. I drank straight from its beating heart. "I left the sword. . . . Erith . . ."

"You don't need to talk," Kendrick says. He slides an arm behind my back and guides me to sit up. "Don't worry about that right now. We can figure out everything when you're feeling better."

I don't argue as he guides me into a bathing chamber. I don't even protest when he gently strips away my clothes. His hands are gentle and he's trying to hide the fear in his voice, but I am dying. I know it. Why fight this when I can take comfort in my final moments?

I'm too weak to stand on my own, so I lean against the wall as they pull at my boots and then my clothes. Unconsciousness beckons, luring me to its oblivion.

Kendrick mutters a curse, and I force my eyes open. Abriella stands between me and a brimming tub, eyes wide. She draws in a sharp breath through her teeth.

They're looking at the gash on my thigh. Every part of me hurts so much, hurts like someone's dragging shards of burning glass through my veins, so much that I'd forgotten about my leg.

"Is it poison or infection?" Brie asks.

Kendrick pales. "See how the redness is spreading all around the wound? And it's hot."

"Monster claws," I whisper. I lean into Kendrick and close my eyes again. His arms tighten around me, keeping me from sliding to the floor.

"Oh no you don't," Abriella says. "Look at me, Jas." She isn't asking as my sister. She's commanding as a queen. I feel her shadows wrapping around me, holding me upright, willing me to consciousness. "Tell me about the monster."

"Like a death dog," I rasp. "But three heads instead of one. With fire like a wyvern."

Even half unconscious I can feel the tension that falls over the room.

"Mordeus's hound," Abriella says. "No one has caught sight of it in years."

"We need every healer in the village," Kendrick says. "Now."

Abriella shouts for someone, and I let my eyes float closed again. I'm too weak to help as they lift me into the tub, and too weak to argue as Abriella takes the sponge and methodically washes all the dirt and blood from my skin. It feels nice to be taken care of. Nice not to be alone. To be more than a quickly forgotten moment in time.

The realization is so unexpected that a wave of emotion washes over me and a sob slips from my lips.

"You're safe," Abriella says. "I'm going to take care of you now."

"I'm sorry." I muster my strength to meet her loving hazel eyes. "I've been so awful and I am so sorry. This ring, Mordeus—it's all my fault."

"You have nothing to be sorry for." She lathers the soap in her hands before starting on my hair.

I try to lift a hand to help, but it's too heavy. Everything's too heavy. "I found Mordeus," I say, and watch as the blood drains from her face. "I tried to kill him, but he's already dead."

She exchanges a glance with Kendrick before schooling her features and looking to me again. "We'll talk about it later. Close your eyes," she says. "I've got this."

So I do. I close my eyes and let sleep pull me under. I dream of fire running along my bones and a cool salve painted on my burning skin. I dream of Kendrick's soothing voice in my ear, his strong arms holding me up as Abriella promises she will get rid of my ring for good.

I dream of arguing, shouting about a stone, someone tugging at my ring and begging the gods.

And then I dream of Mordeus shoving me into a tiny, dark closet, even as his skin hangs from his bones and maggots crawl from his eye sockets. The lock clicks into place and I hear him on the other side, even as I feel the hilt of a dagger in my hand.

My sister's scream of agony echoes in my ears.

I bang on the door, push and shove with all my might, but it doesn't budge. I sink to the floor and curl into myself, trying to hide from the darkness, from my sister's pain.

Then my mother's voice in my mind: *Don't you dare give up now.*

Chapter Eighteen

Jasalyn

Coming back into myself is like crawling to the surface from the deepest, darkest depths of soupy water. Like there's a vortex pulling me back with every inch of progress I make.

Don't you dare give up now. Fherna? My mother? Abriella? I don't know who the words are coming from, but I listen.

I push. I crawl and fight, and the moment I shove Mordeus's consciousness away and take control over my own body, I see it: Abriella with her hand clutched to her stomach, blood gushing through her fingers. There's a bloody dagger at my feet, and Finn's screaming for a healer, one hand stretched out as if he's casting magic in my direction.

My wrists hurt, my hands trapped behind me, held immobile—Finn's shadows, I realize, pinning them there. Because I was the one with the knife? Because I did that to Brie?

Someone's holding me by the shoulders, saying my name, and I blink up to see Kendrick.

"Don't you dare give up now," he's saying. "Come back to me, Slayer. You're stronger than him."

"What did I do?" Frantic, I look back and forth between Brie and Kendrick. Exhaustion hangs on every inch of my skin, willing me to close my eyes. To rest.

Kendrick's grip tightens, like this alone can keep me in my body. "She's back."

"How do you know?" Finn asks. "It could be a trick."

"I *know*," Kendrick roars, the rage so heavy in his voice it rattles the windows.

One hand still clutched to her stomach, Brie reaches toward me with a smooth stone the size of her palm. "It has to be her," she says. "This magic is tied to her life. She has to be the one to use the stone."

"Release her," Kendrick tells Finn. "She can't try the spell herself with her hands pinned behind her back."

"No." I shake my head, trembling all over as I meet Finn's silver eyes. They're so much like Mordeus's that I always avoid them, but I can't risk that now. "*Don't* release me," I say. "We don't know if he'll be back."

Finn's eyes glaze over, and I realize the Enchanting Lady has her hold on him. He won't disobey me.

"Thank you," I whisper. Even words are hard. Whatever magic was in the wolpertinger's blood, it's gone now.

Kendrick shakes me gently, but I can't take my eyes off my sister or the blood coating her hands. "Listen to me, Jas," he says. "This is the Stone of Disenchantment. If you don't want Mordeus to take over your body again, you have to get this ring off. It strengthens the connection between you and Mordeus and makes it easier for him to control you."

I blink back up to him. Do I understand what he's saying?

That I could be rid of this ring? That I could be remembered again? That I could stop sleeping away the little that's left of my life? "How?" Keeping myself upright is harder than ever.

You almost died, and this ring is holding you at death's door.

"You have to ask Finn to free your hands so you can take the stone," Kendrick says.

"Have you already tried this?" I look back and forth between him and Brie, ignoring Finn's adoring, starry-eyed gaze, but I can see the answer in my sister's desperate stare. "If it didn't work for you, how do you know it will work for me?"

Kendrick strokes a thumb across my cheek, the touch so gentle it nearly brings tears to my eyes. "You have to try."

"You have to *want* to be rid of the ring," Abriella says, wincing as she takes one labored step toward me and then another. "You hold the stone and you ask it to free you of the magic."

"I don't want to hurt any of you."

"Then it's time to take off the ring," Abriella says. She takes one more step, holding the stone before me.

"Finn," I say, my voice cracking as I take in my sister's bonded partner. "Pick up that dagger and toss it in the hall, then close the door." He obeys. He's fighting the ring's magic, but I have him in my thrall. "In a few seconds, I'm going to ask you to release your hold on me. If I do *anything* to try to hurt Abriella, restrain me *immediately*."

"If that's what you want."

"It is," I promise. Tears prick the back of my nose. Finn is one of the strongest, most noble males I've had the honor of meeting. There should be no magic that takes away his will like this. I should never have sought out such a power, should never have given that witch what she needed to create it.

"You ready?" Kendrick asks.

What if it doesn't work? What if Mordeus is in my mind, waiting for the right moment to strike again?

What if this is my only chance?

I give a jerky nod. "Release me, Finn."

My wrists and hands fall free at my sides, and I reach for the stone. It's slippery with her blood, but that only strengthens my resolve.

All eyes are on me as I grip it hard, feeling it pinch against the ring. "Free me of this ring."

I can't explain it, but I feel the moment it happens. I feel the magic loosen its grip—still there but more in my control than it has been in months.

I fumble to pull the ring from my finger and the stone slides from my hand and hits the floor with a thump.

When I pull the ring from my finger, it's like being released from a tether. As if it was both reining me in and holding me up. I collapse.

When I open my eyes again, it doesn't take the effort it did before. I'm back in my bedroom at the Midnight Palace. The curtains are drawn but a candle burns at my bedside and scatters flickering light across the room and onto Abriella's face. She's lounging in a chair in the corner, a book open against her chest as she stares out to the night sky.

"Abriella? You're okay?"

"Jas." She sits up and moves her book to the side. "How are you feeling?"

"Me?" I look her over, searching for signs of injury. "*You* were bleeding last time I saw you."

"My healers do good work. And being fae . . ." She shrugs.

"You saved me," I whisper. "If you and Kendrick hadn't found me when you did . . ."

Her eyes well. "I hope you know by now that I'll *always* come for you. No matter how long it takes."

A soft knock sounds at the door. "It's me," Kendrick calls.

Brie swipes at her cheeks before standing. "Come in."

The door opens and when Kendrick steps into the room, my breath catches. He still fills a space with his presence, still grabs ahold of my lovesick heart with both hands. Even when I know I've brought nothing but heartache into his life. Even when I know I have to let him go.

I don't have much time left and Elora needs him.

His broad chest expands as he looks me over. "You're better. Thank the gods."

I shove aside the conflicting tangle of emotions. "Where was I when you found me?" I remember the ash, the charred beams.

Brie cocks her head to the side. "You don't know?"

I shake my head. "I wanted to go back to the cottage where I'd been staying but the sword didn't work right."

"The Sword of Fire? You found it?" The hope in Kendrick's voice crushes something inside me.

"I did."

"What do you mean it didn't work right?" he asks. "It's supposed to take you anywhere you desire."

I blow out a breath. This is the easy part. "I mean I don't know where it sent me."

"You were lying in the charred remains of our old house in Elora," Brie says.

"Because that's where I wanted to be," I whisper. I may have been trying to think of Fherna's house, but the moment Erith made my childhood bedroom appear, I wanted to be there more than anywhere else.

"So it did work," Kendrick says, a bit sadly, and I nod.

Brie sighs. "We had to heal you in Elora—at least enough that the goblins would agree to bring you back here. We worked on disenchanting the ring the moment we arrived at the palace, but it turns out we needed you to do it yourself."

I stare at my bare finger, waiting for relief that doesn't come. Getting the ring off my finger doesn't change anything. I can't undo the deal I made. I can't bring back those I killed in my futile search for vengeance.

"What did Natan say about the ring itself?" Brie asks Kendrick, and I realize they've been busy finding answers while I was sleeping.

Kendrick bows his head. "The ring's magic remains. The only thing the stone nullified was whatever spell was holding it on Jas."

"I don't understand," Brie says. "Do you think maybe the magic of the ring is too strong?"

"It's certainly more powerful than any magical artifact I've seen before."

"Do you have to have all of the magical items for the stone to work?" I ask.

Brie's brow wrinkles. "What do you mean?"

Kendrick curses softly and drags a hand over his face. "The ring was one of a pair. We couldn't nullify its magic because we only had half."

"You're sure there's another?" my sister asks.

"I saw the other ring on Mordeus's finger."

Brie draws in a sharp breath. "You saw Mordeus. He's resurrected? It's real?"

"He's a rotting corpse," I say, breathing through the revulsion that shivers through me at the memory.

"For now," Brie murmurs.

Kendrick looks to Brie and then back to me. "May the princess and I talk? Alone?"

I bite my bottom lip.

"It's up to you, sister," Brie says. "I can stay while you talk or I can go. Or I can kick him out, though if I get a vote I think you should listen to what he has to say."

She's giving me the most patient and understanding smile, and all I can think is that I don't deserve that from her. I've let her down so many times and in so many ways. But now Kendrick is on the list of people I've let down, and I need to tell him what happened with Erith and the sword.

"You can go," I say.

"I'll be right outside if you need me." She pads to the door and closes it gently behind herself.

I push my blankets aside and climb out of bed, surprised to realize my injuries are gone. Magical healing is incredible. But even more miraculous than the absence of lingering pain is the absence of that ever-present weakness I felt when the ring was stuck.

Though I haven't found the courage to meet his eyes, I feel Kendrick's gaze on me with every move I make. I pull the curtains wide, desperate for any moonlight I can get.

"You're staring," I say without turning around. Maybe it's that I almost died or that I nearly killed my sister. Maybe it's the date of my eighteenth birthday looming so close, or maybe it's that I'm finally free of the ring but still feel trapped by my own choices. Whatever the reason, my emotions are humming at the surface, and I don't know what I'll feel if I hold his gaze for too long.

"When we found you . . ." His soft steps scrape across the floor, and in the window I can faintly make out his reflection as he stands behind me. He cups my shoulders and slides his warm hands down my arms. "Do you realize how lethal the Cerberus's poison is? How close you were to death?"

So close I could hear her call my name. "Do you realize how close I am now?"

"Don't say that. You're here. You're better."

"Sometimes I feel like I'm already dying. And I don't just mean the ring." I stare out at the night sky and try to find the words, but I can't. "It was like that before the ring too. Like the world was too loud, so I did everything I could to drown out the noise, and then . . . after a while, it was all muffled, even when I didn't want it to be. It's like what happened with my sister—I kept her at arm's length because I was too broken for her to be any closer, but then I was so lonely it hurt because she was never close enough."

"There have been moments, though." He rubs circles on my back with one big hand. "Moments when you felt alive, even after Mordeus?"

I close my eyes. Remembering those moments. Most of them

involve Kendrick. His smile. His hands. His mouth. "Yes."

He turns me around and pulls me into his arms. "Then it's not over. You're still here. And we're going to keep it that way."

I nod against his chest. Maybe because I don't want to hurt him any more than I already have. Maybe because I want to believe it. "You rescued me?" It comes out as a question because the memory is so foggy.

"We came for you as soon as we knew where to find you."

"Do you remember?"

"The ring's magic is strange. The memories are there, but you're not. Abriella and I took turns keeping record of everything. We didn't want to risk losing you."

"There were parts . . . I don't know if I was dreaming up things about you." I look up at him and take in his pointed fae ears. The tattooed crown he's shown me only once is glamoured away and there's no sign of the wings I think I remember pulling us from the rubble.

He cocks a brow and I get a flash of dimples. "Do you have a question?"

"Were the wings a hallucination or real?"

"They're real enough when I want them to be."

I step out of his arms. "You hid those from me too." I don't mean for it to sound like an accusation, but it does.

His face falls. "They're a gift I have to conjure. I don't like revealing them unless I truly need to. They're just another part of being fae, not another secret." He lifts a hand, and just when I think he might pull me back into him, he drops it and leans against the wall. "I promise things won't be the same as they were. I won't hide from you. Not anymore."

I study him for a long time, but I already know I believe him. I trust him. Maybe that makes me a fool or maybe it means I was a fool to ever leave.

"It must be a relief to have the ring off," he says. "How did you navigate the sickness all these months?"

"The wolpertinger's blood acts as an antidote to the sickness caused by the ring." I risk a glance up at him, though I'm sure the guilt shows on my face. "I had to hunt it and . . . it was horrible."

Understanding dawns on his face. "We've all had to do horrible things to survive."

"I couldn't go after the sword while feeling that weak."

"You really found the sword?" he asks, and I nod. "You said so when we found you, but I didn't know if that was the fever talking. Where was it? Where is it now?"

I fill my lungs, searching for courage. "It was just hidden behind that three-headed monster less than a mile from here, and when I found it I told it to take me to Mordeus."

"You used it?" His face lights up, and my stomach sinks. I trust him and he saved me, and now I have to let him down. They need the Sword of Fire to get to Erith—possibly even to defeat him—and I lost it. I may have cost him his kingdom.

"Did you know the Sword of Fire is literally made of fire? I burned my hand on it when—" I lift my hand but it isn't wrapped anymore, and when I examine my skin, I see no sign of the burns. "They healed my burns?"

Kendrick shakes his head. "You didn't have any burns. Your hand was wrapped when we found you. We removed the dressing when we were cleaning your other wounds but there was nothing there."

"It was burned. It was raw and blistered and . . ." I stare at it, as if the injury I remember might reappear if I look long enough.

"Did you go to a healer?" Kendrick asks. "Or perhaps it healed while you slept."

"I'm human. I don't heal like the fae. And if I somehow found a healer, why wouldn't I have had them heal my leg?"

"Jas." He steps forward and takes my hand in both of his, rubbing his thumbs along the sides of my palm and onto my wrist, where he traces a circle. "Didn't you have a scar here?"

"I . . ." I blink at the smooth skin. *With your blood you can overcome the flame.* "I did."

"The sword healed you."

"Kendrick, it didn't. I'm telling you, that sword nearly killed me. I would never have touched it a second time if I hadn't been sure I'd meet my end in Erith's presence."

"What do you mean it nearly killed you?"

"It burned off my skin. I saw it with my own eyes. I *felt* it."

He closes his eyes. "There's so much about our history that even we don't know."

"Meaning?"

"Meaning I've been searching for the sword for years with no idea I'd be unable to wield it."

"Not without burning yourself at least," I say, but I don't understand that look on his face, like he's puzzling something out.

Suddenly, he strides for the door and flings it open. Brie is standing on the other side, pale and staring at us both. "It's time to tell her," Kendrick says.

CHAPTER NINETEEN

JASALYN

"Tell me what?"

Brie moves slowly as she steps back into the room. "Jas, you need to understand something about your powers."

I close my eyes. I don't know what it's going to take to convince my sister that I'm not like her. Even now, knowing what I gave up, she still wants to believe I'm more fae than human. "I don't *have* powers, Brie."

"You do, though. I asked Pretha to look inside your mind, and she saw them there. I didn't tell you because I didn't want to scare you."

"Why would my power scare me?"

Brie pauses for a long time before answering. For so long I'm not sure I want to know what she's about to share. "Because you're a phoenix, Jas."

I stare at her, waiting for this to make sense. "Is that supposed to mean something to me? Because you just said I'm a magical bird, and I am confident I would've noticed something like that."

"It means you have the power to burn to ash and arise again reborn." She holds my gaze, as if willing me to accept this. "That's why Mordeus needed you. The phoenix is rare, and if he can have it for himself, he can return."

"No," I breathe. I look to Kendrick, ready to see him argue with my sister, but I see the truth on his face. This power of mine can bring Mordeus back for good. I hear Fherna in my head. *With your blood you can overcome the flame.* "I gave up my magic when I gave up my immortality." I shake my head, willing it to be true. I can't stomach the idea of one more part of me helping that monster come back.

"You still have it inside you."

Kendrick moves close and nods to my hand. "You said the sword burned you, but where are your burns?" When I don't answer, he brushes his fingers across the inside of my wrist, where the circular scar used to be. "And of all your scars, the only one that has suddenly disappeared is the one that was in the flame."

I stare at the smooth skin.

"You've been made new where the fire burned you," Brie says. "Just like a phoenix."

I feel like I'm falling and everything I grab ahold of disintegrates in my hands. "Fire almost killed me when Brie and I were children." I turn to her. "If you hadn't come for me . . ."

"We don't know what would've happened in that fire if I hadn't come for you, and I'd never choose to find out. But I need you to understand what I'm telling you. If *you* don't harness the power of your phoenix, Mordeus will. And he will use your body to lead this realm, and we will have lost you for good."

"Lead the realm?" I frown. "I'm not the queen. Don't act like you're going to die, Brie. I won't hear it."

"What better way to have the access he needs to kill me than to come at me as my beloved little sister." She gives me a sad smile. "It's not like he hasn't already tried."

"And that's exactly why I shouldn't be here."

"You aren't stuck in that ring anymore," Kendrick says.

I bite my bottom lip. "I don't think it's worth the risk."

"I *can't*." She flexes her fists, then releases them. "I can't fail you again," she whispers, and her voice is ravaged. She lifts a shaking hand toward my face before dropping it again, and I realize she's looking at the scar that hooks around my eye. "I took too long getting to you. I thought you were safe. I . . . I didn't know."

She means when Mordeus had me imprisoned in his dungeons. My chest aches. "I didn't want you to know."

"But I shouldn't have been so naïve. I should've realized you were so haunted for a reason."

"Tell me what you mean. How is Mordeus going to use me to rule the realm?"

"You already know," she says. "You've known for a long time that he's using you. That you do things during your blackouts you'd never choose to do if you were in control of yourself."

"Yes, but what does this have to do with my supposed powers?"

"We don't believe his plan was ever to be resurrected in his own body."

The words knock me in the chest, stealing my breath. "That makes sense." I squeeze my eyes shut, remembering the smell of rot and the way his flesh hung from his bones. "Because I found him. He's a corpse. A breathing corpse. I couldn't kill him because he's already dead."

Brie flinches, almost as if she'd hoped I'd argue. "We've been operating under the assumption that at some point, probably the moment you turn eighteen and . . ." She clears her throat and shakes her head, as if she can't bring herself to finish that sentence. "At whatever moment his physical vessel fails, his spirit will have to take over your body completely."

"I don't know how. I don't . . ." Numbness creeps over me, inch by inch, saving me from feeling too much. "I tried to kill him and I failed. If I can't kill his body, how can I . . ." The idea of him inside me makes me want to crawl out of my skin. "How do I get rid of him? How do I make sure he can't use this phoenix?"

"Right now, he's using that rotting body to hold his consciousness because he can't claim yours yet, not completely. Maybe *he's* not ready. Maybe *you're* not. Maybe the deal you made when you got that ring was part of the equation that brings him back and he can't take you until the moment the years you handed over begin. We don't know why, exactly, but we do know how much time we have left to figure this out. How much time we have to stop him."

"Tell us everything that happened when you saw him," Kendrick says. "You said you told the sword to take you to Mordeus and then used it to escape him. Where is it now?"

Slowly, I turn to him. "Erith has it."

He schools his expression, but not before I see his face fall. "You saw Erith?"

"I told the sword to take me to Mordeus, and it dropped me into this place that looked so much like his dungeons, but it wasn't. Erith was there. I tried to use the power of the ring on him, and it didn't work. Erith said he's the one who made the ring."

Kendrick and Brie exchange a look. "They *are* working together," Kendrick says.

"We just need to know why," she says. "What does Erith stand to gain from all this?"

"He said he'd been waiting for me to bring him the sword. Told me to go home and that Mordeus wasn't ready for me yet. And when I tried to kill him . . ." I turn toward the windows and lean my head against the glass as I let the memory replay in my mind. "I plunged my dagger into his chest and he didn't even try to stop me. He didn't react, didn't bleed. Nothing happened until he pulled it back out."

"Your blade is made of adamant and iron," Brie says. "If you struck his heart . . ."

I wrap my arms around myself. "He said, 'Isn't it fun when prophecies come to pass? Make sure you tell your friend who fancies himself the king of Elora. He's been waiting for the moment you'd put this blade in my chest.' He pulled the blade free and there wasn't even a mark where I'd stabbed him. Then he showed me our childhood bedroom and tried to convince me to rest there. I wanted to so badly, but it wasn't real. It was an illusion made from my memories—someplace I wanted that was made to trap me." I blow out a slow breath as I remember how hard it was to resist the call of that space.

"So how did you end up at our old house?" Brie asks.

"I was able to get the Sword of Fire back long enough to create a portal out of there. When I used it I must've been thinking of home, so that's where the portal took me." I make myself look at Kendrick when I say the rest. "At the last minute, he wielded his magic to take the sword back, and I couldn't hold on. I lost it."

Kendrick pales, and he drops into the chair Abriella was sitting in earlier. When he tips his face up to the ceiling, I can practically see him trying to process what I've just cost him and Elora.

"I'm sorry." I look back and forth between him and Brie. "I failed you both—by letting Mordeus live, by losing the sword. And now I don't know where or how to find either."

"Don't think like that," Kendrick says, snapping his gaze to me. "You never should've felt like you had to take any of this on alone."

"This isn't your fault, Jas," my sister says, and the words are so patently untrue I nearly laugh. "I mean it. None of this is your fault—if anyone's to blame, it's me for not getting you out of his dungeons sooner, for believing the lies I saw in that mirror."

"You aren't responsible for what he did to me."

She comes closer and lifts her fingers to hover above the scar on my face. "And neither are you."

Chapter Twenty

FELICITY

Between the ball, retrieving the stone, and having the palace healer mend me, last night was a blur. I only got enough rest to retake Jasalyn's form before nightmares pulled me from sleep. Nightmares of my own again, where I plunged my blade into Erith's heart only to have him transform into Kendrick while I watched blood bubble from his lips.

At Abriella's request, I spent the day in the form of the princess, awaiting Ezra's possible visit. He never came, and now the sun has long since set and I need sleep, but I'm avoiding going to bed.

The princess is beautiful, and maybe I should feel lucky that I get to pose as her yet again tomorrow. It's not like it's safe to take my own form when my brother is likely hunting me.

But when I stare in the mirror, I resent that the reflection isn't mine, resent the dark thread of hair waiting to magically keep me in this body when I wake up.

"Quit staring at that pretty face and come with me," someone says behind me. I don't even startle. Maybe because Skylar doesn't scare me or maybe because my mind and body are too tired. "Hale wants to talk to us."

"I'm dressed for bed," I mutter. I'm cranky and just want to complain. The truth is I'm grateful for the excuse to avoid sleep for another hour or two.

She opens my armoire, grabs something from inside, then tosses a silky dressing gown to me. "Put this on."

With a sigh, I shove my arms into the sleeves as I follow her out of my chambers and down the hall toward a starlit terrace that overlooks the capital. Natan and Remme are already there, sitting at a glass-topped dining table. Natan has a pipe between his lips and Remme has a bottle of wine in his hand.

"Hope you're planning to share," Skylar says, dropping into the chair across from them.

Remme shrugs and offers her the bottle. "Help yourself."

Skylar is chugging straight from the bottle when Hale steps onto the terrace.

"I suppose I should've specified that this was a meeting and not a party," he says. The chair squeals against the stone as he pulls it away from the table, a sound as unpleasant as his apparent mood.

Must be something in the air.

"How's Jasalyn?" Remme asks when Hale sits.

"She's better. Awake but a little weak still. The ring's off and her fever is gone. The poison seems to have cleared her system, but we should know for sure if she's stronger tomorrow."

"Well, regardless of what happens," Skylar says, "we got the queen her sister, and it's time for her to pay up."

I gape at her. "Skylar!"

I didn't need to say a word because Hale's withering glare speaks volumes, and Skylar holds up both hands. "I apologize. That sounded heartless. I'm glad the princess is okay, believe it or not."

"We see this through," Hale says. "We will offer our assistance to the queen however we must to protect this court. Ridding Jas of that ring isn't the end."

"But *after*," Skylar says, "right? Don't we still have our own mission? Our own realm to save?"

"The fate of Elora might be more intertwined with the fate of the shadow court than we realized," Hale says. "We have confirmation that Erith and Mordeus are working together."

"So let's do this," Skylar says. She slaps the table twice. "Everybody take notes. We're making plans to kill Erith—for the sake of both realms!"

"There is no *we*," I whisper. "I'm fine with asking Abriella for access to her Hall in exchange for retrieving the stone, but I'm not going to the Eloran Palace—at least not to kill my father."

"This again?" Skylar groans.

Hale turns his tortured eyes on me. "We still need you, Lis. Now more than ever."

Natan sighs. "If you get the queen to take us to her portal, we can try it without you, but you know the odds aren't in our favor. *No one* has been successful in killing him, and it's not for lack of attempts on his life."

Skylar's glare used to intimidate me, but today I ignore it. If she were in my shoes, she'd make the same choices I have. "Fine," she says. "Once the princess is feeling better, we'll take *her*."

"Jasalyn can't do it," Hale says, eyes on the table.

"We'll protect her, Hale," Remme says. "We won't let anything happen to Jas. If Felicity won't do this, then Jasalyn is our only—"

"That prophecy already came to pass." His words are clipped and his face is hard. This is the Hale who will take no arguments. This is the male who the oracle chose as our king. "Jas saw Erith when she went to kill Mordeus. She stabbed him in the heart with an iron blade."

Skylar shakes her head, confused.

Natan and Remme watch Hale cautiously, and my stomach feels like it's sunk to somewhere deep beneath the earth. They can see it as clearly on his face as I can. Nothing is over. Nothing is better. Everything just got a hell of a lot more complicated.

"What happened?" Natan asks.

"It didn't kill him, didn't even hurt him," Hale says. "She plunged that blade in his heart and he didn't even bleed."

"How?" Remme asks. "Is she sure he was there? Could it have been some kind of illusion?"

"She's sure. And when the blade failed to kill him, he told her to tell me about it. If I didn't know better, I'd think the bastard found a way to have godlike immortality, and he wants us to know it."

The blood drains from Remme's face.

"No," Skylar breathes. "But the oracle showed you the princess slaying him. Was she wrong? Have we been tricked into chasing a fate that can't come to pass?"

"What *exactly* did the oracle show you, Hale?" Natan asks. "Did you see him die by Jasalyn's hand?"

"Fate can change," Remme says. "This doesn't mean she's wrong about anything, just that—"

"*I'm* the one who was wrong," Hale barks through gritted teeth. "I went to the oracle feeling hopeless, like we were fighting a losing battle. I asked her who could help us tip the scales in this revolution, and she showed me Jasalyn's face. Then she showed me Jasalyn plunging the blade into Erith's heart."

"And he died?" Remme asks. "In that vision? Did he die?"

His expression is so bleak, it makes my heart ache. "You know how the oracle works. The visions aren't complete. They're snippets. Moments in time. When I saw her sink the blade into his chest, I believed the oracle was telling me she could kill him for us."

Remme mutters a curse.

"We need to find out more about the original prophecy," Natan says. His expression is distant, and I already know he's thinking through a plan—where and how to gather the information he needs. "Erith has survived every attempt on his life and come out unscathed. That's why the prophecy led us to believe that perhaps no one could take Erith down but his daughter. And even when the oracle gave Hale the vision of Jasalyn, we all knew it could have been Felicity in Jasalyn's form." He drums his fingers on the table, thinking. "Which means if Felicity still can't bring herself to kill Erith, our only option is—"

"We need the sword," Remme says. "Even if an iron blade can't kill him, he can't survive the Sword of Fire. I'll wield it myself."

"Erith has it." Hale tips his face to the sky, as if he can find a solution to this mess written in the stars. "He took it from Jasalyn when he found her trying to kill Mordeus."

The group goes silent and the weight of all we've lost hangs in the air.

"You're up, kid," Skylar says, and they all turn their attention to me. "We tried everything we could to let you off the hook, but here we are."

"How do we know the same thing won't happen when Felicity tries to kill him?" Remme asks. "How do we know that the oracle didn't show the same thing in that original prophecy as she did with the princess?"

"We have to try, though, right?" Skylar says. "We can't just sit on our asses and—"

"I can't," I whisper, and everyone looks at me. The weight of their stares might as well be the weight of all of Elora on my shoulders. "You don't understand."

"Then make us understand," Remme says. "Please."

Even if this future she foretold comes to pass, it won't be because of you, Misha said. I need to trust that my brother and his friends will feel the same. "The oracle said I would kill my father, yes, but when *I* visited the oracle, she showed me plunging the blade into his heart and then running and . . ." My eyes burn and my vision goes cloudy with tears. I've held this secret for too long.

I meet my brother's gaze. "In that version of the future, you're bleeding out on the floor, Hale. In that version of the future, you're dying."

Skylar's face goes as white as the moon.

"What?" Remme says. "By whose hand?"

Natan's eyes are sad as he studies me.

"I don't know. She didn't show me that." I bite the inside of my cheek, then force myself to look at my brother again. He's stoic, and I can't read a single emotion on his face. "I never wanted to tell you. I knew you'd say it was a necessary sacrifice. I've always known you believed this cause is bigger than you, and I wanted to find a way around that prophecy." I press my palm to my chest; my heart races beneath my fingers. "Call me selfish, but I won't do it if you are the cost. Elora needs you. Our future queen needs you. I need you." Tears prick my eyes. "I wasn't born into a loving family like you. I had to get lucky and be given one. I don't take that gift for granted and I won't squander it. So, no. The destiny I was shown is not one I'm willing to fulfill. Not at that price. I will help you in any other way I can, but if you intend to kill Erith, you will have to find someone else to do it."

I tear my gaze away from Hale's and stand. The eyes of the other three are trained on me, different levels of shock in each pair, but for the first time they all hold something I never anticipated: understanding.

When I turn my back on the stars and the night sky and head back into the palace, no one tries to stop me.

Misha's leaning against my chamber door, arms crossed over his chest.

"What do you need?" I snap. I just want to bathe and fall into bed and forget the look on my brother's face when I told him the prophecy that's haunted me for years.

Misha frowns as he looks me over. "You finally told them."

"Isn't that what you said I should do?" Then it registers what he said and why he would know. *Storm.* I didn't look for the hawk while we were on the terrace, but he could've easily been close enough to take in the scene without us noticing. "Really, Misha? You're spying on me and my friends now?"

He lifts a shoulder in a completely unapologetic shrug. "You and your friends are still outsiders who currently have easy access to the shadow queen. It would be negligent of me *not* to observe when I have the opportunity."

I shake my head and reach for my doorknob. I don't have the energy for this. "Well, I hope you saw what you wanted," I say, storming past him and into my room. I peel off my robe and toss it on the bed.

"Not really," he says, and because he's apparently determined to make me lose my temper, he follows me into my room. "But I think I understand you better now." He scans my face. "You said you were afraid that Kendrick would ask you to kill your father anyway, said you thought he would be dismissive of any personal consequence."

I huff. "Of course. Have you met him?"

He shakes his head. "But that's not the real reason you've kept this from him for four years. That can't be it because just like they wouldn't force you before, they won't after learning what the oracle showed you. Telling them doesn't change that at all."

"Maybe I wanted to wait so I could find a way around it, so I could find a way to what they needed me to be. Maybe I needed to find a way to make amends that wouldn't put Hale at risk."

"Make amends for what?"

The heat of my temper drains away, and I wrap my arms around myself, trying to ward off a sudden chill. "I am their enemy's daughter. I am the rea—" My voice breaks and I swallow back a sob. "I am the reason the man who raised us is dead."

"That's not how they see you."

I step back and fold my arms across my chest. "Stay out of my head, Misha. I don't want you there."

His fingers are gentle as they sweep across my cheek and tuck a lock of hair behind my ear. "They love you." His throat bobs. "You are so easy to love."

My stomach twists because I want these words more than he could possibly understand. "You don't have to say that."

"I am *king*." His lips quirk into a crooked smile. "I don't have to say anything I don't want to."

The sight of his smile feels like the summer sun after a long, brutal winter, and my irritation with him melts away. "Oh, pardon me. I didn't mean to suggest otherwise."

"This power of yours, the one that lets you sense how people feel about each other. Are you able to use it when you're one of the parties in question?" His smile has fallen away but the warmth is still there. "Do you know how I feel about you?"

"You hate me." The words are weak. I haven't tried using my gift when he's around. I'm too afraid of what I'd find. But I know him well enough to know he feels many things when he's near me, and hatred isn't even in the vicinity—hasn't been since he had me locked in his dungeons.

He lifts his chin. "So that's a *no*?"

"You hated me enough to lock me away when you found out the truth. Hated me enough to ignore me when I told you they'd come for me."

"I'm not a monster, Felicity. You deceived me and had unfettered access to much of my court because you did it so well. I have a kingdom to protect, and I reacted accordingly."

"Right."

He studies me for a long time, the way he does when I think he's trying to see the real me, and I wonder if he wants to. I've been so hung up on him wanting the girl he thought he fell in love with, I haven't let myself consider that maybe he wants *me*. Or that maybe he could.

He finally sighs and steps back. "It's been a long day. Get some rest."

CHAPTER TWENTY-ONE

JASALYN

I BARELY RECOGNIZE THE GIRL in the mirror—not because of the scar that hooks around my eye but because I never bothered with mirrors after moving into the Midnight Palace. I'm no longer the person I was when Brie brought me here, and I'm no longer the person who ran away to hunt down Mordeus.

I sweep my hair off my neck to tie it back. The undercut Skylar gave me grew out while I was sleeping and is several inches long now. I should have her cut it again. Or maybe I shouldn't bother. I can't kill Erith for Kendrick, and when I lost the sword I lost my only way to get to Mordeus. I have six days and a power I don't understand. A power that's going to allow Mordeus to steal my body and my life for good.

I'm still staring at my reflection when I hear a soft knock on the door and the sound of it sweeping open.

Kendrick strides into the room, but his steps falter when he spots me. "What are you doing?"

I chew on the inside of my cheek and shrug. "I wondered if I stared at my reflection long enough, if I might see him in there."

His shoulders sag, and pity etches lines around his mouth. "I don't think he's moved in just yet. They said that he won't fully possess your body until he commands the power of your phoenix. Now that the ring isn't part of the equation, he doesn't have the same kind of access to you as he did before. You are *you*, Jas."

I bow my head. "Except when I'm not."

"Look at me." He pads softly across the room and gently cups my face. "You're here with me right now. He's not."

Kendrick's eyes are such a pure light blue they remind me of the sky on a perfectly clear summer day. All sunshine. No darkness looming in nearby clouds. "For now," I answer.

He drops his hand and studies me. "Now is all we can control anyway."

I swallow. "Did you tell your friends? About Erith? About how I lost the sword?"

He nods, stress tugging on his features.

"I'm so sorry. I shouldn't have—"

"We'll figure it out." Kendrick pulls me out of the chair and draws me against his chest.

I let myself melt into him. His breath is warm in my hair and his heartbeat is steady beneath my cheek.

"I still can't quite believe you're here," he says, hands splayed wide across my back. "For months, I couldn't think about anything but finding you, and then we did and you were barely hanging on. Burning up with fever, delirious. I'd finally found you and was sure I was going to lose you again."

The knot in my chest pulls tighter, and I bow my head. I swallow the lump in my throat. I won't remind him what's coming. Not when we just had this conversation a few hours ago.

"Tell me what you're thinking," he says. When I don't reply, he tilts my face up until my gaze meets his. "Please?"

"I'm just glad I'm here with you." It's true, even if it's not the whole truth.

His gaze drops to my mouth. Lingers there for so long my heart tugs toward him like a magnetic force.

"You have no idea how much I've missed you. How amazing it feels to have you here."

"Even though I've ruined so much?"

He frowns. "What do you mean?"

"The sword? My utter failure to kill Erith? The way I've practically handed Mordeus the keys to my sister's court?"

"None of that is your fault."

I swallow. They keep saying that, but surely they can see as clearly as I can that my decisions got us here. "I'm going to fix it. Somehow."

He strides across the room to the chaise in the corner, where he unbuckles his bandolier of knives and drapes them over the back of the chair.

"What are you doing?"

He shucks off his boots and tucks them neatly by the wall. "I'm sleeping here. You don't have to share your bed, but I'm staying close."

He peels off his shirt and folds it, and I try not to stare at all that beautiful tan skin, but my eyes seem to have a mind of their own. I remember the warmth of that skin. How it felt under my hands.

"We've shared a bed before," I tell him. "I know you can't remember."

He catches me staring and returns to my side. "I might not have access to the memory, but I wrote about it in my journal." He skims his thumb over my bottom lip. "How it felt to touch you, to hold you. Then you left me. You believed the worst and left me."

I draw in a ragged breath. "I was hurt and scared."

"I should be the one you run to when you're hurt and scared. Not the one you flee."

I want to kiss him so badly, but even though the ring no longer endangers him, I don't know if I should. I don't know if I have any right to his kisses—not when I'll be gone so soon and when he's to marry someone else. *His queen.*

Instead, I lift my hand to his bare chest and press my palm against the comforting rhythm of his beating heart. "I feel well. You don't need to worry that I'll fall sick again in the night."

His full lips twist into a smirk. "You think *that's* why I don't want to leave your side?" With a single step back, he drags his gaze over me, from my head all the way down to my bare toes.

I'm acutely aware of the thin material of my sleeping gown, of the way he could see nearly everything if the light hit me right.

His ice-blue eyes darken. He takes a lock of my loose hair, sliding it between two fingers. "I just got you back. Nothing short of an act of the gods is going to tear me from your side tonight." His throat bobs. "Unless you don't want me here."

I lift my hand to his wrist and lean into his touch. "I want you here."

"I was so afraid I'd never see you again." He searches my face. "I was afraid I'd never be able to tell you how I feel."

I press my fingers to his lips and shake my head. "Don't. Don't say it now. Not until there's . . . a reason."

He snaps his teeth playfully, nipping at my fingertips. "I have more reasons than I can count." He bends, trailing soft, toe-curling kisses down the side of my neck. "Let me say it," he murmurs in my ear. "I need to tell you."

Suddenly my eyes burn. "Why bother with words that promise a future we can't have?"

"You don't know that. We are going to find a way to reclaim the life you traded."

"Kendrick." I hold his face in my hands, relishing the feel of his short beard beneath my fingertips. "Even if we do, you are going to be the next Eloran king. You will spend your life with the next Eloran queen. Save your pretty words for her."

Something flashes in his eyes. "Don't do that."

"Do what?"

"Don't cheapen this by pretending I can pass it off to the next person. I feel what I feel for *you*. No one else."

I shrug and step away, but he grabs my wrist and tugs me back. When he crashes his mouth down on mine and plunges his hands in my hair, I'm right there with him, angling my mouth under his, pushing onto my toes to get closer, as close as I can.

He smells like the clear night sky, like the night he took me in his arms and flew me to safety, and he tastes like wine. I part my lips and skim my tongue against his bottom lip, relishing the groan that vibrates in his chest. His hand drops to my waist, squeezing and pulling me closer.

As he deepens the kiss, I let myself remember our night together in Ironmoore, the way his lips felt on my heated skin, the pleasure of his hand between my legs. How desperately I wanted his mouth on mine. I want to re-create the kiss we couldn't have that night, but this kiss can't be the same. This is so much more because so much has changed. Because even if he doesn't want to admit it, we're running out of time. This kiss is a promise, an oath that he will keep me here by sheer will alone.

Gripping my hips, he lifts me onto the vanity, sending bottles and pots crashing to the floor, his mouth never leaving my skin as he steps between my legs, the heat of his bare chest seeping through my thin gown. I let the world fall away, become sensation, aware of nothing more than the scrape of his callused fingers, the heat of his breath, the soft press of his lips. Across my clavicle, along the top of my sleeping gown, over the ribbon between my breasts.

When he pulls away, he closes his eyes and touches his forehead to mine.

"What are we doing?" I ask, chest still heaving, as if I haven't bothered to breathe for the last two minutes. I squeeze my eyes shut. "This isn't right."

"Before you were back in my life, nothing felt right. When I touch you, it's the only thing that does."

I trail my fingertips across his forehead and along the tattooed crown he keeps glamoured away. "Why hide this now that I know?"

He takes a beat before answering, as if trying to pull himself together. "It draws too much attention. The glamour wasn't about deceiving you." He cups my face and traces my jaw with his thumb. "I wish I'd handled it all differently. Not just you but . . . my sister. I've always been so sure I was making the best choices, but now I feel like I was a fool for thinking I knew enough to lead my realm into a new era. Maybe it was never meant to be me."

There's a lump in my throat. I hate that his feelings for me have made him doubt himself. "When did you get it?" I ask. "I mean, you didn't always know you'd be king."

"It appeared after the oracle told me. But now . . ." He shakes his head.

"Now what?"

He steps out from between my legs and gently helps me off the vanity and back to my feet. I don't take my eyes off him, but don't rush him to speak either. He studies the mess on the floor and sighs. "Now it's fading, and I'm not sure what that means."

"Do the others know?"

"Natan, Remme, and Skylar do. They know almost everything relating to the throne." He stoops down and begins picking up the bottles of tonics and pots of face creams, placing each carefully back in their space. "Crissa was the first queen the oracle named in centuries, and I was the first king. My job was to protect her, and I've failed in that. I can't even find her."

"You used a tracking spell to find me. Have you tried one for her?" It hurts to ask, and that hurt makes me mad at myself. Why does it matter that Crissa will be his queen when I won't be around much longer anyway? Crissa deserves someone amazing to protect her, to live by her side and give her a good life. Kendrick saved me in those dungeons, but I wouldn't have been around to be saved if Crissa hadn't been there first.

"I don't have anything of hers to do it."

"Like what?"

"For Felicity, we used the blood that was on the clothes she wore when she was looking for the Hall of Doors. Of course, she wasn't here or in Elora, and when we started checking other realms the blood wasn't fresh enough to be as effective. Misha was instrumental in bringing her back. I don't even like to think about the number of minds he broke into to track her down."

"What did you use to find me?"

"We used the blood you left on my pants the last time you visited me." He frowns and finally looks at me again. "What was that from?"

I let out a shaky breath as I remember the wolpertinger fighting back, spikes tearing into my hand. "The creature I used to overcome the sickness from the ring."

He nods, but I can tell his thoughts are somewhere else. In Elora, perhaps, or perhaps with the oracle. "It's not impossible to track someone without their blood, but we haven't been successful."

He turns to the bed and pulls back the covers. "You should get some sleep. I'll be here if you need me." He nods toward the chair.

"Kendrick..." I don't know what I want to say. That I want him to share the bed with me? That I changed my mind and maybe being together isn't a mistake? That I hope he finds his queen? None of that is a lie, but none of it is fully true either.

"I've not been fair to you," he says, voice raspy. "I won't be asking for anything you aren't ready to give." When he turns to me, there's so much sadness in his eyes. So much sadness that I'm responsible for. And I'm only going to bring him more. "Get some sleep, Slayer. The sun will rise again tomorrow," he says, but for the first time there's no conviction in those words.

CHAPTER TWENTY-TWO

JASALYN

My desk at the Midnight Palace always contained a calendar of the coming moons, but before I traded my immortal life for that ring, I never paid much attention to it. This morning, it was the first thing I looked at after climbing from bed. I have five days left. Five days to figure out how to fix what I've broken. Five days to make sure my mistakes don't destroy my sister and her entire court.

The weight of it could break me, but that's what *he* wants. Broken, pathetic, terrified Jasalyn, willing to sacrifice everything to hide from her fears. So I don't let my thoughts linger. I can't. The people I love deserve better.

Kendrick was already gone, and my handmaiden had left breakfast by my bedside, but one look at the calendar had me dressing and heading out. I refuse to spend my day hiding. I downed a few cups of coffee while I dressed, fortifying myself for the day ahead. For my mission. I'm not going to hide in this castle while my friends fight to fix something I broke. I'm going to help, whether Abriella likes it or not.

I look up from my feet just in time to catch myself before running into an ancient female fae with a cane. I dodge but then turn to look at her again as she continues down the hall. Like mine, her mind seems to be somewhere else, but I think I recognize her. I just can't place her.

Maybe I've seen her in the palace before, or maybe I've even talked to her during those days when the whole world was passing me by in a fog. I could let it go at that, but there's something about her that makes the hair on the back of my neck stand up.

"Karmyn?" The name slips from my lips before I even realize I thought it.

She stops and slowly turns to me. "May I help you?"

It's the eyes that snap everything into place for me. That milky bluish white of the iris, the way they seem too big for her face. I've seen those eyes in my dreams—in Mordeus's memories. "You . . ." My heart leaps into a sprint. What is someone who worked for Mordeus doing in my sister's palace? "Guard!" I shout at the uniformed sentinel stationed at the top of the stairs. "Take this female into custody until I can speak with my sister."

He strides toward us, frowning. "May I ask why? Madame Karmyn is—"

I stare in the female's panicked doe eyes. "A seer. I know. I don't know why she's here now, but she worked for Mordeus, and I want her detained until I can speak with my sister about it."

Fear flickers over the female's face, but she doesn't try to run or resist as the sentinel magically binds her wrists.

Another uniformed male jogs down the hall to join us. "What's happening?"

I lift my chin. The guards are looking at each other. They think I'm crazy and I don't care. "I need to speak with my sister. Now."

I don't know what kind of mental magic these sentinels have

or how it works, but several breaths later, my sister appears in front of me. I blink at her. "You can move like a goblin?"

"Anywhere within the palace, and then small distances outside it." She shrugs, then frowns at the guard holding the old female. "What is happening here?"

I point a shaking finger at the old faerie. She's trembling and squeezing her eyes shut. "Why is she here?"

"Karmyn is one of several seers I have on staff, Jas. She came on board while you were . . . away."

"And you aren't at all bothered by the fact that she worked for *Mordeus*?"

The confusion falls off Abriella's face, replaced with the cool and calculating mask of the shadow queen. The taps of her hard-soled boots echo along the corridor as she strides to stand before the restrained female. "You're sure about this?"

"I wouldn't be bothering you if I weren't. Mordeus's memories come to me in dreams, and I saw her—saw her prophesying for him. She's the one who told him he wouldn't live to rule from the Throne of Shadows."

There's no more sympathy left in Abriella's eyes now. "Open your eyes and look at me," she commands the old faerie.

Karmyn obeys, tears slipping down her cheeks. "If you must kill me, please make sure my family is cared for."

Brie's brows lift. "*Should* I kill you? Have you done something that warrants execution?"

"I have never betrayed my queen, if that's what you ask."

"But you worked for Mordeus." It's not a question, and my heart squeezes at how easily she believes in me. "And then *you* came to *me* looking for work."

"I did, Your Majesty. It's true."

Brie looks her over. "I consider that kind of omission a betrayal in itself, Karmyn."

"I cannot blame you, Your Majesty, but I hope you'll remember that I am the one who told you about the Stone of Disenchantment. I am the one who helped you find it so your sister would be free of the ring's magic."

"And why? Why help me after working for him?"

"I watched the faceless plague sweep through my village and I knew what was happening. I wanted to come here because you're a good queen, and I couldn't stand to see his plans play out."

"What plans?"

"His resurrection. His use of this girl here"—she nods to me—"to steal the throne and retake rule of the Court of the Moon."

Abriella's guards are too well trained to visibly react to this information, but I feel their eyes on me. While Brie's inner circle knows the details of Mordeus's connection to me, she's shared it with no one else.

Brie lifts her chin. "We should talk." She turns to the sentinel nearest Karmyn. "Please take her to my office for questioning. I'll be there shortly."

The guard ushers the female down the hall, and Brie watches, only turning to me when they're out of sight. "I will get to the bottom of this. I'm sorry it happened at all."

She begins to walk away, and I grab her arm. "You aren't questioning her without me."

"I'm not going to have you sit there while we talk about him. I won't do that to you."

"Brie, do you really think that female can hurt me while you're in the room?"

"No, but I have to ask her about Mordeus and—"

"Meaning you're literally trying to protect me from something that already happened," I say. And she shuts her eyes, as if this truth is too much to take. "We can't go back. We can't change it. What's done is done."

She swallows. "Fine. You can come, but if it ever feels like too much—"

"Let's go."

The old faerie's eyes are distant as she sits across from my sister, her gaze on the window and the big blue sky beyond. "I only wanted to help."

"Tell me what you know about Mordeus's plan for the princess."

She blinks rapidly. "He didn't know she was the princess. He didn't understand why she was so special. He didn't care to ask the right questions. All he cared about was the throne, the crown, and the power that came with both. I should've done what all the others did and lied about the future. Or simply avoided telling him the truth. But I'd heard the rumors of what he did to seers before me, and I thought honesty would be best. I regret that my gifts helped him in any way. I did what I thought I must to save my son, who was rotting in Mordeus's dungeons, and to keep my grandchildren from starving."

"Why don't you start at the beginning," I say gently. "You're the one who told him he would die before ruling from the throne. Is that when it all started?"

She presses her hand to her chest, fumbling until her fingers grasp hold of a silver pendant. "He was so angry. He would've done anything to get the answers he needed. Even death couldn't stop his hunger for power, so when I revealed the truth of his impending demise, he took me to Elora to see the oracle. He wanted to know who would kill him and how, but she wouldn't tell him. All she gave him was the face of the girl who had the power to bring him back—a girl he already had in his dungeons."

"How did he know what to do?" Abriella asks.

"Mordeus gathered his most powerful magic wielders to find a way to make it happen, but it was Erith, Patriarch of the Seven, who put it all together for him. He was the one who introduced him to blood magic."

"But you said he didn't know her lineage. How was he able to put his plan into place without knowing how it would work—without knowing my sister's powers?"

"He didn't need to know everything so long as he had people in place to carry out his plan. And he did. So many people who would trade their souls for a sniff of real power."

"Including the witch who gave me the ring." It's not a question. I'm sure of it. I never doubted that the woman could deliver what she promised. Power radiated off her in a way I'd never felt before.

"I imagine so," Karmyn says.

"Who was she?" I ask, grasping at a fleeting hope. "Who was the witch?"

"I've never gotten a vision involving her, so I don't have that answer."

"You haven't shared a vision with me since you told me about the stone," Brie says, narrowing her eyes at Karmyn. "What aren't you telling me?"

"The future is volatile right now. Every vision is accompanied by a conflicting one. You are dancing on the knife-edge of fate."

"What do the opposing futures look like? Tell me what two ways this can go."

Her laugh is brittle and jaded. *"Infinite ways,"* she says. "But there are three I see most often. One way, you continue to rule; another, Mordeus rules in your sister's body."

"And the third?"

"In the third, you all lose. And so does the shadow court. Civil war without strong leadership results in carnage, not change."

"Anything else you need to tell me?" Brie asks. "If you're truly here to help put a stop to Mordeus's plans, you need to give me everything you can."

The female frowns at her queen. "I see a path where your sister escapes her bargain, but she must still endure the pain to triumph." She blinks over to me and cocks her head to the side. "He will be shocked by your strength and fortitude." She lifts a gnarled finger toward me. "You can't win unless you accept who you are."

I glance to Brie, then back to Karmyn. "I know. They told me about my gift."

"Not the phoenix. You've always appreciated fire. You have to be *all* of who you are. Even who you don't want to be."

"What does that mean, Karmyn?" Brie asks.

"It means she's more like you than you realize."

CHAPTER TWENTY-THREE

FELICITY

The queen's briefing room is packed, and the moment I step through the door, I already wish I could leave.

I'd barely finished breakfast before I was summoned, and it looks like others chose to eat their meal here. The table in the center of the room is piled with pastries, fruits, and platters of cheese. On one side are Hale's people. Remme's sitting back in his chair, legs spread wide and lip twitching as Skylar tells him a story from the seat beside him. On the other side of Remme, Natan sits with one ankle propped on his knee, scribbling notes in a leather-bound journal. I know it makes me a coward, but I can't bring myself to meet their eyes after what I confessed last night.

Opposite my friends is Abriella's team. I recognize the queen, Misha's sister, Pretha, and King Consort Finnian, but they're flanked by a sharp-eyed, pale-skinned faerie and a terrifying horned male with red hair and unsettling black eyes with red pupils.

"It's a party," Misha says behind me.

I startle at the sound of his voice, as if I've been caught spying.

Misha scans my face. *Any useful dreams last night?* he asks in my mind.

How do you know I'm me and not her?

His lips twitch. *Jasalyn doesn't look at me the way you do.*

Heat crawls up my neck. I refuse to ask what he means by that, since it's embarrassingly obvious.

Ready? he asks.

What if I say no?

With this group? I couldn't blame you.

It's not them. It's me.

Don't be a coward. It doesn't suit you. He extends a hand into the room. *After you.*

I move to do just that when I hear a squeak behind me and turn to see Jasalyn and Hale waiting behind us. The princess is staring at me with wide eyes. She's in a light blue dress that makes her ivory skin glow, and I have to concentrate so I don't stare rudely at the new scar around her eye.

I cut my gaze to Misha for half a beat. *Really? You know who I am because of the way I* look *at you? Not because of the scar on the real princess's face?*

He shrugs, smirking at my annoyance. *Little of column A, little of column B.*

Why is she here? Shouldn't she be recovering somewhere?

She wants to be involved, and the queen is doing her best not to smother her.

"Jasalyn, I presume you remember Felicity," Misha says.

Jasalyn gives me a polite smile. "Good to see you again," she says, though judging by the way she keeps looking me over, she's forgotten how odd it is to see someone else in her form.

"Thank you, everyone, for coming today," Abriella says from the head of the table. She sits with her head high, in full queen mode. "If you could all take a seat, we'll get started."

The rest of us file into the room. Jasalyn and Hale sit in the spots beside Natan, and when Misha slips into the seat next to the horned male, I'm left with no choice but to take the empty chair beside him.

Relax, Misha says into my mind. *I don't bite.*

You must forget the vines you used to restrain me at Castle Craige. Those bit a great deal.

Oh, but now that I know you're not a danger to my kingdom, my vines would be much softer.

I scowl at him. *What in the world have I done to make you want to tie me up again?*

His lips twitch and somehow the intensity of his gaze scraping over me makes me feel like he's seeing *me* and not Jasalyn.

The warmth in my cheeks notches up to inferno. *Forget I asked.*

Unlikely.

The Midnight Palace's clock tower chimes for the hour, and Abriella clears her throat, pulling my attention off the infuriating king beside me and onto her. She looks to each person at the table before she begins—a look that makes me feel simultaneously intimidated by her presence and proud to deserve her attention. A queen indeed.

"Every one of you played a role in helping us find my sister and rid her of that ring, and before we discuss what comes next I just want to take a moment to say how grateful I am." She directs her gaze to Jasalyn, who bows her head uncomfortably. "She is my heart, and I couldn't do this without her."

"Welcome back, kid," the red-eyed, horned male calls out.

"Good to see you," Pretha says softly, nodding toward the princess.

"You are all here because you care about my sister as much as I do. In the case of many of you, you also care about this kingdom as much as I do. Unfortunately, ridding Jas of the ring can't undo what's been done. Her life is still tied to Mordeus's, and we have every reason to believe that in five days, on her eighteenth birthday, he will take"—her words hitch with emotion, but she schools her face and lifts her chin—"take over her body. And at that point he plans to take over the court. We also now know that Mordeus and Erith are working together."

"Erith or all of the Seven?" Remme asks.

"We don't know," the queen says. "We only know Erith for sure. But while we don't know all the parties involved or the extent of what they have planned, we have reason to believe that the future of both Elora and the shadow court hang in the balance."

Beside the queen, Finn props his forearms on the table and leans forward, gaze scanning the Elorans opposite him. "We are aware that you all have a mission of your own—to bring down the Seven and restore the Eloran monarchy—and after Mordeus has been handled once and for all, we want to help you do that."

"And in return, you want us to keep Mordeus from taking over your court?" Skylar asks.

I can't help but admire the way Abriella meets Skylar's

antagonistic gaze. "First, we need to establish two things. One, I support your mission. I want to see the Seven removed from power and Elora returned to a more equitable society where children can enjoy free childhoods instead of finding themselves in lifelong servitude under those unjust contracts."

"Hear, hear," Remme says, and that earns him a rare smile from the queen.

"Two, you've given me more than I could ever ask by helping me get my sister back, so my kingdom's support of your cause isn't contingent on anything else from you." She takes a breath and looks to Skylar. "But, yes, if you're thinking I plan to prioritize dealing with Mordeus and protecting this court and that I would like your help in doing that, you are correct."

"That's understandable," Hale says, his gratitude shining in his eyes. "We hope that Elora and the shadow court can have a long, healthy alliance."

"Even if the queen weren't offering her support," Natan says, giving a respectful nod in her direction, "we should move forward operating under the assumption that our respective kingdoms aren't only both at stake but that their futures are tangled together—whether through whatever deal Mordeus made with Erith to get him to assist in his resurrection or through some arrangement the two made long before that. In short, by helping each other, we are helping ourselves."

"I wasn't *against* it," Skylar says defensively. "I just like to know what kind of deal I'm making before I get all sucked in."

Abriella nods. "That's fair, but there's no deal just yet. I didn't bring you here to command you on your next moves. I brought you here so we can determine our next moves together."

"The first thing we need to keep in mind is that Mordeus can't take over the shadow court as a corpse," Hale says. "He needs Jasalyn to complete what he's started."

I watch Jasalyn, waiting for her to shrink in on herself at the mention of Mordeus like she would've a year ago, but she keeps her back straight, even if her eyes are averted.

She's changed, I tell Misha through our connection. *Before I met her, she would've avoided this meeting altogether, but look at her now.*

I was thinking the same thing.

"Judging by what happened when Jas went to kill Mordeus," Abriella says with a quick glance to the princess, "Erith needs Mordeus's plans to play out as much as anyone. If we're going to stop Mordeus from using her any more than he already has, we need to understand what he's put into place."

Natan nods and flips the journal in front of him open to a different section. "So far as we can tell, the magic Mordeus used and is using has three main components: the blood magic he used on Jasalyn when she was his prisoner, the lives Mordeus's followers pledged to him, and the ring she received from the witch. Thanks to Jasalyn, we now know that Erith created the ring, but that may just raise more questions."

"Like who was this witch?" Remme asks. "What kind of witch—fae or human—would Erith trust with such a tool? And what kind of magic could he have used to create it to begin with?"

"All good questions," Natan says, "and I'm using all my resources to dig into it. I have to believe that if we understand the ring's magic, we would know so much more about what we're up against."

"We think that was why Mordeus made the blood magic rituals as horrific as he did," Hale says, turning his attention on Jas. "Blood magic rituals don't have to be torture, but he needed you to be angry and afraid. He needed you to wish for vengeance so you'd want his people dead and do the work of funneling the life force of his pledges to him through the ring."

"How do you explain the blackouts?" Skylar asks. "If she didn't have to be conscious to slay rooms full of his followers, why have her willingness to kill his followers part of the plan at all?"

Abriella grimaces. "I don't have an answer to that, but the question is fair and noted. Maybe the answer is that she was being too selective with her kills or that she wasn't killing them fast enough or in great enough numbers."

"Or maybe," Natan says with a respectful nod to the shadow queen, "the plan all along was for Mordeus to use the ring to control her once he had enough strength from the initial kills."

"Regardless," Abriella says, "we have every reason to believe that they *wanted* Jasalyn to be suffering from the effects of wearing it during the day."

"They wanted her sleeping and out of the way until her eighteenth birthday," Hale says. "Were they simply trying to protect her, to preserve the vessel for Mordeus? Or was there something that they needed to keep her from doing in order for their plan to work?"

"Exactly," Abriella says. "If we can figure that out, maybe we can undo all of this."

Skylar drums her fingers on the table. "Maybe they don't want her to learn to wield her powers."

I can't help but study Jas. Her stoic expression gives away nothing of how she feels about them talking about her as if she isn't in the room. It's almost as if she's observing this conversation from afar.

"I don't know if she could access them if she wanted to," Natan says. "She has them buried so deeply, I couldn't find any sign of them when I looked."

"I found them a few years ago," Pretha says, frowning, "when she was fifteen. They were buried, but they were there."

Natan considers this. "But that would've been before her scars began appearing?"

"Right," Pretha says. "So we assume, what? That by the time you searched for her magic, he'd pulled on so much of it through calling on the blood magic that there wasn't a trace to be found?"

"Nothing recognizable at least," Natan says. "Her magic exists in the limbo between their consciousnesses—that space where she isn't herself but she also isn't yet him."

"Meaning that theoretically she could access it," Pretha says. "Perhaps that's what they're trying to avoid?"

Natan shrugs. "It's still hers, so I would certainly think so. With work."

"Is there any other reason they might want her out of the way all these months?" Remme asks.

What is it? Misha asks in my mind. *You look like someone just kicked your puppy.*

I stare at my hands, stomach twisting because I know exactly why Mordeus wouldn't want Jasalyn conscious for any longer than necessary. It's the same reason he put my brother into that cell across from her.

You might as well say it, Misha says through our connection.

I sneak a glance at Jasalyn. She's watching me curiously, as if she doesn't have any idea what's so obvious to me. I could say it. I could explain to the whole group that Mordeus knew she was trying to end her own life when she was in his dungeons, just as he—or someone working with him—knows that she may very well end her life now. From everything I've learned about Jas through her memories, I know she would do it to protect her sister. If the alternative is Mordeus taking over her body and her life, I don't think she'd hesitate.

I could say it, but it's such a painfully private truth. And one that it's not my place to expose—at least not in this setting.

I won't do that to her, I tell Misha through our minds. *Not here. Not now.*

"Whatever the reason," Brie says, "I choose to consider it a gift. Because we removed the ring, Jas is awake and well."

"You never explained how my phoenix plays into all this," Jasalyn says, shocking everyone in the room by speaking for the first time.

I wonder if they forgot she was here or if they thought they could continue to speak about her without her saying a word. Given how quiet and hidden she's kept herself the last few years, probably the latter.

Abriella clears her throat. "We think your phoenix is the fourth element of his plan," she says. "Although Mordeus wouldn't have known or understood it when he put this into motion, the gift of the phoenix is the gift of resurrection. Through your gift and by taking over the immortal life you traded, he can rise from the ash." Abriella holds her sister's gaze for a long time before letting out a breath. "I believe that's what the seers mean when they say, 'Claim the princess and control the court.'"

The room goes too quiet, but I have to give Jas credit. She keeps her chin up.

My brother clears his throat. "Additionally, there are questions regarding Felicity and the Seven," he says. I knew we'd be talking about the Seven in this meeting, but I didn't realize I would be part of the conversation. "We all agreed that Erith and the future of Elora could wait until after Mordeus is dealt with and the shadow court is stable. However, now that we know Erith is integral to Mordeus's plans, we can't ignore how he plays into this.

"When Erith's people snatched her from Misha's dungeons, nearly everyone expected that was the end for her." He meets Misha's gaze for a beat, and I can almost feel their common bond over being two, if not the only two, who refused to believe I'd been killed. "We're grateful they didn't kill her, but we need to think about *why*. They kept Felicity alive for a reason. If we want to both protect her and know how Erith's plans connect with Mordeus's, we need more information."

Hale leans back in his chair, his chest expanding as he draws in a deep breath. "Which is why it's time for me to go back to Elora and return to the oracle."

Remme straightens in his chair. "With everything happening,

you shouldn't be in Elora. You're more vulnerable to the Seven there."

"I can go," I say. "I've been before. I know how to do it."

My brother's gaze softens when he looks to me, and the regret I see there slices into my heart.

Have you two talked yet? Misha asks in my mind.

No. I avoided all of them this morning.

"I appreciate the offer, Lis," Hale says, "but if you want to help, I have something else I need you to do. We need you to go to the Eloran Palace."

My stomach sinks. "I already told you, I can't—"

"I'm not sending you to kill Erith," he says. "In fact, all of our intelligence tells us he's been away from the palace for almost a year." He looks to Jas. He doesn't have to say it for us all to understand the significance of the timeline. He's been missing from the palace since Jasalyn got her ring. "We need you to get us any information you can."

"Everything that happens in the Eloran Palace is recorded in the Chronicles," Natan says. "For a group that has destroyed as many ancient texts as they have, they sure are diligent about maintaining their own histories, and the beauty of the Chronicles is that it's fueled by truth magic. There's no way to cheat history there."

My gaze bounces between Abriella, Hale, and Natan, then back. "The only people who can access the Chronicles are—"

"The Seven," Hale says with a nod. "Or in your case, someone who has taken on their form completely."

I swallow. I said I would help. Now isn't the time for cowardice.

"Whose form will you have me take and how will we make sure we aren't both seen while I'm there?"

Misha holds up a finger and then pulls a small envelope from his pocket. "This hair belongs to Sol. She's—"

"Second only to Erith. I know."

"She's been trying to get a private meeting with me for months. Something about the future of Elora and my court." He places the envelope on the table and slides it toward me. "I got this at our preliminary meeting. If you choose to take her form, I will call her to Castle Craige. That way you don't have to worry about two of you being spotted at the palace at the same time."

I stare at the envelope. I've been avoiding the palace for so long. Going there now feels like walking right into the belly of the beast.

"While you're there," Abriella says, "keep your eyes open for the Grimoricon."

At first that word means nothing to me, but then I remember the dream I had where the witch asked Jasalyn for the Grimoricon in exchange for the ring. I'd offered Brie that information when Misha had me in a cell—proof that I was who and what I said. "You think it's at the Eloran Palace?"

Brie nods. "We assume the witch passed it off to Erith, and I imagine there's no more secure place for them to keep it than the palace. It might prove helpful in researching everything that's happening here."

"You'll let me know what to look for?" I ask. I only know of the book from that memory of Jas's, but I've never seen it in any of her memories.

"I'll meet with you later and explain the book and its . . . idiosyncrasies."

"I'll do it," I say. The table goes quiet, and I scan the faces around me, noting the varying degrees of respect, worry, and curiosity on each. I take a shaky breath. "I'll search the Chronicles and gather as much information as I can about what the Seven have planned with Mordeus."

"You shouldn't go alone," Natan says. "Even in Sol's form, this is enemy territory. If someone were to discover your true identity . . ."

Skylar leans back in her chair and props her feet on the table, crossing them at the ankle. "So spying, stealing, and killing. I'm down."

Across the table, the red-eyed male growls and glares at her feet.

"Seriously, Sky," Hale mutters.

She rolls her eyes and removes her feet from the table.

Hale shakes his head. "They likely have the palace warded against you after the stunt you pulled five years ago."

She grins. "I'm damn proud of what I did that day. A couple minutes sooner and I would've caught every one of the Seven in that blast."

"His point is that we need to send someone who can move around the palace without sending up alarms," Remme says.

"I'm going with Felicity," Misha says. "End of discussion."

CHAPTER TWENTY-FOUR

JASALYN

"I have something to discuss," I blurt, "before everyone leaves?"

The room goes quiet.

"Of course," Brie says. "Tell us."

"I'm going to find another way to get back what I traded. Just like Karmyn said I could."

Brie's eyes are still sad when she nods. "Do you have any idea how to do that?"

"The goblin who helped me when the ring had me stuck in sleep? She said something about the bargain not being complete. They need my immortality for Mordeus but he can't take it yet because it's not available. Not until the moment I turn eighteen. She said only a fool would give in so easily to a bargain that's incomplete. I didn't know what she meant, but after talking to Karmyn, I think she was referring to my deal with the witch. The one I made for the ring." I look around the table, at the faces of so many people who care about me and don't want to talk about what I traded for that ring. "So how do I get out of a bargain with an Eloran witch?"

Remme shakes his head. "You're asking the wrong question."

"Then tell me the right one."

"The question is, how do you get out of a bargain with a *faerie* witch."

"We're sure she's fae?" Skylar asks.

"I can't imagine any realm where Erith would've entrusted a ring that powerful to a human," Natan says. "I'm confident."

Remme nods. "And getting out of a deal with a faerie is much more complicated."

"Could we just track her down and kill her?" Skylar asks.

Remme shoots her a look. "Why are your solutions always so violent?"

She shrugs. "I like to keep things simple."

"Usually that would backfire," Natan says.

"What about going over her head?" Pretha asks. "Is there a more powerful faerie that she answers to—someone who could overrule the deal?"

"We'd have to know who she is to find who she might answer to," Kendrick says. "But I'm all on board with this line of thinking. Find a way out of the bargain and you don't have to give what you offered."

"What about Mab?" Skylar asks Brie. "She's some relation of yours, right?"

"Mab can't interfere," Brie says, "and after speaking to her when I was trying to reunite the crown and the throne, I never assume her solutions are the best."

Natan drums his fingers on the table. "There are two tried-and-true methods of getting out of a deal with a faerie: trick them or offer them something they want more."

"We know that Erith and Mordeus are working together, but we don't know how this witch works into the equation," Remme says. "Is she working for Mordeus or Erith?"

"Does it matter?" Kendrick asks.

Remme turns up his palms. "It does if we need to offer her something she wants enough to let Jasalyn out of the deal."

"So we have to start by finding the witch," I say. I look to Kendrick. "I plan to leave for Elora in the morning. You can come with me if you want, or I can do it alone."

My sister stiffens. "We can send someone else. I can't keep you safe in Elora."

"You tried keeping me safe inside this palace and I was miserable for three years."

Abriella flinches as if she's been struck. I pull in a fortifying breath and make myself continue. "You can't protect me. I know you want to. I know you would lay down your own life if you believed it would keep me safe, but this world doesn't work like that. And even if it did, don't I deserve a chance to believe I've done something *good*? I don't have much time left, and the way I see it, I have two choices. I can languish in my room and contemplate the atrocities committed by my hand or I can help the two best people I've ever known rule their kingdoms. That's no choice at all."

Abriella's gone pale, but when Finn places a hand on top of hers, she seems to breathe again. She looks to him and they hold eye contact for several beats. They can't communicate mentally the way Misha can with others, but they are bonded and tethered and completely aware of what the other is feeling. I've watched them have silent conversations more than once.

Finally, Abriella breaks the silence. "I would rather you send someone else, but I respect that you need to do what is right for you. And I agree that we need to find this witch. If Karmyn and Jasalyn's goblin friend both see a way out of the bargain, then we need to find it. Quickly."

"I'll go with her," Kendrick says. "I'll help her find the witch, and I'll keep her safe."

Brie's eyes soften. "Thank you." Then she straightens and surveys the table and claps her hands. "We all have work do to. No sense in sitting around here any longer."

Chairs scrape against the floor as everyone stands and slowly disperses toward the door.

"We'll leave at first light," Natan is telling Kendrick as we all flow out into the hall. "There's an open portal just north of the swamps that we can reach in five hours on horseback."

"My goblin would take you," my sister says, coming to walk beside us.

"We only use goblins when it can't be avoided," Natan tells her. "They already know too much, and we don't want their movements getting back to the Seven."

"That's fair," she says. "What about the Eloran portal in my Hall of Doors? It's not nearly so far to ride."

"That would be *amazing*," Skylar says, but Brie's attention is on Kendrick. She knows who's in charge of this group.

"Thank you," Kendrick says. "That would help a great deal."

Abriella flashes me a weak smile. "I'm trying to be supportive," she says, "even if every instinct is telling me to stay here and protect you."

"I know," I tell her.

With a nod, she disappears into thin air.

"Gods, I want to be able to do that," Skylar says.

Remme grunts. "Eat your vegetables like a good girl and maybe someday you can."

Skylar makes a vulgar gesture that makes the whole group laugh.

"Pack light," Kendrick says. "I don't know how long we'll be gone, but we can get anything we need while there."

Anticipation hums in my veins at the idea of another adventure with this group. Whether the next five days are my last or the precursor to an entire immortal existence, I know one thing for sure: I don't want to spend them locked up in my room at the Midnight Palace.

"Skylar?" I call when she turns down a hall away from the group.

She spins, her brows shooting up. "What's up, kid?"

I pull my hair up, holding it loosely at the crown of my head. "Could you fix my hair like you did last time?"

Her eyes light up. "The princess is back in her fancy palace with her fancy servants, and she wants *me* to do her hair?"

I scowl. "I could call someone else, I just thought—"

"Don't you dare. They'll try to do some spell to grow it all even or something. My way suits you better. Way more badass."

I arch a brow. "You think I'm badass?"

"I've never met anyone who's fought a Cerberus and lived to tell the tale. If that isn't badass, I don't know what is." She waves her hand. "Follow me."

CHAPTER TWENTY-FIVE

FELICITY

THE MORNING AIR IS COOL. It feels good after being cooped up in that meeting room. We have a plan for tomorrow, finally, and though it might be a death wish, none of us can stomach not trying. I came straight to the terrace, hoping fresh air could clear my mind. The birds around the Midnight Palace chirp and sing, as if celebrating the reappearance of the sun.

"There you are," someone says from the open doors behind me. I turn and hold my breath as Hale joins me. "Natan wants to meet with you and Misha tonight to talk plans for your trip to the Eloran Palace."

"He's going to Elora with you and Jasalyn in the morning?" I ask.

Hale huffs out a breath, amusement dancing on his lips. "They all are. You know this group." He cocks his head to the side. "You look thoughtful. Want to talk about it?"

I shrug. "Nothing to talk about."

He arches a brow. "I know we've been separated the last few years, but you think I don't remember what you're like when you're upset about something?"

I blow out a breath.

"This is about what you told us last night."

I cut my gaze to him. I want to deny it, but it's the truth, even if only part of it.

"I'm sorry," he says. The words come out rough, as if they're scraping against all the days he willed me to kill Erith. "I should've known you had a good reason for refusing. I wish you would've told me sooner."

I shiver. "I didn't want you to sacrifice yourself." I shake my head and rest my elbows on the stone ledge. "And I didn't want to be the reason my big brother wasn't in this world anymore."

"Yeah." He stares at his boots. "I get that."

I scoff. "Really? No speech about how there are things bigger than ourselves? About how the ends justify the means?"

He huffs out a breath and laces his hands behind his head, pacing in front of me. "I'm twenty-one, Lis. My life has hardly started and most of the years I've had have been spent busting my ass and trying to prove I'm worth this gods-damned crown." He drops his hands and turns to me. "You know what's crazy? Before, I thought I was okay with it. With the crown. With the burden. With having my wife picked for me. A wife who, let's not forget, I'm supposed to watch age and die while I enjoy fae immortality."

"You thought you were okay with it before what?" I ask. "Before you knew what the oracle showed me?"

"Nah." The corner of his mouth twitches in sardonic amusement. "I probably would've accepted that, or at least told myself I did."

"Before your princess," I murmur, and his throat bobs. "I'm

sorry, Hale. It isn't fair, the way the monarchy works."

He braces his hands on the stone ledge and looks out at the capital beyond. "I know we're fighting a losing battle here. I know we're trying to get back something Jasalyn already gave away. I know that it makes no sense for me to reject my fate—whether it be death or ruling beside a human queen—until we know if Jas can get out of this bargain. If the woman I love is ultimately lost to us, why do I even care that bringing down Erith could mean the end of me even before we get to see the monarchy restored?"

"You care because there's more to you than the male who loves the princess."

When he turns to me, his eyes are bleak. "That's where you're wrong. There's no part of me that exists apart from loving her. I care because I can't accept that she'll be gone. I know the facts and yet . . . my mind rejects them. And so, no. I won't be telling you to kill that bastard despite what the oracle showed you—at least not without some well-thought-out safeguards. Because if there's any chance at all that Jasalyn's going to be here when this is all over, I'm sure as hell going to do everything in my power to be here too. Maybe that makes me selfish. Maybe it makes me unworthy of this crown."

"Or maybe it just means that you've fallen in love, and it's changed you," I say.

"It feels as if it's changed everything. From the way I breathe to the color of the sky." He drags a hand through his hair, making a mess of it. "It sounds absurd but it's true."

I know what he means, but given my situation with Misha I'm too embarrassed to share as much. "So tomorrow you all head back to Elora to find the witch. And if you get the princess out of this bargain, what's next?"

His jaw ticks. "I need to see the oracle. I need to figure out what I'm missing. Why would she show me Jasalyn's face as the key to turning around this revolution, why show me Jasalyn plunging that blade in Erith's chest if she can't even kill him?" He makes a fist and presses it to his chest. "And why did the Mother make me feel this if I have to let her go?"

My heart aches for my brother. Elora has always asked too much of him. "Do you think she'll see you again?" I ask. "When you've been so recently?"

"I have to try."

I bite the inside of my lip, thinking of everything that could go wrong for all of us in the coming days. I'm still bothered by what I didn't tell the group in our meeting. Maybe I should have told them that Jas is a risk to herself—maybe they need to know in order to protect her. "If you don't find the witch, I think you need to understand why they wanted Jas sleeping until the time Mordeus can overtake her body."

His brow furrows. "What do you know?"

I hesitate. Not because I'm unsure but for the same reason I hesitated in our meeting. This is such a raw truth. I'm exposing her darkest secrets.

"Tell me," Hale urges.

"He wants her in a deep sleep because he needs her alive," I say. I swallow. "The only thing that could stop Mordeus from coming back the way he has planned is if Jasalyn didn't make it to her eighteenth birthday. And Mordeus knows from the time

Jasalyn spent in his dungeons that the biggest risk to Jasalyn's life is Jasalyn herself."

Hale's expression turns bleak, his eyes so sad. "We'll find the witch and get her out of this bargain. I won't accept anything else."

"I've been curious about those memories your brother planted," Natan says. Natan, Hale, Misha, and I decided to meet over lunch so the group could spend the evening ironing out their own plans. "How true to life were they?" He waves a hand over the table and the surface transforms into a map of interior rooms.

I've never been to the Eloran Palace before, but Natan's suggesting that I might be familiar with it from the illusion I was trapped in. I scan the rooms and corridors reflected on the table and feel like I'm looking at a map of my own home. "Very." I point to a bedroom, then trace my finger down a hall and into the throne room. "This is exactly as it was in my dreams."

Natan beams. "Perfect."

Misha grunts and frowns at the map.

Is he thinking the same thing I am? "Why would he do that? Why not create a fictional place? Why risk giving me information that puts them at a disadvantage?" *Why keep me alive?* My mind keeps circling back to that.

"For the same reason he didn't create fictional people," Natan says. "I'm not familiar with the magic he used to create and maintain such an elaborate illusion, but I imagine it works best with as many details as possible. Chances are, Konner has spent the majority of his life in the palace—or at least has never stayed in another place long enough to mentally re-create it. He used what he knows to make sure it felt fully real to you." He waves a hand and the image on the table changes. "Now what about this? This is the southern pillar of the Eloran Palace and the place we suspect they keep the Chronicles."

I study the new collection of rooms and corridors and shake my head. "I don't recognize that at all."

"He isn't a complete idiot, then," Remme says.

"It makes sense to use what he knows and create memories in the less secure areas of the palace. But the knowledge she was given—the familiarity those memories will give her to the palace—will still prove useful for getting around with the kind of confidence Sol would have. And I can tell you how to get here," he says, indicating an area on the map I'm unfamiliar with.

"And we're sure this Sol will leave the palace so there aren't two of her walking around when Misha and I arrive?"

"I invited her to join me at Castle Craige tomorrow," Misha says. "She thinks I want to discuss an alliance between the Elora Seven and the Wild Fae."

"I bet a bag of coppers that she thinks she's on the short list to be the next queen," Skylar says with an eye roll. "Not that you've done anything to disabuse her of that notion."

Misha seems unbothered by this jab. "I did what I needed to do to get close to her so that we would have everything we need."

What he had to do. Why does that have my hackles up? It's not like he's actually interested in her or as if he has any plans to make her his queen, but my stomach turns at the idea of them getting close enough for him to subtly take her hair. "You don't think anyone will think it's odd that the Wild Fae king is suddenly visiting the Eloran Palace?" I ask.

"I won't be, though," Misha says. "Not as far as anyone there will know. I plan to stay hidden during our visit."

"Okay, let me make sure I understand." I drum my fingers on the tabletop. "Misha gets Sol to visit Castle Craige again and detains her—which I'd like to point out is risky business if you'd like to avoid war with the Elora Seven, but I'll leave that for now—"

Misha scoffs. "I'm insulted that you think I would detain her in a way that *feels* like detainment. Pretha and Amira are going to help keep her happy until I can return."

"Well, that's good at least," I say. "Then, with me as Sol and you planning to stay unnoticed, we'll use the queen's Hall of Doors to access the palace?"

"That's right," Hale says. "She's offered to let us use them to get to Elora as well."

"So Misha and I enter the Eloran Palace. There, I find the Chronicles to discover everything we can about Erith, then search for the Grimoricon, then we get out of there and get Misha back to Castle Craige so Sol never suspects that Misha played her."

"Sounds right to me," Natan says.

"So why not send me alone? Why risk calling any unwanted attention to ourselves by sending Misha?"

"I already told you I'll stay hidden," Misha says.

"You aren't going alone," Hale says, worry creasing his brow. "Not there."

"We have one more hiccup to consider," Remme says, watching me from his post behind Hale.

My brother frowns over his shoulder at him. "What's that?"

"I'll be okay," I say, nodding.

"What's the hiccup?" Hale asks again.

Remme lifts his chin, telling me he's going to allow me to explain this myself.

I stare at the map so I don't have to look at their eyes. "You know my twin, Konner, planted memories in my mind—an illusion where he and I were close and I loved my life in the palace. They haven't fully faded yet, but I can do this. I won't let an illusion affect my resolve."

"It might not be so simple," Remme says gently. "If you find yourself confronted with your brother or a friend he planted in your mind, the illusion could be just enough to make you hesitate. A moment's hesitation can be the difference between life and death."

"Is this going to be a problem, Felicity?" Hale asks. "Because if we need to find another way—"

"No." My chair cries against the stone floor as I push it back. "I can do this. I want to do this."

I head for the door and the nearest balcony. Misha follows me.

"It's okay to admit if you're worried about this," he says behind me.

"Anyone reasonable would be," I say. I pull the envelope from earlier out of my pocket and wave it between us. "How did you get Sol's hair anyway?"

"Pretty much the same way you got one from Ezra. I got close and made sure she was too distracted to think about what my hands were doing." He shrugs. "It wasn't that complicated."

My stomach twists. "I'm sure that comes easily to you. Distracting females."

He cocks his head to the side. "Are you jealous, Felicity?"

I scoff. "Why would I be jealous of a power-hungry member of the Seven?"

The corner of his mouth twitches. "Maybe because you liked it when my hands were in *your* hair."

I should blow this off as just another jab, but I'm tired and can't. "Your hands were never in my hair, Misha. Only Jasalyn's."

His gaze drops to my mouth, and I can't breathe. "And why do you persist in believing that I wanted it that way?"

My mouth goes dry, my heart racing. "When you look at me like that, I don't know what to feel."

"When I look at you," he says, "*I* don't know how to feel."

I glance down at myself—at Jasalyn's body, Jasalyn's arms. "I'm sure it's confusing."

"Confusing?" He huffs, then his face softens. "I dream about your kiss," he says, rare vulnerability weighing on his words. "It haunts me."

"About my kiss, or about the princess's?" We both know there's a difference.

The rough pad of his thumb skims across my bottom lip and he bends down to speak softly into my ear. "When you're in my dreams, you never look like the princess."

I let my eyes float closed and focus on the sensation of his fingers in my hair and his breath on my neck. I hook my fingers into his belt, holding him close. I want his kiss so much that I'm trembling from my fingertips to all the way inside my belly.

He bends down and tucks his face into the crook of my neck, breathing me in. Every inch of my body is in tune with every move he makes. Jas's body is too small for his, fitting awkwardly against his towering frame, and I can't help but wonder what it would feel like to be pressed up against him like this while in my own skin. If my taller stature would allow me to tuck my face into his neck instead of his chest, if his strong hands would make the body that always feels too big, too curvy, feel *right*.

When he traces two fingers down my neck, a shiver travels down my spine. I've missed this. Missed it as much as I miss waking in my own skin.

Then he steps back, and I go cold.

"I can't," he whispers. "This isn't what I want."

My stomach plummets to the floor, but I won't let myself follow. No matter how much I might want to. "I understand."

He takes another step back and searches my face. "I don't think you do."

"I know you don't hate me, but I betrayed you and you can't forgive me. I'm not so bold as to think the last few days are enough to overcome that."

His mouth opens and then closes again before he looks away from me.

I can't stay here and look at him after he's rejected me. I'm too confused about what just happened and too afraid I might beg for affection I'll never get. "I'll see you in the morning," I say, then turn and stride into the room.

"Felicity."

I freeze. I will never tire of my name rolling off his tongue. But

I'm not strong enough to look at his face as he douses me with pity. "You don't need to explain."

"I have no desire to kiss Jasalyn's lips," he tells my back. "Or have Jasalyn's scent in my nose or Jasalyn's body under my hands."

Everything inside me winds tight. Hopeful.

"I dream of you as you truly are. I've dreamed of you since before you arrived at Castle Craige and fooled me into thinking I was falling for the shadow princess." I feel him come closer. Feel the hairs on the back of my neck shift when he draws in a shaky breath. "I want *you*. I crave *you*. And rather than settle for a substitute, I'll wait until I can have you. The real you." He trails two fingers from my nape and between my shoulder blades, and over the thin material of my gown all the way down to my waist. I shiver.

Then his touch disappears, and when I turn to make sure this isn't a dream, he's gone.

I pluck a thread on my goblin bracelet, then settle onto the floor with my playing cards as I wait for Squird to appear.

"Oh goody!" Squird says, his voice registering before he's become fully corporeal. "I've been learning to play. I was hoping I'd get to show you."

Folding my legs under me, I pat the floor beside me, then begin to lay out the cards. "You know the rules, then?"

"Yes. My brother taught me." Squird drops onto the floor and mimics my posture, his bony knee poking into my thigh. "I'm not very good yet."

I complete the game's starting spread and hand the rest of

the deck to him. "That's the thing about solitaire. You don't have an opponent so you can't lose."

He frowns, sticking his tongue out of the corner of his mouth as he studies the cards. "That's not what my brother said. He told me I lost over and over again."

I shrug. "When I play cards with my brother, high score wins. When I play alone, I always have the high score."

He flashes me a wide grin that shows all the gaps between his pointed teeth. "I like the way you think." He plays a card from his hand and studies the next.

"Tomorrow I'm going to the Eloran Palace," I say.

Squird snaps his head to the side to look at me. "Why would you do that?"

"Erith and Mordeus are working together, and the fate of Elora and the shadow court are both at stake. We need more information." I feel guilty for exploiting his youth and naïveté, but it's necessary. If Erith discovers I'm there, he will kill me. I take a breath and go for it. "And this is my best chance to get it since Erith isn't at the palace."

He wags a finger at me. "That's smart. Several days yet before he'll return."

I exhale slowly as his attention turns back to his game. I made the mistake of asking too many questions last time and I scared him off. When I decided to call for him tonight, I knew I'd need to approach the conversation carefully. "We don't know where he is. Only that he guards Mordeus's body."

Squird nods and plays another card. "But your friend has been there—the princess."

"Did you know she plunged a blade into Erith's chest and he didn't even bleed?" I shake my head, as if I'm just passing on some juicy gossip and not hunting for answers.

"That's because she used the wrong blade," he says, a grin spreading across his face when he plays another card.

"True. But she didn't know." I bite my bottom lip and decide to go for it. "I wonder if even *I* could kill him without the Sword of Fire—you know, given the prophecy and everything."

He plays another card, then shakes his head before looking at me. "You already know you could. No part of the deal he made said his female descendants had to use the Sword of Fire to kill him. Just that they could."

I swallow and try to keep my expression blank, but my mind is swimming. What deal? And female descendants? Not just me? "I can't take that risk, though. Not with what the oracle showed me."

He stares at the spread of cards for a long time before sweeping them into a pile and sighing. "You would do anything for Kendrick the Chosen, and Erith knows it. Until recently Kendrick's fate was the only thing keeping the Patriarch of the Seven safe. But now a new variable has entered into the mix. Erith doesn't know yet, though."

"What new variable?" I ask.

Squird cocks his head and studies me. "Your brother didn't tell you?"

"No, but Hale has been very busy the last few days."

"Not that brother, your blood brother."

My heart clenches as I think of the Konner from the illusion. Blood brother and best friend. I swallow the lump of emotion and keep my voice casual. "He was too busy keeping me in stasis to tell me much of anything."

Squird nods and hands over the deck of cards. "He has a reason for his secrets. A bigger reason than he's ever had for anything. Now, if you don't need anything tonight, I should go."

I might have more questions than I did when I called him here, but I still want to hug him. Goblins are a little finicky about affection, though, so I only offer him a smile. "It was good to see you, Squird."

"I can't enter the Eloran Palace, so be sure you have everything you need before you go."

My heart swells. Nigel would be proud of this kid. "I will."

CHAPTER TWENTY-SIX

JASALYN

"Jas? Jasalyn, are you okay?"

I feel like I'm being pulled from a thick fog and shake my head to clear it.

"You all right there, girl?" Skylar asks, one brow arched.

"I . . ." I blink down to the cold stone beneath my hands—the ebony stone of the Throne of Shadows—then jerk them away. "How did I get here?"

Skylar frowns at me. "I was cutting your hair and you told me you'd show me that funky mirror of your sister's I've heard so much about."

I nod. Yes. I remember that. She wanted to see the Mirror of Discovery. I remember Brie sending us to retrieve it from the throne room, but it all gets foggy after we started walking—like when I would be doing a repetitive sewing project for a client and my mind would wander. Suddenly it was hours later and the stitching was done.

"Are you okay?" Skylar asks. She holds out the mirror—when did she get that? "Here, you can put it back. I just wondered if it worked the way they said."

I take the mirror, numbly turning to place it in the case on the dais where it belongs. When I turn back, Skylar's watching me carefully.

"Feeling okay?"

"Did I . . ." I bite the inside of my lip. "Did I do anything? Hurt anyone or—" I pat my pockets. "Or take anything?"

She cocks her head. "Since we got here from down the hall?"

"I don't remember," I whisper. "I don't remember coming in here."

She scrunches up her nose as if she's about to argue, but then it must hit her the same way it hit me. I don't remember. Just like I don't remember all those nights before the ring got stuck, nights when Mordeus took over my body and used me to assassinate hundreds. "You were a little quiet, but that's not strange for you. You aren't exactly the chattiest girlie I've ever met."

"I didn't think he could use me without the ring." My stomach is a giant knot. "I didn't think I'd have to worry about that until . . ."

"Until your birthday." At least Skylar doesn't beat around the bush. I appreciate that right now. "You didn't do anything other than fondle that throne a little inappropriately, but I think you can both get past it with time."

I want to laugh. I do. But instead, dread has a hundred tiny bugs scuttling through my veins. "I need to leave," I say, even as I sink to sit on the edge of the dais.

"Do you want me to get someone?" She looks around the empty throne room. "Kendrick!"

I rest my head in my hands. I have to close my eyes. Just close my eyes and breathe and the world will stop spinning.

"I'll be right back."

I barely register the sound of her steps rushing from the room. I'm too busy counting. In, two three four, out, two three four.

I don't know how much time has passed when I sense someone in front of me, but when I open my eyes, Kendrick is there, down on one knee before me, hand on the edge of the dais as if he's intentionally waiting to touch me until I know he's there. "There she is," he murmurs, holding my gaze.

"He's already here," I whisper. "It's already happening."

"*You* are here. He doesn't have control." He takes my hand and skims his thumb across my knuckles. "You feel that?"

I nod jerkily.

"You're here. I'm not going to let anything happen to you."

"What if he had gotten to Brie?" I shake my head. "I can't risk her, Kendrick. I need to leave. I need to get out of this palace before . . ." My bottom lip trembles. I can't even say it.

"We can pack our bags and leave right now if that's what you want."

My throat bobs as I swallow. "Really?"

He smirks and I'm treated to the flash of a single dimple. "We were going to leave in the morning anyway. I don't mind moving it up a little." He squeezes my hand, and I realize he never let go.

That's what it's always been like between us. Me spiraling and Kendrick holding on. I want to be around long enough to be the one who holds on when he needs it. I will find a way out of this bargain. I have to. "I'm sorry."

I know he doesn't understand what I mean, but I don't have the strength or focus to explain.

"Enough boo-hooing," Skylar says from behind Kendrick. I don't know how long she's been standing there. "We've got a long day ahead of us if we're going to go to Elora tonight. We don't have time for that."

Kendrick stands and guides me to follow. "We'll go tell your sister and then get packed."

Find the witch and make a new deal. Everybody wants something. We will find out what she wants and give it to her. We can do this.

When I shift my focus off all the unknowns and concentrate on my next step, my pulse steadies and my breathing slows, so that's what I'll do.

"You're sure you wouldn't rather go by goblin?" Abriella asks. The portal to the Unseelie Hall of Doors is deep in the Goblin Mountains, near the River of Ice, and she insisted on coming this far with us. But unless she's going to go to Elora with us, this is where we have to part ways.

She's wearing her worried mother hen face, and for the first time in a long time I appreciate it for what it is. My sister has hovered and coddled and fussed over me for almost four years, but it's the only way she knew to love me. She's always been more mother to me than someone so young should ever have to be.

"We're sure," Kendrick says. I can't help but think how odd he looks with the rounded ears of his human glamour now that I've gotten used to his fae appearance. They all took a potion from

Natan before heading for the portal. Being fae in Elora is too dangerous. I always knew that, but it never struck me as sad when I didn't know anyone personally affected.

"The Hall will dump you hours from Fairscape and you'll have to get horses and find a place to stay."

"We've got it covered," Skylar says. "Don't fuss. I promise we'll take good care of your princess."

"We have friends in the Handres territory of Elora," Kendrick tells her, patiently giving her the explanation that she needs. "We'll meet up with them tonight and head to Fairscape first thing tomorrow."

She nods jerkily before turning to me. "You'll be back before your birthday?"

"I . . ." I cut my gaze to Kendrick before looking back to her. "If we don't find—"

"We'll bring her back after we find the witch," Kendrick says. There's so much confidence in his voice, and I could curl into it like a hug. I wish I could hold the same assurance that he speaks with and believe that fixing this is a foregone conclusion.

"Come here," I say, stepping forward and wrapping my arms around my sister. I feel her choked sob more than hear it, and I squeeze her a little tighter. "Thank you for everything you've ever done for me. I know I was horrible and—"

"You weren't."

I scoff. "I was. And you deserved better. I want you to know that I—"

"Stop." She shakes her head. "Don't do this. We aren't doing goodbye. This isn't the end."

I pull back to look at her. My fierce, beautiful sister who slayed a cruel and evil king for me. Now it's my turn to find a way to slay him for her. I squeeze her shoulders. "I love you."

Tears slide down her cheeks, leaving streaks on her porcelain skin. "I love you too."

I want to hold on a little longer, but I make myself let go and turn to Kendrick.

"Ready?" he asks, extending a hand.

I nod and take it, and as we walk through I hear Brie behind us. "Take care of her, ple—" But then she's cut off and we're somewhere else. An expanse of dark night sky that seems to stretch on forever and makes me dizzy. There's no floor, no ceiling, and no doors. Just mirrors on either side of us.

There's a pressure in my ears and a whooshing all around me that might be a noise or moving air, but it all just feels too *wrong* to be sure of anything.

"How do we know which one goes to Elora?" I ask the others.

"Your sister said we'd know it when we see it," Remme says, stepping around us.

He leads the way forward. When we stop briefly before each mirror, it shows us a reflection of ourselves in a new setting. There are floral meadows and cold stone dungeons. There are grimy village streets and the starlit sky of distant lands.

But he's right. The moment we stop in front of the portal to Elora, I know we've found it. Nothing about the wood-paneled room beyond looks familiar, but I feel it somewhere in my chest.

I glance to Kendrick. "This one."

He nods. "I feel it too."

"How does that work?" I ask.

"The Hall knows why we're here," Natan says. "It's answering the question we're asking."

"Totally rad," Skylar says.

The moment we step into the mirror, the whooshing stops, the pressure in my ears disappears, and a tavern materializes around us, complete with the stench of stale beer and the cacophony of drunken patrons. The portal brought us into a dark corner by the back door, and no one seems to notice, but Kendrick reaches for my hand and quickly leads me and the others outside nevertheless.

In the dark dirt-path alley behind the bar, a man waits by the stables. His face lights up when he spots us. "You made it!"

"Thank you for meeting us," Kendrick says, throwing an arm around him in a quick but firm embrace.

"Anything for you all. You know that."

Kendrick tugs me forward gently. "Jasalyn, this is Hector. Hector, this is Princess Jasalyn."

I offer my hand, but Hector pulls me into a hug. "We are so grateful to have your help. You could make all the difference in this revolution."

I pat him on the back, awkwardly returning his hug before pulling away. "I haven't . . ." I look to Kendrick, wide-eyed. Does this man know I can't kill Erith? Does he know I lost the Sword of Fire? "I haven't done anything useful. I'm not sure I can."

Hector's eyes sparkle with delight. "I trust in the oracle and you should too."

I bow my head to hide my shame. Kendrick's people will hate me when they find out the truth. That I lost the Sword of Fire.

That I plunged the blade into Erith's chest, like the oracle said I would, but that he still lives.

"Have you returned to the oracle?" Hector asks Kendrick. "Maybe this one can be our new queen."

"She's fae," a woman croaks behind Hector, stepping out of the shadows where she was hidden before. She's thick in the hips and waist and has the keen eyes of someone who's spent most of their life on guard. "The Eloran queen was always a human."

"That's Loryn," Kendrick says, "Hector's wife. Loryn, this is Princess Jasalyn."

Hector flashes Loryn a look that speaks of years of frequent exasperation. "Do you ignore all the gossip about Faerie? This girl is the first *human* Faerie princess."

"But she's not human for long. She's a descendant of Mab." She turns an apologetic expression toward me. "Sorry, child. It's not personal. It's tradition."

"It's fine," I whisper, dropping my gaze back to the ground when I spot Kendrick watching me.

"It's a dumb tradition," Hector says. "Don't you think the monarchy would've been stronger if the king and queen had been able to age together? If they'd been able to choose each other because of love and not because of some prediction by the oracle?"

"You don't get to pick and choose which traditions we keep just because your friend is lusting after some hot young princess." She wrinkles her nose at me. "Again, no offense, darling."

I open my mouth, but I don't know how to reply. I don't know what's worse—this man wishing things for me that can never be, this woman pitying me for what she believes to be the reason

Kendrick and I can't be together, or the look in Kendrick's eyes because he knows the truth.

Before I can figure out a response, Skylar speaks up. "She *is* hot, isn't she? It's the haircut. Pretty damn good, if I say so myself. And the clothes, for which I can also be given all the credit."

"We've had a long day," Kendrick tells Hector. "Could you show us to Amelia's?"

"What am I thinking?" He shakes his head and waves us toward the road. "The ley line is just a few blocks this way."

"Ley line?" I ask Kendrick as the group begins to follow.

"Ley lines are paths of magical power that run through the realm and can quickly take you from one point to another without you having to physically travel that distance."

"Like a portal," I say.

Hector flashes me an endearing smile. "Ah, but unlike a portal, the ley line is part of the earth, which means the Seven can't take it away."

"That's incredible." I frown. "But why didn't you just tell my sister we'd be using ley lines so she didn't have to worry about us being so far from Fairscape?"

"We don't make it a habit to share *all* our secrets," Remme says, "especially not with those from Faerie. Though if I were to choose someone to trust with them, your sister would be high on the list."

"Right there," Hector says, pointing to a maple tree on the side of the road. "Walk just to the left of the tree but so close your shoulder brushes the bark."

"I'll go first," Skylar says, jumping ahead of us.

I watch as she walks along the left side of the tree, her shoulder rubbing against it, and then she's gone. Natan follows, and then Remme.

"You go next, and I'll be right behind," Kendrick says.

I roll my shoulders back and copy the others, brushing the tree so close it scratches my skin. I expect it to feel like goblin travel—the stomach flipping and world spinning—but it's as if I just walked by the tree and my surroundings suddenly changed. The roads here are stone and the streets have oil lanterns along them.

Remme grins. "Kind of cool, yeah?"

"So cool," I agree, returning his smile.

The others join us and Hector jogs to the front of the group, hurrying us along, but Loryn walks backward and scans the group again. "Your glamours—are those from mage magic?"

Kendrick nods. "Natan cooked up more of his potion."

Hector nods approvingly. "Good. The Seven are more sensitive than ever to the use of elven magic. I've seen people dragged away for as little as a minor lighting spell. Be on your guard. It's not worth using anything that might put you in their sights."

"Noted," Kendrick says as Loryn bounces up the steps of a modest two-story cottage.

She opens the door and waves us inside, where a woman is standing at the stove and the smell of stew fills the warm space and makes it feel cozy.

"Amelia!" Skylar shouts, and the woman turns away from the stove and toward us. She's beautiful. Nearly as tall as Kendrick, with dark hair and smiling eyes. The full figure beneath her leather pants and vest looks like it's been trained for fighting, and I'm instantly a little jealous of the aura of strength and competency she exudes.

"You made it!" She drops a spoon on the counter and rushes toward us, hugging everyone eagerly before finally making it to me.

I stiffen as she looks me over, gaze flitting down my body and back up before focusing on my face. I wish I'd asked Natan to glamour away my scar. I'm not up for explaining it to a stranger.

"No wonder he's in love with you." She grins, shaking her head. "You're stunning. Your babies will be heartbreakers."

Confused, I look back and forth between her and Kendrick. "I'm sorry. I think you might have me confused for someone else." Like Crissa. Like his queen.

She levels Kendrick with a look. "Did you bring some other woman to my house? This isn't Jasalyn?"

Kendrick's cheeks are tinged pink. "Jasalyn, this is Amelia. She's known for her melt-in-your-mouth meals, her mean right hook, and her inappropriate comments."

"Don't forget my beautiful hand-stitched clothing," she says, then to me adds, "I sell them in the storefront next door."

"Indeed," Kendrick says. "Amelia, this is Jasalyn, who hasn't yet come around to the idea of having my babies so maybe cool it on that for a few years so you don't scare her off?"

My stomach does some sort of flip-flop tumble maneuver that leaves me feeling a little lightheaded. "Sorry. I thought maybe you expected . . ." I swallow. I don't want to say her name.

Amelia squeezes my shoulder. "He was a mess when they couldn't find you. Glad you're okay."

"Thank you," I whisper.

"Could you tell me where we can wash up before dinner?" Kendrick asks.

"Top of the stairs, first door on the left," Amelia says.

"Hale can take the room on the far end of the hall," Loryn says.

"Hush, woman." Hector nudges his wife with an elbow. "He can sleep wherever he pleases."

She grunts, and Amelia turns her attention to me. "Bathing chamber is on the opposite side of the hall. We all share. I apologize I can't offer you better."

I hate that my shadow court title makes her feel like she needs to. "You're offering more than enough. I grew up sharing a bathing chamber with my cousins and sister—and my sister and I were only allowed to use it when our cousins were out of the house. This will be more than sufficient."

Hector's eyes soften. "What a sweet girl."

Kendrick intertwines his fingers with mine, and I let him lead me up the stairs and into the room Amelia indicated would be mine. It's small but it has a big window behind the bed. There are plenty of candles for light while I sleep. I should feel safe enough if Kendrick wants to save Loryn the aggravation by sleeping in his own room.

He drops his satchel on the floor in the corner and then shuts the door. "I'm sorry about Loryn. She means well, but she's toeing the line. I'll talk to her."

"You don't need to do that," I murmur, but I'm distracted. The room seems familiar to me, and at first I can't place it. "You brought me here. After I confronted Erith and you found me in the rubble of my old house."

"We needed somewhere safe in Elora, and I knew Amelia would accommodate us."

"But she didn't know me. She wasn't here?"

"Not that day, which is for the best. She would've lost her cool at the chance to meet your sister. She's completely enamored with the idea of an Eloran human rising to power in Faerie and thinks your sister is the quintessential badass."

I smile. "Well, I can't blame her for that. Do Hector and Loryn live here too?"

He shrugs. "They stay sometimes, but this is Amelia's home. They are emissaries for the movement, so they go from town to town in Elora to check in with our people and keep things organized." He digs a piece of chalk from his satchel and walks to the corner, marking something on the wall.

"What kind of things?"

"Killing Erith is only the first step to putting the realm to rights," he says, moving to another corner. "We have a long fight ahead of us, so it's vital that we keep our supporters in the loop—letting them know what to expect and how they can help." He moves to the third corner and I realize he's drawing runes on the walls.

"What are those for?" I ask.

"It's a barrier to keep unwanted guests out of this room. In Faerie I'd just use my own magic to create wards around us, but here it's safer to use mage magic."

I want to ask if he always warded the spaces where I slept when we were together, but I already know the answer. Kendrick's protected me from the day we met. "I didn't expect your friends here to know about me," I admit.

After marking the final corner, he wanders to the window and stares out for a long time before answering. When he finally does, all he says is "They care about me, and I care about you." He looks me over one last time, as if he's trying to convince himself I'll be safe here without him. "Natan and I need to run out to see someone, but we'll be back in time for dinner."

He heads through the door, and I blurt, "I don't want them thinking I'm a threat to their queen."

He turns around slowly and leans on the doorjamb, scanning my face. "I've never wanted to fight for anything the way I was willing to fight for Elora."

"I know. And they know that too. I just want you to know, I won't ruin—"

"But that was before you. Everything's different now."

Everything in my chest twists tight. It's hope I have no right to hold on to. "Kendrick..."

"You're fighting for your life, and there is nothing that's more important than that. That's why I haven't pushed this thing between us." He swallows. "But, for the record, I reject any future that doesn't include you. I'm not willing to give you up, not so long as you'll have me."

I stride across the room and tuck my hand into his belt to tug him forward. Rising onto my toes and pressing my mouth to his, I slide my hand behind his neck, and he slides his behind my back. He's warm and soft, and his kiss makes me believe this will all be okay. We will find the witch and undo the deal. We will find a way to save Elora from the tyranny of the Seven that doesn't require me to watch the male I love marry someone else.

Kendrick angles his mouth over mine and pulls me closer. I melt into him and brush my tongue against his. He groans, removing the hand I've slid up into his shirt and against his warm skin without thinking.

I laugh and pull away. "Sorry."

"Never apologize for that." He leans back in to nip at my bottom lip, then backs out the door, dimples flashing just long enough to promise *soon*.

CHAPTER TWENTY-SEVEN

JASALYN

Kendrick and Natan are out longer than expected, but Amelia distracts me from my worry by telling me about her family and life in Elora. She asks me questions about where I grew up and what it's like to live in the Midnight Palace. By the time Kendrick and Natan appear, she feels like an old friend.

"Did everything go okay?" she asks, pushing out of her seat to pour two fresh mugs of tea.

"More or less," Kendrick says. "We've been gone too long. People start losing faith that change is coming when they don't see progress."

"It was fine," Natan says. "He's just in his head about everything."

Amelia nods, but I can tell she's fighting back a frown. "Natan, Remme is sitting out back. He said to send you out there when you got home."

Natan's eyes brighten, and he hoists his mug in the air. "Does he already have one of these or should I take one for him?"

"He's chosen the kind of refreshment you drink straight from the flask tonight," she says, winking.

"Ah, in that case . . ." Natan pours a second mug of steaming tea, and Amelia watches as he heads out back.

"I've missed them," she says softly before turning her attention back to Kendrick. "Hurry and save the realm so I can have my brother back, okay?"

I put my mug down. "Natan is your brother?" But as soon as I say it, I realize my mistake. She and Remme have the same dark hair and deep brown eyes. "You're Remme's sister."

She shrugs. "Natan is a bit of an honorary brother, but yes. I share blood with Remme."

"A few short years ago, she wouldn't have admitted to that so easily," Kendrick says.

"He was a pest to grow up beside. Just ask Felicity. He tormented her nearly as much as he tormented me." She smiles into her tea. "But I suppose after seeing him so rarely in the last few years, I've learned to appreciate him."

"I hope he gets to come home soon," I say. "He and Natan both. Someone as kind as you deserves to have her family around her."

She flashes me a grateful look and then draws in a shaky breath and slaps the table. "Anyway! Enough about me and my depressing life. You must be exhausted. Go put on your pajamas and I'll find some extra blankets since it's getting cold tonight."

I laugh. "We packed light. Didn't exactly bring pajamas." I glance down at my riding clothes and shrug. "I can just sleep in these."

She scoffs. "You have a night with the handsome and charming Hale Kendrick and you're going to spend it wearing stinky riding clothes? No. I won't have that. Come follow me."

I rise obediently, following her toward the stairs. I sneak a glance at Kendrick, who merely winks before leaning back in his chair with his tea.

"I don't have anything fancy," she says as she leads me into the bedroom. She pulls open a drawer and rifles through it. "How about this?" She pulls out a piece of silky cyan fabric and holds it up for my inspection.

My cheeks flare hot as I take in the slip. Truth be told, there's not much to it. "I do hope you have those extra blankets if I'm going to wear that."

"The client I had in mind for this is a bit fuller bodied than you, so it might slip off the shoulders, but with this style it doesn't much matter."

I drag my bottom lip between my teeth. "Do you think he'd like that?" I've had so little time for vanity in my life. I was far too fixated on revenge and fear to worry about how I look or if a male might find me attractive, but right now I very much want to wear something that Kendrick will like me in.

Her bit-back laughter puffs out as a light snort. "Oh, I think so." She nods toward the door. "Why don't you go across the hall and get cleaned up and changed? There's some water waiting by the fire. Should still be warm enough. I'll send Kendrick up to join you in a few minutes."

She heads for the door.

"Amelia?" I look down at the silky blue fabric one more time before meeting her curious gaze. "Thank you."

She flashes me a grin that reminds me so much of Remme I'm not sure how I didn't see it before. "I am more than happy to assist in matters of seduction."

My cheeks heat. "Not that . . . well, that too, but thank you for being so friendly." I swallow. "I haven't had a lot of friends, and I don't know whether the oracle will help us with what we need so I'll have the chance to make more. For what it's worth, I'm grateful I met you."

Her expression turns solemn. "If the oracle doesn't give you the information you need, you'll find it somewhere else. I believe that." She pulls open the door to my bedroom and waves me inside. "As for the rest, I am honored to be your friend. We'll have lots and lots of nights where I can tease Hale about how much he adores you. I can't wait to spend years watching the way he lights up whenever you're in the room." She backs into the hall and gives me a final nod. "Rest well."

I take my time washing up. The water isn't hot, but it's not so cold it leaves a chill either, and after being in my riding clothes all day I'm more than grateful for the chance to have clean skin before slipping into such a lovely gown.

When I return to my room, I release my hair from the high tie and take my time brushing it out.

The top section has gotten long and nearly falls to my waist now.

A soft knock sounds at the door and a tiny shiver races from my belly to my sternum. "Come in?"

The door slowly opens and Kendrick steps inside the room, looking uncharacteristically bashful, his gaze pointedly not straying from my face, which means there's no way he's missing my eyes on him. He's clearly done his own cleaning up before joining me. He's shirtless and wearing a pair of soft breeches that show off his strong thighs. His golden chest has a spattering of light brown hair on it and my gaze snags on the line of characters tattooed over his heart.

"Hi," he says softly. Shyly.

There's no point in pretending this hasn't been a very calculated evening, so I stand and wave a hand down my body. "How do I look? Amelia thought you might like this."

His pupils dilate and his tongue darts out to touch his bottom lip. "I like *you*. Doesn't matter what you wear."

"You like me." I catch myself crossing my arms in front of my chest and drop them. "But maybe I hoped you'd *want* me."

"I have wanted you since the moment Remme and Skylar brought you to our cabin eight months ago. I wanted you when you were angry with me and when you were scared and when you were reckless. When you were in your dress from the palace and when you were in those outfits of Sky's." He strolls forward, letting his eyes sweep over the slip, and my bare thighs, before he stops in front of me and traces one strap of the slip with a callused fingertip. "A nightgown couldn't make me want you more than I already do. That's just not possible."

"Amelia will be disappointed all her thoughtfulness was for nothing." I sound a little breathless. I *feel* a little breathless.

"I'm not so concerned about what Amelia thinks. I'm more interested in the fact that you wanted to wear this. And you want me here?" It comes out as a question, and I realize he's still not sure where he stands with me. Still not sure where *we* stand. And that's my fault.

"I always want you to be wherever I am."

His throat bobs. "Happy to oblige." His gaze skims over me again. "I do think this suits you, though. You deserve more time in pretty things." I shiver and he glances to the fireplace. "Though if that's really what you're going to sleep in, I should get some more wood on that fire."

I admire the roll and pinch of the muscles in his back as he works, and when he turns to me, he catches me staring. His grin is all dimples and crinkled eyes and I feel more in love than ever.

This, I think. *If I get to live, I want more moments like this.* The simple joy shared between two people who see each other, the quiet moments somewhere cozy.

And if I live but Kendrick serves on the Eloran throne married to another woman?

After being doused in Amelia's optimism, it's easier than ever to push that thought away.

"Tell me what's going on in that head of yours," he says, rising to stand before me.

I scan his face, study the kindness I recognized in his eyes from the first time we met. "I'm thinking about *not* thinking too much, actually."

He brushes his knuckles against my cheek. "What happens if you think too much?"

"I get hung up on things I can't control." I swallow. "I'm not going to trade this moment's happiness for worries of something that may or may not happen tomorrow."

"Happiness." He traces my bottom lip with the pad of his thumb. "Is that what this is for you?"

"I think it might be. Ridiculous, given the circumstances, isn't it?"

He drops his hands to my hips and pulls me close, bending

down to rest his forehead against mine. "I think that's how we know it's happiness. It isn't contingent on everything around us feeling easy." He releases a breath. "Though I would like a little easy, even if just for a while, if you're going to keep looking at me like that."

I breathe him in. He smells like soap and pine. Like *safe*. "How am I looking at you?"

He cups my face, skimming the bridge of his nose over mine. "Like you might want me to kiss you." He takes my hand and places my palm against his chest, right over the steady thump of his heart. "Like you might want to touch me as much as I want to touch you."

"That makes a lot of sense, since both are true." Relief washes over his face and I have to shake my head. "I know I pushed you away, but it wasn't about you."

He puts a finger to my lips. "I was wrong to ask anything of you when I hadn't made it clear I was offering more."

I find his mouth with mine and kiss him while I relish the rhythm of his heart against my hand.

His lips are gentle as they explore—parting and closing, nipping and sucking—but then I thread my fingers through his hair and tug him closer and he growls into my mouth. "If I had the magic to stop time, I would use it to stay here with you. Let the rest of the world carry on without us." He bends to slide his hands to the back of my thighs, then lifts me off the floor. I instinctively wrap my legs around his waist. He lowers himself into the chair, keeping me on his lap.

"I don't think I'd argue with that," I admit. "I don't want to be anywhere but here."

"Good." He grips my hips tightly, like he's trying to pull me even closer. I can feel the hard length of him through his soft sleep pants.

I like this angle, looking down at him, our bodies flush. It's intentional, I realize. He's giving me complete control.

I draw back enough to watch his face and pull the silky slip off over my head.

His throat bobs, and his gaze drops, roaming over me.

"I feel beautiful when you look at me like that."

His eyes flick back to my face. "You should always feel beautiful."

I shrug. "It never mattered to me before. And maybe it shouldn't now. It's such a superficial thing, beauty." I drop my gaze to his chest and trail my fingers across his collarbone. "But I think I need to know you see me. Not despite the scars and not because of them, but just that when you look at me, you see all of me."

"I do," he says, voice rough, "and it's the greatest honor of my life." With a hand slid roughly behind my neck, he pulls my mouth down to his and kisses me fully, like he's trying to pour everything he feels into one kiss, like he's trying to convince me with his lips and tongue alone that I am *all* he sees.

The fire crackles beside us, warming the room and the bare skin he's exploring with the tentative brush of fingertips up my back and down my side. One palm presses to my ribs and drags up to cup my breast.

He breaks the kiss and meets my eyes. "This is okay?" I love the rough edge to his voice, the one that lets me know how much he wants this, wants me, while also reassuring me that if I stopped things now, he would absolutely follow my lead.

"If it's okay with you." I sit back, giving his hands more room to move and his eyes more room to explore.

His breath catches. "Nowhere else I want to be."

He drags an open mouth down my neck and across my clavicle, tongue warm against my rapidly heating skin. When he picks me up again, he takes me to the bed and lays me down on top of the covers.

I reach for him and he takes my hand in his, squeezing as he brings it to his mouth for a quick kiss. His eyes stay on me. He shucks off his sleep pants and climbs onto the bed, lying beside me, propped up on one elbow and scrutinizing my face.

I smile. "Don't look so worried. I'm okay."

He shakes his head. "I want you to be better than okay. I want you to be good—great, amazing." His gaze slides down my body again and his breath hitches. "I want to make sure you're feeling even a fraction of how I am right now."

I can't keep my smile from stretching across my face. "I'm good, great, amazing."

"Hmm. I'm not convinced yet." He trails fingers between my breasts and over my stomach.

I arch into his touch, and when his hand finds its way between my legs, I drag in a shaky breath.

"You've thought about this." It isn't a question. He knows I have, but he still wants to hear it. "Since the last time."

"Yes." My hips lift—seeking, pleading—as he teases me. "You?"

"I hate that I can't remember, but I think about it anyway. All the time."

I melt, tomorrow and all the what-ifs falling away in the face of sensations that start in one spot and seem to radiate out to my whole body.

When I can't stand any distance between us anymore, I loop an arm around his neck and tug him toward me, guiding him to position his body over mine. The weight of his hips settles between my thighs, and the tenderness in his eyes turns back to fire. I sigh happily.

"I want to give you so much more." He nuzzles the side of my neck. "I *will* give you more. I'll find a way."

His whiskers are rough beneath my palm as I urge his face up and press my lips to his. The broad expanse of his back feels like a dream beneath my fingers, warm and taut. "I want this," I say, in case it's not clear. "*No matter* what tomorrow brings."

He shifts his position over me. I feel him against me now and tense in anticipation. "I will always choose you," he says. "No matter what tomorrow brings."

He angles his mouth over mine and kisses me so deeply I let the tension evaporate. He feels the change and grunts softly as he moves into me. Slowly. So slowly I could push him away. So slowly I don't need to. My body is warm and pliant and ready to give everything his asks. Then we're joined, and he's looking down at me like I'm a miracle and I think I'm looking up at him the same way.

CHAPTER TWENTY-EIGHT

FELICITY

I dreamed of my brother again. Of that other life he planted in my mind. Of being in my own body and never having to hide. Then I dreamed of a beautiful dark-haired faerie passing me a cherubic blue-eyed baby girl, and when I held her in my arms, I knew I would do anything, sacrifice anything, to protect her.

Misha skims his gaze over me a few times before shaking his head. "I wouldn't think anything could take me by surprise after how well you impersonated Jasalyn, but every time you take a new form, it's still hard for me to believe it's you."

"It's probably best that you forget," I say, glancing down at myself. Sol's tall and lean and has dark hair that's loose around her shoulders and flows down to the middle of her back. Because watching someone move and talk is better than being told, Misha let Storm into my mind to show me his brief interactions with her. It's more than her traditional beauty, though. She has an air about her that exudes confidence and power. It's the perfect match to Misha's energy.

It's the first time I've seen him since what he told me yesterday afternoon, and while I would've loved nothing more than to wake in my own body and put his words to the test, I couldn't do that—because I assume my father's still looking for me, and because I need to be Sol today.

"Learn anything useful in your dreams?" Misha asks.

Focus, Felicity. "There's a child—a baby girl. I think Sol is a grandmother. And I think she would do anything to protect that child."

He flinches.

"What is it?"

"That's the kind of information I hope we never have to exploit," he says. "Let's go. Pretha said Sol just arrived at Castle Craige, so we need to hurry."

"You're sure we have to go back that way?" I ask Misha as I glance toward the mirror we just walked through—a mirror that now looks entirely ordinary. There's nothing ordinary about where we just came from. The Hall of Doors is worse than the sanctuary he took me to while I was staying at Castle Craige. When we walked down the corridor toward his revered elder, the Jewel of Peace, I didn't think I'd ever be in a place as disconcerting as that. I was wrong.

"As far as we know, that's the only way in or out of the Eloran Palace." After a quick survey of the room—a space that looks like a rarely utilized office—he opens the door to the hall. *Does any of this look familiar to you?* he asks, switching to speaking into my mind.

We pass room after room and I don't see anything I recognize until— "In here." I tug him to follow me and turn into the library.

My mind is flooded with memories of playing in here when I was a child, of my mother reading to me, of—

Illusions. These are just illusions.

"There." I point to the opposite side of the library, where another doorway leads into a hall I know from my memories.

"This is as good a place for you to remain unseen as any," I say, looking around.

"It wouldn't be impossible to explain it away if I was seen here with Sol."

"And if we run into Konner? And what about anyone else who might know you're the one who rescued me?"

He sighs. "Keep your mind open to me. I can get to you quickly if you need me." He gives my hand a hard squeeze.

"It will be okay," I say. I'm not sure why I feel the need to reassure him, but he seems more on edge today than usual.

The moment I turn out of the library, my surroundings click into place in my mind. It's eerily easy to navigate through the palace's maze of hallways. It doesn't feel like a strange place I only know from maps. It feels like . . . like *home*.

"Sol," someone calls from the hall to my left. I freeze. "Where have you been? I've been hunting for you all morning."

I turn slowly and have to focus on keeping the shock from my face when I realize it's Konner. "Hello."

He grins. "Come with me. I have a surprise."

I grimace. "I'm in the middle of something. Surely it can wait."

What do I do? I ask Misha in my mind.

"It can't, though," Konner says. "It won't take long at all." He takes my hand and tugs me along like a little boy excitedly dragging his mother toward some new toy. "You want to see this. I promise."

Calm down and use your gift, Misha says in my mind.

Using my gift is what got me into this mess.

Not your Echo gift, the other one. Feel out their relationship. How does he feel for Sol? Is this just professional or is it personal?

Misha's right, and I'm more than a little embarrassed I didn't think of it myself. Konner seems almost giddy as he pulls me through the halls, and I realize my thought of him as a little boy was coming from their connection. She's like a mother to him. Interesting.

"What's wrong?" he asks.

"Nothing," I say, forcing a smile. "I'm just busy today."

"I promise this is worth it."

I let him lead me down the hall, then follow him into a room at the back of an isolated corridor. When he opens the door, I'm met with sunshine and the smell of clean laundry and milk.

A young fae woman with long, dark hair sits in a chair by the window, a babe with white curls cradled in her arms. Her eyes light up when she sees me, and though she strikes me as familiar, I can't quite place her. "Did you tell her?"

"I thought she might want to see for herself," Konner says.

I look back and forth between them, trying to act as natural as possible. Who is this female and why did Konner bring one of the Seven to see her and her baby? "See what?"

Konner laughs. "You *are* distracted today, aren't you? I think this is the first time I've had you here that you didn't immediately demand to hold her."

The female brushes her hair behind her shoulder and spins the baby to face me. The infant's chewing on her fist, drool rolling down her chin.

"Act like you're leaving, Mom," she says.

Mom. That is why she looks familiar. I saw them in my dream. She's Sol's daughter, and this is Sol's grandchild—Konner's daughter.

My niece, I realize with a flip in my stomach.

I reach toward the door behind me and open it, pretending to leave, as instructed.

Konner lifts the baby from the mother's arms. "You have to wave and say bye," he instructs me.

The baby girl looks up at him with wide eyes and says, "Bye-bye!" opening and closing her chubby little fist.

"That's right," Konner coos. "Tell Mamaw bye-bye!"

"Bye-bye," the baby girl repeats with a giggle.

"Precious," I breathe, and heat pricks my eyes.

"See why I didn't want you to miss it?" Konner says, but his full attention is on the child in his arms.

"She's so beautiful." I do want to hold her, just as Sol would, but I'm afraid if I do I'll never be able to convince myself to let go.

These people are my family. No matter how I feel about the Seven or my brother, that will always be true. They're my family and this might be the only time I ever get to see my niece.

"Now all we need is Konner's sister to do her thing and maybe we can stop hiding," the child's mother says.

"She's scared," Konner says. "The oracle told her that her brother would die if she killed Erith."

She presses her lips into a thin line. "*You* are her brother."

He looks almost sad. "Not in any way that counts."

"I still think we should tell her about Leia. Maybe she would help us to protect her."

Konner shakes his head. "We can't trust her. No matter how much we might want to. She was raised by our enemies and brought up to believe that the Seven should be abolished." His throat bobs. "You should've seen how quick she was to kill Orlen. She wouldn't have done that if she was interested in understanding me or capable of believing that we're all not like Erith."

The young female looks to me and I realize I'm just staring at them—staring and trying to piece everything together. "Mom, what's wrong with you? Isn't this where you usually go into your tirade about how the concept of the Seven has been corrupted and how you have a vision for the future that brings it all back to where it belongs?"

I swallow hard and sigh. "I'm feeling a little off today," I say, hoping this response isn't completely out of character.

Konner frowns at me. "She's worried about the alliance with King Misha."

Sol told Konner about her plans, then. "Can you blame me?"

"But it was still worth it, right?" the female asks. "Seeing Leia one more time before we leave?" She stands and wraps one arm around Konner, leaning her head on his shoulder. The sight of him with a baby in his arms and his partner at his side makes me sentimental for a life that might've been—a life where I was close to my brother and friends with his wife, where I got to watch his children grow up. Tears prick at the back of my nose.

"Mom!" she says, stepping away from Konner and pulling me into her embrace. "Don't cry. I'll be fine, though I wish I could tell you where to find us."

"Tulle, we talked about this," Konner says.

"It's better that I don't know?" It comes out like a question. I'm off my game, but neither of them seems to notice.

"We'll see each other again soon." She looks to Konner. "Just as soon as someone meets her destiny."

I squeeze her in return and let myself imagine that other life for just a beat longer than I should. When Sol realizes we made her miss this goodbye, she'll hate us for sure. And I can't even blame her.

Konner hands the child off to her mother and kisses her on the cheek. "I'll be back in a few," he says before leading me out of the room.

Once we're several steps down the hall, he blows out a long breath. "I know we don't really have a choice, but I don't want her to go."

"What else can you do?" I ask, because it seems like a safe response and because I want to know more. Is Leia the secret Squird mentioned? Is she the new variable?

"It was one thing to have them here when Leia was smaller and no one would question who their father was, but . . ." He gives a bashful shrug.

"She's starting to look like you," I say.

"Exactly. And Erith will be back soon." He scrapes a hand over his face. "It's better to hide them until this is all handled."

"I . . ." I swallow hard. "You're so young." This is my *twin* brother. I can't imagine thinking about children yet, and meanwhile he has one he has to keep hidden.

He coughs out a laugh and shakes his head at me. "I thought you were done with that lecture once Leia arrived."

I flash what I hope looks like a concerned, maternal smile. "Call it motherly concern."

"I wish we'd understood the prophecy better before. Wish we'd have taken the time to think about where his power came from. But we didn't, and I can't regret her."

"Neither can I," I say softly.

"I hate all of this. I wish I could've just talked to my sister when I had her. I wish there'd been a way to make her understand—to make her see it from my point of view." He stops in front of the double doors of the library and shoves his hands into his pockets. "Thank you for meeting with Misha today. I would've gone with you, but after everything with Felicity..."

"I understand," I lie.

"You go soon?"

"I'm supposed to be there already," I say. "But he can wait."

"I'll be here when you return. I want to hear everything."

"Of course."

He steps out of the way, and I should let him go, but instead I hear myself call out, "Konner?"

He turns back to me and my heart swells. "Thank you for taking me to see her. I would've hated to miss that."

"I know." He winks and then strolls away, leaving me with nothing to do but return to my mission.

My head spins as I step into the library to cut through to the hall where Natan told me I'd find the Chronicles. I find the hidden stairwell behind the back row of books, and when I'm sure no one is watching, I climb up and duck inside the dark room at the top of the steps.

I feel the power in the room before I even find what I'm looking for. It pulses like a living thing and calls me toward the panel on the opposite wall. My hand shakes as I lift it to the screen, but a low hum buzzes through the room and the walls before me slide away, revealing another wall of books.

The Chronicles.

"What do you think you're doing in here?"

I freeze, mid-reach, too scared to turn around. *Sol wouldn't be scared. She belongs here and has as much right to the information on these shelves as anyone else.*

I make myself face the male behind me with confidence and fury in my eyes. I'm planning to give him a piece of my mind until I see who it is.

"Shae." His name slips out before I can catch myself. *Shit. Shit shit shit.* I better hope Sol is supposed to know his name. I school my expression and fold my arms. "Why do you think I'd take orders from you?" I ask, sneering as I look him over.

There's no reason he should recognize that I'm not really Sol, but I've never used my Echo abilities in front of Shae when he didn't already know it was me.

"You think we don't know what you've been up to?" he asks. "All the whispers and the sound shields and the secret meetings. 'Sol thinks she can save the world from greed and tyranny just because her grandmother was one of the original Seven,'" he mocks, then chuckles. "Don't worry. A lot of people fall victim to that. I know because I was raised around them. Thank the gods Erith offered me the deal of a lifetime or I'd still be stuck with those idiots."

"You don't know what you're talking about."

"Don't you get it? None of this matters. The threads of fate are stitched too far now. There's no going back."

I need him to leave if I'm going to access the Chronicles, but how? I lift my chin. "Did you need something?"

He frowns and looks me over. "You seem different today...."

"That's because I'm trying to decide how to execute you." It takes everything in me to still my hands, and all the shaking I'm stopping on the outside seems to have relocated to my stomach. If he realizes it's really me, I'm as good as dead.

He cocks his head to the side, then in the next second, he's behind me, his dagger to my throat. "How did you get in here, Felicity, and what did you do with Sol?"

CHAPTER TWENTY-NINE

JASALYN

"This is where you grew up?" Kendrick asks as we walk the streets of Fairscape.

Last night was so special, I was reluctant to face the day when the sun rose this morning. I relished those moments alone with Kendrick, and I hated to return to our mission—the heavy reality of the task before us.

"After my mother left, yes. We lived just outside the city before we moved in with Madame Vivias, our aunt. It was a little quieter there, but there were still a lot of people who didn't have nearly as much as they needed."

We rode horses from Amelia's to the outskirts of Fairscape, but only the rich own horses here so we left ours with our friends and decided to walk the rest of the way into town.

I look around and try to see the city from Kendrick's eyes. There's so much poverty here—obvious in the litter, the state of the homes, and the unbathed children begging in the street. So much need for basic necessities. I know Abriella has sent sentinels in disguise as humans and had them leave packages of food on porches, but without big changes at the top, there will always be too much suffering in this realm we used to call our home.

Kendrick tucks a handful of coins into the bag of a begging boy, and the child's face lights up for a brief moment before he pulls away, scared. "I can't give you nothing for this, though."

Kendrick shakes his head. "I'm not asking for anything."

The boy looks skeptical, but we keep walking, and when I glance over my shoulder I spot him tucking the coins into his trousers and running away.

A few minutes later, we reach a familiar gravel lane, and I point to the front stoop of a straw-roofed hut a few doors down. "That's where the witch was when she called me into her cottage." An icy chill runs down my spine as I remember that day. How could I have given up so much? How could I have let my fear and rage control me so completely?

"Want me to go investigate?" he asks. "You can wait here."

"No." I lift my chin. "I need to do this. She can't hurt me." I'm not even sure that's true, but it doesn't make sense that she would. Not this close to the deal being completed.

Kendrick looks at me for a long time before nodding and offering his hand. "We'll do it together."

The street is lousy with people making their way to the market. We weave our way through them to get to the house on the other side.

The three rickety wooden steps in front of the door aren't big enough for us both, so Kendrick steps to the side of them while I go up to knock.

I rap three times before dropping my hand, but nothing happens. It's too noisy out here for me to know for sure, but I can't even make out any sounds inside the small cottage.

"Who're you?" a redheaded little girl with pigtails calls from the stoop next door. She's combing the yarn hair of a battered hand-stitched doll. "You know thems who live there?"

"I'm looking for the lady who lives here," I say, descending the steps to get closer to her so we don't have to shout. "Do you know if she's home?"

The little girl shrugs. "They never come out. Don't think she's there no more."

"Dimpsy, who're you talking to?" A young woman sticks her head out the door and scowls at us. She has dark smudges under her eyes and flour on her apron. "What do ya need?"

"We're looking for the woman who lives next door," Kendrick says. "Could you maybe help us out?"

"What woman? Isn't nobody living in that dump." She leans down and takes her daughter by the arm, urging her into the house.

"It's been about a year since I last saw her," I say. "She was maybe in her sixties and had long, dark hair and walked with a cane. If you could help me find her, it would really help me out."

She nudges her child the rest of the way into the house before coming onto the stoop and closing the door behind her. "I don't know anybody round here like that, and the man who bought that place hasn't been around in ages. Must be nice to have so much money you can just buy houses and leave 'em to rot."

"Do you know anything about the owner?" Kendrick asks. "His name or where we might find him?"

She grunts. "Nah. He kept to himself, but I wouldn't have

wanted to know him if I could've. Game me the creepy-crawlies, always watching my girl, always smirking."

"What did he look like, if you don't mind?"

She shrugs. "Long white hair, tall and rail thin, but not in a hungry way, ya know? He acted like somebody who didn't know what it was like to want for a darn thing."

Kendrick and I exchange a look and I know we're both thinking the same thing. *Erith.*

"Thanks for your help," Kendrick says, reaching forward to shake her hand. She accepts it reluctantly, surprise registering on her face when he passes over several coins.

"What now?" I ask as we walk back toward our friends at the edge of town. "I feel like that got us nowhere."

"We have our answer on whether the witch was working with Erith or Mordeus," he says. "But if no one has been there since that witch met with you, then I'm not sure we're going to find her through any of the neighbors. We'll go back after dark and see what we can find inside."

CHAPTER THIRTY

FELICITY

"You really thought you could come to the *Eloran Palace* and go unnoticed? I'll give you credit. You're more ballsy than I ever would've guessed. Good for you."

"Who's Felicity?" I snap, but it's too late. Shae knows me too well, and even though I can school my features with the best of them, I'm failing miserably at controlling my heart rate.

"You and your brother and his friends—you're all delusional, thinking you can bring down the Magical Seven. Elorans *adore* the Seven. The common people don't know jack about the monarchy you all hold so dear."

"A monarchy *you* fought for once."

"I fought for the same reason everyone else does—I was sick of being poor and powerless. But I'm neither of those things now. Something much better came along than bowing to *Kendrick the Chosen*." He singsongs my brother's name like it's a joke.

"Something better? Is being Erith's errand boy so great?"

"We all do what we have to. This will be worth it in the end. Leading the Seven will be worth it in the end."

I sputter out a laugh. "*You?* Leading the Seven? In what

pathetic kind of world would that happen?"

"You think you're so smart, and Hale thinks he's so special, but you don't know anything about the way this world works. About how the Seven work. Erith has all the real power and he can hand it over to anyone he chooses."

"Is that what he promised you so you'd betray your friends? His position among the Seven? And you think anyone in the palace will stand for a piece of crap like you ruling them?"

"I could kill you right now," he growls.

"But you won't." He would've killed me back at Castle Craige if he could have. Maybe before that. "You can't ascend if you have blood on your hands."

"That's the only reason you're not dead already. Don't worry. Daray is on his way. He'll take care of you for me."

Misha, I call. *Misha, I'm in trouble.*

I grasp for our mental bond, but I don't feel him there. How long has he been gone?

"You should've died when you faced that cave demon, but it turns out little miss sweeter than sunshine isn't too good to let her goblin die for her."

His words are like a knife, hot and twisting in my chest. I never would've chosen for Nigel to sacrifice himself for me and Shae knows it.

"Seamus!" someone shouts behind us. "What do you think you're doing?"

Shae keeps the blade at my neck and spins us both around. Konner is standing there, eyes wide as he looks back and forth between us.

Hope bubbles in my chest.

Konner. He wouldn't let Shae kill his child's grandmother, but how much did he hear?

"What's happening here, Seamus?" He prowls forward slowly, drawing a dagger from his hip, but Shae doesn't move his blade.

"She's not Sol," Shae shouts, his voice frenzied and the knife digging into my neck enough to draw blood. "This is your piece-of-trash sister and she came to kill your father. We can't let that happen."

Konner's eyes are hard as topaz when they meet mine. "Don't. Move." It's a warning, and I'm trembling.

"Yes. We should get rid of her before she can get to anyone else. Who knows, she may have already killed Sol—if not, where is she?"

"I have a question," Konner says, taking another step forward, gaze on Shae now. "What's the point in holding the blade to her neck if you aren't willing to follow through?"

Konner looks at me, and maybe I imagine it, but I think he nods ever so slightly, as if to say, *Move now.* And I do. I use the maneuver Misha taught me while I was staying at Castle Craige, pulling down on his arm and dropping my weight to the floor. Sol is taller and much stronger than Jasalyn, so I don't need any help to send Shae to the floor on his back. I sidestep as Konner approaches behind me, as sure of his next move as if we'd trained together a dozen times.

Konner drops and puts his blade to Shae's throat. "Oh, Seamus. You know what's nice about never aspiring to sit among the Seven?" he asks, adding just enough pressure that blood pearls along the blade. "I can kill anyone who threatens my family."

But just as he draws back to strike, Shae disappears.

Konner releases a string of curses that would make even Remme blush, but all I can do is stare at the spot on the floor where Shae used to be.

When Konner guides me to a chair in a sparse sitting area of even sparser living quarters, I'm still shaking.

Maybe he's brought me here to torture information out of me. Maybe I should've run from him the moment Shae disappeared. But just like I knew he would take care of Shae if I got out of the way, I know he has no intention of harming me now.

He strides to a small armoire and throws the door open, shoving uniforms aside and reaching to the back. He pulls out a bottle and walks it over to me. "Drink this."

I frown at it. Brown, foggy glass. The gods only know what inside. "Why?"

"Because right now, the only person other than me who knows you're not who you say is on the run. Drink before someone who knows better spots you—someone I'm *not* willing to kill." He shakes the bottle. "It doesn't hurt. I've used it a hundred times."

"This will allow me to return to my true form without sleep?" His words sink in, and I flick my gaze back up to his. "You're an Echo too?"

"We're twins, remember? I'm guessing there are a lot more similarities between us than you realize." He paces back and forth in front of me, eyes darting to the door every so often as if he's afraid someone's going to charge through it. Maybe they will.

"Do you think Shae will tell someone?"

"He's not a favorite around here, and that will work in our favor. But yes, I think he'll tell Erith's favorites exactly what happened today. Luckily, I can plead ignorance and say I thought he was trying to kill one of the Seven."

"You would've really killed him for me, wouldn't you?"

"Happily. Though I've been looking for an excuse." He scoffs and stops pacing to scowl at me. "What do you think you're doing here? Are you alone? Are you a complete fool?" He drags a hand through his white hair. There's real fear in his eyes. "You're lucky you're alive. Seamus is Erith's proxy. Through the power Erith handed him when he left, Seamus would've had the right to have you executed."

"I know." I squeeze my knees. I'm not used to this. Hale's the one who's always running into dangerous situations, the one risking his life, the one having to think on his feet to survive.

Konner folds his arms. "Where is Sol? Did you do something to her? Did—"

"She's fine. She's at Castle Craige being wined and dined by the former queen and the king's sister." And probably growing more and more irritated that Misha hasn't shown up to the discussion she was promised.

"She was hoping for an alliance. But after this?" He waves a hand up and down to indicate my form. "I don't know if she'll trust him."

"Why would he want to ally with one of the Seven? Why help anyone who keeps someone like our father in power?"

Konner grabs the wooden chair from the desk and drags it in front of me before dropping into it. Once we're eye to eye, he says,

"There are many among the Seven who want a change, but few who are as brave as Sol. We could make it happen if Erith were out of the picture. Sol has been pushing for reform for decades and gotten nowhere because everyone is too afraid to stand against our father. And now that she has something of her own to lose . . ." He blows out a breath.

"You never wanted me dead."

"I tried to tell you that before." He shakes his head. "I need you too much."

"For your daughter?"

He stares at me with wide eyes, and I can feel the panicked beat of his heart as if it were my own. When he finally speaks, his voice is a low rasp of desperation. "*Anything* for her."

"Erith can't be killed by anyone but me, can he?" I ask. "I can kill him, and when your daughter is grown, she could too—if he lets her live that long."

He takes half a step back. "So you know?"

I shake my head. "Not enough. I'm just trying to piece it all together."

He licks his lips and looks toward the window thoughtfully. "When the oracle told our father that our mother would give him twins, a boy and a girl, and the girl would kill him, only some of that information was new to him."

"What do you mean? Had it already been prophesied?"

"Our father has never been satisfied with his lot in life. He was given the power of the Seven, and he wanted more. He was given the immortality of the fae, and he wanted more. Godlike power, godlike immortality. He would have done anything for that.

"Long ago, after Father had ascended to the Seven but before he had been named as patriarch and before there was any prophecy about him being killed by his daughter, he found an evil, ancient spell that would give him true immortality and magical power greater than anything we've ever seen. To this day, no one can prove what he did or what—or rather *whom*—he sacrificed for it, but I've had my suspicions for years, and I think the source of his sacrifice is the source of his greatest weakness."

"What do you mean?"

He swallows, gaze still unfocused, as if he's looking back into a time long ago. "I don't think you were his first daughter. When I was young, Mother was not well, and Father would send her away for long stretches of time. To 'heal' her, he said. He wanted everyone to believe she was crazy, but I think he made her that way. I've found evidence that he sacrificed their firstborn—a daughter. He cast a spell for power and immortality well beyond what the gods would naturally gift the fae, but the crux of the spell was the unthinkable: offering his daughter, a mere babe, in exchange for the power he sought."

My stomach pitches, then I shake my head. "He wouldn't have been able to ascend if he'd done that."

Konner holds my gaze. "Except he would've already been one of the Seven at this time."

My heart feels too clunky in my chest. Like a smashed wheel that is fighting to turn. A sister. We had a sister that he sacrificed for nothing but power.

He gives a subtle nod, as if he can see my thoughts on my face. He probably can. "I think our mother knew that and that's why she risked her own life to protect you when we were born."

"What kind of horrible magic works in such a way?"

"The kind that is very old, very dark, and very ugly," Konner says. "And anyone who wields it becomes the same. The hunger for power like that is a curse. There's never enough."

It might be a curse to him but it's worse for the rest of us. He destroyed our mother. Killed our sister. And Elora is falling apart under his rule. "What can we even do in the face of that kind of power? That kind of evil? He's a true immortal, then?"

"Close, but no one but the gods can be a *true* immortal. He can be killed, but only in two ways, the first being the sacred Sword of Fire, which Mordeus promised to return to him if he brought him back to rule from the Unseelie throne. His other weakness was a punishment for what he was willing to sacrifice. He could be killed by a female down his bloodline."

"*Any* female," I say. "Meaning that if he knew about Leia, he'd have her killed." Imagining anyone hurting that precious curly-haired baby makes my chest ache. I can't imagine having something that precious brought into your life knowing there's someone who wants to take it away.

Konner closes his eyes, and for a beat I see years of worry written on his face. "Yes."

As ridiculous as it is in the face of all this horrible information, I find myself flooded with relief. Relief that the Konner in this world isn't so different from the one in the illusion. Relief that my brother is a good enough male to want to stop my father. "And that's why you captured me? To keep me alive so I could kill him before he found out about your daughter."

He nods. "I knew you hated me, that you believed I was your enemy, and that you were raised to hate everything the Magical Seven stood for. I hoped that what I planted in your mind would help you see I'm nothing like Erith."

"But how could I trust that when I had no reason to believe I could trust you?"

"I get that, but if that king hadn't shown up, if I'd had a chance to talk to you . . ." He stands and starts pacing again. "I was jealous when I found out about you. Jealous that you got to have a family—a real family, not this toxic servitude our father tries to pretend is family. I wished that Mother's nursemaid would've sent us both away." He straightens and his wistful expression fades. "Our father is a monster. He's exploited so many in Elora and still he's hungry for more power. I know you fear him, but if you will do this, I will be by your side. I will protect you with my life. Because by protecting you I'm protecting my daughter."

It's not that simple, I want to argue. *I can't risk Hale*, I want to argue. But can I risk that sweet baby girl? My niece? Hale's fate can change. We have the advantage of forethought to protect him, but so long as Erith lives, my niece will always be in danger.

How ironic that when Hale finally agrees that I shouldn't kill Erith, I find myself wanting to risk it. "We'll find a way," I finally say. "I won't let him take another family member from me."

The relief on Konner's face is immense, and I feel it too. After years of running from my fate, it almost feels good to embrace it.

"I need time to prepare and to speak with my friends"—*time to find a way to protect Hale*—"but I'll find a way."

"Erith's away for now. All we know is that he'll be gone

until Mordeus's return—that he's facilitating the resurrection somehow—and that he left that prick Seamus as his proxy. Wherever he is he's using so much of his already considerable magic that he can't monitor what's happening here."

I look down at the drink I have yet to taste. "Does that mean if I take my true form, he can't track me?"

"Not until the Unseelie king's resurrection is complete."

The relief of that washes over me like cool water on a hot day. It shouldn't matter in the midst of everything that's going on, but my true form calls to me. Being in my own skin is a comfort I desperately need right now. "That's why you came for me months ago instead of him. He wasn't even tracking me anymore."

"Wherever Erith is, he's confident no one can get to him, including you. Seamus was supposed to be keeping tabs on you, but once I took you from the dungeons of Castle Craige, he couldn't do that anymore. He didn't even know I was the one who had you all that time. He could've had me killed if he'd found out."

"And why Shae—why did Erith give him so much power? Why does he trust him to act in his stead? Is he really so powerful?"

"Seamus is nothing more than a pawn. He offered up information on you and your family years ago to earn Erith's trust, and he's been his devoted sycophant since."

"I thought Mordeus was the one who told Erith about me," I say, searching Konner's face for the lie, part of me hoping I'll find it.

"I'm sorry," he says softly.

Maybe I shouldn't, but I trust him. I drink from the bottle, swallowing the potion fast. It fizzes on my tongue and when it hits my stomach, I immediately feel more alert.

Konner smiles. "See?"

I blink down at myself. "How was that so fast?" I turn the bottle in my hand and study it. "Where did you get it?"

"Our father formulated it. He doesn't have the patience to sleep every time he wants to return to his own form."

"He's an Echo too?"

Konner nods. "Believe me when I say that's the least of his talents."

"What do we do now? What do we do until I can get to Erith?"

He stops pacing and turns to me, chest expanding on a deep inhale. "We do what your people have been waiting so long to do—we set our sights on tomorrow and plan for an Elora without the Patriarch of the Seven."

A crack echoes off the walls. We turn to the door just as Misha throws himself through it, chest heaving, eyes wild. He throws out a hand, sending magic pulsing across the room. Konner flies through the air before hitting the wall and falling to the ground.

"Misha! Wait!"

He throws himself in front of me, still glaring at Konner.

"Don't hurt him." I grip Misha's shoulder. "I'm fine."

He spins and looks me over, blinking when it seems to register that I'm unharmed and in my own form. "You're okay. I've been searching this whole damn palace for you, but you're okay."

Konner gingerly picks himself up off the floor and glares at Misha. "You know how to make one hell of a first impression," he mutters.

CHAPTER THIRTY-ONE

JASALYN

NATAN PLACES HIS HAND OVER the doorknob and it glows red, lighting up the dark stoop of the old cottage.

I look around nervously. "Are you sure this is a good idea?" I ask for the third time.

As Kendrick promised, we waited until after dark to return to the cottage, but we brought Natan with us this time.

"He'll be able to check the house for magic," Kendrick said. I didn't question the vague explanation. Natan seems to always have a way to get more information, and I trust this time is no different.

Unlike earlier, the streets are quiet, but the Fairscape sentinels aren't known for being understanding and I hate to think what could happen to my friends if we're caught.

"Come on in," Natan says, nudging the door open with a smile.

We file into the small cottage, Kendrick staying close to me and Natan making quick work of casting a floating orb of light into the air. I expect the room to be like it was when I was here before, but there's nothing more than the table the witch stood behind when I brought back the book. There's no sign of the tattered library I remember stacked against the back wall, and there are no shelves or apothecary supplies littering the tabletop. "She moved everything out," I say, looking around slowly.

Natan scans the room, then slowly walks its perimeter, sprinkling something along the edge of the floor as he goes.

"That will help him see what kind of magic was used and created in this space," Kendrick explains. "Anything more than common magic will leave its mark behind."

"So you're saying that's magical dust," I say, cocking a brow. "But won't the people looking for magic users notice this?"

"By the time they track it to this cottage, we'll be long gone," Natan says. He dumps the last of the dust and steps into the middle of the room, standing near the table. Right when I'm about to ask what he's looking for, slashes of colorful light streak around the room.

"That's from magic?" I ask, watching the light move. There's a blue streak by the front door and red and yellow particles seem to dance around each other where the apothecary shelves were.

"What does all this mean?" I ask, trailing the moving lights in awe.

"First, you can see that it's Eloran magic," Natan says.

"How do you know that?"

He shrugs. "Lots of experience, mostly. Eloran magic and Faerie magic leave different marks behind. But this"—he points to a swirl of lavender and blue floating in the middle of the room—"this is the trail of Echo magic."

"Echo magic? Like what Felicity does?"

"That's right," Natan says.

"Do you two see that?" Kendrick asks, nodding to a place on the wall where the light outlines what looks like a doorway.

"That wasn't there a minute ago," I say.

Kendrick narrows his eyes. "*That* doesn't look Eloran."

Natan steps toward it and cocks his head to the side. "You're right. I don't remember there being a door here, do you?"

"There weren't any doors. At least none we could see," Kendrick says, stepping up to the outline and pressing on the wall. The wall falls away, and a burst of light fills the room, blinding me to everything else.

When my vision returns, I can make out a small room behind the hidden door, and in the corner, a book sits, calling to me.

"The witch left it here," I murmur, shocked.

"Is that what I think it is?" Kendrick asks.

I nod numbly. "That's the Grimoricon." It's sitting in the corner in its true form, surrounded by magical wards so intense I can feel the energy rolling off them.

"Do you think it's a trap?" Natan asks.

"Oddly, I don't." I remember how it felt to have that book in my hands, remember how it called to me before I picked it up. This time is no different. If anything, it's stronger now—that rightness and sense of home. Maybe because of my connection to Mab. Maybe because the book literally contains the keys to my salvation.

"Why would she leave it here?"

Giddiness bubbles in my chest. "She wouldn't have. Not unless she didn't have a choice. Not unless it refused to go with her." Natan and Kendrick are both staring at me, waiting for an explanation. "It changes forms. When I brought it here, it fought like mad to avoid going to the witch."

"It will take some time to pull down those wards," Kendrick says. "Maybe you should go back to the house until—"

I shake my head. "Can you tell if those wards are set to keep us out or keep the book in?"

Kendrick extends a hand, then takes one of mine and stretches it forward. "You tell me. What do you feel?"

At first I don't think I can feel one way or another, but I focus and realize there's an energy that's pulsing outward. "They're keeping us out, which means the book can come to us."

Kendrick nods. "How are you going to—Jasalyn, what are you doing?"

I step into the room, getting as close to the wards as possible. Dropping to my knees, I click my tongue like I'm calling to a cat.

"Be careful," Natan says. "If you touch those wards, they could hurt you."

I glance at him over my shoulder. "Hurt me how?"

"Depends on the magic. Some burn, some snap bones, some get into your head and plant horrific nightmares, some just throw you across the room. None of the possibilities are a good time."

I nod as if this makes perfect sense. "If we make it through this, I want you to teach me how to make wards like that." I tsk a few more times, then start humming under my breath. It's an old song my mother used to sing to us at bedtime.

"We've gotten this far," Kendrick says. "A few more hours to bring down the wards won't—"

The book transforms into a long-haired gray cat who licks her paws.

Kendrick curses. "What just happened?"

"Come here, baby." I extend a hand as close to the wards as I dare, cringing at the repulsive energy that tells everything in me to back away. "Let's take you home."

The cat yowls, and her tail flicks like she's swatting away flies.

"I'm sorry," I tell her. "I should never have given you to that mean witch. I promise it won't happen again."

This time her meow is more curious than angry, and she ambles toward me, hesitating before she reaches that wall of magic.

"It's okay," I whisper. "You can come here. I just can't go there."

She leaps into my arms, and I barely react fast enough to catch her.

"Gods above and below," Kendrick mutters. "You just sweet-talked a book into coming to you."

I scratch the cat behind her ears as I stand. "She's partial to Abriella and me—partly because of the enchantments Abriella placed on her and partly because of our lineage."

"Are we going to carry the cat when we ride back to Amelia's?" Natan asks.

Suddenly my fingers are scratching at nothing, and the cat is gone. In my palm is a golden locket on a long chain.

Kendrick releases a puff of air. "Look at that. I think she wants you to wear her."

I slip the locket over my head and back out of the tiny room.

Natan waves a hand and the colorful lights fall away. "We

should get out of here before someone from the Seven's legions comes to investigate the magic we just used."

"But we still don't know where to find the witch," I protest, reaching for the locket for comfort. "If the witch was using Echo magic, then what she looked like isn't relevant at all. She could've been anyone."

"Yes and no," Kendrick says. "That is an exceptionally rare gift. There are maybe half a dozen living fae who possess it." He looks at Natan, who nods.

"I'll have a list for you by morning," he says.

"Wouldn't the fae with this gift keep it a secret?"

"Generally speaking," Natan says, "but I wouldn't have a job if I wasn't best at finding information that's believed to be secret."

Kendrick squeezes my hand. "We'll also head for the oracle first thing. She'll be able to help us."

I should school my expression, but I can't find the energy and feel my face fall. "And while we're there, you can ask about your queen and your crown."

Kendrick takes my chin in his hand and tilts my face up to his. "I will ask her how I can support Elora without betraying my own heart."

Natan clears his throat. "I'll wait out front."

I don't bother watching him leave. I'm too busy soaking in the determination in Kendrick's eyes. Exhaustion and relief run tandem through my blood, sapping all the adrenaline away. I lean back against the wall, muscles limp.

He braces his hands on either side of my head and leans over me, dimples flashing as he studies my face, then the locket I keep twisting in my hand. "You did it. You got it back."

I bite my bottom lip and press my hand to my chest, where hope bubbles like sparkling faerie wine, just as intoxicating. "I feel good about this. I feel . . ." I squeeze my eyes shut but can't hold back my smile. "I'm hopeful for the first time in a long time." When I open my eyes again, he's staring at me, something like awe in his eyes. "What is it?"

"Your smile. I forgot how much it lights up the room. It could light up the whole damn world if you wanted it to."

My cheeks heat and I bow my head. "You're the one with the dimples people swoon over."

His mouth twitches, like he's trying to keep those dimples from showing and failing. "Anyone in particular doing that swooning?"

I roll my eyes. "Are you fishing for compliments when I just gave you one, Kendrick?" I smack his chest playfully and he grabs my hand and holds it still against the steady beat of his heart.

He searches my face before letting his gaze fall to my lips. I tilt my face toward his, and he wastes no time lowering his mouth to mine, the warmth of his lips melting my already loose muscles completely.

"That will never get old," he says, smiling against my mouth before tugging me out of the cottage and into the cool night air. With my hand in his, I realize, the dark doesn't bother me much at all.

CHAPTER THIRTY-TWO

FELICITY

Konner gave me riding pants and a tunic to change into since Sol's dress wasn't exactly giving me the room I needed to move freely, then we agreed to meet at Castle Craige at first light to convene with Sol. Konner said he had his own way of getting there, though he refused to divulge what it was, and Misha and I decided that using the Hall of Doors was still the fastest and safest way for us to return to Faerie. Much like the first time, I was ready to get out of the Hall the moment we stepped into it.

"Why are we heading back to the palace instead of going straight to Castle Craige?" I ask on our way back to the Midnight Palace. It's past sunset, and I can imagine how irritated Sol is to still be waiting for Misha.

As soon as we stepped back through the portal and into the mountain ridge by the River of Ice, Misha let out a low whistle that brought a wild horse trotting up to us. He nuzzled Misha's hand and patiently allowed us to climb onto his back. Misha explained it was one of his gifts, but when I asked why those gifts didn't include the ability to call a horse for each of us, all I got was a wink and an extra squeeze from the arm he had looped around my waist.

"I have a standing portal between the Midnight Palace and Castle Craige that we need to use to get back."

I crane my neck to look up at him. "You too, huh?"

"What?"

"My brother doesn't trust goblins, but I didn't realize you felt the same."

His jaw ticks. "My goblin isn't responding to my summons at the moment."

I shift my weight to one hip to get a better view of his face. "Why not? Do you want me to call mine?"

"Do you *want* to call yours?" he asks, brushing his thumb across my ribs. "Because there was nearly an hour in that palace where I was pretty sure I lost you, and I'm enjoying the reassurance of having you in my arms."

My whole body goes taut, then loose all over. "I was never truly in danger. Not from anyone but Shae, at least."

"He's the one who betrayed your friends, isn't he? The one they believe called the wyvern's attack?"

I give a jerky nod.

"How long have you known him?"

"Since I was a kid. He was one of Hale's friends, but I . . ." I shake my head. "I fancied myself in love with him, but I realize now that I was in love with the idea of him. He was always a little edgy, a little dangerous, and because his parents were killed when he was young and he was brought up by a cousin of his mother's, I thought he might understand me in a way the others couldn't."

"Did you feel misunderstood a lot?"

"Not exactly. Just a little out of place. I always felt like the

Kendricks were doing me this big favor by taking me in."

"Did they make you feel like that?"

"Never them. Neighbors said some things. And then when Erith found out about me and one of his sentinels killed my father—my adoptive father . . ." I draw in a steadying breath. "They didn't have to say anything then. I knew what I'd cost them."

"Did you and Shae ever . . ."

I cough out a laugh. "Are you kidding me? I was this wide-eyed little girl waiting for him to notice me, and he never did. At least not until I was in Jasalyn's body." I flick my gaze up to him and then away. "I won't pretend I didn't like the attention it brought me—being beautiful like her—but there's a cost to attention you get for false reasons. I knew that before you, but what happened between us was a much-needed reminder that the life I live in someone else's skin is never truly my own. Even if part of me longs for it to be."

"Odd to hear you say it that way. I don't think Jasalyn's life is anything to be envious of."

I feel a flood of sympathy for the girl I've gotten to understand through her dreams. "It's not. Life has been cruel to her in many ways. What I really mean is that it was easy to wish I could look like her all the time. I haven't had more than a couple of days in my own skin since I was sixteen—not while I was conscious, at least—and that means I never had the chance to come to terms with my body."

"I don't understand that," he says. "You've said it before—that you'd like to look like Jas." His voice dips a little lower, a little softer. "Why would you want to change anything about yourself?"

I open my mouth, then snap it shut again. I wish I could see his face. I'm almost positive that's a trick question. "You can't deny you looked at me differently when I was in her form."

"You only say that because you don't know how I would've looked at you as you are."

Why are you saying these things? Why are you making me wish for things I can't have? "I suppose we'll never know."

"My point is, you shouldn't want to be anyone but yourself. Not even for a minute." He tucks his face into my neck and breathes deeply, making me shiver with want.

We ride the rest of the way in a silence loaded with so much tension that by the time Misha urges the horse to stop at the palace gates I feel like I might explode from being so close to him and wanting so much more than his arm around my waist and his thighs bracketing mine.

Misha dismounts, and when he reaches up to help me down I hesitate, fully expecting to feel awkward about my body under his hands, but then his hands are on my hips and they don't make me feel too big or too wide. They curl around me and make me feel like I'm exactly what I need to be.

When he guides me down, I keep my eyes on him, and I could swear the thrum of his pulse in his neck quickens.

"Thank you, Loki," he murmurs to the horse, giving it a quick pat on the hindquarters before it races back to the woods.

"Loki?" I ask. "How do you know his name?"

His eyes crinkle in the corners. "Because he told me." He leads me through the gates, exchanging brief greetings with the sentinels on guard before pulling me around to a stone fountain in the garden. "Ready?" he asks, nodding to the pooling water.

"That's the portal?"

"The energy from the flowing water helps keep it charged so I only need to use my magic to open and close it upon use. It's significantly less cumbersome than creating a new portal each time."

I'm not keen on the idea of getting soaked and wonder how he'd feel about me circling back to the suggestion that we call on my goblin.

He chuckles when he sees my hesitation. "I promise none of the water will touch you. You'll be as dry when you arrive as you are now."

"If you say so."

He takes my hand, as if it's the most natural thing in the world, and we step over the ledge of the fountain together. He's right. I don't feel the water, but it doesn't feel like any other portal I've used before either. While most portals feel like taking a step from one spot right into another, this one yanks us back mid-step and we tumble, falling onto the cold, rocky ground in a space that is definitely not part of his castle.

Misha jumps to his feet, jaw tense as he surveys the craggy cliffside.

"Where are we?"

"Not at Castle Craige." He tugs a hand through his hair and mutters a curse.

"I noticed." I stand and brush the dust from my pants. He looks more angry than surprised. "What's happening, Misha?"

He swallows hard and his jaw ticks. "My magic is . . . it's not cooperating."

"What do you mean by that?"

"Some of my magic isn't mine alone. It comes from my court. It's the magic the land grants to the king and queen so that they may protect their people." He scoops a handful of rock from the ground and waves it beneath his nose before dropping it back to the ground. "For several months now, I've been having some trouble harnessing that magic consistently."

He looks around and sighs. "And now we're stuck here for the night because goblins won't travel to this part of my court. I won't have the strength to get us back to the castle until I get some sleep."

"Do you know where we are?"

"Yes. That, at least, I am useful for." He crooks a finger at me, then nods to the boulder just in front of him. "I'll show you."

When we climb atop it, I can see a panorama of the sun setting over the distant mountains. Misha steps up behind me and loops an arm beneath my chest. "See that mountain ridge down there that looks almost blue?"

I close my eyes for a beat, loving the warmth of his back pressed against me. Misha's close. And not just close to whatever form I happen to be in. He's close to *me*. "Yes," I murmur, forcing myself to focus.

"In the morning, fog rises off them, and it looks like smoke. They're called the Blue Smoke Mountains. Judging by how distant they look from here, I'd say we're in the far west of my territory." He drops his arm from around my waist and I immediately miss it.

When he steps away, I turn to him. "Sol will be wondering where you are, but at least the sun hasn't set yet. How long will it take us to get back to the castle if you called a wild horse in?"

He shakes his head. "Too long, even if it weren't this close to dusk. We're better off staying here for the night." He scans my face, as if trying to gauge my reaction to this. "My greater magic may be lessening, but I promise I'm still strong enough to keep you safe in my own mountains."

I'm still stuck on spending the night with Misha after the things he said to me on our ride to the Midnight Palace, but I say, "I never doubted it."

His gaze softens, and his eyes flit over me again and again.

"What?" I ask.

"I don't think I've ever seen anything as beautiful as you in this moment." His tongue touches his lip. "You're stunning in the light of the setting sun."

I'm still searching for a way to reply to this when he turns, jumps down from the boulder, and starts collecting what I can only assume are supplies for a fire. I watch him work for a minute, then gather with him, earning a wink and a smile. He waves me over toward a soaring pine and I make piles of kindling, sticks, and small logs while he trims low branches on the pine tree, carving out a little shelter.

"It'll keep the wind off us," he says before turning to build the fire.

"Come here," Misha says, patting the ground between his legs. The sun has fully set and we're settled around the fire he skillfully assembled in the cave-like space he created for us beneath the soaring pine. "You'll be warmer if we stay close."

I scoot closer until we're shoulder to shoulder. "I didn't realize how cold it gets in the mountains at night," I say, shivering.

He chuckles. "That's not going to do much." He shifts and the next thing I know, he's sitting behind me, my backside snug between the V of his thighs. It's like we're on the horse again, only this time we have the crackling fire before us and the stars peeking through the branches above.

My pulse kicks up. There is absolutely no way I can play this cool, but I'm going to try. "I swear if I didn't know better, I'd think you were trying to seduce me, King Misha."

I feel his warm breath in my hair and his chest shake against my back. "I promise you that when I'm trying to seduce you, you'll know." He wraps one arm around me, big hand splaying across my ribs. With his free hand, he tucks loose hair behind my ear. "Though if I *don't* plan to seduce you, sitting with you this close might be a special kind of torture."

My stomach swoops. "Might? You're not sure?"

He's quiet so long I wish I could take the question back. How embarrassing that I'm pushing him to tell me where he is with all this. "It's been a big day for you—with your brother and Shae and . . ." His arm tightens around me. "If your mind's a little fuzzy because of all that, no one could blame you. So, no. I'm not sure. As much as I'm dying to touch you, *really* touch you, I don't want to take advantage of how vulnerable you are right now."

I turn, rolling to my knees so I'm kneeling between his spread thighs before pointedly arching my brow. "I think you're projecting."

His lips twitch. "You do? Please, indulge me."

I lift one shoulder in a half-hearted shrug, as if this isn't exactly what I've been wishing for since . . . well, since the first time I laid eyes on him, if I'm honest. "I had a lot happen today. It's true. But I'd argue that of the two of us, you're the one who's vulnerable right now."

He props his hands behind him and leans back. "Me? Vulnerable? This I have to hear."

"Well, yeah. You have the whole *I am king* business, but right now those kingly powers aren't even working properly. I'm guessing that delivers a pretty hefty blow to your ego, and while I'm sure it would be much easier to get around without that thing weighing you down, I can't imagine what this would do to your confidence. And given how *old* you are, you might even have trouble—"

He cuts me off with his mouth. A hard kiss that is somehow simultaneously playful and demanding. He guides me down, leading me onto my back and repositioning our bodies so he's hovering over me. When he pulls away, he can't seem to tear his gaze away from my mouth. "I promise, I will have *no* trouble."

I shift beneath him, drawing a knee up so he can settle between my thighs. I feel the proof of his claim pressing into me and draw in a ragged breath.

"I'll admit that I'm perhaps a little vulnerable," he says, his voice suddenly soft. He scans my face. "I've dreamed of you. This face. These eyes." He dips his head into the crook of my neck and breathes me in like I am oxygen and he's been starving for air. "Your smell." He props himself up on his elbows and stares down at me, lust darkening his eyes.

I'm afraid to move. Afraid to blink. Afraid this will all turn out to be *my* dream.

He cups my face in his big hand—thumb tracing across my cheekbone, then along my jaw. "Do you have any idea what a kick in the gut it was to see you like this the first time?" He leans forward and trails the bridge of his nose over mine, our breath mingling, his lips so close. "I had all these feelings for you that I couldn't trust because you weren't who you'd claimed to be."

"I'm sorry."

"I understand now."

But maybe I need to share some of my vulnerability too. "When you saw me like this the first time, you asked if my appearance was supposed to be a joke." I feel his surprised inhale, but make myself continue. "That hurt, Misha. And I've been carrying that around."

He opens his mouth and then snaps it shut again, pure confusion written on his face. "I don't think you're hearing me. When I say I dreamed of you, I don't mean after you went missing. I dreamed of you before you ever came to my castle. After I locked you up and saw you like this the first time, I thought you'd gotten into my head somehow. You were her. You were the female I'd dreamed of so many times. The one I'd convinced myself . . ." He swallows. "I didn't think I'd ever see her outside my dreams, and there you were. I thought you were being cruel. Thought you were taunting me by appearing as the female I'd never met but pined after for months."

I swallow. "So you weren't disgusted by me?"

His eyes go wide. "Are we even speaking the same language?"

His eyes scan my face, down to my breasts and back up. "No. Not at all. Never."

"It's just those words..."

"Were horribly out of context, and I'm sorry." He skims his thumb across my bottom lip. "I thought you were my enemy and when I saw you like this, I wanted you more than ever. You're beautiful, Felicity." He pulls back enough to sweep his gaze down the front of me. "What I feel for you doesn't change when you're in a different form, but when I see you like this, as you truly are, it's as if the clouds have parted."

"Don't just say things like that." My chest is so full of need I can barely breathe. I slide my hand behind his neck and pull him close again.

He leans his forehead against mine and smiles down at me. "If it's not words that you want, is there something else I could offer?"

"Why do you think I was in your dreams? What was I doing?" The corner of his mouth lifts in such a mischievous smirk my cheeks go molten. "That's... well... I suppose I didn't need to feel insecure about that, then."

He rasps out a laugh. "Not at all." He cups my face and strokes his thumb up the column of my neck. "As for the why, I asked myself that for months, and before I saw you like this the first time, all I could figure was that you were some manifestation of my subconscious. That I was lonely and my sleeping mind tried to fix that by giving me this beautiful female whose presence made me feel warm and lustful and... *happy*—content in a way I'd never felt in my waking hours."

"And what do you think now?"

He's quiet for a long time, his expression turning solemn. "I think you were a promise from the Mother. I think she wanted me to know my partner was coming. That with you I wouldn't have the love I'd always hoped to find but something even better."

I slide a hand behind his neck and pull his mouth down to mine, nipping at his lips and savoring the feel of his weight pressing into me.

While we kiss, his hands work their way down the front of me, loosening the laces at the front of my shirt, and I tug his tunic from his pants. He pulls back to let me lift it over his head and toss it to the side. I lift off the ground enough to pull my arms from my sleeves and let my shirt fall to the ground. When I lie back down, he doesn't follow.

Maybe I would feel uncomfortable or insecure, maybe I would feel anything other than undiluted need, if it weren't for the way he looks at me, his gaze sweeping across every dip and curve of my exposed flesh.

"I was wrong," he says, gaze scraping over me with so much intensity I shiver. "I thought you framed by the sunset in my lands was the most beautiful thing, but this"—he cups my breast and sweeps his thumb across the sensitive peak—"you in the firelight, under my hands? Stunning."

Something like bliss blossoms in my stomach, and I think I'm shaking. Not with nerves. With need. With joy. I want to pull him back to me, to kiss him again, but I don't. I wait and let him look at me the way I never would've imagined wanting anyone to look at me. Not the real me.

When he finally lowers to me again, I thread my fingers

through his hair. He skates his mouth along my jaw, down my neck, and back up, tongue flicking across my earlobe before he pulls it between his teeth, drawing a gasp from my chest. As if he needs his mouth to explore every inch his eyes just did, he travels down my body and across my chest, teasing my breasts with such skill I can't focus on anything but how to breathe. He glides his lips across the softness of my abdomen and curls his fingers into the waistband of my riding pants.

He removes them, following his hands with his mouth. Every part of me gets different treatment. I get the scrape of his teeth across the swell of my hips, and the barely there skim of lips and warm breath down the sensitive skin of my inner thighs, a sweep of the bridge of his nose along my shin. When he's kneeling between my feet, he tosses my pants to the side and pauses again. Looking.

Now I'm sure I'm trembling, but I'm no longer nervous about what he thinks of my body, not when the truth is so apparent in his eyes.

He shucks off his own pants before lowering back onto me, and his skin is so warm against mine I can't believe I ever worried about the cold. It could be snowing, and I probably wouldn't notice.

"Too fast?" But he says it like he's asking permission to breathe.

I shake my head and hold his gaze. There's nothing between us, and I've made myself so vulnerable by letting him look the way he did, speaking my truth feels simple in comparison. "I've wanted you for a long, long time," I say. "But tonight, it's different than wanting." I search his patient face. "I need you. I need this."

His kiss is so gentle, his movements so precise. It isn't my first time, but I find myself wishing it were. Not because I think I lost something when I slept with the neighbor boy back home, but because my first time was nothing like this. The tenderness and the care. I've spent far too much of my life believing I was disposable, but in Misha's arms, as he looks into my eyes and joins his body with mine, I feel nothing but precious.

CHAPTER THIRTY-THREE

JASALYN

"We need to stop," Kendrick says after a day of traveling through Fairscape on horseback. The sun is sinking toward the horizon and since there are no ley lines to the oracle, we've been traveling since sunrise. "You're exhausted."

"I can keep going."

He absently strokes my stomach with his thumb. "I could use a full night's sleep too, and I know a place ahead."

My stomach knots at the idea of waiting until tomorrow to see the oracle when we only have three days left, but I know he's as anxious as I am. "If we keep going, could we get there tonight?"

It's just been the two of us all day. Kendrick sent the others back to the Midnight Palace with the Grimoricon so Brie could start combing it for the answers they need. They tried to object, to insist Remme stay with us, but when Kendrick pointed out that taking more than two people to the oracle at once is asking for trouble, they stopped arguing.

"I won't take you to her mountain after dark. It's too dangerous."

I nod. "Okay. Maybe we can get up early enough to make it there by sunrise?"

He presses a kiss to the side of my neck. "I promise I'll get you there." His hand slips under my shirt and his thumb strokes the underside of my breast. "But after riding so close to you all day, I need the break too."

"Is it that bad?" I joke. "I promised I bathed this morning."

He tucks his fingers beneath the waistband of my pants and groans against my neck. "Dare I confess to you how many times I've wanted to stop at a passing just to have you under me again? I thought waking you before the sun would help get me through the day, but it's only making it harder."

My cheeks heat as I remember the way he woke me—slowly and patiently, with exploring hands, then lips, then tongue. By the time I was fully awake, he was kneeling on the floor with my hips on the edge of the bed and kissing me in ways that made the world disappear around us.

"I can't stop thinking about the way you taste." He sucks gently on the side of my neck, his fingers brushing just below my waistband, and I shiver in his arms.

He guides the horse down onto a dirt road and then spurs her ahead, pushing her to ride faster. I cling to his arm, holding on for dear life as he makes us both greedy for a private room, kissing and touching me for the rest of the ride.

When he finally slows the horse to a trot, we're riding through a field of wheat and there's a farmhouse in the distance.

"Whoa," Kendrick murmurs, pulling on the reins and bringing the horse to a halt. He pulls his hands from underneath my clothes and smooths them down before dismounting.

"What is this place?" I ask, looking around as he helps me to the ground.

"This is my home," he says, eyes bright, then nods to the back porch, where the door stands ajar. "This is where my mother lives."

"You didn't!" I smack him in the stomach, then regret it when my hand meets a wall of muscle. "You could've warned me."

He grabs my hand and grins. "What's the problem, Slayer? Nervous about meeting my mother? I promise she won't hurt you. She's protective of her children but—"

"I look like I've been to the Underworld and back!" I brush my ride-mussed hair from my face. "No, I look like something that crawled out of the Underworld!"

He rakes his gaze over me. So slowly my cheeks heat. "I had no idea that place had so much to offer."

"Stop," I squeal. "This is serious."

He's still grinning as he bends, his mouth brushing my ear as he whispers, "She's going to love you because I love you. That's all it takes."

"Hale?" a female calls from the door. She has light brown hair and rosy cheeks, and while she has the rounded ears of a human, I know it's just a glamour to protect her in a realm that doesn't welcome the fae. "Is that really you?" she asks.

He gives me a final encouraging look before turning to the door, my hand still in his. "Mom."

"Oh, the gods are good," she says, rushing toward us with open arms.

Kendrick releases my hand and catches her in a big hug, lifting her up off the ground. When he returns her feet to the earth and draws back, tears are streaming down her cheeks.

"Is it finally done?" she asks. "Can you and Lis come home now?"

His face falls but he schools his expression so quickly I wonder if I even saw it. "Not yet, Mama. We're still figuring it out."

"But you're here, and who's this?" She offers me her tiny hand and I shake it self-consciously. "I'm Georgie."

"This is Jasalyn Kincaid," Kendrick says, and if his mother is waiting for a label to explain my relationship with him, she doesn't get it. What would he call me anyway? *Friend* is too weak a word and *girlfriend* seems ridiculous given how painfully temporary this may all turn out to be.

"The princess," she says, no small amount of awe in her voice. "The oracle said you could help us."

I note that she doesn't use specifics. Because there are people listening or because using Erith's name could trigger some sort of magical surveillance?

"I wish to," I admit, glancing to Kendrick. "But nothing has yet worked the way we hoped it might."

"Hale will figure it out," she says. "He always does."

Kendrick takes my hand again and Georgie's face twists into a nervous grimace. "Oh dear."

"What's wrong, Mom?"

She looks back and forth between us before leveling her apologetic gaze on Kendrick. "A while back I took someone into my care. I couldn't send you word about it for fear of the message being intercepted, but . . . she's here."

My stomach plummets into the soft earth beneath my boots.

A line forms between Kendrick's brows. "Who?"

But I already know, and I hold Georgie's gaze when I say, "Crissa."

Her smile wavers. "You know her?" Her gaze drops to my hand, still in Kendrick's, as if to ask why we're still touching if I know about his betrothed.

Kendrick's hand tightens around mine. "You're sure it's her? Because we've been fooled before."

"Hale . . ." Her gaze bounces back and forth between us. I can't tell if she's confused or upset or feeling guilty. "I'm sure."

I pull my hand from Kendrick's and lift my chin. He's not mine. I've always known he's not mine. "I'd like to see her."

Georgie worries her bottom lip between her teeth. "You're sure?"

"Jasalyn knows Crissa," Kendrick explains. "Mordeus imprisoned them together."

Her mouth forms a small O and then she nods toward the house. "Come this way, then."

Moments ago, I was drinking in every detail of this place. The fields Kendrick grew up running through, the trees he probably climbed with his sister, the porch I can imagine his mother stepping onto to call them in for dinner. Now everything feels gray around me. I shouldn't have let myself get so attached to him. Not when we both knew what was coming.

Yes, he said he plans to talk to the oracle about how he could have a future with me, but is it fair of me to want that from him? She is their queen, and he has dedicated his whole life to becoming their king.

The house is dark and cool, all the shades pulled with none of the wall sconces flickering. It smells like cinnamon tea and fresh bread, and for a beat I imagine a different reality—one where

Georgie was as happy to meet me as she was to see her son, one where she invited us in and served us refreshments as she asked me endless questions about my life and relished the opportunity to get to know the woman her son loves. One where I was a welcome addition and not a problem.

I shake the image away before it can latch on to me and drag me into the darkness.

"How is she?" I ask.

"She's back here," Georgie says, leading us through the house. "Healthier now. She was weak when they brought her to me last month, but she's grown strong with the opportunity to rest and heal."

Kendrick's steps slow until he falls back behind me, but I continue toward Crissa. Toward the reality I should've accepted a long time ago.

Kendrick's mom knocks twice at the door and then opens it a crack. "Crissa? May we come in?"

"Of course." The familiar voice sends me back to that dark dungeon I would've done anything to escape, back to a time when she was the only thing making me hold on.

Georgie pushes the door the rest of the way open, and Crissa comes into view, her long blond hair braided and twisted into a crown atop her head. Her eyes light up, and in a single breath, all my self-pity is forgotten beneath the joy of seeing my old friend. Kendrick saved me in those dungeons. But Crissa saved me first.

Crissa sets her book to the side and stands. "Jasalyn!"

I ignore the feel of Georgie's and Kendrick's eyes on me as I cross the room and Crissa and I embrace each other. She is stronger than the last time I saw her—that time she was so weak from using magic to help me survive.

"It is so good to see you," she says, pulling back and beaming at me. "I knew you'd make it out of there."

"Thanks to you," I say, then chance a glance behind me. "And Kendrick."

Crissa's expression wavers, but she schools it into something unreadable when she gives her attention to her future king. "Hello, Hale. It's good to see you are well."

"Same, my queen." His face reveals a jumble of emotions, but he lowers himself onto one knee and bows his head, and I feel it like a knife dragging through my gut.

The silence is so tense, it thrums through the room.

"Please stand, Hale," Crissa says softly. "You never need to bow to me. The oracle named you as my equal."

The way I spin and rush from the room is probably rude. It's definitely unfair. But I'm going to be sick if I observe another second of this reunion.

Half an hour later, Kendrick finds me on the back porch, looking out toward the swaying fields of wheat.

"I'm sorry," he murmurs. "I had no idea. I . . ."

I wrap my arms tighter around my chest, as if putting pressure on my aching heart might stop the hemorrhaging. "You don't owe me an apology."

He brushes my shoulder. I flinch, and he jerks his hand away. "She and I talked. I explained our plans to visit the oracle."

"We planned that when we thought she was missing. The

fact that she's not is something to celebrate."

"I agree, but it doesn't change anything between us."

I can't look at him. Not if I want any chance of holding myself together. "You're not mine, Kendrick. I've always known you weren't mine."

He takes me by the shoulders and slowly turns me to face him. I stare at his chest, afraid I might break if I look into those blue eyes. "But I am," he says. His hands slide down my arms and he steps closer until I surrender and lean against him. He threads his fingers into my hair, pressing a kiss to the top of my head. "What you think you know is irrelevant. I am wholly and completely yours and no matter what the oracle says, no matter what is or isn't tattooed on my skin, that will be true until I draw my last breath, and it will still be true when I roam the lonely fields of the Twilight waiting for the moment my soul meets yours again."

I can feel Crissa's eyes on me as I move through the room, preparing for bed. I pretend I don't notice, finish my nightly routine, light a small candle beside my bed to burn through the night, and slip between the covers. "Just turn down the lantern when you're ready to sleep," I say, forcing myself to give her a smile. She certainly deserves more than a little gratitude from me.

"You are in love with him, with Kendrick the Chosen."

I hate that title. Every time I hear it, I'm reminded of who he is and who I'm not. He's not mine and I can't be his. "It doesn't matter," I say.

She douses the lantern between our beds and sits on the edge of hers. "If there is a world where love does not matter, I hope I never have to live in it."

I roll to my back and stare at the ceiling, focusing on the shadows my candle's flame has dancing there. "Kendrick is going to be a great king and you will be a great queen. I can love him and not want to interfere with that. This is about something bigger than me. And besides"—I swallow—"he will make a good husband and you deserve that."

Sighing, she maneuvers under the covers. "You don't need to be jealous of me. What Kendrick and I have been chosen to share—it's nothing like what you two have. I am going to grow old and my king will stay young until long after I'm gone. This is the way it was always done before the Seven came into power. It is the best way to keep a human queen protected. It isn't any kind of marriage I would choose. We can't have children. We won't grow old together. And he'll never look at me the way he looks at you."

I shouldn't ask, but I'm too broken to resist. "And how does he look at me?"

"Like he would climb into the sky and rearrange the stars on your behalf."

My heart twists painfully in my chest as I remember the advice Remme once gave me. *Then you go find yourself a world with a whole new night sky.* I swallow hard. "Why is it like that? A fae king, a human queen?"

"Every tradition from the old times was about protecting the queen. She was to be human so that she would best understand and therefore protect the weakest in the realm, and he was to be fae so he could guard her with his own immortality. He was to marry her so he would always be closer to her than anyone else."

"He will make an amazing king," I whisper. "Elorans deserve the pair of you to lead them into a better era."

"It wouldn't bother me if you wanted to stay—if you remained his lover, even after our marriage."

She doesn't mean to be cruel. It's probably the best offer I could ask for. But I'm not the same girl I was during those years I hid inside my sister's palace. I know my worth now. If I am lucky enough to see a life beyond my eighteenth birthday, I won't disgrace that gift by living in the shadows. I deserve a life in the sun. "I'm not interested in that arrangement," I say as gently as possible, "but there is another way you can help me."

She perks up. "Anything. Tell me."

"Tell me how to reach the oracle."

CHAPTER THIRTY-FOUR

FELICITY

When I open my eyes at first light, a heavy arm is draped over me, a big hand splayed against my belly—my soft belly. *Mine.*

I pull in a deep breath and revel in the way it fills my lungs. It feels so good to be in my own skin I want to stretch like a cat. But I don't want to disturb Misha, who's sleeping behind me. I don't know what to expect when he wakes, and I don't want to miss a single moment of him holding me like this.

He hums and his hand slides up my stomach and between my breasts. His hips shift closer and I'm aware of the hard length of him against me.

My cheeks heat and I clear my throat. "Good morning."

He hums again and nuzzles my nape, then guides me onto my back, bracing himself on his elbows above me. I part my legs, welcoming the weight of him as he settles between them.

I explore his chest, then the breadth of his shoulders, with my fingertips, and he shivers above me.

He trails kisses from the corner of my mouth to my jaw to the crook of my neck, and breathes me in. "This," he says, nipping at the sensitive skin there. "This is what you're supposed to smell like." Pushing himself up onto one palm, he uses his free hand to trace my collarbone.

He trails one finger from the hollow of my neck down between my breasts and to my navel. I arch into the touch, silently pleading for more.

"Does it feel different?" He tracks his fingers as they trace invisible paths across my rib cage and beneath my breasts.

"What?"

He smiles. "When you wake in your true form—does it feel any different than when you're shifted into someone else's?"

"Yes." His touch is inching upward. I can barely breathe, let alone think. "When I'm in another form, everything is somewhat muted. When I'm just me, it's—" His knuckles brush across my breast and I gasp, bowing off the ground.

"It's what?" he asks, as if he isn't the one driving me to distraction.

"It's like the clouds have parted," I say, stealing his words from last night.

"Lucky for us the sun is shining today." He lowers his mouth to my neck. Lower. "The things I want to do to you," he whispers against my skin.

"I think you already did." I arch into the teasing sweep of his lips against my belly.

"I've barely gotten started."

I fell back asleep in Misha's arms, and when I dreamed, it was of his hands on my skin and his promises whispered into my ear.

When the birds wake me at sunrise, I'm alone. I crawl out

from under the protection of the big pine and find Misha sitting on the edge of the cliff overlooking the mountain range below. He looks pensive and I wonder if he's worried about the meeting with Sol today. Or, more likely, worried about whatever it is that's happening with his magic.

"Did you sleep at all?" I ask, crouching to sit on the cool stone beside him.

"Some." He turns his attention to me, and the way his expression morphs from worry to tenderness fills me with warmth. He scans my face over and over, as if he's trying to remember it. "How long do I get to see you like this in the morning?"

I glance down and brush pine needles off my shirt. "By 'like this,' do you mean half-dressed and covered in pine needles, or . . ."

He grins. "Not what I meant, but I'm not complaining about that part either."

"Konner said Erith can't track me from wherever he is until Mordeus completes his resurrection."

He grimaces. "Let's hope it's never complete." He blows out a breath and rolls his shoulders back, as if physically moving into a change of subject. "What about you? How did you sleep?"

"I feel well rested." I smile shyly. "I had someone keeping me warm, though."

He takes my chin in his hand and leans forward to press a kiss to my lips. "I want to do so much more than keep you warm."

My heart tumbles into a sprint. "I want that too," I whisper.

"But how much? Because I'm sitting here this morning wondering how reckless I am to want to give you everything."

There's a riot of spastic butterflies raging in my belly.

"Why do you think I need everything?"

"Last night, you let a king make love to you. It seems unfair that tomorrow you could find me as nothing more than a male who lost it all."

I cock my head to the side, trying to understand everything he's not saying. "Is this about your magic? Do you think your court is in jeopardy?"

His throat bobs. "It's possible. No one in Faerie should assume their kingdom is safe until Mordeus has been defeated."

"Do you think they've had any luck finding the witch and making a new deal?"

"I can only hope." He sighs, brushes his hands on his pants, and pushes to standing. "We should get back to the castle before Sol grows too impatient."

"I apologize for the delay," Misha says as we file into the meeting room where Sol and Konner are waiting. Despite Pretha and Amira's efforts to keep Sol distracted yesterday, there's an undeniable tension shimmering around the table. I might have blamed that on our late arrival if it weren't for the four heavily armed sentinels Misha has stationed in the corners of the room.

Did your parents teach you nothing about hospitality?

He quirks a brow at me. *You didn't expect me to let her run loose around my castle, did you?*

Sol shoots us an accusatory look. "You're lucky you had Konner join us this morning, or I might have dismissed any thoughts of alliance after being brought here on false pretenses and made to wait."

"It was unavoidable, I'm afraid," Misha says. "I had an unexpected complication arise in the western region of my territory. By way of apology, I've brought a couple of friends to join us." He leans his head out into the hall. "We're ready for you."

Sol's glare falls away as the queen of the shadow court glides into the room, red hair loose around her face, posture regal.

"Good morning," Brie says, nodding to our Eloran guests. "Thank you for letting me join."

Behind her, Remme steps in from the hall. Misha and I met with Brie and Remme when we finally made it back to the castle and Misha updated them on what we've learned since we last spoke.

"This is my friend Remme," I tell them as Remme surveys Misha's guests skeptically. "He's here to represent the interests of the Chosen Eloran monarchy."

Konner acknowledges him with a lift of his chin, but I don't miss the look Sol shoots him—a look that says maybe she's not so happy about Remme being here.

"We've caught the queen up on everything Konner shared with Felicity about Erith's special brand of immortality," Misha says. He pulls out two chairs opposite Konner and Sol and nods for Brie and me to sit. Remme sits beside the shadow queen, and I expect Misha to take the seat at the head of the table, but instead he lowers himself next to me. "And we're ready to hear what you have in mind for Elora and how an alliance with the Wild Fae Lands might work," he says.

Sol looks to Brie. "What about the Unseelie Court? Are you offering us an alliance as well?"

Brie lifts her chin. "I would need a great deal more information before I could consider that."

When Sol goes stiff, Konner puts a hand on her arm. "In that case, we're glad you're here."

Sol sighs, directing her attention at Misha. "Luckily for you, I find your sister and former queen quite delightful, and Konner has used his time since arriving to convince me to forgive you for scheming against me and to forgive this one"—she points at me—"for taking my form."

Misha nods to Konner. "I appreciate that, Konner. Thank you for your diplomacy."

Konner glances toward the door. "I appreciate you bringing the shadow queen and a representative from the monarchy, but I'd hoped Kendrick the Chosen himself would be joining us for this meeting."

"He's detained in the Eloran realm at the moment, but we will bring him up to speed when he returns." Misha waves a hand and a breakfast spread appears on the table between us, complete with croissants and pastries, coffee, tea, and juice. "Please help yourselves to some refreshments," he says, taking the pitcher of orange juice and pouring himself a glass.

Konner rubs his eyes. "Given Kendrick's vested interest in the direction this conversation goes, I'm almost willing to wait even longer if it means he can join." Brie leans forward to object and Konner holds up a hand. "But we don't have the luxury of time, so we'll have to do this without him."

I fold my arms. "What do you mean? Aren't we here to talk about how we'll put the Eloran monarchy into power?"

"Unfortunately, no," Konner says.

Remme's chair squeals as he shoves back from the table. "I told Felicity this morning that it was foolish to trust anyone from the palace."

Brie puts a hand on his arm. "Let's hear what they have to say."

Remme huffs but seems to relent. He snags a croissant from the tray in front of him and tears into it without bothering with a napkin or plate.

"It's not that I don't understand the efforts of your people," Sol says. "I get it. The monarchy is what came before the Seven, so in your mind the monarchy is the solution."

"But it *is* the solution," Remme says, tapping his fingers on the table. He looks to Konner. "Even you see what has become of the Seven—or were you lying when you spoke to your sister about this matter?"

"I spoke only the truth," Konner says. "But the old system is too flawed, too vulnerable to exploitation."

Misha narrows his eyes, leaning back in his chair, juice untouched. "*Was* it ever exploited?"

"Why do you think the Seven chose to overthrow the monarchy to begin with?" Sol cocks her head to the side. "My grandmother never would've been part of it otherwise. There's a reason people believe we protected them from the fae—the queen was allowing her allies in Faerie to take our humans, to turn them into their unwilling servants."

Remme opens his mouth to object, but Brie stops him with a hand on his arm again. He glares at that hand.

"Why would the oracle choose someone like that to rule?" I ask.

"She didn't," Sol says. She pours herself a cup of tea from the porcelain pot and takes a sip. "The queen who ruled Elora before the Seven came to power wasn't the one the oracle named. Her king didn't even wear the crown of the Chosen."

"How could that happen?" Remme asks.

"The queen and king of that time were called Cora and Fazal, and they schemed their way into power. They knew the male who wore the crown was in love with someone else, knew he was hiding his crown in hopes of staying with her. He didn't want a life with a mortal wife, not when his heart beat for someone else. And the Chosen queen? She was just a scared mortal girl who had seen her sister captured and abused by a faerie. She was terrified of our kind and certainly didn't want to be married to one. Cora and Fazal made them a deal: They would stand in as the Chosen if the true Chosen rulers signed a magical contract promising secrecy."

"The Chosen couple was willing to risk all of Elora for their personal romances?" Remme asks.

I bow my head, thinking of the conversation I had with Hale before he left for Elora. *Maybe that makes me selfish. Maybe it makes me unworthy of this crown.* He carries so much guilt but even that doesn't outweigh his love.

"Cora and Fazal seemed like they would be ideal leaders. They told the true king and queen about all the ways they wanted to change the realm for the better. Apparently they were quite convincing."

Misha gives a sad smile. "And it's easier to believe something when you want to so badly."

"Yes." Sol sighs. "When everything in Elora turned for the

worse during their rule, the true Chosen couple was bound by the magic and couldn't tell anyone the truth about the two on the throne. When they eventually tried to defy the contract and get the truth out, the magic punished them for it."

"They died," I say, my heart sinking.

Misha narrows his eyes. "If they couldn't share, then how do you know?"

Sadness fills Sol's eyes. "Only through the truth magic of the Chronicles did I learn my grandmother's past and that she was the one the Chosen king loved."

"I am so sorry," I say.

She lifts her chin. "She and her friends made our plan to overthrow the king and queen and close the gates between the realms to protect the humans."

"The original Seven," Remme says, clearly softening to the story.

"Yes," Sol confirms. "But by then the fae had done so much damage they knew the humans would never accept them as fae. The decision to pose as mages seemed harmless. But the power changed some of the original Seven, and they became greedy for more—more power, more wealth, more everything. Corruption is sneaky because it infects in small, seemingly inconsequential ways at first, but suddenly it becomes too big to ignore and it expands from there exponentially." She closes her eyes, lost in her thoughts. "My grandmother confessed in her diaries that she wasn't immune to the siren call of power. She justified many decisions that she regretted in retrospect. Destroying the true history of Elora, for example, seemed like the only way to keep what had happened with Cora and Fazal from happening again."

"That's idiotic," Remme mutters.

"Had her regret been enough to undo the mistakes of the past," Sol says, "we wouldn't be here right now."

"So what are you asking of us?" Misha says.

"Erith is power hungry. We've been unable to change anything about the Seven's rule with him overseeing us—especially since two of my counterparts are devoted to him. And the only way he'll give up his power while he's alive is if he's stepping into a more powerful role." She holds Misha's gaze. "Which, I imagine, is why you're interested in forming this alliance. You have as much to lose as the rest of us."

I look back and forth between them, confused. Does she mean because what affects one court affects all of Faerie?

"Felicity has already agreed to help us take out Erith," Konner says.

Remme snaps his head in my direction.

I meet his eyes. "When the time is right. Only once I've met with Hale, and we've taken precautions to prevent any potential casualties."

You didn't tell me that, Misha says into my mind. *What's changed?*

My niece. I can make efforts to protect Hale from Erith, but I'll never be able to fully protect her so long as my father lives.

"You want us to ally with you and help you take out the other two," Abriella says.

"That's right," Sol says. "In return we will help your realm fight what Mordeus has planned."

"How can you do that?" Brie asks.

"I can offer you the assistance of the Eloran Palace infantry," Konner says. "They've been notified to be ready and can be deployed to the shadow court at a moment's notice."

"Don't they answer to Erith?" Remme asks.

Konner shrugs. "On paper, perhaps that's how it works, but I've trained with these soldiers since I was a boy. I was raised to lead them, and they respect me for that."

Sol takes another sip from her tea. "You also need to understand that the humans aren't the only ones who've been hurt. Many of Konner's fighters have lost relatives who were living in hiding in Elora. When Erith discovered them, he used them to get more powerful."

Brie shakes her head. "How could he use Eloran fae to increase his own power?"

"Where do you think Mordeus learned about blood magic?" Sol asks. "Erith has no boundaries, and there is no limit to his hunger for power."

"It will take time to move the infantry to the shadow court," Konner says, "but if we move now, we can get there before the attack."

"Attack?" Brie meets Misha's eyes for a beat before looking back to Konner. "You're speaking of a specific attack and not just of a vague threat."

Konner holds her gaze. "If Mordeus is successful in taking over your sister's body, he still won't be able to take the throne, not so long as you live. His forces will come for you."

The mix of emotions flashing across the shadow queen's face

make me dizzy. She goes from denial to fear to rage to cool calculation in a beat.

She doesn't want to make plans for what happens if Mordeus is successful, I tell Misha through his mind.

I know. But I also know she will. She takes her duty to her kingdom as seriously as I do mine.

"We will accept the help," Abriella says, scooting her chair back and rising. "Now if you'll excuse me, I need to return to my court."

Remme stands too and opens the door for her. He gives me one last searching look before heading out and my stomach sinks. I don't want to risk Hale any more than he does, but we're running out of options.

"Excuse me. I need to speak with the queen," Misha says, standing to follow Abriella from the room.

When the door shuts behind him, Sol looks at me and her face softens. "I know we're asking you to do something scary, but—"

"I need to speak with my brother first. To make a plan to ensure he's safe while I take out Erith. But I can't ask him to worry about that while he's in the middle of fighting for the love of his life. Erith will have to wait until after the princess's birthday."

She holds my gaze quietly for a long time before nodding. "You met our Leia?"

"I did," I say with a wobbly nod.

"So you know what we're fighting for. You know what's at risk if you don't help us get rid of him."

"I do," I say. "My niece. And all of Elora."

CHAPTER THIRTY-FIVE

JASALYN

THE JOURNEY TO THE ORACLE is exactly as Crissa showed me. She projected the image of the journey into my mind, taking me down the dirt road on horseback and through the deep woods toward the rising sun. She showed me the mountain pass as it would look as it perfectly framed the morning light and the steep path up the side she said I'd have to follow to the plateau of contemplation. From there, she said I would have to "follow my heart" to come face-to-face with the oracle.

As I climb the barren mountainside toward the plateau, my heart thuds heavily in my chest, exertion from the hike and wild nerves making me tremble. I've been watching to make sure I'm not being followed. I haven't seen anyone, but I can't shake this feeling. I keep craning my neck to look over my shoulder to make sure someone—or, worse, some*thing*—isn't at my back.

Just keep going, I tell myself as I reach for a gnarled root to hoist myself up.

In the short hours I let myself sleep last night, I dreamed of a woman with long, colorless hair floating on the breeze around her as she sat on my chest and screeched in my face. She pressed her lips to mine and stole the air from my lungs. Her soft fingers dug into my neck as she cut off my air supply.

Upon waking, I knew who she was. The Banshee. Abriella explained it all when she told me the story of how she got me back from Mordeus.

The Banshee visits when death is coming for you.

Of course it's coming. You traded away your life.

But it's one thing to know that intellectually and quite another to feel the life being drawn from your lungs.

When I spot the plateau, I speed up, ready to leave the steep incline and catch my breath on level ground. I reach for the final ledge and hoist myself up, rolling from my side to my back and away from the edge.

It's when I lie there with my eyes closed that I know for sure. *I'm not alone.* Haven't been this whole time. But I've also not been in danger.

"You can show yourself." I push up onto my palms, chest heaving as I stare ahead—right at the spot where I feel the presence of one very angry Chosen king.

Kendrick's form flickers into view before he becomes fully corporeal.

"I realize you don't remember, but you did this at Feegus Keep as well. Do you make a habit of following people?"

"Only when they're putting themselves in unnecessary danger." He offers me a hand and helps me from the ground. "I would've shown myself sooner, but you were clearly set on doing this alone. Which is something *you* apparently make a habit of." A muscle in his jaw ticks in irritation, but I ignore it. Someday he will appreciate that I stepped out of the way so he could claim his fate.

"You didn't tell me it was such a journey to get here," I say, brushing the rocky dust off my pants.

"I didn't think I needed to since we were supposed to come *together*."

I ignore this and give all my attention to my surroundings. As I walk to the edge of the plateau, my stomach flips at the sight of the drop. One wrong step and I'll plunge thousands of feet down into the rocky ravine below. "I thought it would be better this way."

"Jas..." His boots scuff the ground as he steps closer. "Jasalyn."

Slowly, I lift my gaze to meet his, and the pain on his face cleaves me in two. I don't want to hurt him. I want to make this easier for everyone.

He grips my shoulders. "Would you stop being so gods-damned selfless."

"I don't want you to have to choose between me and Elora. I don't want you to have to choose between me and the future you've worked your whole life to see come to pass." *Especially when I might not be here in a few days' time.*

"How do you not understand"—his calloused fingers sweep up the side of my neck, then slide into my hair until he's cupping my face—"that I've already chosen?"

"What if it's the wrong choice? What if in two days you realize it was a never a choice at all?"

"Don't give up on me," he pleads, expression bleak. "Not now. Not when we've come this far."

I could tell him about the Banshee's visit, her screeches a

promise that death is coming soon. I could tell him the future Crissa offered me and why I can't bring myself to take it. I could tell him how much I love him and how scared I am of what tomorrow might bring. But I don't. I don't have enough time to marinate in my feelings. I don't even have enough time to fix what I broke.

"Can we talk about this after I see the oracle?"

He studies me for a long time, as if part of him knows I'm putting off a conversation I never intend to have. "Sure. I'll go in first."

I look around and realize even after coming all this way on my own, I have no idea where the oracle is. "Go in where?"

He points to the spot in the earth that looks like nothing more than a puddle. "She's down there."

"Is it a portal?"

"Not exactly." He shrugs. "Actually, I don't know for sure what you would call it. Come here. Look at it from directly above."

I stand on the opposite side of the puddle and peer down into the pool—into the ice-blue, swirling depths. "How does she talk to you?"

"Telepathically. It's not always words. Sometimes it's images. Sometimes it's like you're watching a play underwater."

"Can you breathe down there?"

He shakes his head. "No. Some think that's why the oracle chose the water—so their time with her can't drag on. Sometimes when people want to draw out the visit, they stay under too long and pass out." He gives my hand a quick squeeze. "Back up a bit."

I hold my breath as he steps into the puddle, water splashing around his ankles. His face falls.

"Was something supposed to happen?" I ask, looking at his wet boots.

"She won't see me," he says, flexing his hands at his sides.

I frown. "Are you sure this is the right spot?"

He swallows. "Yeah. I am."

It's hard to believe anything else could happen if I step into that puddle, but I didn't come all this way to keep my feet dry. "Let me try."

He steps out of the water, disappointment and worry written all over his face. "If she doesn't consider you Eloran—"

I don't hear the rest of his warning because I'm dropping down into a vortex, the world around me disappearing.

There's nothing but darkness all around me. I turn and flail in the water, trying to push myself back to the surface, but I'm stuck. There is no up or down. No surface, no bottom.

Calm, child. The words are spoken into my mind, the voice soothing and melodic.

What is this? I ask, flailing. *Why is it so dark?*

Because if you want to see your future, you first have to face your fears. You need to sit in the dark until you become it. You need to stop seeking nothing but sunlight when your gifts are born of the shadows.

I stop kicking and will my racing heart to slow. *The darkness reminds me of his dungeons.* I don't bother explaining who *he* is. I have no doubt she knows.

Why? It could remind you of a night in your lover's arms or of your sister's court, of her power. The darkness could be a chance to shine your light. Why give it to him?

It's not that easy.

It's not that complicated either. Tell me why you're here.

I'm looking for the witch I made a deal with. Everyone always speaks of the oracle as a female, and I always pictured a delicate fae female, sitting so serene, but she isn't a person at all. She's a presence. And yet there's no doubt in my mind she is female. *I traded my immortal life—every day after my eighteenth birthday—for a magical ring, and I need to get out of the deal to save my sister. Can you tell me where to find the witch?*

The darkness seems to spin, and suddenly I'm in the throne room at the Midnight Palace and Erith, Patriarch of the Seven, is speaking with Mordeus, hands clasped as they make a deal.

But then it's not Erith. It's the witch. And I know. I know as surely as I know myself that Erith and the witch are one and the same.

Erith is an Echo. Like his daughter.

Which means I'm not looking for a witch at all. It was never some elderly woman from Elora. It wasn't even a faerie glamoured to look human. It was Erith slipping into some unsuspecting human's skin so I'd trust him.

If I want to get out of my deal, I need to find *Erith*.

Do you know what I can offer him? What does he want more than my life and my immortality? There's nothing but empty silence for far too long. *Please. I'm trying to save my sister and her court. If Mordeus takes over, I fear it will be the end of both.*

When the words come, they are in my mind and somehow radiate inside me, like music. *There's nothing you have that Erith wants for himself. He is using you so Mordeus will get him what he desires—power, a crown, and a court of his own to rule.*

I thought Mordeus planned to take my sister's court. Will he share it with Erith?

Mordeus will share nothing, but once the shadow court is back in his control, he will reward Erith for his loyalty by using his legions to usurp the Wild Fae throne for the Patriarch of the Seven.

Misha's court?

The court is vulnerable without a queen to balance the power. Erith and Mordeus will work together to exploit that weakness and Erith will finally have the power he has craved for so long.

I'm so busy trying to process this that I nearly miss her next words as she pours them into my mind.

Unless you offer to kill your sister and then find a way to give Erith the Unseelie throne, you have nothing to give that he wants more than what Mordeus has offered him.

My panic surges. *Nothing to offer him. There's no getting out of this deal.*

No. I can't think about that right now. I need to get back home. I need to warn Misha about what they have planned.

I flutter my legs to kick to the surface, but a vision floods my mind, and I freeze. The Midnight Palace is on fire. Flames lick at the starless night sky, flames so tall and so hot they're unaffected by the pouring rain. The gates are down and bodies litter the lawn. Hundreds of soldiers in olive-green uniforms file into every door, through every window with torches, swords at the ready, the symbol of their allegiance to Mordeus tattooed on their necks.

My sister . . . my sister is strung up on the wall, her lifeless eyes looking into the distance as her palace burns behind her.

CHAPTER THIRTY-SIX

JASALYN

No. My lungs burn like I'm running out of air, and for the first time since I sank to these dark depths, I'm conscious of the water surrounding me. I need to breathe, but I can't go yet. *How do we stop it? When does this happen?*

But it's gone. The vision and the oracle—that feeling of presence faded as quickly as it appeared.

Big hands grab me beneath my arms and I'm yanked from the water, pulled out of the watery tunnel and onto the rocky plateau. The sky blurs in and out of focus above me as Kendrick stares down at me, panic lining his blue eyes.

I open my mouth, but my lungs refuse to take air.

"Breathe!" he commands, shoving me onto my side. "Please, Jasalyn! Breathe!" He squeezes me hard around my rib cage, and I gag and sputter as water lurches out of my lungs.

I stay on my side and curl into a ball as I force myself to take one breath after another.

"That's it," Kendrick says. He rubs my back, his touch soothing and gentle. "Easy now. Slow and steady breaths."

Only when my breathing has evened out does he pull me up

and against his chest. He strokes my hair. "You scared me. You were down there too long. I couldn't get to you, and then suddenly I could, but you were kicking and flailing—fighting me while I tried to pull you out of there."

I bury my face in his chest. *Just one more moment*, I tell myself. *I'll let myself find comfort in his presence for just one more moment.*

I breathe him in, and I don't want to move. I don't want to give him up. I don't want to give any of this up. But I have nothing to offer Erith. All I can do now is protect my sister.

I count to three and make myself let him go.

"What did she say? Did she tell you where we can find the witch?"

I shake my head, confused. It feels like days have passed since I was searching for the witch, since my first priority was finding her. "Erith," I say. The ground feels like it's tilting left to right beneath me, so I drop to a crouch, hands in the dirt, close my eyes, and focus on the rocky earth beneath my knees and palms.

"What about Erith?"

"He's an Echo," I whisper. "He was the witch. And the oracle said I have nothing to offer that he wants."

Kendrick's jaw hardens. "We'll find another way, then. A new deal isn't the only path. We can find a way to trick him out of it. We can—"

"We have to get home." I need this numbness to pass so I can act, but right now it's the only thing keeping me from breaking down. "Mordeus's legions are going to storm the Midnight Palace and crucify my sister."

"She showed you that?" Kendrick stoops to his haunches,

studying me. "We can change what's to come. We'll go back and warn your sister. We'll help her strengthen her wards and then we'll find a way to get you out of this deal with Erith."

I blink up at him. "Erith wants the Wild Fae territory. He wants to rule over fae, not just humans. Misha is in trouble too."

He mutters a curse. "We'll warn him, and we'll warn the queen."

My sister. Every time I close my eyes I see her on that gate, blood spilling from her lips.

Kendrick offers me a hand to help me stand and I take it.

As his gaze shifts to the steep path I traversed to get here, I realize what he's thinking—that we'll have to find our way to a ley line that can get us back to the closest portal.

I grip his forearm. "Kendrick, we don't have time. We have to trust my goblin."

"It's not that I don't trust *him*, Slayer. It's that anything he knows, they all know."

"How long to get back to the shadow court if we don't use goblins?"

He draws in a shaky breath. "Half a day's hike to the nearest ley line that can get us close to an open portal to the Unseelie Court. From there, we'll have to find our way back to the Midnight Palace." He shakes his head. "Late tonight at best."

"We can't afford to lose that much time."

He scratches his beard and releases a breath. "You're right. I don't like giving them anything, but I know you're right. I don't want to lose that time either."

"What if we get as far from the oracle as we quickly can? That way they don't know for sure that we saw her."

He stares down the mountainside and I can practically see him tracing potential routes in his mind. "There's a ley line maybe ten minutes down this path. It won't get us anywhere near a portal to Faerie, but we'll be far away from the oracle when we call for your goblin."

"Good. Let's do that." I move to crouch back onto the ground so I can lower myself off the plateau and back onto the path, but Kendrick catches my arm and pulls me back up.

He studies me for a long time, his expression solemn. "You aren't allowed to give up on me. Just because she couldn't tell you something you could offer Erith doesn't mean there's no way out of this."

The grief in his eyes breaks my heart. I take his face in both hands and hold his gaze. "There is no point in me surviving all of this if everyone and everything I care about are destroyed along the way." I drop one hand to his chest to feel the steady thud of his heart. "We start here, with protecting the people we love and a future worth fighting for, and the rest will work out as it should."

"What about me? What can I say to make you find a way to survive for *me*?"

My mind flashes to the battle the oracle showed me. The bodies littering the corridors of the Midnight Palace. Was that Kendrick among the fallen or is my mind playing tricks on me? Is my panic making me imagine he'd been part of the carnage?

"I have to warn my sister and Misha, but I promise I won't stop looking for a solution. Not until this body is no longer mine."

He draws in a breath, and I realize he hasn't since he asked his question. "Thank you."

I swallow. "Kendrick, I need you to make me a promise too."

I can feel how intently he's thinking, plotting, planning a way to get around my fate. "Anything."

"The moment *he* takes over and I'm gone, I need you to end it. To end me."

He drops his hands from my face and steps back. "Anything but that."

"I know it's not fair to ask you, and if we weren't so close to my birthday, I wouldn't. But there's no one else here right now, and in case something happens and we can't get to the others in time, I need to know it will be taken care of."

He shakes his head. "I can't do that. Don't ask me to do that."

I close the distance between us and this time I take *his* face in *my* hands. His facial hair tickles my fingers. "I'm not asking you to kill me. It won't be me in here anymore, and when that moment comes—when he has taken over this body, I need you to kill him before he can use me more than he already has."

His face crumples, and he squeezes his eyes shut and leans his forehead against mine. "How am I supposed to know that you're gone for good? How am I supposed to be *sure* that you aren't still in there somewhere?"

I thread my fingers into his hair and hold him close. "You'll know. I trust you to know."

"I can't." He cups my face and drops his mouth to mine. His kiss isn't tender or giving. It's hard and demanding. This is the kiss of *stay with me*, the kiss of *please don't go*, and it fractures something inside me.

"I'm sorry," I whisper against his mouth. "I never wanted to hurt you. I never wanted to hurt my sister. But none of that mattered when I made this deal with the witch—with Erith. I just wanted..."

"You wanted to stop hurting." He nods, and when he brushes a kiss over each cheek, I realize tears have slipped from my eyes. "I wish we could go back. I wish I could change so much."

I search his face—taking in all the emotions living there. The love and sorrow and fear and desperation. I recognize each one because I feel them myself. "But we can't. The only moment we can change is this one."

Gommid is his usual grumpy self when he deposits us on the back lawn at the Midnight Palace. "More wards are about to go up," he says, sniffing like he can smell them in the air. "You'll have to go beyond the gates if you call me again."

"Thank you, Gommid." I reach into my pocket and hand him the nail clippings I gathered from the trash at Amelia's. I shuddered in revulsion as I did it, but I knew they'd come in handy.

As soon as he disappears, Kendrick and I head into the palace and straight for Brie's study, where we find her—as I thought we might—poring over the Grimoricon.

Her head snaps up as if she senses me. She hops out of her chair and runs around her desk to pull me into a hug. She squeezes me and I squeeze her—so tightly that I believe, perhaps more than ever, that if love were enough, we wouldn't have to carry a single worry for what's to come.

"I'll be just out here if you need me," Kendrick says, and I nod into my sister's chest, not bothering to release her as Kendrick leaves and the door shuts with a soft snick behind me.

"You're back." Brie strokes my hair and keeps herself curled around me. "You came back."

"I came to warn you," I say, pulling away so I can make sure she's paying attention. "Mordeus's militia is going to attack. I saw the oracle and she showed me."

She closes her eyes for a beat. "I know."

"We can't let them get past the palace gates. They will come for you first."

She gives a pained nod. "Our friends from the Eloran Palace are planning to help."

"*Friends* from the Eloran Palace?"

"Turns out we're not the only ones who want Erith and Mordeus out of the picture." Her throat bobs. "I promise to catch you up, but tell me what happened. Did you find the witch? Did you get out of the deal?"

I wish I could lie to her. Wish I could protect her from what I'm so sure is coming. Instead, I just say, "I saw the Banshee. She sat on my chest and I couldn't breathe. My ears are still ringing from her screeching."

Brie flinches—she knows as well as I do what a visit from the Banshee means—but when she schools her expression, she morphs it into a lighthearted smile. "I keep telling her that's no way to make new friends."

I huff out a laugh. "No kidding."

She tucks a lock of hair behind my ear, smiling when her fingers graze the short buzz of my undercut. "You're saying you didn't find the witch, then?"

"Erith is the witch. He took an old woman's form, but he was the one I made the deal with."

The blood leaves her face but she holds my gaze. "Surely there's something we could offer him?"

I let myself squeeze her one last time. "According to the oracle, I have nothing to offer that he wants, so I'm choosing to focus on what I can control. Tell me how I can help you prepare for this battle."

She looks stricken. "You can't give up that easily."

"I'm not giving up. I plan to fight to the end."

"Natan said there are other ways. He said if we find a way to trick the witch—Erith—we might be able to get you out of this."

"Trick him how?"

"What if he didn't fulfill his side of the bargain?" she asks. The hope in her voice weighs heavily on my heart. "Didn't you say it was supposed to take the fear from your heart, but the magic stopped working? If the ring didn't do as promised, maybe the bargain is already nullified."

I am going to break her because of what I've done. "That wasn't the wording. There was something about 'so long as the magic holds.' I remember that because I remember wondering if that meant the ring wouldn't work forever."

I skim my eyes and fingers over the Grimoricon. "I was hoping you'd find a solution in here."

She steps around me and stares down at the book, as if the words are a puzzle and she's sure she'll know how to fix this if she just looks closely enough. "I still might."

Everyone around me is hanging their hopes on *might* and *maybe*.

In the hall, Kendrick's low voice mixes with two others. There's a knock at the door before it creaks open and Misha ducks his head inside. "Apologies, Abriella, but we should meet up with Kendrick's people and bring them up to speed."

"Misha, I'm so sorry." The words are out before I can stop them. I've made so many terrible decisions and he's yet another person who could lose everything because of it.

His expression goes shuttered. "The oracle told you something." He doesn't sound surprised.

"What?" Felicity asks, stepping up from behind Misha and placing a hand on his arm. "What is it?"

I take a breath, not sure if I'm the right person to reveal this information, but Misha gives me a subtle nod. "It's not just the shadow court that's in danger." My words are tripping over each other, so I force myself to slow down. "We've been wondering why Erith has been helping Mordeus and she explained. Mordeus promised to help him take the Wild Fae territory as his own."

Felicity pales and looks to Misha. "That's not possible, is it?"

"I'm afraid it is," Misha says, his gaze shifting to the window beside my sister's desk.

She pulls back as if she's been struck. "You already knew?"

His jaw ticks. "I've been warned that he's a threat, yes."

Brie flexes her hands at her sides and shadows dance up her arms. "The best way we can protect Misha's court is to keep Mordeus from taking this one. Tell everyone to gather in my meeting room in twenty minutes."

CHAPTER THIRTY-SEVEN

FELICITY

THE EVENING AIR COOLS MY heated cheeks, but I still haven't recovered from the blow Jas delivered before our meeting. Misha's kingdom is in jeopardy because of Erith, and he knew. He knew and didn't tell me.

After leaving the shadow queen's office, we met with the others. Skylar, predictably, was horrified by our decision to work with members of the Seven and let their soldiers defend the palace and skeptical of our claim that they want change as much as we do. The queen's people were more focused on the logistics—everyone figuring the attack will likely come on or very shortly after the princess's birthday. Plans were already in motion to move the shadow court's Cursed Horde into place for defense.

Meanwhile, I'm selfishly wrapped up in my broken heart and can't seem to escape the ache of it.

"Why are you out here alone?" Misha asks.

"I'm not alone now," I say, but the words come out bitter instead of welcoming. I can't help it. My heart aches, and there are so many layers to the ache that I can't begin to untangle them all.

"You're upset."

I huff. "Our realms are going to hell. We're all upset."

His fingertips graze my arm. "You know that's not what I mean."

"How could he manage a takeover?" I ask. "You have legions of devoted people, armies and a whole infantry that will defend you to the death." I try to meet his eyes but he's staring at the ground. "Right?"

"Mordeus has armies too," he says, still not looking at me. "And my court is so small in population compared to the shadow court. Assuming Mordeus is able to recruit more troops once he takes the throne, I won't be able to compete with his numbers."

I can't take my eyes off the male who has stolen my heart so completely, and he can't look at me. "Tell me about what's happening with your court. With your magic. Tell me the truth about how this is even possible."

The silence stretches between us for a beat too long and I flinch.

"You don't trust me?"

"It's not that," he says.

"Then tell me."

He drags a hand through his already tousled hair. "Over the past year, it's become increasingly clear to me that something wasn't right within my court. The glitches in my magic became more frequent and more consequential. Those issues only escalated as the months went on. It was only recently that I returned to the Jewel of Peace, and she told me that I severed the magic of my court when I dissolved my marriage and Amira stepped down as queen. There's so much about the magical connections between a court and its rulers that we don't understand, but it seems that since I took the throne with a queen at my side, the magic of the court split between us."

"But you aren't the first to end your marriage, to be without a queen."

"That's true. Typically, upon the death of one ruler, the magic would transfer to the other, but Amira was still well. I'm not the first Wild Fae king to dissolve his marriage, but the others took a new queen almost immediately. Her power didn't shift to me and it didn't have anyone else to shift to either. It's out there in limbo somewhere, and my own magic gets weaker every day because of it."

"Right," I murmur. "Which is why you need a queen, and quickly."

His brow wrinkles, the silver webbing on his forehead glowing faintly. "Would you please tell me what you're really upset about?"

"You *knew*."

Misha's chest rises and falls with a deep breath. "Lark had some visions. I know very few specifics."

My gut twists painfully and I look back to the distant city. As dusk approaches, streetlamps are lit one by one. I can imagine people heading toward their homes, ready to stay in for the night. I'm envious of that—of everyone who has a place to go, who knows where they belong.

"When Konner had me and you came for me, you insisted that you weren't there for *me* personally. That you had other reasons. I didn't believe you because I didn't want to." I squeeze my eyes shut. "And now I see what a threat Erith poses. I see that you need the very thing I alone can promise and I wonder if this was ever really about me at all. Or if it was always about what you needed from me."

"Felicity . . ." The wind howls in the distance, blowing my white hair across my face. "Would you look at me?" He squeezes my shoulders, then he urges me around.

I stare at his chest. I am hurting too much to let myself get lost in those russet eyes.

His fingers skim my jawline. "When I was searching all the realms for the female who tricked and betrayed me, I needed an excuse to want you alive. I couldn't stand knowing you'd fooled me while still knowing I'd do anything to protect you. I told myself that if you were destined to kill this male who would take over my throne, I was allowed to want you to live. I was allowed to do everything in my power to save you." He stoops so we're eye to eye. "But the truth was I wanted you to live because I'd fallen for you, and I was loath to imagine a world without you in it."

My eyes burn as I lift my chin to look at him. "I wanted you to want me so much you didn't need an excuse."

He makes a fist and presses it to his chest. "Erith could die today, and I would still want you. He could take over my court, and I would still want you. He could kill me tomorrow, and I would still want you."

I search his face for the reassurance I need to take his pretty words and tuck them away, but my heart aches so much.

"Felicity!"

I pull my gaze off Misha to see Abriella rushing onto the balcony. "What is it?"

"I need you to become my sister one final time." She hands me an envelope, no doubt containing the hair I will need to do as she asks.

"Why?" Misha asks.

"General Hargova, the leader of the Cursed Horde, is coming to the palace tomorrow. He wants to meet with me and Jas."

"And why not have your sister appear as herself?" Misha asks, glancing toward me as if he understands that every day I wake up as someone else it costs me something.

"Because if he sees that scar on Jasalyn's face, he'll know that the princess I pointed out to him at the ball wasn't really her. He might not forgive the betrayal, and I can't risk that with what's coming."

"Well, well, well, aren't we looking beautiful in our own skin tonight," Squird crows when he materializes in my room.

"I'm enjoying it while I can," I say. Because once Erith is no longer wherever he is to keep Mordeus alive, I'll have to go back to hiding—at least until I find a way to get to him and kill him.

I haven't let myself think about it too much.

I debated for a quarter hour whether I should call Squird, but now that he's here I'm not sure why I tried to talk myself out of it at all. I already feel a little better, and I wasn't sure that was possible today.

"Care for a game?" he asks, whipping a deck of cards from his pants pocket.

"Sure." I sit on the floor, tucking my legs under me. Squird sits facing me, dealing cards between us in the traditional layout of solitaire. I smile, remembering Nigel. Maybe Squird doesn't like to play alone either. "How do we do this together?"

"I move the cards and if I don't know what to do next, I ask you and then I move the cards the way you said."

I bite back a laugh. "Sounds good."

We settle in and I watch him play without my help for a few minutes, but my mind keeps spinning back to Misha and all the reasons he had for making me feel wanted. Within a matter of days, Mordeus's forces will descend on this palace and wreck the future of this court and the lives of people I've come to care about. I should be thinking of how to help with *that*, not dwelling on my stupid hurt feelings.

"Spit it out," Squird says, not looking up at me.

"It's just been a weird day." I bite my lip, then decide to go for it. "What do you know about getting out of faerie bargains?"

"It depends on the bargain."

"For example?" I ask.

"If you agree to give all your meals to a faerie and begin to eat only snacks, he would get nothing."

"What if you agreed to trade your life?"

He lifts his head and sighs. "You're speaking of the princess and what she traded for her magical ring."

"If Mordeus takes over her body, so many other awful things will follow. But if we can prevent it by somehow getting her out of her deal . . ."

"Offer your meals when you have no meals and you give nothing. Offer your life when you have no life and you give nothing."

I bow my head. I'm too tired for this, but he's probably right. It could be that the only way out of this is for Jasalyn to give up her life before she turns eighteen. It's irony in its most heartbreaking form, knowing that might be the best path for someone who finally wants to live after wishing for death for so long.

"Are you going to sit there and pretend this is really all that's on your mind, or are you going to talk to me about your broken heart?"

I gape. "Who told you that I have a broken heart?"

"Can smell it." He wrinkles his nose and waves a hand in front of his face. "No offense, but it's rather unpleasant. Rancid and pungent, like juice left to sour."

"Sorry about that." I point to the next card he should play and watch as he flies through three more moves. "You've gotten better."

"Been practicing." He tears his gaze off the cards to frown at me. "So? The broken heart? Did you break his right back?"

I huff. "No." Then frown, thinking of how Misha looked at me when I walked away from him tonight—like it took everything in him to let me go. "Maybe? I don't know. I just thought someone finally wanted me for myself. No agenda, no ulterior motives, you know?"

He hums and plays another card. "But he does, doesn't he? Nigel told me he could smell the stink of new love on the Wild Fae king."

My heart twists. "That was when he thought I was the princess."

"Oh, so he's said he's not interested in you now, then?"

"No, but—"

"So he's acted in a way that *shows* he's not interested?" He bobs his head. "They say actions speak louder than words, which is odd when the actions are often quiet ones, but I do think they're more meaningful all the same."

Goblins. Literal and logical to such an extreme. Nigel would never let me stew in my feelings either. "I just wish he would've told me the truth about needing me for more than . . ." I shrug, and when Squird directs a confused frown in my direction, I blush. "More than affection. I wish he would've been honest with me about the other ways he needed me."

"Pfft," he says. "Then this romance would've been even shorter lived than it already was. First thing you look for is a reason to believe what he feels isn't real."

Before I can respond, he jumps to his feet and drops his cards, looking around frantically. "I have to leave." He turns worried eyes on me. "I can't be here when it happens, and I can't come back until it's settled. Goblins cannot involve themselves in these matters."

Before I can ask more about what he means, he's gone.

CHAPTER THIRTY-EIGHT

JASALYN

"Did you come up with anything?" Abriella asks later that evening as she and Pretha join us in one of the palace's more comfortable sitting rooms. I've been telling Natan everything I remember about the day I made the bargain for the ring, and Kendrick's been by my side the whole time, willing me to remember as much as possible.

"Nothing yet," Natan says, "but I find our minds work on these problems in the background if we give them what they need. Something will come to me."

Brie's quick glance in my direction is all I need to know that she's thinking the same thing I am. His mind needs to work it out quickly. We only have one more day.

"May Pretha and I join you?" Brie asks. "I've been wanting Pretha to talk to you about your phoenix power. So you can be prepared."

"Of course," Kendrick says, waving to the armchairs across from us. "Please have a seat."

Pretha smooths the wrinkles in her skirt before looking at me. "Since Kendrick and his friends teamed up with us months ago,

Natan and I have been working together to sort out everything we know about the gift of the phoenix, Eloran blood magic, and everything else related to this unique situation."

"I appreciate that," I say softly. I hate to think how much time has been dedicated to fixing my extraordinary mistake, but it's making me realize that even through my dark years holed up in my bedroom here, I was surrounded by people who cared about me.

"In any other circumstance," Pretha continues, "I wouldn't have wanted anyone to tell you about this power. It's one you need to discover yourself—to join with it without searching for it."

"We don't have time for that," Brie says. "She needs to know how to wield it."

Pretha sits back in her seat. "The gift of the phoenix is rare. The ability to wield it is even more rare. We don't know for sure, but many suspect that only a small percentage of those born with the power of the phoenix live to use it."

"Why?" I ask.

Pretha holds my gaze. "Because in order to wield it, you have to be willing to burn, to feel and endure the pain of the flame. Most people are more afraid of pain than they realize."

"So suffering is inevitable?" Abriella asks. "There's no way around it?"

That's my sister. Always trying to find a way to save me from hurting.

"Think of the werewolf and the agony of his transformation," Pretha says. "Once he becomes the wolf and has its power, the pain is gone. But the process—the metamorphosis from human to wolf—that is excruciating every time. The weakest wolves don't survive the pain."

"So you're saying that even though I have this power and I could become flame itself, I could just as likely die trying to use it."

"You *will* die," Pretha says. "The process of the phoenix—burning to ash and rising again—it's a small death." She looks at my hand again. "Well, not so small, I'm sure you can imagine."

"Why are you telling me this? Why would I ever burn myself to ash if there's such a high risk of dying?"

Natan pushes his glasses up his nose. "It might not be you," he says. "We've seen Mordeus take over from time to time, and he will have to use your gift to take over your body completely. You need to be prepared."

"We've dedicated a lot of our time in the last few days trying to work around the bargain—to get you out of it entirely," Pretha says. "Even if you find a way to be released from your deal with Erith, Mordeus may still have access to take over your body through the power of your phoenix. If we don't find a way out of the bargain, he will take over on your eighteenth birthday by burning to ash and rising again. If we *do* find a way out, there's no guarantee he won't still take over."

"How?" Brie asks.

"Through the blood magic Mordeus used on her," Natan says gently. "So long as he lives in any form, they are connected. Every one of those scars is evidence of that."

"He has to be stronger than you—in will and in desire." Pretha folds her arms across her chest and hugs herself tightly. "I imagine that's why he worked so hard to break you. So that letting go wouldn't just be a relief when you were faced with the flames, it would be a gift."

Tears brim in Brie's eyes and one slips from the corner. "This isn't fair."

The despair in her voice rips through me.

"The moment you decide"—Pretha taps her temple—"that life, that your very existence isn't worth the pain, that it would just be easier to stop existing, you lose to the phoenix. In any other person with this gift, that would be it. That would be the end. But in your case, if you surrender and he doesn't . . ."

"Then he wins," I say, my blood turning as cold as it did when I first got the ring. "And if Mordeus wants to claim my body as his own, if he wants to steal my life, then all he has to do—all this male who has already died once has to do—is make me burn and endure the pain better than I can."

"That's right," Pretha says. "You have to want to live. Want it so much that every moment of suffering and agony is worth it."

The fires around the perimeter of the palace lawn are spelled to enhance the wards. I stand in the back garden, transfixed by the sight.

Abriella must've understood that I needed to be alone because she didn't try to come after me when I excused myself from our conversation with Pretha in the sitting room. I've been out here for hours, watching the flames dance and flicker, licking at the night sky. For years, I dreaded the end of day, cowered at the encroaching night. Then I got my ring and I relished it. *Vengeance. Murder. Justice.* I craved them more than I feared the darkness.

The soft scuff of boots on stone tells me I'm not alone anymore, and I know without looking, know even without those keen fae senses the others have, that it's Kendrick.

He wraps something around my shoulders. I close my eyes against the warmth of it, the subtle smell of laundry soap, the comforting brush of his hands as he adjusts the blanket around my neck. "It's getting cold out here."

I twist my neck to meet his eyes. "Thank you."

"May I join you?" he asks.

I shrug, then take a breath and force myself to say what I feel instead of what feels safe. "I thought I wanted to be alone, but I think I'd rather be with you."

He wraps his arms around me from behind, his hands clasped just beneath my breasts, his chest warm against my back. "You never have to be alone so long as I'm around."

I don't bother to bring up Crissa or the fact that I only have one day left. I know his words are a promise he'll keep as long as he can, and for now, for tonight, that's enough.

"I was never afraid of fire," I say, eyes on the crackling piles of brush before us. "I nearly died in a fire when I was a little girl, so perhaps it should've occurred to me sooner that there was some uncommon connection between me and flames, but I never gave it much thought. It's not all that strange to find fires a source of comfort. To want to step closer when they're near or to find peace in the crackle of burning wood. And then, after Mordeus, I was so afraid of the dark, and fire gave me light. It broke the thing I dreaded so deeply. So I never questioned this pull toward flames."

He bends down to rest his chin on my shoulder. "And now

you think it's because you're a phoenix."

"Maybe." I shrug. "Or maybe I just fear the thing that broke me more than I fear the thing that could have."

"I already told you: You aren't broken," he says.

"That remains to be seen." I extend a hand toward the too-hot flames and let them heat my skin. "I think I fear the darkness because it changed me. It became part of me. Ask anyone who knew me before. I believed there was so much good in the world. So much to look forward to. And he locked me in that cell and then trapped me in my own body, and I stopped believing that."

My hand has gone from pale to pink to red from the heat of the fire.

"I would've died in that cell if he hadn't forced me to eat, if he hadn't forced water down my throat. I would've found a way to end it if Crissa hadn't used her magic to soothe the chaos and panic in my mind. Or after, if you hadn't arrived. I heard a hope in your voice that I recognized from the girl I'd been before he'd taken me—the girl I used to be—and instead of wanting to escape my body, my life, you made me dream of escaping that cell. And that was exactly what he wanted."

"I can't be sorry that you survived," he says, his voice a gritty rasp. He takes my hand in his, and when he brings it back to our sides, he holds it there, as if he can absorb the burning sensation. "I'm sorry that it happened in a way that helped him, but I refuse to apologize for keeping you here."

I swallow the lump in my throat. "I don't want you to. I get it now. I understand why you made the choices you did." My eyes brim with tears, but I laugh. It sounds crazed. "He almost won.

If that little girl he locked up were about to face what I am, it wouldn't have mattered if there was a way out of the bargain. I would've gladly surrendered to the pain. He wanted to break me. He needed me to be so fragile that when the flames burned me to ash, I'd surrender. He wanted to make me weak, but he didn't realize he was teaching me just how much pain I can endure and survive. I am so much stronger than he is." I stare into the flames, imagine I *am* the flames.

He turns his face into me and brushes his lips at the sensitive spot where my neck meets my shoulder. "Then why do you seem so sad?"

"I'm not, not really. Just contemplating what I want."

"What's that?" His voice is so soft, almost like he's afraid he might not like my answer.

I wiggle until he loosens his grip enough that I can spin in his arms. He takes my face in his hands and brushes tears away with the rough pads of his thumbs. "I want to live."

CHAPTER THIRTY-NINE

FELICITY

The Grimoricon was a heavy book when Jasalyn took it from the Midnight Palace, but in the time it's taken her to call her goblin, get to Elora, and walk to the witch's hut, it's changed into a slime exuding the stench of rotting flesh and a heavy stone so big she had to use her cape to drag it behind her. Now it's a cat that's burrowed itself against her chest and is purring loudly enough to block out the cacophony of the noisy village of Fairscape.

The moment she steps into the witch's cottage the purring stops and the cat curls its claws into her flesh, hissing. In the next second, Jas is holding a black rat with red eyes and a long, fat tail. She drops it without thinking, and it scurries to the door they just came in. The witch throws up a hand and the door swings shut before the rat can escape.

"You found it," she says, stepping around her worktable and reaching for the creature. It shrinks down to mouse size and skitters up Jasalyn's skirt.

The witch glares. "You want your ring? Give me that book."

Jasalyn's stomach twists. She suddenly isn't so sure of anything. Will her sister forgive her when she realizes the Grimoricon is missing? Will this witch's ring really work? Could anything *take away* the fear she carries around all the time? "You'll give the book back, though, right? After you've made the ring?"

"I never promised that."

"But my sister—"

"Will never suspect you stole it." Her smile is anything but kind.

The mouse has its claws deep in her flesh beneath the skirt, but Jas doesn't attempt to pull it away.

"Do you want this ring or not?" the witch snaps.

She swallows but the lump of dread doesn't leave her throat. "What *exactly* is the deal again?"

The witch slides a roll of parchment out from behind the clutter of apothecary bottles on the wall and unrolls it on the table between them. "By accepting the ring," she says, tapping the page, "you agree to forfeit your immortal years by surrendering this life of yours on the eighteenth anniversary of your birth. In return, for as long as the magic holds true, whenever you wear the ring, you will carry the kiss of death on your lips and have numbness replace the fear in your heart."

The deal says nothing about Abriella never getting the book back. Maybe she will. Or maybe it will find its way back to her.

As if already sensing her decision, the mouse drops to the floor and runs to the door. The witch intercepts, scooping up the creature. It squeals and sinks its big teeth into her finger. The witch curses and mutters something in a language Jas has never heard before. A small girl emerges from the corner and holds out her hands, her eyes full of terror as she takes the rodent from the witch. They exchange a few more words in that unfamiliar tongue. The *girl disappears into the darkness again and the witch turns her attention back to Jas. "I need an hour to complete your ring, then you can come back for it"*—she taps the unrolled scroll—*"and our deal will be complete."*

Chaos rules every hall and passage of the palace today, and it's after lunch before I finally find a space that isn't already occupied with Konner's soldiers or Brie's advisors or some other group of people I don't have the energy to talk to.

The room is small—the only door off a tucked-away alcove—and I exhale in relief as I sink into a chair and soak in the silence.

I shouldn't be here. I should be tracking down the queen and figuring out what I should and shouldn't say when the general comes. But the truth is, I don't know what I'm going to say if I run into Misha.

Hey, it's okay that maybe you wanting me was like seventy percent about me and thirty percent about what you need from me. That's more than I ever could've hoped for anyway.

Or, *I was too busy being angry yesterday to hear all the sweet things you said, but I think I need to hear them so could you just run that down again?*

Or worse, *I don't care why you want me because I don't know how not to want you.*

"You okay there?"

I look up and see Konner lowering himself into the chair across from me. He blows out a breath. "Felicity," he says. "I almost thought you were Jasalyn, but"—he taps the skin around his eye—"that gives you away. Why are you in this form today?"

"A favor for the queen. What are you doing here?"

"Looking for a quiet spot to clear my head, if I'm honest. You?"

"Same."

"I've been wishing we had time to talk, but it seems like there are too many fires to put out or coming storms to prepare for."

I huff. "No kidding."

His eyes soften and I think of all the times he got that look on his face in the illusion. "I know you probably still haven't forgiven me for putting you in that stasis, but I'm dying to know what it was like."

I lean back and fold my arms. "That seems like a weird thing for *you* to ask, given that you're the one who put me there."

"It was a risk, you know, giving you an alternate reality to make you understand me better. Who knows? Maybe I was a jerk and it could've worked against me."

I frown. "Alternate reality? Don't you mean illusion?"

"It's nothing I constructed, if that's what you mean. I can't choose what you see when you dream."

I'm baffled because his face is all sincerity. "Then how..."

"I can focus on a moment in the past and change one thing about it. Then you'll dream the life you would've had if things had unfolded from there."

Everything inside me slows down. "And what did you change for my dreams?"

He cocks his head to the side. "You already know."

When I close my eyes, I can practically feel our mother's hand on my shoulder, the warmth of her hugs and the beauty of her smile. "Our father—this was if our father had died. And that was why Mother was still alive." My heart twists as I look up at Konner. "And our sister, Aster."

He draws in a breath. "That's right." His throat bobs. "What was it like? That life?"

A flood of emotion makes me want to hug Konner. *My brother.* "Mom raised us in the palace, and we . . . you and I were close." *And I was being courted by the king of the Wild Fae, who wanted me just for being me.* "I thought it was an illusion. I thought you'd crafted this whole life and all the details. . . ."

He shakes his head. "No. I focus on a single moment. In this case, I went back to the ritual our father did for power and immortality. I imagined him failing and dying as a result. It was a risk, but I hoped you'd have a chance to see me for who I really am, perhaps even see how good a world without Erith could be."

"I've never heard of such a power."

"You're given a memory in a dream when you take another's shape, right?" he asks, and I nod. "Well, I think this is a variation of that power. It takes the memory, the history, and spins in a different direction."

"That's . . . fascinating."

"It makes a weird sort of sense to me," he says. "For instance, you know how when you get your dream, it can be different than what the person remembers?"

I frown. "It can?"

He nods. "Well, yes. Our memories are imperfect. They're an impression of that moment that's obscured by all the things we're thinking and feeling at the time. But what an Echo gets in the dream isn't really a *memory* so much as a recounting of the event as if we're reliving it. The Echo is aware of the subject's emotions while also seeing the truth of it."

The hair on the back of my neck prickles. "Konner, that's it."

"What's wrong?"

My mind races as I mentally recount the words from my dream over and over. I have to be sure. If I'm wrong, it could be catastrophic. "I dreamed of the day Jas gave the Grimoricon to the witch and finalized their bargain."

"She misremembered the terms, didn't she?"

Offer your meals when you have no meals and you give nothing. Offer your life when you have no life and you give nothing.

My stomach flips with nerves and adrenaline and *hope*. "I need to find the princess."

CHAPTER FORTY

JASALYN

"Turn your attention inward," Pretha says, focusing so intently on me I wish I'd never gotten out of bed this morning.

It was late when Kendrick escorted me to my chambers, and when he tried to say good night and leave for his own, I pulled him inside.

"Are you sure you want this?" he asked as I pulled his tunic off. And I understood why. When we found out Crissa was alive, I'd pushed him away again, too afraid my own existence would ruin everything for him. But last night, with my birthday looming so close and the ring of the Banshee's cry still echoing in my ears, I didn't have it in me to be selfless, didn't have it in me to sacrifice the little time I have left with him in favor of some noble act that may never matter anyway.

So he stayed, and we said everything that needed saying with our hands and mouths and bodies. It was beautiful and sad and comforting and painful. It was everything it needed to be.

When I woke up in his arms this morning, I should've stayed there. Should've ignored the knock on my door and insisted we ignore the world.

One more day.

That's all I have. I don't want to spend it here, failing tremendously as Pretha tries to get me to tap into my power, to find this supposed "inner fire" I need to activate my phoenix.

"Just focus on that kernel of flame deep inside of you and draw it out to your fingertips," she says.

I stare at my fingertips, search for a flame that isn't there, and will fire to flare from my skin nevertheless. Nothing happens. "I'm sorry."

"It's okay," Brie says, stopping her incessant pacing behind me. She's trying not to smother me, but she's definitely hovering. "We'll keep trying."

I want to ask *why*. We haven't found a way around the bargain, so my ability to wield my phoenix is irrelevant. When I close my eyes and turn my attention inward this time, I'm not searching for flame but for *patience*.

"Jas!"

I look up to see myself running into the room. Not me, *Felicity*. Does her gift give her my abilities when she's in my skin? Maybe she could tell me where to find this kernel of flame that supposedly burns inside me.

"The deal you struck with the witch," she says, breathing hard like she ran here. "I think you misremembered the wording."

All eyes in the room turn to her. My sister rushes to her side, and my heart sinks. *Don't give her false hope.*

"You dreamed of that day," Brie says. "The day she made the deal."

Felicity turns to me. "The witch said you would 'forfeit your immortal years by surrendering this life of yours on the eighteenth anniversary of your birth.' *That* is what you agreed to."

I bow my head, shame burning hot in my cheeks. "Sounds about right."

Pretha drags in a shocked breath, and I'm not sure why because they already knew this.

Brie looks back and forth between me and the me-who-isn't-me.

I release a ragged breath. *Why does it matter?* "I guess I don't remember the exact words."

"Eighteenth anniversary of her birth . . ." Pretha presses her fingers to her lips. "You think that if she ends her life before her birthday, by the terms of the deal, he can't take over."

"That's not an option," Kendrick says at the same time as my sister says, "I'm not letting her give up until we know without a doubt—"

"I don't want her to kill herself," Felicity shouts. "Not in that way, at least."

My sister's nostrils flare. I'm not the only one lacking patience today. "Explain."

"I thought they wanted her in stasis until her birthday because they didn't want her to end her life, and I was right, but there's more than one way she can end her life and, by doing so, invalidate her deal with Erith. She's a phoenix," Felicity says. "When she burns to ash and rises again, her life begins *anew*. She can end this life *before* she would have to surrender it to Mordeus. And when she rises again, he'll have no claim on that new life."

The room goes hushed but can't compare with the complete silence inside me. *This is the way out.*

"She has to harness her power before the moment she turns eighteen," Pretha says, "and she has to wield it—burning to ash and rising again before the bargain's terms can be recognized."

Kendrick's throat bobs. "But you said that very few people survive the transformation of the phoenix." His gaze bounces around the group, looking for someone to reassure him. "How do we know Jas can survive it?"

Pretha's quiet for a long time. "We don't."

"But there's another way," he says. "There has to be another way."

Abriella's face is pale but even she shakes her head. "If there is, we haven't found it yet."

"Even this isn't a guarantee, thanks to the blood magic," Pretha reminds him. "Until *this* life of hers ends, Mordeus is connected to her. When the agony of the fire begins, he will do everything he can to be the one who can hang on the longest."

Panic marks Kendrick's face when he turns back to me. "I need you," he says, voice as soft as a whisper. "I need you to beat this thing."

I want to promise him I will. I want to give him all the reassurance he needs. But if I can't even bring a single flame to my fingertips, how am I supposed to burn myself to ash? "I won't stop trying until my last breath."

A shadow passes over the room and the mood shifts with it. Gray storm clouds have blocked the afternoon sun, and it's given a weight to the very air in the room. In the distance, thunder rolls.

"They're coming," I say, eyes fixed on those dark clouds.

"My generals haven't said anything." Brie rushes to the

windows and looks right to left. "Do you see them?"

"This was in what the oracle showed you?" Kendrick asks.

"The storm. They take the palace during the storm. By nightfall they . . ." I push out of my chair and go to my sister, taking her by the shoulders and turning her to me. "You need to leave. Get out of here. They are coming for you first. I saw them string you up at the gates."

The ferocity in my sister's face softens. "I won't leave the palace. I can't."

"Please," I whisper. "Please go. For me."

"I won't leave that throne unattended for Mordeus to steal. I will stand and defend my court."

Someone clears his throat and we all turn our attention to see my sister's horned advisor stepping into the sitting room, his red eyes burning bright as ever. "My queen, the general has arrived."

CHAPTER FORTY-ONE

FELICITY

GENERAL HARGOVA, THE LEADER OF the Unseelie Court's Cursed Horde, gives me the creeps. While Brie said he wanted Jasalyn at this meeting, my presence seems to make him uncomfortable. I keep catching him staring at me—at Jasalyn.

"We expect the attack to come tonight," the shadow queen says.

"Tonight? Why do you say that?"

"Our seers have had a number of visions," she says, the lie smooth as butter. As far as I know, the only reason they have to believe this is happening tonight is because of what Jas saw at the oracle, and even she didn't know a day for sure. We're reading a lot into some gray skies and distant thunder.

He arches a brow and glances toward the window. "Where are these armies that are supposedly going to overwhelm your palace? I saw no sign of them on my way in."

Brie doesn't cower under his scrutiny or his doubt. She merely shrugs. "I would rather be prepared too early than too late, wouldn't you?"

"Tell me again why Mordeus's followers believe he's been

resurrected. Tell me why they think this dead man can steal your throne." He cocks his head to the side. "Didn't he try this before and fail because he didn't have the crown?"

She narrows her gaze. "I can't speak to why his legions are so convinced of his return. However, his failure to sit upon the Throne of Shadows didn't prevent him from wreaking havoc on this court for two decades. As you know."

He smiles. "Fair." His gaze shifts to me again, and again, I want to shudder under the weight of it. "And other than my horde, what other defenses do you have for the palace? I don't want to risk my people if this battle is a lost cause."

"I wouldn't ask you to," Brie says. "The palace brigade is on the ready. They will be stationed at the gates and throughout the palace. Our Midnight Raiders are stationed throughout the capital, waiting for signs of attack. They will be our first line of defense and hopefully keep the insurgents from reaching the palace gates."

"That's all?" he asks. "These visions have made you so convinced attack is coming but you only have the standard Unseelie guards to protect you?"

"We have another group of troops," she says. "Provided by an ally. They will be just inside the palace gates."

"Queen Abriella," someone calls from the doorway. "I am so sorry to interrupt but you asked me to get you if there were any developments during the training happening down the hall. I think you need to come see this."

Brie pastes on a calm smile and pushes to her feet. "My apologies, General, but I promise to be back as quickly as possible. I'll send in some refreshments for you." She waves me forward. "Jas, would you mind keeping the general company while I take care of this."

I glance between them. "I'm happy to."

The general flicks his gaze to the queen and then back to me. "I can wait alone," he says. "Don't worry about me."

I don't know why, but my gut tells me it's important that I stay. Something isn't right. And while I haven't seen Misha all day and desperately want to talk to him after what I learned from Konner, the best way I can help Misha and his court is to make sure Abriella's doesn't fall. She needs the general's Cursed Horde.

"I could use some tea," I say, "and you can tell me about how this horde of yours stays invisible when they're not fighting."

Hargova chuckles uncomfortably. "I can't reveal my secrets."

Brie holds my gaze so long that I'm sure if she could mentally communicate like Misha she'd be telling me something important right now. "I will be back as soon as I can."

"What kind of training is happening that she needs to leave a meeting to observe?" Hargova asks when the door swings shut behind the queen.

"I'm not sure. Perhaps training to prepare for the attack."

The wind howls outside. "It seems a bit late for that."

More storm clouds roll in, so many that the world goes dark as night, though it's hours to sunset. The lanterns in the wall sconces magically flicker to life to compensate for the lack of natural light. The next boom of thunder makes the palace tremble around us.

He grimaces. "I apologize, but I'm wondering if you could direct me to the nearest lavatory?"

"Oh." I paste on a smile to cover my panic. Is this a trick? Should I know where the nearest toilet is? The Midnight Palace is massive, and I haven't spent much time on this end. "Of course. I—"

A maid steps from the shadows and nods in our direction. "I will escort you, General."

"Thank you so much." He pushes out of his armchair and follows her without a single suspicious look in my direction.

Calm down. You've done this a hundred times.

I lean back in my seat and close my eyes, thinking what I'll say when I find Misha after this. The truth is, I'm a little embarrassed about how I reacted yesterday, but I'm also still hurt that he wasn't honest with me.

The sitting room door creaks, and as if my thoughts themselves summoned him, Misha pushes into the room, a tray of tea in his hands.

"Misha." My heart stumbles at the sight of him. "I wanted to talk to you."

He glances toward the door, then back to me, before answering in my mind. *Now might not be the best time*, he says into my mind, before adding aloud, "Where's the General?"

"He needed to excuse himself for a minute. Let me help you with that," I say, watching the windows as they are pelted with rain. I push out of my seat as he settles the tray on a table at the side of the room. *I don't know if I want to apologize or explain myself,* I say into his mind. *Maybe both.*

His eyes are soft as he sweeps them over me, mouth twisting like he's looking for the female beneath Jasalyn's skin. *You don't* owe me an apology. If you don't know my feelings for you are sincere then perhaps I haven't done a good enough job proving them.

I melt a bit and give a small shrug. *In any other circumstance, I'm not sure that would be true, but I'm aware that much of my reaction was about* me *and not about you.*

He glances over his shoulder at the closed door, then whispers, "I'm sorry I wasn't honest. I was afraid you'd walk away from me if you knew, and by the time I accepted my feelings, I couldn't stomach the idea of losing you."

I bow my head and when I lift it, he's staring again. *What?*

Just wondering if you have any of that potion of your brother's—for after the general leaves. His lips quirk in sardonic amusement. *I'd rather look in* your *eyes when we have this conversation.*

My cheeks heat. *Maybe I could sneak away for a short nap later.*

Maybe I could join you.

CHAPTER FORTY-TWO

JASALYN

"I can't!" My objection comes out as a bellow that shakes the room—or maybe that's the thunder.

Pretha isn't fazed. "I think you're getting in your own way. Let's circle back to those deep-breathing exercises and then try again."

This has been going on for *hours*, and every minute that passes without me summoning flame is another minute I'm closer to losing my life to Mordeus. Another minute closer to my sister losing her court.

"We need to take a break," Kendrick says. "She's exhausted."

"Of course," Pretha says, but I don't miss her glance at the clock. We are all much too aware of the clock.

Kendrick offers me his hand, then guides me from my chair. His arm snakes around my shoulders as he leads me past two guards and to the door.

One of them grumbles something behind us, and everything seems to happen at once.

Kendrick suddenly spins, lunges for the sentinel, and pins him against the wall. "What did you just say?"

Iron sings as the other sentinel pulls her blade, but she hesitates, clearly unsure if she's supposed to protect her brother in arms or the queen's guest.

"Everyone calm down," Pretha says, standing as slowly as someone surrounded by angry wild animals. "Kendrick, what happened?"

"This piece of shit opened his mouth."

"Not helpful," Pretha mutters.

"I'm sorry," the sentinel says, eyes never leaving Kendrick's. "I shouldn't have said anything."

The steady thud of boots on stone grows closer and my sister appears in the doorway. "What's happening here?" Brie asks, looking between Kendrick and her sentinel.

"Tell the queen what you said," Kendrick says, eyes blazing with fury.

The room glows brighter for a beat as lightning flashes outside.

"I didn't mean it," he blubbers.

"Kendrick," my sister says coolly. "Please put down my sentinel and back away."

Kendrick sneers at the male one last time before doing as she asks. Brie smoothly slides between them, mouth in a thin line as she looks over the now-trembling guard.

"Tell me what you said that upset my guest so much," she commands her guard, cocking her head to the side.

The sentinel's throat bobs. "I shouldn't have said it. I didn't mean it."

"Tell me."

He glances to each person in the room, as if someone might save him.

"Look at *me*," Brie says, each word directed at him like a blow. "I am your queen and I asked you a question."

"The princess has been unsuccessful in wielding her flame," he says, his voice trembling as much as the hands at his sides. "I foolishly asked at what point we consider the *other* way to make sure there's no life for Mordeus to take."

I flinch like I've been slapped. Not because I can't handle the cruel words of some random shadow court sentinel but because he's only highlighting what everyone in this room has probably been thinking for hours—my inability to find the power that supposedly lives inside me could mean the end for everyone here.

"I didn't mean it, and I shouldn't have said it," the sentinel blubbers. "I was only thinking of my queen, worried for my court, and I spoke recklessly. Please accept my apology, Your Majesty."

"Prenley," Brie says, coolly addressing the other guard. "Please escort Yarrow to my dungeons."

"My queen," Yarrow begs. "Please understand. I wouldn't—"

She holds up a hand and though his mouth keeps moving, his words make no sound. "You do not *want* me to make a final decision about what to do with you right now." Her voice is cool but the shadows weaving around her ankles and wrists give her away. "Trust me when I say you are safer in the dungeons with the rats than you are in my presence. Be grateful." She drops her hand and he gasps.

"Yes, my queen." His lips tremble. "Thank you, my queen."

Prenley returns her sword to its sheath and guides Yarrow

away without risking a single questioning glance in her queen's direction.

"I'm sorry about that," Brie says to me when they're gone, jaw ticking.

Mortification sits like lead on my chest. I want to scream that he wasn't wrong. That maybe we should stop looking for magic that isn't there and start looking at other options. "You didn't have to do that."

She arches a brow, still the haughty queen. "But I did. I expect better behavior from my sentinels. I can't and won't allow them to disrespect their princess." She takes a deep breath and as she releases it, some of her vengeful ruler demeanor falls away. She glances between me, Kendrick, and Pretha and her expression grows somber. "No progress?"

Pretha shakes her head. "None of the strategies we've used thus far have worked."

"She needs a break," Kendrick says.

Fast, thudding steps sound in the hall and another sentinel rushes into the room. "Your Majesty," the male says, "General Hargova sends word from the palace gates. There are soldiers approaching the capital now."

Brie frowns. "The general is at the palace gates? When did he . . ." Her face goes pale, but she wastes no time before turning away and sprinting down the hall.

I grab Kendrick's hand and we follow her down one corridor and into another sitting room, where Misha and Felicity—in my form—are standing and seem to be having a silent conversation.

"Where's the general?" Brie demands, scanning the room.

Felicity pales. "He needed to use the facilities. The handmaid took him."

"How long ago was that?" Brie asks.

Felicity looks to Misha, panic all over her face. "I'm not..."

Brie turns to one of the sentinels standing by the door. "How long ago did Hargova leave this room?"

"It's been maybe a quarter of an hour, Your Majesty. The maid took him toward the lavatory around the corner."

"What is it, Brie?" I ask.

"General Hargova just sent word from the palace gates. Which means the General Hargova I met with this afternoon was someone else." She looks to each of us before turning her full attention on the sentinel. "There's an impostor in this palace disguised as the general, and we need to find him."

"A shifter?" the sentinel asks. "I apologize for not noticing, Your Majesty. Next time, I'll—"

"Not quite a shifter," Felicity says, voice weak. "He's an Echo. You couldn't have known."

"I'll sound the alarm," the sentinel says, and within seconds the halls are filled with guards searching for our intruder.

"Erith?" Misha asks Felicity.

"I think so, yes."

"Aren't you the only one who can kill him?" I ask Felicity. "Surely he knew you were staying here, even if he thought I was the one in the meeting. Why get so close to the only person who can kill him?"

"Because we took back the Grimoricon," Brie says. She rushes from the room and toward her office, and I follow after her, Kendrick following after me.

"Jasalyn," he says. "We need to get you somewhere safe. Erith is incredibly dangerous."

"Brie!" I shout, but she turns the corner to her office before skidding to a stop, frozen.

I see why a moment after she does. In the hall in front of Brie's closed office doors, four sentinels and a handmaid lie pale and lifeless—looking every bit like victims of the faceless plague.

I check my hand to make sure the ring didn't come back somehow.

"This was Erith," Kendrick says.

Brie reaches for the door handle and is thrown back against the wall. "Wards," she seethes. "Wards around my own damned office in my own damned palace."

Screams tear through the air and echo through the palace halls, so loud and piercing they mask the ceaseless thunder rolling overhead.

Confused, I look back and forth between Kendrick and Brie. "What is—"

Three males come around the corner, blades drawn. Their eyes go wide when they spot us—or rather, when they spot the shadow queen, who is still scrambling to her feet after being thrown by the wards.

Blades sing all around me as the males lunge for us. Kendrick shoves me behind him and plunges his sword through the chest of the first in line. The other two roar, and charge.

Brie throws out her hands and shadows wrap around them, holding them in place while Kendrick slices his sword across their throats.

They fall to the floor with a wet thud that turns my stomach, but I make myself look. At their drab olive uniforms, at the upturned crescent moons tattooed on their necks.

This is the consequence of me not finding my powers. Mordeus's forces will attack my sister and her people until the palace is theirs.

Kendrick takes me by the shoulders and turns me to him. "Are you okay?"

"Kendrick!" I try to shove him aside as the next attacker turns the corner and throws her dagger, but Kendrick is faster and puts himself between me and the flying steel.

It hits him in the side of his arm, making him drop his sword.

As Kendrick crouches to retrieve it, his opponent lunges with her own sword, only to freeze mid-swing, then fall to the ground.

Remme's chest heaves as he scans each of us—looking his king over twice. "You're hit."

"I'm fine." Kendrick rises, sword in hand. "What is *happening*, Remme? Where did they come from?"

"Portals are opening all through the palace, and dozens of these assholes are pouring out of each one." He looks to Brie, who's leaning against the wall as if wielding enough shadow to paralyze those two fighters used up all her magic.

"Brie, are you okay?"

"The wards," she says, nodding to her office door. "They zinged my power a bit, but it's trickling back."

Remme curses. "How is this happening?" He glances to the door. "Who's in there?"

"Erith," Kendrick says. "He got into the palace by taking the form of General Hargova and has locked himself in the queen's office."

"Why?" Remme asks, scanning the area again and again, as if waiting for more of Mordeus's forces to attack.

"The Grimoricon is in there," I tell him.

Brie nods. "He's the one opening the portals."

CHAPTER FORTY-THREE

FELICITY

Misha shoves me in a closet and steps in behind me, pulling the door shut as screams fill the corridor outside the sitting room.

"What's happening?" I ask.

"Intruders," he says.

"But how? There are wards all around the palace gates. How did they get in?"

Misha curses. "Portals. There are portals opening all over the palace." I don't have to ask to know he's mentally communicating with someone to get that information. "Erith is in the palace. He's locked himself in Brie's office with the Grimoricon to allow the fighters in."

He turns to face me. I can barely make out his features in the darkness of the closet. "Will you stay here? Hide until I can send someone to protect you?"

I shake my head. "What? Not without you. Where are you going?"

"I have a gift for portals. What can be opened can be closed."

"A gift that has been *failing* you," I cry.

"I know," he whispers. "But I have to try or they'll keep coming.

I'll find my sister. She and I work best together."

Another wave of screams comes from the other side of the wall.

I curl my hands around his biceps and squeeze. "Please don't go. Please stay here. You just said *Erith* is in the palace somewhere. He wants your court. He wants you *dead*."

Misha cups my face in his hands and lowers his mouth to mine, kissing me hard. "Stay safe. I won't be able to focus the way I need to if I'm worried about you."

"Misha." A sob rips from my chest. "Please."

"Abriella's entire defense strategy revolved around keeping them out of the palace. If they keep coming, none of us will survive." He reaches behind him for the doorknob. "Please stay safe." He slips out and shuts the door behind him.

Sinking to the floor, I put my face in my hands. *Please stay safe. Please come back to me.*

I can't listen to the horrible sounds outside this closet. Can't think about what could be happening to him. I cup my hands over my ears and feel tears streak my cheeks as time crawls forward.

I force myself to stay still. To keep myself safe for Misha's sake.

I jerk awake and knock my head into the wall. I must've dreamed because I'm in my true form. My dress is suddenly much too small and I can barely breathe.

Reaching behind me, I quickly release the laces of my corset and unloop the top button of my skirt. But it's not enough. Something feels *off* in the air, like breathing in a space that's running out of oxygen.

I've been in here too long. Has it been hours? My muscles ache from crouching in this tight space. I can't just sit here anymore. *Erith* is the reason all this is happening, and I'm the only one who can kill him. I can't stand by and let him ruin lives any longer.

I crack open the door and peek out into the sitting room. The windows are dark, the lanterns on the wall flicker and cast shadows across the room, but I don't see anyone here.

Slowly and quietly, I slip from the closet and creep toward the hallway door. It's gone eerily silent compared to before Misha hid me in the closet. All the shouts sound distant. Because the fighting's moved to a different part of the palace or because everyone in this wing is dead?

I can't let myself think about it.

Even out here the air still feels *wrong*.

Then I realize what it is. This is how it felt when Misha rescued me from that cell and Konner's silencer friend blocked our magic.

The storm continues at a low rumble outside the palace walls. I turn in the direction the queen ran when she found out the general wasn't the general at all. Most of the lanterns out here have been extinguished, and I nearly fall on my face when I stumble over something on the floor.

A body. A friend? I can't let myself look. I wish I could cast light in front of me, but I know without trying that it wouldn't work. I feel the suppression of my magic like a blanket thrown over my face when I'm trying to catch my breath. Maybe it's for the best that I can't. I don't want to call attention to myself.

I slowly move forward, one hand along the wall, feet shuffling to find anything on the floor before it trips me.

Someone grabs me from behind and puts a hot, sweaty hand over my mouth. "Look who we have here."

"That's not the princess," someone else says. I kick and flail, trying to squirm from his grasp, but he's huge and his hold on me is too strong.

"No, but it's the next best thing. Erith wants this one dead and he will reward me for finding her."

"What are you waiting—"

The sound of steel slicing through flesh fills my ears. I'm dragged to the floor as the male holding me falls. We land in an awkward heap, him half on top of me, and blood soaks into my dress.

Someone shoves him off me with his boot and grabs my hand to pull me up.

"Hale?" I'm almost positive, but I can barely make out his silhouette, much less his face. "It's so dark. How did they know who I am?"

"Orcs see better in the dark than we do." He glances back and forth, watching for trouble. "Are you okay?"

No, but I won't saddle him with that when there are a thousand things wrong with this moment. "I'm fine. You?"

"Fine. I got separated from Jasalyn, though—earlier when the portals opened and all hell broke loose—and now I can't find her."

That's not the princess, one of the orcs said. "Those orcs were looking for her. You think one of Mordeus's people took her?"

"They would want to if they could."

Of course. Because they need to secure the vessel for the king to return. "I'm looking for Erith. His magic is behind so much of this mess." I wish I could see Hale's eyes, that I could hold his gaze while we had this conversation. "Hale, if I can find him, I need to do this."

He finds my hand in the dark. "Don't worry about me. Any fate that's going to end me tonight won't be stopped by you sparing that sonofabitch."

"Do you know where he is?"

"He was in Abriella's office last I knew, but he was guarded by wards. I don't know if he's moved since. A few of Konner's sentinels are silencers and they're working together to cut off magic to the whole palace—that scared most of the insurgents outside. Misha and Pretha are working together to keep wards up around the palace walls so they can't get back in."

"I'll start at her office."

"I'd go with you, but I need to find Jas."

I think of the vision the oracle gave me, the image of Hale bleeding out on the ground, and shake my head. "No. It's better if you're not there."

"Everyone's gathering in the throne room," he says. "Come there when you're ready."

I take a breath, but I can't make myself let go of his hand. "Please be careful. Hide if you have to."

He releases a dark chuckle. "Don't have it in me to hide, sis. Now get your dagger ready and get out of here."

Where are you, Erith?

As I round the corner to Abriella's office, lightning cracks outside, illuminating the hall. Half a dozen bodies litter the floor in front of the busted-down office door. My heart is racing, and I focus on steadying my breaths to even it out, waiting for another flash of lightning so I can see more.

I don't have to wait long before the hall is lit up again. Thunder follows immediately, shaking the floor beneath me. The storm must be right on top of us. The light lingers just long enough for me to make out a trail of blood, leading around another corner.

I follow it in the dark, moving slowly and using every fae sense I have to listen for others.

That's when I hear the voice in the distance. A voice that sends shivers down my spine.

"You are a disgrace to my palace," he's saying. "Did you ever ask yourself why I started sending you to do my killing when you were barely ten and three years?"

A beat of silence and no response. I creep closer.

"I knew you would never amount to anything, never be worthy of ascending. I knew it from the day you were born. Your mother coddled you."

I'm getting closer. His voice is getting louder.

When I peek into the next doorway, I find a room illuminated by candlelight.

Erith has his back to the door as he uses his knife to carve into his victim's skin.

Konner's skin. I bite back a gasp. Is he doing blood magic? Does blood magic work when powers are muted like this?

Erith jerks his blade across Konner's gut and my brother releases the weak grunt-cry of someone barely hanging on. "Tell me where she is, and I'll spare you," our father says. "You know I'll find her one way or another. Wouldn't you rather I end her now, while she's too young to have spent her life fearing me?"

"Never," Konner rasps.

Not blood magic. *Torture.* Erith knows about Leia somehow and he's torturing Konner for her location.

I pull my dagger from my boot and curl my hand around the hilt. Konner's eyes flutter open and he meets my gaze over Erith's shoulder. He nods almost imperceptibly. *Do it.*

I charge forward, ready to plunge my blade into his back, but before I can cross the threshold into the room I'm jerked backward and thrown against the opposite wall. My skull cracks against the doorframe. My dagger goes flying as I crumple to the floor.

"Look who finally came out to play," a familiar voice says as I struggle back to my feet.

The room is spinning and my head throbs. I no sooner get my feet under me than they slip out again. Blood, I realize, leaning my head against the wall while I wait for the world to stop spinning. There's blood all over the floor.

"Sorry, Lis. I can't let you fulfill your destiny today. Or ever." Shae stalks toward me, a sneer curling his lips. "Looks like this is the end of the road for you."

"What are you going to do? Kill me?" I say, mustering all the courage that I don't feel. "You can't ascend to be one of the Seven if you've killed."

"I can't kill you, but there's no rule about making you wish you were dead while I wait for my friends to come do the job for me."

He grabs me by the front of my shirt and yanks me upright as he draws a dagger from his hip. He shoves me against the wall, leaning forward, his hot, foul breath against my face. "No one will miss you, Felicity. That's what's really sad." He drags the tip of his blade down my cheek and a hot bead of blood rolls down to my chin. "You've tried so hard to win Kendrick's love, the approval of his friends. But the truth is you could never give them the one thing they really wanted. Even now, when you've finally mustered a tiny bit of courage, you're failing."

"I thought I loved you," I say, looking up into his eyes.

"How pathetic." He's so busy laughing, he doesn't even see me move for his blade. The ease with which I take it from his hand only proves how greatly he underestimates me—has always underestimated me.

He's the reason the man who raised me is dead. *He's* the reason I've had to be on the run for so long. To be alone for so long. And if he has his way, he'll be the reason I never walk out of this palace again.

I plunge the small blade into Shae's chest.

The shock registers in his eyes a moment before he stumbles back, his hands going to his chest, to the wound the iron-and-adamant blade left gushing blood.

"Now I know better," I whisper, shoving him against the wall, where he slides to the floor.

"*Please*," the desperate plea sounds from the room where I found Erith. "Please, don't."

"Konner," I breathe. I run back to the room and collide with something hard.

My already aching head snaps back and my ears ring. When I lift my gaze, I meet my birth father's eyes. Wide and panicked.

He's a buck in the woods, staring down the archer's arrow. But why is he so afraid when he's armed? When he's bigger and stronger and more powerful than me?

Time seems to stop when I look into the icy blue depths I've run from for so long, and I see the truth. He can't hurt me. I'm not only the one who can kill him; whatever twisted magic got him here made it so he can't harm the few who can harm him.

In that split second, I have him at my mercy and see what could've been—a life in the palace with the mother he killed, a sister, a bond with the brother I never had.

I see years of fear, of guilt and loneliness. All because of this male who put his power before everything and everyone else.

And then I see the family I was given. The friends I made along the way. The strength I've found in myself.

Letting him live should've never been an option, but I've always done everything I could to protect those I love, and that doesn't end today.

I plunge my iron blade into his heart.

Erith's eyes go wide. He grabs a handful of my hair and pulls, trying to drive me to the floor, but I'm immovable. This was my destiny all along. This moment needed to happen, and the world will be better for it.

I pull my blade free and plunge it into the side of Erith's neck for good measure, stumbling back out of his grasp. He falls to the floor with a garbled gasp for air, blood trickling from his lips. "I deserved better than you, and I got it. But Konner deserved better than you too. And so did my sister."

I shove his body to the side with my boot and crawl over him to get to Konner. "Are you okay?" He looks so pale in the flickering candlelight.

"You did it," he says, voice weak. "May the gods bless you for all your days."

He's bleeding all over, covered in evidence of the torture he endured. "I couldn't risk him hurting Leia." I need to find a healer and get him outside these palace walls, where they can use magic to mend him.

"I will thank you forever from the Twilight," he rasps. "I owe you everything."

"What? Konner, no." I pat his chest and sides, as if I could stop the death that's creeping into his voice if I find the wound. But there's too much blood and I can't tell which spot is fatal. "You stay with me. You have a little girl to raise, remember? That's what all of this is for—so you can watch her grow up. She can hold your hand when she takes her first steps, and laugh with you over stupid jokes, and cry on your shoulder the first time her heart is broken."

He grunts softly. "You'll have to stand in for me. Make sure she knows how much I loved her—*love* her—how I would've battled every monster in every realm to protect her." He coughs and blood leaks from his lips. "If she's like us, make sure she understands how to use the gift. Don't let her use it against people she loves."

"Please." I curl my body over him and cling to his hand as his blood saturates my clothes. "Don't do this. Tell her yourself. I just got you. You *can't* leave me."

"Leia is safe. Nothing matters more than that."

My vision blurs and tears plop onto his cheeks. "You asked me what it was like in that alternate world you put me in." I swallow a sob. "It was wonderful. You were my very best friend. You knew me better than anyone, and I never felt alone."

"You never were," he says. His hand goes limp in mine.

CHAPTER FORTY-FOUR

JASALYN

"There you are!" Kendrick pulls me into his arms and out of a panic-induced stupor. "I've been looking for you everywhere."

He has? I don't know how long we've been separated. Minutes? Hours? I was searching for my sister but—I look around the dimly lit hallway—I don't remember how I got here or where I was before this. I recognize this corridor as belonging to the main level of the palace, between the ballroom and the throne room. Sounds of fighting and destruction come from outside. "Where are the others?"

"Everyone's gathering in the throne room." He ushers me toward a bit of flickering light at the end of the hall.

"Is Brie there? I've been looking for her."

"I don't know, but she might be." He stops right outside the throne room doors and turns me to face him. "Listen, I don't know if you can feel it, but Konner had some silencers cast their magic across the palace."

"Silencers?" I still feel off. Like I'm not quite one with my body.

"They block magic. It was the only way to quickly close all the portals Erith had opened. That means that when it's time, you're going to have to get outside these walls so your magic can work."

"Time for what?"

His throat bobs. "Time to activate your phoenix—so you can rise before the clock strikes midnight and your birthday gives Mordeus the power to take you himself."

But I still don't know how. I glance toward a set of windows that have been blocked by a wooden headboard, dampening the sounds of chaos beyond the wall.

"I'll go with you," he says, pulling me through the throne room doors and into a candlelit space. "I will *make sure* no one can touch you. When you burn, when you go through that rebirth and shed that bastard's control once and for all, I will protect you. I can do that."

"And who will protect *you*?" I ask. Walking feels strange. Like stepping on solid ground after walking around on a boat for hours.

"I'll handle it," he says.

"And if I still can't figure out how to call on my inner fire and make myself burn to ash? What then? Because I don't know *how* to do this. I can't."

He grips my shoulders and I see hope in his eyes right alongside his fear. "I've been thinking about this, and I realized something about your power. Something we haven't considered yet."

This is important, and I watch his lips move and will myself to listen, but I'm feeling dizzy. Maybe because I haven't eaten anything today. Maybe at the idea of Kendrick protecting me while surrounded by our enemies.

"Are you listening to me?" Kendrick says, but the room is going blurry and I'm having trouble focusing. "Think about the Sword of Fire. That flame wasn't yours."

There's a dull humming in my ears. I feel like I'm sleeping and floating. Like I'm a spirit without a body. I put my hand on his chest and see the ring there.

The ring that strengthens the bond between me and Mordeus. The ring I had to use magic to rid myself of. Did I put it back on? Where did I find it?

Kendrick is trying to tell me something, but he needs to know the ring is back. I lift my hand to show him what I can't find the words to explain.

"Jasalyn!" Strong fingers curl around my wrist and I'm pulled back into myself.

"Kendrick?"

He looks down at me in horror, eyes panicked, mouth agape. His fingers loosen from my wrist. "Fight. It."

Blood pools hot and sticky over my hand, and when I tear my eyes from his to look down, I see my dagger plunged into the middle of his chest, my ringed hand wrapped around the hilt.

"Kendrick." My voice shakes. "No . . ."

"I . . . I love you," he gasps before he falls to the floor at my feet.

I'm frozen. Shaking.

"What happened?" Skylar rushes to us, eyes on Kendrick, but she stops when she sees me. "Are you okay?"

"Help him!" I screech. I reach for the ring and yank it from my finger, letting it clatter to the ground.

Skylar drags her eyes off me and drops to her knees. "Kendrick," she sobs, putting pressure on his wound. She shouts for help, then people are running all around me, but I can't move. *How did I get here? When did I pull out my dagger? Where did the ring come from? Why . . .*

The dark, familiar chuckle at the back of my mind gives me the answer I should've already known. *Mordeus.*

Remme shoves me away and I stumble backward as he drops to his haunches. He rolls Kendrick to his back. "He's still breathing," he says.

"What did you do?" Skylar asks, her voice climbing to a pitch I've never heard from her.

"She missed his heart," Natan says, "but we need to remove that blade before it can do more damage."

"No," I whisper. "This isn't fair." As if *any* of this has *ever* been fair.

"Remme, you pull the blade," Natan is saying, "and Skylar, get down here and help me put pressure on this wound."

"Get out of the way!" Skylar says, shoving at my legs until I stumble back a few steps.

I drop to my knees and crawl toward him. *I stabbed him. I stabbed Kendrick.* "Please be okay. Please, Kendrick, please," I sob.

Natan turns to me and takes me by the shoulders. "Let us help Hale. You need to go tap into your power. It's somewhere in there, Jas. Find it and win. Win for *him.* Beat the bastard who tried to kill the male you love." He looks over his shoulder and when I follow his gaze I realize he's looking at the big clock on the other side of the throne room. Fifteen minutes until midnight. Fifteen minutes until my birthday. Fifteen minutes until I have no way out of this bargain.

Even if I can find this inner flame, how can I endure the pain knowing I have to come back to a world where Kendrick is gone because of me?

"Natan, we need magic," Remme says. "He's not going to make it without a healer."

"We need to get him outside," Skylar says.

"He'll be a sitting duck out there," Remme says, "never mind the amount of blood he'll lose if we try to move him. No way. We need magic *here*."

"He's dead!" All heads turn to Felicity as she runs into the throne room, her cheeks streaked with tears. "Erith is dead. I killed—" She stops in her tracks when she sees her brother on the ground. "No," she breathes. She runs to his side and drops to the floor, pressing her hand to Kendrick's pale face. "No, no, no."

My heart is being carved out. *Please, Kendrick. You don't have to live for me, but you need to live for them. They need you. They love you.*

"We need magic," Remme tells Felicity. "I need you to find Misha and the Eloran silencers—they're on the north tower. Make them lift the shield."

She gives a shaky nod and runs from the throne room.

"I don't know how long it's going to take before Felicity finds Misha," Natan says, squeezing my shoulders. "You can't count on having the time to use your magic here. You still need to go to the lawn."

"I don't know *how*—"

"You *are* the phoenix," Remme shouts. "*We* will take care of this. Get beyond these walls, keep to the shadows, and find your inner fire. Give him a reason to wake up, Slayer."

I don't know how to do this, but I can't stand here and do nothing. I sprint for the door, pumping my arms and legs so fast my lungs burn. *Get to the lawn. Get to the lawn and find your power. Get to the lawn and* try *to find your flame.*

Brie told me once that when she was first learning to wield her shadows, she found them easiest to grasp when she was angry. Later, she learned better ways to control them, but maybe if I focus on my anger, my rage—

I charge through the doors and toward the lawn at the back of the palace and stumble back at the chaos before me, all illuminated by flames that line the perimeter. The dozens of raging bonfires that were lit to fortify the wards have grown in size. The flames lick at the night sky, the crackling so loud it sounds like breaking bones, and the heat so intense I can feel it from a good hundred yards away.

Soldiers fight with swords and fists and magic, and everywhere I look there is death. Dead soldiers being stomped underfoot while others fight. Soldiers struck by blades and magic and arrows and falling to join them.

"We have the queen!" someone shouts, and the insurgents flooding the lawn cheer. Several of the Midnight Raiders turn, distracted by the incoming horde, and are struck because of it.

I tuck myself into the shadows and watch as five males carry my sister over their heads. Her arms are bound to her sides, her legs tied together. I can't breathe. They're going to hang her from the gates, just like the oracle showed me.

I want to chase them down and tear her from their grasp. I roll the ring between two fingers. If I put it on, I could save her. I could command them and they would do as I say.

Wait. I drop my gaze and nearly drop it because my hands are shaking so hard. I took it off in the hall with Kendrick. I didn't pick it up, did I? I don't *want* to wear the ring again.

Though, maybe I should. If I'd put it on sooner, who's to say I couldn't have stopped all of this?

But last time I wore it, I hurt Kendrick and he may not survive. If I put it on now to save my sister, who's to say Mordeus won't take control and kill her with my hands?

It takes every bit of my focus, but I hold it tight and hurl it toward the flames that line the lawn.

The best way I can help my sister now is to keep Mordeus from taking it all, and the only way I can do that is to tap into the power I can't seem to find inside myself.

I blow out a shuddering breath, ignore every instinct that tells me to run after my sister, and will myself to find that fire Pretha swears is waiting inside.

Someone grabs me by the hair and yanks me backward. "Finally!" he mutters. "We find the vessel. Come with me."

I let him push me along toward a group of soldiers near the gates. The air grows hotter the closer we get, and I have to squint against the glare of the flames.

Burn now, I tell myself, *burn and take this bastard with you.*

I dig, looking deep toward my anger, thinking of every day Mordeus stole from me because of what he did in those dungeons—not just the days I was there but the days after. Fury pumps through me, but I still see no flame.

The vessel. They know Mordeus's plan. And if that's the case then they know that their king plans to take over this body.

If this continues, I lose, and all my efforts were for nothing. But if they think I *am* Mordeus . . .

"Enough!" I shout, and everyone in the group pulls to attention.

"Is this how you look at your *king*?" I jerk from the soldier's grasp and spin to glare at him.

"Mordeus," he breathes, bowing his head. "Forgive me, I—"

"Give us something so we know it's you in there, Your Majesty," someone says behind me.

What was Kendrick trying to tell me before Mordeus pushed me from my own consciousness? Remember the Sword of Fire, he said. Does he think it's here somewhere? That Erith brought it with him? Maybe it could be used to ignite my power or—

"Yeah," the male next to him says. "It's not midnight yet."

"Exactly. And your job is to protect this vessel until it's *complete*," I spit, spinning to glare at the others.

"Of course," the first male says. "We will keep you safe."

The clock on the Midnight Palace sounds its first chime for midnight. If I don't move now, this is over. *Think about the Sword of Fire*, Kendrick said. *That flame wasn't yours.*

Pretha wanted me to find my inner flame, she thought that was the way to use my power, but what if that's not how this works at all.

Maybe we've been wrong all along. Maybe I can't wield flames like my sister can wield shadows. Maybe there's no fire burning inside me but only the ability to survive it. Or not survive but return.

I don't know any other way to do this. "You know what I have to do," I tell the males. They exchange worried glances, unsure.

Before they can stop me, I walk to the closest raging fire and right into the flames.

CHAPTER FORTY-FIVE

FELICITY

Misha, Pretha, and the silencers are on the top of the north tower, just where Remme said I would find them. Misha and Pretha are holding hands and facing the lawn from the back of the rooftop terrace, focusing intently. The three silencers stand in a triangular formation. They're in the uniform of Konner's men and are glistening with sweat, a sickly greenish pallor to their skin, as if blocking out the magic in the whole palace is taking everything out of them.

"You have to drop the silencers!" I shout. "We need the magic!"

The silencers look at me, then at each other, but do nothing.

I turn to Misha. "Tell them to let magic back into the palace."

Misha's eyes flicker open and he gives a delirious half smile at the sight of me.

"Listen to me!" I shout. "Drop the silencers now! Hale is dying. We need magic to win this!"

Misha blinks several times. "Too dangerous."

"Erith is dead. He can't reopen the portals."

He gives a slow nod, as if it's taking his mind much longer than usual to process this information. "You can stop," he tells the others.

The female of the trio looks to him, her head rolling to the side as if she lacks the strength to hold it up. "You're sure?" Her voice is barely a whisper.

"Yes," Misha says.

The trio lets go of each other and collapses to the ground. They're all dragging in big, ragged gulps of air like they just kicked their way to the surface after being trapped underwater.

In the next moment, I feel it—the ripple of power and magic and life returning to the palace.

"Junius!" Pretha calls, and the sentinel on the stairs turns. "Bring Goliad and hold these wards for a while."

I run to the tower's edge to scan the yard below and lose my breath. The queen is being strung up on the palace gates, and—

"That's Jasalyn," Pretha says from beside me. Misha moves to stand at the edge with me.

I follow her gaze as the clock clangs once, signaling we're mere seconds from midnight—from the return of Mordeus—and we all spot the princess just as she steps into the flames of the raging bonfire.

Pretha grabs my arm and squeezes hard. "What is she doing?" she asks, her voice barely audible. We all know what Jas is doing even before her blood-curdling screams echo through the night. Through the capital. Through the whole world.

Everything seems to fall away but that single point in the distance where Jasalyn walked into the fire. This doesn't feel real. It's all too much like a horrible dream. "Can it work like that?" I ask Pretha. "Can she burn from a fire that isn't her own? Can she rise again this way?"

"I don't know," Pretha says. "If she can command the flame, we know she can wield the phoenix, but if the flame isn't hers . . . I just don't know."

We watch. All I see are raging flames. All we hear is the sound of horrific cries tapering off into the night. My gaze scans the horizon and my breath catches.

"Is that what I think it is?" Misha asks.

He sees it too. A mass of bodies marching toward the palace gates.

"How many of them are there?" I ask.

Panic fills Pretha's eyes. "We've lost too many men to survive numbers like that."

But then something strange happens. The insurgents who are filling the palace lawn begin running out to attack the new forces.

Mordeus's soldiers begin falling. One after another.

"Who?" Pretha whispers.

I press my fingers to my lips. "Crissa. The Eloran queen. She brought her battalion to help us fight."

CHAPTER FORTY-SIX

JASALYN

Pain surrounds me. Consumes me. *Becomes* me.

There were no blades in Mordeus's dungeons that hurt like this. There were no moments when my hope for tomorrow was *this* bleak.

My mind tells me not to fight. Begs me to surrender. My body has nothing left to fight with. I am agony and flame and despair, and I don't know *how* to rise.

"Wake up, little human. Open your eyes and look at me."

I recognize that voice from my memories—from my nightmares.

The room spins, and even with my eyes closed I know it's dark. Even without obeying that horrifically familiar voice, I know that the only light here will be from the unnatural glow of his silver eyes.

"Come, little pet. Wake up so we can play."

The stone floor is ice cold beneath my cheek, and I focus on the sensation as I try to pull myself from the heavy grip of sleep. *Wake up.*

Darkness. Stone floor. The whimpering of the woman down the hall.

I'm back in Mordeus's dungeons. *The knives and cuts and blood and pain.*

I'm in the dark. And I'm all alone.

I can't make myself look around. Can't make myself confirm what I knew the moment this place appeared around me.

I can't stop the sobs that tear from my chest. Because of the pain consuming every inch of me. Because of the terror. But mostly because I've come this far, and I still don't know how to win.

This is just another one of Mordeus's games.

No. Abriella killed him. I was freed from that horrible place, and Mordeus is nothing more than a rotting corpse now.

I open one eye, angry with myself for the way I'm already shaking—a trembling that starts in my gut and radiates out to my fingertips.

His boots are in front of my face. How is he standing? How is that body supporting him? Was it healed? There is nothing weak about that voice or about the presence of the male in front of me. And I know as surely as I knew it back in his dungeons that he could obliterate me with his magic if he wanted to.

I push myself off the floor and force myself to look at him—to face the male I fear most—but before I can get my feet beneath me, a wave of shadow sweeps through the room and grabs me by the throat. I gasp, choke, splutter. The grip is too tight and when I claw at my neck to pull the squeezing hand away, my fingers sweep through nothing but air.

The shadows throw me against the wall. My head snaps back against the stone and pain sears the backs of my eyes. *Burning. Why is everything burning?*

Ignoring the ringing in my ears and the terror in my blood, I meet his eyes. The maggots are gone, and the silver is back. The decay is gone, his face as healthy and unmarred as it was the day we first met.

"Such a sweet little human. So full of power. So ignorant of how to use it." His repulsive chuckle sends a dozen spiders crawling up my spine. "This doesn't have to hurt," he murmurs, stepping closer. And closer. He lifts his fingers to my cheek, and I am frozen. I am paralyzed like I was during all our visits. Unable to control my own body like I was when he forced food and water down my throat. "I don't need your suffering any longer, little human."

I need to *think*. Where are we? What's happening?

His soldiers captured me, and I pretended he was in control, and then . . .

"Let me help you," he says, and the hands of the shadows that hold me ease up a bit. "I don't need to hurt you anymore."

I don't bother to control my glare. "Then *why*?"

His eyes flash. "I didn't say I *won't* hurt you. I said I don't *need* to. Not if you make this easy for both of us."

"I don't understand." Where we are. What he means. How this is even happening.

"Don't you? All you need to do is surrender. Surrender and there's no more pain. Surrender and all of this goes away."

Because he'll take it. He'll take my body and my life. "Never," I breathe.

"Never?" He laughs. "Says the girl who was all too eager to hand over her life to the Eloran witch. Says the girl who prayed to her gods' deaf ears for death when she was living in my dungeons."

He scoffs. "*Never.* You don't have the *backbone* for *never.*"

But that's just it. We're not in some stony dungeon, and Mordeus isn't up and walking around in his old body. He hasn't been magically healed and we aren't truly in this room.

None of this is real. Except maybe this unceasing agony.

This is some sort of limbo. Some *between* one future and another. The fact that I'm with him and not dead proves I just *might* have more backbone than he ever anticipated, proves I wasn't too late, proves I have a *chance.*

All I have to do is take it.

"None of this is real," I snap.

"What is *real*, little human?" A shadow darts out and wrenches my arm behind my back, twisting until my shoulder feels like it might bust out of my skin. "Is this not real? Or do I need to make you bleed to believe it?"

The pain isn't just in my shoulder. It's everywhere. And it burns and I want it to stop—*need* it to stop.

I don't know how to wield this phoenix that lives inside me, but I've been taught how to shield by the best. If none of this is physically happening, maybe, just maybe, I could use those mental shields to gain an advantage. I gather my power, coiling it tight, until it's too big to hold, until it's vibrating with the need to be free. Then, like attacking with a shield, I scream and release it, shoving it toward his shadows.

The invisible hand releases from my neck, and I drop to the ground and gasp for air.

Every inch of me burns and I'm not sure I have the strength to stay on my feet through the pain.

Mordeus licks his lips. "*There's* the power I've been waiting for."

"The power you'll never touch."

He stalks in a circle around me and looks me over. "I don't think you understand what's happening. There are two of us here—two souls entangled in a battle for a body that cannot hold us both. Not fully. And I am unable and unwilling to live on scraps anymore."

"If you want a second life so badly, you're going to have to live it in that rotting corpse."

Shadows dart forward and shove down my throat, so much like the food he forced me to eat to sustain me. I choke and gag. "This is not a battle I will lose, little human."

I hurl my shields—*my power*—toward him. It's energy and I feel it, feel its potential and its magic, but all I can do is blindly shove it in his direction. His shadows surge to deflect as easily as swatting a fly, dancing around his fingertips as he circles me, but I'm no longer the little mouse who can do nothing but run. *I* circle him too, hands raised in front of me, open and ready to strike.

"You are a disgrace to faekind," he says, sneering. "Rejecting your magic, rejecting your immortality, hiding from darkness. Mab must be rolling in her grave to have the world connect your weakness to her strength."

"You're the disgrace," I say, letting my power fill me. "You were born with great gifts. Magic that could change the world and you used it for greed and power."

He strikes, a ball of darkness plunging into my belly. The air rushes out of me as I'm thrown back. I teeter, struggling to find my balance when my lungs refuse to take a new breath.

"You've come a long way." He looms over me. "The little girl from my dungeons would've been begging for death by now."

A jerky inhale finally gives my lungs the air I need, and I roll to dodge his next strike. Anger boils inside me, and I hurl amorphous power at his face, completely missing when he spins away. "I'm not that little girl anymore," I shout.

"What do you want to live for anyway?" he asks. "I watched what was happening at the palace. Everyone you care about is dead. There is nothing and no one left for you."

"*Liar.*" They aren't dead. Not yet. I can't believe that. "They are going to fight and they are going to survive. Unlike *you*."

Shadows swirls around his feet as he cocks his head to the side. "Your pretty Eloran male is dead, is he not? Because you drove your blade into his chest."

Grief and panic steal my breath—the memory of Kendrick on the ground, blood oozing from his chest. I shove it aside. Mordeus is trying to make me give up. If I have nothing to live for, he wins. "If he's gone, I fight for him. I will defeat you to honor him." I gather my power, preparing for my next attack.

"That's so sweet. And your sister too?"

I freeze. "What about my sister?"

He waves a hand and an image appears behind him. Abriella's body, strung up at the gates of the Midnight Palace, her neck snapped, her head hanging limply at an unnatural angle. "While you've been here, fighting for a life you don't even want, my army finished the job. The revolution is here. You've already lost."

His shadows fill the room, stealing all the air and pressing in on me. Darkness deeper than anything I've ever seen. This is the darkness that will swallow me. This is the night where I'll meet my end.

I fight to breathe, but there's nothing there. My lungs ache, compressed and empty and desperate for air.

"Surrender." The word is a scream that comes from between my ears. It's a plea that comes from the little girl who didn't know how to fight the monster who was torturing her. It's there before me, a path, after so much pain and suffering and fear, to the peace I've craved.

And I don't want it.

I strain to push my power back against his darkness, but I can't. There's nothing for my fire to feed on. There's nothing but shadow and night and fear.

You can't win unless you accept who you are. Karmyn's words come back to me. *Not the phoenix. You've always appreciated fire. You have to be* all *of who you are. Even who you don't want to be.*

I thought she meant I needed to be fae, but maybe she means I'm more like Brie than I ever thought. My sister embraces the darkness and manipulates shadows like they're her own personal infantry. I, on the other hand, have always run from the shadows and cowered from the approaching darkness.

I don't need to fight Mordeus's shadows to win—not when I can command them for myself.

This time, when I breathe, I invite the shadows into my lungs, into my core, into my very essence. I don't need to be the Enchanting Lady to face the darkest parts of myself. They're still there, even when the ring is gone. I am not just a scared child, and I'm not just an avenging girl with a magical ring.

I am anger and vengeance.

I am love and acceptance.

I am power and strength.

I am grace and wrath.

I am fearful *and* fearsome. And I can command the shadows that I've spent years running from.

When I invite the shadows in, they swirl into every corner of my mind, my self, and my soul, and they wait for my command.

The room clears and Mordeus looks around in a panic. "What did you do?" he asks, and now it's my turn to smile.

"You created me," I whisper. "Everything you did to use me, to defeat me, made me into who I am today." Flames flare to life around the edges of the room, licking up the sides of the walls, igniting the wooden beams in the ceiling, crackling all around us.

There's too much heat. It's melting my flesh, and I know the scream piercing my ears is my own.

The flames were never something I could wield, but they are something I can endure.

I feel him pulling at his shadows, calling them back. "We're connected," I say. The pain slices through me, willing me to surrender, but I tighten my hold on the darkness. "Your power is my power. *You* did that."

The flames crawl toward him now, catching on his robe and racing up his back. I feel my own clothes burning. I don't let myself look.

His scream pierces the air and tears through me. I feel his pain because it's mine too. There is no *his body* and *my body*. There is only this one body we are wrestling over, and the white-hot burn of the flame eats away at flesh and bone, ripping into my soul. It's destroying him. It's destroying *me*.

Instead of hiding from it, I wrap my arms around the torment and invite it closer.

I close my eyes. *We're connected.* I cannot destroy him without destroying myself.

Abriella's gone, a small voice whispers between whimpers of pain. *You're too late. Don't do this. Surrender and the pain can end.*

I open my arms and invite the flames to feast. It doesn't matter if I'm too late for Brie. I'm not too late for the rest of the court, for the people who would suffer under a wicked king's rule.

Kendrick is gone. You will have to live with knowing you *killed him. That pain will make this look like nothing.*

But he can't be the only reason I endure. Neither can my sister.

The flames race up my arms. I let them engulf me as they fill the room. Let them engulf *Mordeus*.

His screams fill my ears. They become *my* screams.

I won't surrender to the monster, and I don't hide from the suffering. I let it hurt. I invite in the pain until I am nothing else. I am melting flesh and bubbling skin. I am charred bone and the glowing embers at the root of the flame.

I am the danger in the darkness. I am the scream of the nightmare.

I leave my body long before it turns to ash, but I see it, like I'm watching from a distance.

"And then what happens, Mama?" Abriella asks. Her hand squeezes mine.

I look down. I *do* have a body. I'm a little girl again, tucked into bed, night stars twinkling through the window.

"Then the little princess knew she'd destroyed the monster," our mother says, and the sound of her voice, after so many years without it, is like a balm to my aching soul, "but her fight wasn't over."

CHAPTER FORTY-SEVEN

FELICITY

When morning comes, the sun comes with it. The battle and the storm ended late in the night, leaving nothing but carnage and smoldering fires on the palace lawn.

Misha and I haven't moved from the tower. We watched the battle from up here, watched as Crissa's battalion wiped out most of Mordeus's legions and made the rest run. We waited through the end of the storm and the rising sun, our friends visiting to share updates about Hale's and the queen's condition every so often. Maybe I should be down in the infirmary with my brother, but sitting at his bedside holding his hand feels like *goodbye*, and I refuse to accept any eventuality that doesn't include another *hello*.

So I sit in his stead, watching the final flames on the lawn burn down and willing the princess to appear, for the sake of my brother, for the sake of the shadow queen, for the sake of my friends who fought so hard and deserve something to believe in.

"Your queen is here," Misha says, referring to Crissa, who's been in the palace since helping us defeat Mordeus's forces. "What will your brother do if the princess comes back?"

"The same thing he'll do if she doesn't," I say, and I know it's true. "He'll love her forever. Elora will have to find another king."

He's quiet for a long time and then surprises me by pulling me into him, wrapping me into his warmth, his strength. "How lucky he is to have a sister who understands and accepts this about him," he murmurs into my neck.

I turn my head. "Don't you think Pretha understands you?"

His throat bobs. "I'm the one who didn't understand her. I didn't understand how love could overpower duty. Now it's so clear that I never should've married Amira for the sake of the crown, not when what she and Pretha had was so real, so pure. But I didn't understand it then because I'd never . . ." He releases a slow breath. "I understand it now."

My insides shimmer with something that could be happiness. One day soon, even. Once we aren't perched on a rooftop waiting to see if we have another friend to grieve. "They made it back to each other, though," I say. "That's something to celebrate."

"Indeed it is." He presses a kiss to my neck.

"And what will you do now that there's not an immediate threat to your throne?"

His arms tighten around me. "You know what *I* want to do. What happens next will depend on what you want. Your home realm finally got its revolution. Change is coming. Maybe that's where you want to be." He swallows. "But if you decide you'd like to stay with me, I'd jump at the chance to prove my love to you."

"I didn't tell you." I spin in his arms and look up at him. His hair's a mess and his tunic is half untucked. He's still irresistible like this, disheveled from a night of wielding unimaginable power to protect a kingdom that isn't even his own. "I thought the dream Konner locked me in was an illusion."

"It wasn't?"

I shake my head. "No. It was an alternate reality—it was the way life would've been if my father had died during his attempt at gaining godlike immortality."

His face falls. "And you were so happy there. In that dream. Perhaps a life at the palace—"

"Misha, I was in love."

"You mentioned that," he rasps.

"Did I tell you *who* I loved?" I touch my fingertips to his face and smile, soaking in the flickers of hope in his russet eyes. "I was in love with the Wild Fae king and ready—eager, even—to leave my home and spend my life with him."

"And what about in *this* reality? What are you eager for here?"

"The same thing," I whisper.

He presses his mouth to mine and kisses me hard. Like he's trying to freeze this moment in time. Like he's trying to hold it tight so he can take it with him everywhere. "I love you," he says against my lips.

"I love you too."

The scuff of boots on the stairs pulls my attention from Misha. "Hale, should you be out of bed?"

His knuckles are white as he uses the rail to pull himself up the last few steps. Behind him, the shadow queen follows, her king consort at her back. Hale and the queen are both still pale, and should be resting, but I know they need to be here even more than I do.

"Any sign of her?" my brother asks.

I shake my head weakly. "I'm sorry."

"Word came from beyond the gates," Abriella says, her voice faint. "General Hargova had a group of Mordeus's pledges he planned to bring to my dungeons. They're all gone."

"They escaped?" Misha asks.

"No," Hale says. He scans the ground below. "They collapsed. They're dead."

"We think Mordeus is gone for good," Brie says. "We think that they died the moment his spirit was finally completely cut off from the world of the living."

I glance toward the fires on the lawn. "So she won? She beat him?"

"We don't know that," Brie says. "All we know for sure is that he didn't survive it."

"That's where she stepped into the flames?" Hale asks, nodding toward our hours-long point of focus.

"Yes," I say.

Hale braces himself on the stone ledge and looks toward the ground, where servants and sentinels deal with the battle's fallen, sorting their people from their enemies. His gaze quickly flicks past them and beyond, to where embers of the fire glow hot, even in the morning sun.

"Even if she didn't survive, she still saved so many," I tell him, hand on his arm. "Her sister, the future of this court, countless others that would've been impacted by the ripple effect of Mordeus's return."

"She'll rise," he says.

Misha and I exchange worried glances. "How do you know?" I ask.

His jaw is hard, his eyes steely. "I just do."

CHAPTER FORTY-EIGHT

JASALYN

"It's easy to want the good days," Fherna says, flipping through the pages of her book. "It's the others that make the decision so hard. The bad and the painful and the gray and the numb. You can't just imagine a happy life and decide it's worth it; you have to choose all of it."

Wind whips around me, snapping my hair against my tearstained cheeks. "I know."

"No one can promise you any future. No oracle can see every path; no seer can speak a truth that won't change with tomorrow's tide."

"I know."

"So you would choose this uncertain, painful existence even if it might be any of these?"

"Any of what?" I ask. I look around and see only darkness. But then I look again and realize I was focusing on the wrong thing. There's so much more than darkness. There are all these stars—swirling and changing like a kaleidoscope before my eyes.

A million images, sensations, and emotions swamp me all at once. I am in the mind of the person I become in a dozen different turns of fate.

In one, I see my sister holding a baby, and the joy that fills my heart as his chubby fist wraps around her finger makes me feel like I might float off the ground. But in this same fate, I'm keenly aware, as I look into the baby's silver eyes, that a child is something I will never have. Because I'm alone. Because Kendrick died the night of the battle and I can't bring myself to make a family with someone else—no matter how much I may want one. The pain is an ache that starts in my heart and lives in my bones. I carry it with me everywhere.

In another, I'm looking into Kendrick's eyes as someone ties colorful ribbons around our wrists and murmurs a prayer about the Mother blessing our union. I'm so happy in that moment, but time goes too fast and before we're celebrating our fifth year together, he's slain when he steps in front of a poisoned blade to save my sister from assassination.

I die too young.

I die too old.

I find love.

I know loneliness with an intimacy no one in my life can understand.

I have children who have Kendrick's eyes and children who die in my arms.

I have an achingly empty womb, and I have children I orphan when I die too soon.

I know friendship and betrayal. I know the comfort of the magical bond between two faeries.

I know pleasure. I know pain.

I bury my sister and become queen of the shadow court, Kendrick by my side. Then no one by my side.

I move back to Elora and live on a farm with Kendrick.

I move back to Elora and nearly starve on the streets when I can't find work.

War comes and takes everything that matters. From me. From the people I love.

War comes and change follows. Revolution that feels worthy of the sacrifice it demanded.

I bury my friends. My friends bury me.

Every existence has pain and joy and sacrifice, and I know them all at once.

I can no more pick from these myriad futures than I can pluck a single grain of salt from the sea. I can't choose. My stars may feel cursed or my fate may feel charmed, but my reality will inevitably be a little of both.

"Do you see?" Fherna asks. She's behind me and I meet her eyes in the mirror before me.

I touch the scar hooked around my eye and nod. "They're part of me. They aren't the pain or the memory. They are simply a sign of where I've been."

"You could let the fire take them, pretend they were never there."

My heart surges into my throat and I shake my head. "No. They're mine. I endured."

She lifts her chin, pride shining in her eyes. "You're ready," she says.

"Yes." My mind and body are ravaged from the grief of the losses in a hundred different fates, but my heart is full of the gifts that came from choosing one more day. "I am."

She gives me a slow smile that looks nothing like a goblin's and everything like my mother's, and when she speaks again, the words are in my head because she's disappeared.

Then this is the part where you rise.

The ash on my bare skin is gritty and hot. My body feels weak, like I've been sleeping for a year, but when I open my eyes, a full moon shines down on me and the stars are spread in a blanket across the sky. They appear closer than ever, like I can make out the edges of each individual one.

I sit up, pushing myself off the ground and out of the ash surrounding me. I'm on the palace lawn, in the same spot where I stepped into the fire and nearly surrendered to escape the agony of the flames. The battle is over now. The pain gone. All that's left is this ash, the clear night sky, and a collection of stars that feel brand-new.

A few feet away, Kendrick's body lies limply in the grass, and my heart sinks. *He didn't make it.*

When I chose to rise, I knew nothing was promised and accepted that, but that does nothing to spare me from the grief of knowing—

Wait.

His chest gently rises and falls. I lean closer to make sure I'm not imagining it, and tears turn my vision blurry. *He's sleeping.*

I roll to my knees, crawling across soot and silt, through bits of charred wood and scorched earth, to get to lie by his side. I can't help myself, so I stroke the side of his face, let his stubble tickle my fingers, let his breath tickle my ear.

When his eyes slowly open, his lips part and he places a gentle hand on either side of my head. "Jasalyn."

I take him in, those blue eyes, his full mouth, the steady beat of his heart beneath my hand. Every sense is so heightened. It's like I can see him with all my senses. "Kendrick," I say in return, then more softly, I try, "Hale."

"I love my given name on your lips." He scans my face over and over and shakes his head in wonder. "Is this a dream?"

"If so, I think it's mine," I say. "You're alive." My voice is full of awe and gratitude, but it doesn't come close to matching the magnitude of what's happening inside me.

He lifts shaking hands to cup my jaw, his touch so tender, as if he thinks I might disintegrate if he's not careful. "*You're* alive," he says.

I smile. "Are you surprised?"

"I refused to believe anything else, but Jasalyn . . ." He squeezes his eyes shut for a beat. "It's been days."

I try to imagine what that was like for him. For Brie. Waiting for days and not knowing if I was gone for good. "It felt like many lifetimes." Maybe someday I'll tell him all I endured to get back to him, to get back to this life, but not tonight.

"But you made it. You beat him. I knew you would."

I nod. Yes, someday I'll tell him that beating Mordeus was the easy part, but for now . . . I look toward the palace. "Abriella?"

He must see the worry on my face. "Your sister is well."

Relief washes over me, opens my lungs for a long, shaky breath.

"She was injured but recovered quickly. Crissa's battalion showed up and saved our asses."

"Your queen," I murmur. There's no bitterness in my voice. How could I be bitter toward the girl who saved me once? Toward the girl who saved my sister and my friends?

"Elora's queen," he says, then runs a finger across his forehead. "I think the Mother accepted that I won't be taking any throne."

"It's not glamoured away?"

He shakes his head. "This is me."

"And that's what you want?"

He kisses me hard, as if to ask how I could doubt him. When his kiss turns softer and longer, I moan against his lips. "I don't want any life without you by my side," he says when he finally pulls away. "And anyway, I don't need a throne to change Elora."

"No, you don't." He's so amazing and I wonder at how lucky my home realm was that they had him fighting for their future. "How long has it been? Since . . ." I glance toward the ashes.

"Three days. The soldiers who were clearing the lawn tried to shovel out the ash and your sister lost it on them." He bows his head but can't hide his smile. "I'm pretty sure she would've made them leave it here for a century even if there'd been no sign of you. And she was right. *We* were right. Because here you are."

"And you slept out here? By a pile of ash? For days?"

"There was nowhere else I wanted to be." He shrugs, then flicks his gaze down my body. "And seeing you naked in the moonlight isn't doing anything to make me regret that decision."

I stifle my smile. "I'm covered in ash."

He arches a brow and gives a self-satisfied shrug. "It looks good on you."

"You're ridiculous," I mutter, but my insides are dancing. I'd missed his words. His eyes. His laugh. Three days for him, for my sister, for my friends. Lifetimes for me.

"Are you hurt?" he asks.

"Not anymore."

"Good." He puts one hand behind my head and one behind my back and rolls us so he's on top of me and there's nothing but soft grass at my back. His thigh settles between my legs, his weight on his elbows. He kisses me tenderly, drinking me in in sips before he angles his mouth over mine to demand more. Every inch of my skin is more sensitive than I remember and I shiver beneath him.

He pulls back. "You're cold. Do you need some clothes?"

"Not cold," I promise, looking into his eyes. "But the clothes might be a good idea."

"Debatable." He winks but sits back on his heels and peels off his tunic, helping me sit up so I can cover myself with it. The buttery-soft material slides over my sensitive skin. It smells like him. Like home.

"What about everyone else?" I ask.

The delight instantly flees his expression. "We lost a lot of people, but our closest friends, our family, they made it through."

"Erith?" I ask.

"Gone. Felicity made sure of that." He frowns. "Unfortunately, Konner, Felicity's twin, didn't make it."

"I'm sorry to hear that," I whisper, my heart aching for her.

"You are the talk of your sister's court. The reason that Mordeus is gone for good, they're saying."

"There were so many ways we could've lost. Infinite potential heartbreaks. We are so lucky."

He nips at my lips. "Luckier than I could've ever hoped."

"We should probably go inside."

His dimples flash. "Probably," he says, but he doesn't resist in the slightest when I lie back on the grass and pull him with me.

The door to my bedchambers rattles when it slams against the wall.

I push up in bed, eyes bleary. Abriella marches into my room and stands beside my bed with her arms crossed.

"Seriously?" she says, looking back and forth between me and Kendrick.

Kendrick rubs his eyes and blinks at her. "Morning," he mutters. She swats him on the side of his head, and he flinches, then tugs me onto his lap. "Protect me, Slayer."

"My sister has been back long enough for you to come back inside, sleep, and"—she waves a hand—"gods know what else, and you *didn't. come. get. me?*"

"We were a little busy with the gods-know-what-else part," he says, then ducks behind me when she makes to swing at him again.

I nudge his hands off me and climb out of bed. "You were sleeping," I explain, "and I needed a bath."

She looks me over, taking me in like she wasn't sure she'd ever get to again, then her eyes fill with tears and she drags me into her arms and hugs me tight. "I was so afraid we'd lost you."

I wrap my arms around her and hug her back. "I'm sorry. Apparently resurrection isn't as speedy as we expected."

Her chest shakes against me with silent laughter. When she

pulls back, her cheeks are streaked with tears but her eyes are clear. When she touches my face, she traces the scar around my eye. "I don't know why I expected these to go away when you rose from the ash."

I study her for a long time, thinking of the shadows we share and the trials we've both had to endure to get where we are. "They could have, but I wanted to keep them."

She cocks her head to the side. "They're a reminder of how strong you are," she says, answering the question for herself. "Yes, that's what makes them so beautiful on you. The fae ears are a nice touch too."

I jolt upright. I hadn't even thought about that. "That's right. I'm fae now." That explains everything I was feeling last night. Fae senses are supposed to be extra sensitive. "Interesting."

"*Interesting?*" she says. "That's it?"

Kendrick doesn't even try to disguise his smug smile.

Brie blows out a breath. "Get dressed and come have breakfast with me? I'll cancel my meetings."

"What meetings are those?"

She shrugs. "Nothing important."

I look to Kendrick.

"The remaining four of the Elora Seven are here," he says. "They're eager to discuss the future of the realm."

"But it can wait," Brie says.

She opens the drapes, then stares at me as she backs toward the door.

"What?" I ask.

"I'm just happy," she says, then she disappears.

I crawl back into bed with Kendrick. "I can't believe you didn't say anything."

"About what?" he asks innocently.

"The ears? My fresh immortality?"

"Didn't think I needed to." His eyes soften. "And didn't want to put a damper on our reunion if you weren't happy about it."

"I . . ." How do I feel about being fae? I knew this was what was coming but I never let myself think this far ahead. "I'm glad we're both fae. One human lifetime couldn't possibly be enough."

His eyes heat and he tugs me down toward him. I go happily.

"Also"—I block out the morning sun with my shadows—"this comes with cool tricks."

CHAPTER FORTY-NINE

FELICITY

"We didn't fight this long and sacrifice so much to keep the corrupt Seven in power," Remme says, slapping a hand on the table. "I can't believe we're even having this conversation."

Sol presses her palms together, the picture of patience. "But have you stopped to consider what that's going to be like? The vast majority of Elorans think the Seven are their saviors. Maybe that would change once you prove all the centuries of lies, but people *want* something to believe in. And the Eloran people? They *need* something to believe in. They will fight you if you try to take that away—even if your reasons are all the right ones."

"So what's your solution?" Skylar says. She's been frowning so hard Mom would say her face was going to get stuck like that. "Keep the status quo? Accept that the world is full of injustices just because change would be *hard*?"

Sol exchanges a look with her daughter, who came along for this meeting and informed us that she'd be taking her *husband's* seat at the table. I hugged her and apologized for not being able to save Konner. Her eyes were bright when she told me I saved the thing he cared about most instead. And then she passed that squirming, giggling baby girl into my arms.

"We're suggesting," Tulle says, "that you don't change the system but the people inside of it. We've culled the rot and the greed from the Seven, so it's the perfect time to replace them with humans. Leaders of their own right who know better than anyone stuck in our palace exactly what their people need."

"Humans," Remme says, like he's never heard the word before.

Sol steps in. "Your old monarchy was headed by a human queen—so why not a human Matriarch of the Seven? Then we don't have to fight the people to give them what they need. We work together, elves and humans, to create a world where both can live."

"You make it sound so easy," Skylar says.

"It won't be easy," Sol admits. "Not at all. When has lasting change on a scale this big ever been easy? But would your full revolution be any easier?"

"If I could say something?" Crissa says, her small voice breaking, the first bird chirp before sunrise.

"I would love to hear your thoughts," Sol says. She sounds sincere. About *all* of this.

"We have three groups of people in Elora," Crissa says. "You've spoken of the first two—those who believe the Seven are their saviors and those who know the true history and want the monarchy restored—but I think you're forgetting about everyone else." We all wait expectantly for her to tell us, but it's Jasalyn who speaks first.

"Those who are too busy trying to survive to have an opinion about any of it," the shadow princess says. My brother beams at her, sappy and in love and so good for my heart.

Crissa nods. "It's easy for you all to look down on them for failing to take a stand in a world that has been so unjust to them, but protest is a luxury. Having an agenda is a privilege. These people are focused on finding their next meal and keeping a roof over their children's heads." She takes a breath. "So, yes, there are those who still believe in the grace and goodness of the Seven, but there are also plenty of people out there who have either been working to help restore the monarchy or who are so jaded they don't believe in the current system anymore. Those people need something to believe in too, but something new might be easier for them to swallow."

"You're proposing a *new* system?" Sol asks.

"I'm proposing," Crissa says, "that we don't choose." She gives a small shrug. "We rebuild the Seven, as you suggested, replacing those who supported Erith and Mordeus with human leaders from Elora, but there's no matriarch and no patriarch. The Seven worked best when they all ruled equally."

"Hear! Hear!" Sol says.

Crissa goes on. "Then we have the Seven publicly support new monarchy. A callback to the old days. A blending of the old and the new. We work together and support each other. And most importantly, we keep each other in check."

"You'd still be our queen," Skylar says, stars in her eyes.

Abriella glances toward my brother. "And who would be your king? Will you ask your oracle?"

Crissa's eyes are bright as she turns to the shadow queen. "Did you know that in the early days of the Eloran monarchy, the Chosen was simply the one who protected the queen? The markings along his forehead weren't considered a crown but a symbol of his fate being tied to the crown. Along the way, some people decided a woman shouldn't rule alone and insisted the Chosen marry the queen and rule beside her."

"You're *kidding*," Skylar says.

"She's not," Natan says. "Those days were long ago, but you'll find record of them in the Chronicles."

"The oracle will give me a new protector if we request one, but I've realized"—she flicks her gaze to Jas and smiles—"that love isn't something we push aside for when it's convenient, and it's not something that should have to hide behind a public marriage. If it's real, it's part of who we are, and with it we are better.

"I plan to marry the man I love—a human, for what it's worth. We will marry and make a family, and I will lead Elora into a better day with him at my side." She turns her smile on the shadow queen. "As you do with your love."

"A queen and the Seven," Remme says slowly. "Four fae and three humans make up the Seven, plus a human queen."

"I like it," Skylar says, leaning back in her chair. "I think it could actually work."

"And since we are supporting each other," Sol says, "it avoids the nasty bloodshed that so often comes with change."

"I suggest we reconvene after dinner to discuss the best way to choose who sits among the Seven," Crissa says.

The group disperses, but Hale doesn't go anywhere so neither do I.

Jas kisses his cheek, then flashes me a smile before following the others out of the room.

"So what's next for you?" I ask. "Where do you go after this?"

"Jas and I want to live in Elora. And while I hate to take her from here . . ." He scans the room, and I know he's seeing the opulence and wealth of the shadow court, thinking of everything he won't be able to provide her. "She says she wants it too."

Hale's brows lift. "And what about you, sister?"

"I plan to stay in the Wild Fae Lands. With Misha."

"Why am I not surprised?" He grins. "Damn, sis, wouldn't that make you his next *queen*?"

"Nothing that was in my plans, I promise."

"You'll be good at it, though. The best. I'd bet money on it."

My chest feels too full. I wonder how much closer Hale and I could've been if I hadn't always been so insecure, so sure I had cost him and his family—*my* family—more than I was worth. I won't let my future be darkened that way, not when I've come to realize who I really am and how much I have to be proud of.

You almost ready to say your goodbyes, so I can take you home? Misha asks in my mind. He must be waiting in the hall.

Almost.

"Sol offered me a job," I admit. "If the Wild Fae Lands and the Elora Seven are going to be allies, they need a liaison who has interests in both realms."

He beams. "You'd be good at that."

I clear my throat. "Yes, but I believe the role of Wild Fae queen might keep me a bit too busy, and perhaps a bit biased as well? I suggested you."

He blinks at me, looks around the room like maybe he's the butt of a joke, then *gapes* at me. "You're suggesting that after a life crusading against the Eloran Palace, I *join them*?"

"What better way to keep them honest and focused on the right things? And anyway, you wouldn't work *for* them, nor for any particular court in Faerie. You'd be an intermediary."

"Thank the gods for that," he mutters.

Misha's back in my head and I can practically feel him tapping his fingers impatiently. *Please don't forget we have plans for tonight*, he says.

I haven't forgotten.

"You'll think about it?" I ask Hale.

He gives a jerky nod that tells me he's already thinking.

When I stand to go, he jumps up and hugs me. "Don't let your important new life keep you from visiting. Mom wouldn't forgive me if I let that happen."

"Don't worry," I whisper, eyes hot. "I have a lot of reasons to visit and an eager young goblin to escort me anytime I need."

"Good," he murmurs, voice rough. "Until then, I'll miss you."

"I'll miss you too." I turn to the door and see Skylar standing in the doorway, waving her eyes dry. "You okay?"

"Not one word," she snaps, pointing a finger at me.

"I wouldn't dare."

She sniffs and gives me a quick hug. "Be safe and take good care of that delicious king of yours."

"I plan to."

"How were the rest of your goodbyes?" Misha asks when his goblin finally leaves us at our destination a short ride from Castle Craige.

I smirk. "They were fine, though you didn't do the best job disguising your impatience."

"It's not that I'm not sympathetic," he says, opening the door for me. "It's that I happen to know we're all going to be in the same room together before the next full moon."

"Hale and Jasalyn's bonding ceremony?" I ask.

He scoffs. "As if the princess would want guests for something like that."

"Good call." I wave to Fancee and she scurries up front from the kitchen.

"Welcome," she crows, eyes bright. "I have the perfect dinner prepared for you two. Just follow me."

The back patio is set up as it was over eight months ago when I was in Jasalyn's form and Misha and I shared such a lovely meal here.

"This okay?" he asks, pulling a chair out for me.

I take a seat and tilt my head back to smile up at him. "Misha, it's perfect."

He drops a kiss to my lips. "You're perfect."

"Not at all." I laugh, shaking my head at him as he walks around to his side of the table. "So tell me why you're so sure we'll see everyone soon?"

"Because Pretha and Amira are getting married, and they want their favorite people there."

I snort. "And that includes Skylar?"

"Amira, shockingly, thinks Skylar is incredibly charming." He turns up his hands. "It must be an empath thing."

"She's a badass on the outside and a softie on the inside. It's true, but she'll punch you if she finds out you know, so don't mention it."

He chuckles and Fancee reappears with a bottle of wine.

"Faerie wine for the special couple." She fills our glasses and then plops a basket of bread between us. "I'll get your meal started. You enjoy."

I trace the rim of my wineglass. "Faerie wine, huh?"

His eyes sparkle. "Only if you want it."

"Is it wise to lower my inhibitions around you, King Misha?"

He pulls his chair around to my side of the table and leans into me. "You never know." His gaze drops to my mouth. "I might kiss you, confess my undying love, and trick you into being my queen."

I lift out of my chair, just enough to press a kiss to his lips. "Sounds like the perfect dinner."

Chapter Fifty

JASALYN

"You're sure you don't want to take more clothes? Maybe your riding gear or some of the bedding you love so much?"

My sister, the shadow queen, is fussing over me. "I have everything I need. And anyway, I can't take a bunch of fancy dresses to Elora. You know how it is there."

The worry on her face morphs to tenderness. "I do. And that's why I'm grateful to know change is coming—to know you'll be there to make sure things are better for the little girls of the next decade than they were for us."

"They will be, Brie. I really believe it."

"We have the right people in place. I'm not sure it will take a whole decade."

"Let's hope not." I squeeze her hands. "I will miss you, but I will visit soon."

Gommid appears at my side, ever the prompt servant.

"Take good care of her," Brie commands.

"I always do," he grumps.

"Hey, Gommid?" I ask. "Do you know a goblin named Fherna?"

He wrinkles his nose. "What kind of name is that? Fherna."

"So you don't know her?"

"There isn't a goblin named Fherna. If there were, I would know her." He offers his hand. "Ready?"

I hold up a finger and turn back to my sister. "What would you say if I told you that when I was stuck in stasis with the ring, I think our mother came to me as a goblin to get me to wake up?"

"I would say that sounds like one of the fairy tales Mom would tell us when we were kids."

Warmth spreads in my chest. "I thought so too. Then she was there again after I walked into the fire. Before I came back."

Brie shivers. "Do you really think it was her?"

"I think it could've been, and when I was stuck in limbo before I came out of the ash, I think I needed to believe it was her. But either way, I know she would've done something like that if she could have."

"Yeah," she says softly. "How do you remember her so well?"

I shake my head. "I don't. I just remember her some but then see that magnified in you, which makes me feel like I remember her a lot."

"Stop." She waves her hands in front of her face. "Dang it, Jas! Finn bet me I couldn't get through this without crying and I *really* wanted to win."

Laughing, I open my arms and we hug each other tight. "See you soon," I promise.

"So soon."

I've barely released her and taken Gommid's hand when the world disappears around us and we're falling and spinning and lurching into nothingness and then suddenly standing in Amelia's living room.

"She made it!" she shouts, jumping up from the sofa and running to me.

"Sorry I couldn't come with Kendrick yesterday," I say. "I needed to help my sister with a few things in the shadow court."

"You're forgiven. But your guy is upstairs and a little grumpy, so you should probably go share those apologies with him." She winks at me and turns for the kitchen. "Dinner in an hour!"

"I'll come back down and help in a few."

"Don't you dare," she says. "Tonight, you're my guest. Tomorrow you can start with chores."

Warmth fills me. "Fair." I jog up the stairs and down the hall to the room I shared with Kendrick last time we were here together.

The door's cracked but I knock on the jamb anyway.

"Come in," he says, voice low.

I nudge the door open and it creaks on its hinges. "Why so glum?" I ask.

The frown falls off his face and he stands. *"Finally."*

"It's been one single day." I'm teasing him, but it felt too long to me too, and when he kisses me hello, I decide it's been *much* too long.

"But I missed you."

"Me too. So much."

"The position as liaison pays a nice wage," he says. "We'll be able to move out of here and into a place of our own soon."

I narrow my eyes at him. "Is *that* what has you down? You're worried about where we're living?"

"I am taking you from all the comforts to—"

I press a finger to his lips. "You've taken me from the pit of despair and back to hope. You've taken me from loneliness to love." I shake my head. "I don't need more than you, Hale Kendrick."

He takes my hips in his big hands and pulls me toward him, tucking my head under his chin and lining our bodies up flush. "I thought I couldn't have you, and then I thought I couldn't keep you, and then I knew I wouldn't let you go but thought I'd lose you anyway." He bends to bury his face in my neck. "Forgive me if I act like a fool sometimes when I'm trying to understand how I got so lucky."

"How *we* got so lucky," I say, pressing a palm into his chest so I can push back and see his face. "And it won't all be sunshine and rainbows. There will be hard moments—but I guarantee you, spending a few weeks bunking with a lovely friend doesn't qualify."

His lips quirk. "Amelia's pretty happy to have you here."

"Well, I'm pretty happy to be here."

"And when those moments come," he says, "when it feels like it's been too long between the sunshine and the rainbows, we'll remind each other that the sun will rise again."

"Don't forget I'm not so scared of the dark anymore."

He smiles against my mouth. "How could I forget your secret dark side?" He kisses me, and I reach across the room with my shadows and shut the door.

ACKNOWLEDGMENTS

I took a chance with this duology. I wanted to write about depression and anxiety and the kind of darkness that is so deep it feels inevitable and unending. Of course, I also always want to write a book people *want* to read, and "HEREIN LIES MENTAL ANGUISH!" is not the best advertising campaign. I knew, though, that my readers would jump in for more adventures in Faerie and that some not only needed Jasalyn's story but would champion it—getting their friends, followers, and coworkers to read it too. That is exactly what happened with *Beneath These Cursed Stars*, and I am so grateful. I hope this conclusion is everything you hoped for and more. Thank you for coming to see me on tour, for the DMs and emails, and for always reminding me that my words are reaching you. My readers are the reason I get to do this.

My father, who had dementia, was on hospice care while I drafted this book, and he passed only a few days after I turned it in to my editor. I am so grateful to the team of aides and nurses with Gentiva Hospice and Harrison's Crossing who cared for him during those months. Knowing so many were working to make his final weeks as pain-free as possible was such a gift to me and my family. And, Dad, thanks for letting me get to the other side of that first draft before you said goodbye. You're the one who taught me not to believe in coincidence. Don't think I didn't notice that one.

Thank you, always, to my husband, Brian, who is my rock and my best friend, and who should write a book on the care and feeding of the neurotic writer. You, sir, are a pro! Thank you to my kids, Jack and Mary, who amaze me every day with their talents, intelligence, and ability to make me laugh. My little family is the best and I'm grateful for the three of you every day.

Thank you to my friends for cheering me on. Special thanks to the writers who had to endure my deadline crankiness while we were working at the beach together. Amanda Berry, Asa Marie Bradley, Elena Aitken, Jayne Rylon, Kait Nolan, Katie Dunneback, Mira Lyn Kelly, Selena Blake, Trish Loye, and Zoe York, you are great retreat partners and I can't wait to do it again. Special thanks to my longtime BFF, Annie Swanberg. When I was stuck, she rushed through reading an unpublished version of book one so she could help with some panic-plotting of book two. I am forever in your debt, Annie!

To my agent, Dan Mandel, who remains one of my favorite cheerleaders, thank you for all you do!

I am grateful for the team at HarperCollins and Storytide, and to all my foreign publishers, who launched *Beneath These Cursed Stars* with a flourish and made this duology shine. Special thanks to Tara Weikum for adopting me when I found myself orphaned mid-duology. Losing an editor is stressful, and while it's happened to me way too frequently, I can't complain when I end up with such incredible people. Tara, your feedback was spot-on, and you and Christian Vega are a joy to work with. Thanks to John Sellers, publicity director, for pushing this series and for organizing the incredible tour for book one, and to Michael D'Angelo for all your marketing efforts. Charlie Bowater, thank you for the gorgeous artwork for the cover—I love it so much!—and thank you to Chris Kwon and Jenna Stempel-Lobell for bringing it all together in the cover design. My gratitude also to Erika West. I appreciate all you do!

ABOUT THE AUTHOR

LEXI RYAN is the #1 *New York Times* bestselling author of sexy contemporary romance and action-packed YA fantasy. Her novels have sold over a million copies and been translated into over a dozen languages. She is the recipient of the Romance Writers of America® RITA® Award for her novel *Falling Hard*, and her debut YA fantasy, *These Hollow Vows*, was a Goodreads Choice Awards finalist. Lexi is known for her love triangles, her plot twists, and for making everyone she knows read her favorite books. She's happiest when at home in Indiana with her husband and two teenagers, where you can find her reading copiously, hanging out with her family, and thanking her lucky stars.